BLOOD COUNT

Artie Cohen Mysteries:

Londongrad
Fresh Kills
Red Hook
Disturbed Earth
Red Hot Blues
Hot Poppies
Bloody London
Sex Dolls

Somebody Else
Comrade Rockstar

BLOOD COUNT

AN ARTIE COHEN MYSTERY

REGGIE NADELSON

WALKER & COMPANY
NEW YORK

Published by Walker Publishing Company, Inc., New York

All papers used by Walker & Company are natural, recyclable products
made from wood grown in well-managed forests. The manufacturing processes
conform to the environmental regulations of the country of origin.

Library of Congress Cataloging-in-Publication Data

Nadelson, Reggie.
Blood count : an Artie Cohen mystery / Reggie Nadelson. — 1st U.S. ed.
p. cm.
ISBN 978-0-8027-7767-6
1. Cohen, Artie (Fictitious character)—Fiction.   I. Title.
PS3564.A287B57 2010
813'.54—dc22
2010015534

Visit Walker & Company's Web site at www.walkerbooks.com

First U.S. edition 2010

1 3 5 7 9 10 8 6 4 2

Typeset by Westchester Book Group
Printed in the United States of America by Quad/Graphics, Fairfield, Pennsylvania

For Justine with love

Until last week the Red Cross, acting on orders from the services, refused to accept blood from Negro donors, although there is no physiologic difference between Negro and white blood plasma. Negroes, proud of Dr. Charles R. Drew who headed the Blood for Britain service, protested. Negro blood donations are now accepted, but the plasma will be segregated for exclusive use of Negro casualties.

Time, February 2, 1942

With many thanks to Norman Skinner, for telling me about Sugar Hill, its grand buildings and the history of the area; to Curtis Archer, for walks around the neighborhood and much more; and to Frank Wynne, for sorting it all out.

Harlem, November 4, 2008—
Election Night

On a dark side street in Harlem, a silver van suddenly appears out of nowhere. Its wheels spinning, it seems to move with a life of its own, down the empty street, past the quiet brownstones and the old trees shedding their leaves.

I've been driving around for a while, looking for a place to park. Election night. A balmy Indian summer night in November. The sounds of the city getting ready to explode with joy, especially here in Harlem. Overhead, long beams from the arc lights on 125th Street play on the sky, the night lit up like day.

From somewhere close by comes the noise of celebration: shouting and laughter, fireworks, sparklers, music. From someplace, music—R&B, rap, Dixieland, all-enveloping—drifts through the open window of my car as I turn into 152nd Street, see an empty spot, cut across the street to grab it.

It's tight. I back in sharp as I can, trying to fit my ancient Caddy, big boat of a car, into the space, and it's only then I notice the van.

It comes from around the corner, comes up behind me after I've parked, I think. Gathering speed, it passes me, rolling down the hilly street toward Harlem River Drive.

Up here in Sugar Hill, on good days, if you're high up in a tall building, you can see down the broad boulevards to the midtown skyline, almost down to Ground Zero, the hole in the city that's still empty after seven years.

If I hadn't found a spot to park that night, if I'd just given up, gone home, watched the election returns on TV, maybe none of it would have happened—not what happened then, not what followed six weeks later.

Parked now, I watch the van roll, seemingly out of control, as in a dream.

It's new, a slick new Ford just out of a showroom, probably bought cheap now everything's hitting the skids, car dealers selling off what they can, waiting for letters from Ford or Chrysler, or GM, telling them it's all over, the good days gone, you're done for, forget the ten, twenty, thirty-seven years we've been in business together.

Stop!

Why doesn't the driver stop?

I can't see a driver. It's as if the van's driving by itself, nobody in it, just a silvery box on wheels hurtling down to the river.

Maybe it's the booze. I've been out drinking all evening, getting up enough nerve to come here, find a place to park, go over to the club on St. Nicholas Avenue. Is it the booze, a hallucination, this driverless ghost van that rolls by me faster and faster, in and out of the white pools cast by streetlights on a dark Harlem street?

But I know it's real. I watch until it disappears around a corner as fireworks explode overhead.

SATURDAY

CHAPTER 1

Who died?"

The night when I finished a case, closed it up, got the creep who killed pigeons in the park for pleasure—and the homeless guys who liked to feed them, I went to bed early, spent a luxurious hour in the sack drinking beer and watching a rerun of the Yanks' 2000 World Series win on TV.

As I tipped over into sleep, I realized I'd forgotten to turn off my phone. When it rang a few hours later, still mostly asleep, I ignored it, until the voice on the answering machine crashed into my semiconscious brain.

"We got a dead Russian. Get yourself over here," said the voice, and I wasn't sure at first if it was real or I was trapped in that nightmare where you're buried alive, pushing up on the coffin lid, hearing a phone ring, unable to get to it.

At the foot of the bed, the TV was still on—pictures of Obama in Chicago—and I realized I was safe at home in downtown Manhattan, and then the phone rang again. It was only Sonny Lippert.

"Who died, Sonny?" I was pissed off.

"Didn't you get my message? I told you, a Russian," he said. "Get your ass over here, man."

"Not now."

"Now," he said. "Right now. My place."

"It's the middle of the night."

"Listen. Friend of mine uptown in Harlem, he needs some help, right? One of his detectives found a dead guy up in his precinct with some kind of Russian document stuck to him, skewered with a knife, like a shish kabob. He's asking can I get it translated. Asked if I could call you."

"Where is it?"

"What?'

"This document?"

"I have it."

"So fax it over."

"I want to do this in person," said Sonny, and suddenly I knew he was lonely and wanted company.

"He's white?"

"Who?"

"The dead guy."

"Why?"

"You mentioned Harlem."

"I told you, man, he's Russian. Probably Russian."

Still naked, I went and looked out the window and saw the light on in Mike Rizzi's coffee shop. "I'll buy you coffee, OK? Rizzi's place," I said.

I was surprised when Sonny said OK, he'd come over, couldn't sleep anyhow. Sonny Lippert had been my boss on and off for a long time, right back to the day when he picked me out at the academy because I could speak languages, or at least that's what he always says.

These days I humor him because of the past. He still drives me crazy some of the time, but we're close now. He helped me with some really bad stuff last summer. When Rhonda, his wife, is away, he sits up alone until dawn reading Dostoyevsky and Dickens, listening to Coltrane, drinking the whiskey the doctor says will kill him.

Shivering, I went back to my bedroom. I yanked on some jeans and a sweatshirt, shoved my feet into a pair of ratty sneakers, grabbed a jacket and my keys, and headed downstairs, where it was snowing lightly, like confetti drifting onto the deserted sidewalk.

Who was dead? Some Russian? All I wanted was to go back to sleep.

* * *

"Morning," a voice said, as I walked out onto the street, and I looked up and saw Sam, the doorman from the building next to mine. It was also an old loft building that dated back to the 1870s. But the owners had transformed it into a fancy condo—marble floors, doorman.

A black guy in a good suit, Sam was a presence on the street now. He was a quiet man. Didn't say much, though once in a while we compared the stats of our favorite ballplayers. I said hi and went across the street to Mike's coffee shop.

When I tapped on the window, Mike looked up from behind the counter. He grinned, unlocked the front door, waved me to a stool. There was fresh coffee brewing. Some pie was in the oven. It smelled good that time of morning. From the ceiling hung a string of green Christmas lights.

Mike Rizzi pretty much runs the block: he takes packages, watches kids, serves free pie and coffee to local cops on patrol.

In New York, everybody has a coffee shop, a bar, a restaurant where they hang out. It's the way our tribes set themselves up, claim their piece of territory. To eat, I go over to Beatrice at Il Posto on East Second Street; to drink to my friend Tolya's club in the West Village, or maybe Fanelli's on Prince Street.

"What's the pie?" I said.

"Apple," said Mike. "You're up early, man."

"Can I have a piece?"

He was pleased. Mike's obsessed with his pies.

"*Deck the halls with boughs of holly,*" came a voice over the sound system Mike rigged up years ago.

"Who the fuck is that?"

"Excuse me? That," he said, "that is Nana Mouskouri, the great Greek singer." Mike, who's Italian, is crazy about the Greeks. Over the ziggurat of miniature boxes of Special K, on a shelf against the back wall, he keeps signed pictures of Telly Savalas, Jackie Onassis—he counts her as an honorary Greek—and Jennifer Aniston. "You know her real name is Anastasakis," Mike says to me about once a week.

"*'Tis the season to be jolly . . .*"

"What are you doing around at this hour?" Mike looked at me intently. "You just got home from some hot date? You found a nice woman yet, Artie?"

"Sonny Lippert. Needs me for something."

"Jesus, man, I thought Lippert retired."

I ate some pie. "That's really good, Mike."

"Thanks. So, you ever see her?"

"Who?"

"Lily Hanes. You could bring her over to me and Ange for supper. Ange always says, 'When's Artie going to marry Lily?' "

"Sure."

"What, you met her, like, ten, fifteen years ago? I know you've dated plenty of women, and we liked Maxine and all when you got married to her, but you weren't the same with her like with Lily." Mike was in a talkative mood.

For ten minutes while Mike pulled pies out of the oven and set them on the counter to cool, while I drank his coffee, we exchanged neighborhood gossip. I agreed to go over to his house in Brooklyn—he drives in every morning, around two a.m.—for dinner. But all the time we were making small talk, I could see there was something on his mind.

"What's eating you?"

"Nothing, man."

"You pissed off because McCain didn't get in?"

Mike's a vet, served in the first Gulf War, volunteers at the VA hospital. McCain's a god to him.

"I got over it, more or less. It was that broad's fault, Palin. Geez. Who invited her to the party?" Mike looked over my head toward the door. "You got company," he said.

CHAPTER 2

Wrapped in a camel hair coat, Sonny Lippert took off his brown fedora and climbed on the stool next to mine. His hair was all gray now. He had finally stopped dyeing it. He tossed a sheet of paper on the counter in front of me and greeted Mike, who brought him a mug of coffee. "Anything to eat, Sonny?"

"You got a poppy bagel?"

"Sure."

"Yeah, so can you do it well toasted, with a little schmear, but not too much? OK?"

"You got it." Mike reached for some cream cheese.

I picked up the piece of paper—it felt thin and greasy, like onionskin—and when I unfolded it, I saw it was printed in Russian. "This is what you called about?"

"Yeah, man, I need you to translate it, Art. OK? They found it stuck in his chest with a knife, like I said, right near his heart," said Sonny, pointing at the paper. I saw the edges were brown from blood.

"Where'd they find him exactly?"

"Harlem, up by the border with Washington Heights. Church cloister. Half buried, dirt all over him."

Mike put a plate down in front of Sonny. He picked up the bagel, spread the cream cheese on it, and bit into it. "Nice," he said to Mike. "Thanks."

"They whacked him before they buried him?" I said.

"They cut him up good, with a curved boning knife, it looks like, same as they used to stick the paper to his heart."

"You said he was still alive when they buried him?"

"I said maybe." Sonny ate another bite of his bagel.

"Who told you?"

"An old pal name of Jimmy Wagner, he's the chief of a precinct uptown, the Thirtieth. One of his homicide guys found this guy a couple days ago. I think. I think Wagner said a couple days. He thinks it's mob stuff. Drugs, maybe. Some kind of extortion."

"Why's that?"

"He didn't say, just asked for me to get him a translation," said Sonny. "Just read it, Art, OK?"

"*Don we now our gay apparel, fa la la la la la la la la . . .*"

"What the fuck is that music?" Sonny said.

"Mike likes it. She's Greek," I said. "The singer."

"Yeah, right. Just translate the fucking Russian," he said. "Please."

I gulped some coffee. I put on my glasses. Sonny was amused.

"They're just for reading, so shut up," I said.

While I looked at the blood-stained paper, Sonny made further inroads on his bagel. Mike poured him more coffee. I read, and then I burst out laughing; I couldn't help it. This was stuff I knew by heart, but you would, too, if you'd grown up in the USSR, like I did. I didn't leave Moscow until I was sixteen, and the stuff had been drilled into me like a dentist going down into the roots.

"You find it funny, Art? It's a joke?"

"Yeah, I *so* fucking do." I read out a few lines.

"In English, for chrissake."

I read: " 'Freeman and slave, patrician and plebeian, lord and serf, guild master and journeyman, in a word, oppressor and oppressed, stood in constant opposition to one another, carried on an uninterrupted, now hidden, now open fight, a fight that each time ended, either in a revolutionary reconstitution of society at large, or in the common ruin of the contending classes.' "

"Jesus," said Lippert. "It's the fucking Communist Manifesto."

"Yeah, your parents would have appreciated it," I said. Lippert's parents had been big Communists back in Brooklyn—it's part of Sonny's history; it never leaves him. Now, he stared at the paper and shook his head, deep in some memory of childhood.

"Does that help?" I said. "Is that it?"

Reaching into his coat pocket, Sonny took out two pictures and tossed them on the counter and said, "Take a look at these."

In one photo was a dead guy on a slab at the morgue. The second was a close-up of the guy's upper arm where there were some tats, Russian words circling his bicep.

"Same guy as they found the paper on?"

"Yeah," said Sonny.

Naked, the dead guy had a huge upper body, heavily muscled arms, a slack face. A lot of Russians who work security in the city were once Olympic weight lifters, though I'd picked up at least one hood who'd been a nuclear physicist. Times change.

What were you? I always ask them. What were you back then, before the empire collapsed, before everything changed?

"What about the tats?" said Sonny.

I held up the picture.

"Jesus," I said. "I never saw Russian tats like this, but it goes really well with what's on the paper."

"Yeah? What?"

"'Workers of the World Unite. You have Nothing to Lose But Your Chains,' you know that one, right, Sonny? I mean, ask yourself, is this guy the last crazy Commie true-believer left on planet Earth, except for maybe a few elderly ladies holding up pictures of Stalin on the street in Moscow? Maybe he belongs to a gang of old Commies. Maybe he strayed, turned capitalist, whatever." I yawned. "I'm going back to bed."

"You'll help me with this one, won't you, Art?" Sonny asked. "You could do me a favor and drop in on Jimmy Wagner."

"What's your interest? You're retired. What do you want this for?"

"I'm consulting on certain cases that come my way."

I saw now that Sonny was looking thin, old, his face lined.

"You feel up to working?" I was worried. Truth is, I love the man.

"I'm taking a few things on."

"Why's that?"

"Why's anyone hustling right now? Tough times."

"You have your pension, right? You told me you had some investments."

He stared down at the remains of his breakfast.

Once upon a time, Sonny Lippert was the most connected guy in the city. He could raise anyone on a dime. You'd say, Sonny, I need a lawyer for a friend, I need somebody in forensics, a contact with the Feds, and he'd say, No problem, Artie, man, just give me a few minutes.

He had to be in bad shape financially. The meltdown was killing the city. Madoff had been arrested, but I didn't figure Sonny for a big enough player to have put his money with the bastard.

"Sonny?"

"Just say I'm doing some consulting work, OK? Can we leave it at that, Art? OK? Please?"

"Sure."

Sonny got up, put his hat on, tossed a five on the counter, thanked Mike for the bagel and coffee. "So I'll figure on hearing from you by the beginning of the week, right? Just plan on working with me a couple days, maybe more, right, man?" he said. "And Artie?"

"What's that?"

"Answer your phone."

I went home, got into bed. Warm under the covers, drifting off to sleep, I forgot about Sonny's case. I'd left the answering machine on again, too tired to bother. When it rang, I said out loud, "I'm asleep."

The phone rang again. The answering machine clicked on. I was sure it was Sonny, and I yawned. And then I heard her voice. I grabbed for the phone as fast as I could.

"Artie? Are you there? Pick up the phone, please, Artie? I need you. Please. Hurry." It was Lily.

need you." Lily's voice echoed in my ear as I got in my car.

I tried playing back what she had said, but I knew from her tone she must be in big trouble. I was still groggy with sleep, and all I had really heard was that she wanted me to hurry. I looked at the road. Saturday morning, early. No traffic.

I'd scribbled the address, in Harlem, on a scrap of yellow paper I put on the dashboard. 155th Street. I drove too fast, breaking the speed limits on the FDR.

Everything was gray, the tin-colored river where chunks of ice had formed, the buildings on the Queens side of the East River, everything except the red neon Pepsi sign. It was cold. I turned on the heater and put the radio on for the forecast. Snow. Fog. Cold. Sleet fell on my windshield.

I drove. I tried Lily on my cell over and over, but she didn't answer. The only time I'd seen her in a year had been six weeks earlier, election night, the Sugar Hill Club in Harlem.

That night in November, when I see her, she looks wonderful. Her red hair sticking out from under a gold cardboard tiara, Obama's name spelled out on it in glitter, Lily is wearing a white shirt, collar turned up in her jaunty way. She's laughing. She doesn't see me at first.

"Lily?"

"Hi, Artie," she calls out to me, spotting me near the bar. "Hi," she says, smiling, and then, for a moment, she's swept away into the crowd.

This is why I'm here. This is why I drove uptown, why I had

jammed my car into the tight spot on 152nd where I saw the silver ghost van.

I knew she'd been working on the Obama campaign, living uptown in a friend's apartment. So when my pal Tolya Sverdloff had said, "Let's go to Harlem election night," I was OK with it. "I'll meet you at the Sugar Hill Club," I had said. I'd been here with Lily once or twice to listen to music. I figured she might show up.

In the club, the tension is electric, everybody waiting for the results. In the club I see white faces, black, Latino, Asian. People are yakking in Russian, Italian, French. Tonight everybody is a believer. Once Obama is elected, everything will change, people say. If it happens; when it happens. Soon.

The results are coming in, slowly at first. Inside the club, the TV hangs overhead like some ancient oracle, and with every win, the crowd turns to look.

Yes we can!

"Lily?"

Almost a year since I've seen her. It's a year since we agreed to stay away from each other. No calls. No e-mails. I've kept tabs on her as best I can. We know some of the same people.

For a while I went to bars and coffee shops I knew she liked. Sometimes I went past her building on purpose and felt like an idiot standing on the corner of Tenth Street, watching out for her.

How long have I known her? Almost fifteen years, on and off.

The only thing I'd had from her all year was a handwritten note when Val died. Tolya's daugther Valentina died and Lily wrote to me. Just that once. Only then.

Now, Saturday morning driving through the gray city dawn, sleet coming down on my windshield, Lily, her desperate phone call earlier, election night, were all rattling through my head. Like a maniac, I drove to Harlem, dialing her phone number over and over, hurrying to see her, to help her. Lily needed me.

"Artie? You knew I'd be here, didn't you?" Lily says when she spots me at the club on election night. She's close enough I can smell her perfume. "It's wonderful, isn't it?" She gestures at the TV. "I mean, if we win."

"You're superstitious?"

"Yeah. I'm not hatching any chickens before they're cooked." She laughs. "That's not right, is it? Oh, God, I'm so happy. Hello, Tolya, darling," she says, hugging him as he appears, diamond Obama button blazing on his black silk shirt, magnum of champagne in his hand, pouring it in her glass, in mine, in his. Lily gulps her drink.

"God, I wish they'd hurry the fuck up." She glances at the TV screen. "So you guys thought I'd be here?"

"Luck," I say. Lily smiles. Tolya laughs. He knows I'm lying, knows I picked this joint because I thought Lily might come. He keeps his mouth shut. We've been best friends a long, long time.

Suddenly, the noise in the club dies down. There's a sudden hush. One more state. He's almost in, somebody whispers.

The anxiety is so solid it forms a sort of invisible shelf everybody seems to lean on. We're glued to the TV. Lily clutches my arm. I smell her perfume again. Joy. It's perfume I gave her.

"What time is it?" somebody calls out. "Eleven," somebody yells back. The bartender gets up on top of the bar so he can see better. In one hand is a red-and-white-checked dishcloth. In the other, a martini glass, as if he was in the middle of making a cocktail. He stands there, suspended, waiting.

As I drove uptown on my way to Lily that Saturday morning, the weather guy on 1010 WINS was reporting lousy weather—snow, cold, sleet, airports shutting down, flights cancelled.

Sudenly, I skidded. For a few seconds I was out of control. Like the silver van on election night.

I got through it, kept heading north, trying to get to Lily as fast as I could. Where was she again? 155th Street? I knew she was in big trouble. I had heard it in her voice. Call me, I yelled into the phone, even though I was alone in the car.

I was heading for a part of town I didn't know at all. It made me edgy. If something went wrong—a crime, a death, an accident—I'd be a white cop in a black neighborhood at the other end of the city, where I didn't know anybody, the Saturday before Christmas with a storm coming. Last time I'd been uptown was election night and that didn't count, that had been a night out of real time when the whole city had dropped its tribal attitudes and celebrated together.

Maybe I should call somebody, make some kind of contact in case I needed help, I thought. But until I knew what was wrong, I didn't want to involve other people. Maybe Lily was just unhappy. She wouldn't call me for that. Would she?

I turned the radio up. The news was all bad. Financial shit, the system coming apart, Madoff's arrest. The election, the blaze of optimism, the joy, already seemed a lifetime ago.

"We did it!"

Eleven o'clock. Eleven p.m. Somebody yells it out: "He's in!" The club goes nuts. Somebody pounds out "Happy Days Are Here Again" on the piano. Up on the screen, I can see people going crazy, not just in New York, but in places like Iowa! Iowa!!

Everybody is hugging and kissing, we're all drunk, the bartender pops corks on bottles of pink champagne, somebody hands me a huge glass of bourbon. A girl in a silky red dress jams an Obama hat on my head and kisses me on the mouth. She's drinking flavored vodka; she tastes like pears. Outside, cars are honking, people singing. Inside, everybody is yelling, crying, hugging, singing, high-fiving.

Tolya, bottle in one hand, is dancing with a pretty woman almost as tall as him, in a silvery top, silk pants, high heels. A girl who looks like Beyoncé—at least she does to me, drunk as I am—bumps into me, and apologizes and laughs, and Tolya pours her some wine, too, and she says, "It's sweet, isn't it? Tonight it is so sweet."

"Where were you on election night 2008?" people will ask, the way they still ask each other about 9/11 or about the day JFK was shot. When I was a kid in Moscow, older people sometimes asked, Where were you when He died? and they meant Stalin. Where were you?

But this time, this night, we'll remember it differently, this life-changing event. We did it!

On the TV, there are all the faces, people crying, older black people unable to stop crying. There's Jesse Jackson in Chicago, face swamped with tears. Enough to break your heart.

"We want Obama," a guy near me in the club shouts. He says something in Italian. In English he adds, "Fuck Berlusconi, we want an Obama." An Irish guy is hanging all over me, moaning, "I love this place. I love you guys."

"Now I can stay in America," says Tolya. He's never loved America the way I do, but tonight it's different. He hugs me. "Now I can stay here." In Russian, he adds, "Maybe I buy nice house in Harlem. Become black Russian." He laughs and can't stop.

I put my arms around Lily. I can smell her hair, feel her against me. I kiss her. She doesn't seem to mind, maybe because everybody is kissing, and for a moment, she's with me again, and I'm lost.

"'Where were you that night?' We'll say that, won't we?" she says, half to herself. "We'll be able to say to each other, 'Where were you that night?' And we'll be able to say, 'I was there. I saw him elected.' We did it."

"I was thinking the same thing."

And then Lily is pulled away from me, dancing now with a good-looking black guy, a young guy.

They're holding each other tight on the floor, and I tell myself it doesn't mean anything, that tonight everybody's dancing, everybody's in love, it doesn't mean anything at all. Does it?

For a second I lose sight of her, then she surfaces near the bar, her back to me.

I think to myself: If she turns in my direction in the next five minutes, I'll go to her. If she turns around, I'll go over, I'll tell her how I feel.

But she doesn't. She doesn't turn around.

By the time I got off the Drive, the snow was coming down heavy, and I took a wrong turn. I found myself on the Harlem side street where I'd parked on election night, then turned the car around. For a second or two, I was lost. I felt uneasy. The streets were empty.

Finally, I pulled into Edgecombe Avenue. I found Lily's building. Over the front door a plaque read THE LOUIS ARMSTRONG APARTMENTS. I looked up. The tall building was made of old brick. From a second floor overhang gargoyles—grotesque stone animals—leered down at me. The snow had settled onto the creepy figures.

I got out of my car, left it near the front door, and ran up the steps to the building, bumping into an elderly man in a tweed coat and cap, who muttered at me. A woman trying to get a little girl zipped into a pink jacket looked up at me and looked pissed off, maybe because I was parked in a delivery zone, or maybe she didn't like my looks. Or my color. Dog walkers emerged from the building, one of them stopping, fussing with her hand to get the snow off her shoulders. Except for me, everybody was black.

I dialed Lily again. No answer. Anxiety, the kind that feels like a gust of icy wind on the back of your neck and along your spine, suddenly got to me. I stopped for a second, then I went inside.

CHAPTER 4

Red hair held back with a rubber band, face white, Lily looked frightened. Green sweatpants, an Obama shirt. She was waiting for me as I came out of the elevator on the fourteenth floor.

"God, I'm so glad you're here," she said, taking hold of my sleeve. "Thank you for coming." Her voice was flat, but she was shaking. With cold? With fear? She led me down the long corridor, stopped in front of a door marked 14B and hesitated.

"This is your place?"

"Yes."

"Let's go inside. It's cold."

"No. Across the hall." Lily gestured to the door opposite hers.

"What is it?"

"Come with me." She unlocked the door. We went into the apartment.

"Whose place is this?" I said.

The woman lay on a worn brown velvet sofa. Lily, who had locked the apartment's front door behind us, pulled back a purple shawl to reveal her face.

"She's dead, isn't she?" said Lily.

I felt the woman's neck for a pulse. "Yes."

"I didn't know what to do. I never saw a dead body, not somebody I knew. Wars and stuff, but when you're a reporter, it's different. I thought I should cover her face."

"You did the right thing."

"She was my friend." Lily shivered. The room was freezing. "Who left the terrace door open?" Lily asked nervously.

I went to shut the terrace door, where heavy silk curtains the color of cranberries—that Russian color somewhere between wine and blood—billowed in the bitter wind. When I turned around, Lily was staring at the dead woman.

"She always said she could only sleep in a cold room because she was Russian," said Lily.

"Who is she? "

"Marianna Simonova. She was my friend." Lily put her hand on the oxygen machine that stood near the sofa. I had seen one like it before. The oxygen tank was enclosed in a cube of light-blue plastic. It stood on wheels. A coil of transparent tubing ran from the tank to the woman's nose. The oxygen was still on; it sounded like somebody breathing.

"I left it like that," said Lily. "I didn't want to touch her." She started to cry silently.

"She was sick," I said.

"Yes." Lily stumbled a little, moving back from the sofa. I got hold of her hand to keep her from falling.

Her hand was ice cold. I rubbed it to make it warm. I could feel the electricity between us even now. It had always been like that with Lily and me, and I knew she felt it too. Abruptly, she pulled her hand away.

"I shouldn't have asked you to come," she said. "It's not fair."

"I'm glad you called. Talk to me."

"Marianna was so sick, and I couldn't help her."

"What with?"

"Her lungs were shot. I think her heart couldn't take it. She drank. She smoked like crazy. You can smell it everywhere."

I looked around the room with its high ceilings and fancy plaster moldings. The building must have gone up around 1920. The apartment needed a paint job. The yellow walls were grubby. The stink of cigarette smoke was everywhere; it came off the furniture, shabby rugs, the red silk drapes, off the dead woman.

"What should I do?" said Lily.

"Tell me what's going on. You said she was your friend."

"Help me." Lily sat down suddenly in a small chair with carved wooden arms; she sat down hard, as if her legs wouldn't support her.

I asked if Lily knew who the woman's doctor was.

"What for?"

I told her somebody had to sign the death certificate. She said there was a guy in the next-door apartment who was a doctor. Maybe he could sign it. "They were friends," Lily said. "Him and Marianna."

"Didn't she have her own doctor?"

"Of course. Sure."

"You have a name?"

"Why?"

"It's better if somebody who was taking care of her signs the certificate," I said, and wondered why Lily was suddenly wary.

"Lucille Bernard," she said finally. "Saint Bernard, Marianna called her. She could be pretty funny. She was funny."

"You met her? The doctor?"

"Yes."

"You have a number?"

"I took Marianna to an appointment once or twice," Lily said. "At Presbyterian. Bernard's office is in the hospital. I might have the number."

"Let's call her."

"Why can't we just get Lionel? I'll go next door and get him." Lily's eyes welled up. She wiped her face with the back of her sleeve.

"Lily? Honey? It was you who found her?"

"Yes.

"How come you didn't call 911?"

"Marianna was sick. I didn't think it was an emergency, not if you die from being sick. Was that wrong?"

"Of course not. Did anybody else see her like this? I mean before you found her?"

"Why does it matter?" she said.

"What about last night?"

"I don't know. I don't know why you're interrogating me. She was sick. She just died. I'm sorry I called you out." Lily seemed half out of her mind now. This dead woman on the sofa had obviously meant a lot to her in a way I didn't understand.

"Come on, honey," I reached for her hand. "Let's get the doctor's number."

Lily didn't move. Didn't let me hold her hand.

"Come on."

"Don't nag me."

I sat on the floor near Lily's little chair. "Is there something else going on?"

"I'm just sad."

She was sad, but she was scared, too, and I had to know why. Was Lily lying? My gut told me she was holding stuff back. I switched on a standing lamp with a fringed shade. The low-wattage bulb spilled a dim pool of yellow light on the body.

Marianna Simonova's getup was like a costume. Her head was wrapped in a purple silk scarf, she wore a white shirt with a high neck, Cossack style, a long skirt, and over it all, a heavy brown velvet bathrobe with fancy embroidery. Around her neck was a gold cross with red stones.

Her hands were clasped across her body, one of them curled in a fist. I figured she was arthritic.

It was as if she had been arranged—or had arranged herself—for death. There was no sign anyone had hurt her, no actual sign of her dying, either, except that she was dead. She was as composed as one of the icons on her mantelpiece.

Kneeling by the sofa, I saw she wasn't so old, no more than seventy. Her face was still smooth, and it was a long, imperious, oval face with a weirdly high forehead, thin, plucked eyebrows, a skinny nose.

The fingers of her left hand were cold but still pliant. Rigor hadn't set in yet. I touched the other hand. It wasn't arthritic after all, just curled in a fist. I pulled back the fingers. Something she had been holding fell out. It was a horn button from a man's jacket. I put it in my pocket.

Simonova wasn't a victim. Was she? This wasn't some case I was working. But I took the button anyway, and then I touched her face. The skin was soft, almost alive, like one of those dolls they sell at fancy toy shops, the kind with the creepy feel of human flesh.

On the floor was a biography of Rasputin in Russian, and a paperback, an English mystery, the kind my mother used to love, which she read secretly in her kitchen back in Moscow. She hid them in a kitchen cupboard with the potatoes. I remembered them all.

A little table near the sofa, black and inlaid with mother-of-pearl, was piled with pill bottles, a half-empty liter of cheap American vodka, a pack of Sobranies, most of them already smoked, a glass ashtray full of the butts. A small glass with water still in it had red lipstick on the rim, and there was a bottle of perfume. I took out the stopper, smelled it. From the low chair where she was sitting, Lily watched me.

"Artie?"

"What?"

"Please cover Marianna up," Lily said. "I feel like she can see me."

I put the shawl back over the dead woman's face, which is when I noticed something I hadn't seen before: the tip of the woman's left ring finger was missing, and the flesh where it had been cut was thick with scar tissue.

"Lily?" I wanted to ask her about the finger, but she suddenly got up and left the room.

CHAPTER 5

Along with the stench of cigarette smoke in the dead woman's apartment was a heavy flower smell. It came from dried rose petals in a brass bowl on an old mahogany table. Candles, most of them almost burned out, gave off a cloying stink, too, clove and cinnamon. When I touched one, it was still warm, the wax soft. Something else in the room stank in a different way: age or death.

Lily, who said she had gone to the bathroom, had reclaimed her seat in the little chair. I knew she needed time. I'd let her sit for a few more minutes. I didn't ask about the dead woman's missing fingertip, not now. Instead, I walked around the enormous room. Only half consciously, I was looking for clues. There was something wrong about Lily's shift in mood from flat to frantic, something wrong the way the dead woman was posed on the sofa, something wrong in the way the place stank.

Across the room from where Lily sat I saw that part of the ceiling and wall were wet. A plastic sheet on the floor caught the water that dripped from the roof through the ceiling. Chunks of crumbling plaster lay in wet pools on the plastic.

A rickety card table held a gold-colored bust of Pushkin. The cracked marble mantelpiece was jammed with pictures, some framed in leather, some in silver. I reached for one of them.

"Leave it," Lily called out. "Just leave it all, OK?"

I crossed the room to where she sat. "What is it? Lily? Honey?" I had never seen her so out of control, tears creeping down her cheeks.

All the years I had known her, Lily had almost never cried, unless you counted election night, and that was for joy. Not even when she was out reporting on the sex trade in Bosnia and was beaten up so badly by thugs she almost died. People think Lily's remote, even cold, obsessed with her work, unyielding in her opinions. And she is. Sometimes. She has a temper. I didn't care; I never had.

Seeing her in the sweatpants, her hair a mess, her face pale and wet, I realized that nothing mattered to me as much as being with her. Nothing.

"Hey."

"What?"

I touched her sleeve lightly. "I'll help you. I'll fix it. Whatever it is." I put my arms around her. She didn't pull away this time.

Just come home with me, I wanted to say. Just come downtown, we'll go to my place, I'll be with you, I'll take care of you. But I didn't. I couldn't take the chance she'd say no.

"Marianna was so sick." Lily's voice was barely audible. "She was in such pain."

"What happened?"

"I sublet the apartment across the hall when I decided I was going to work for Obama over on 133rd Street. I wanted a change anyway, so I rented the place from a friend who was going to Chicago for a year," said Lily. "A few weeks after I got here, I met Marianna in the hall. We talked. She invited me for a cup of tea. I could see she needed help, so I got into the habit of stopping by. I put out her meds every night, and made sure the oxygen was working right, and then I'd come by most mornings to check in on her again."

"I thought the doctor next door was her pal."

"He helped. But his wife didn't like Marianna." Lily looked at me. "Also, I brought Marianna vodka. She used to say, 'So I die sober, I die drunk, first way I die happy.'"

"What else?"

"In the beginning, I helped her out of, you know, my ridiculous sense of duty," Lily said, almost smiling. "Then we became friends. Marianna told these really great stories, about her life in Russia, and about Harlem when she first got here. People she had known. She just needed somebody to talk to. I guess she was trying to make sense of her own history, and I listened."

"Go on."

"You know who that is?" Lily pointed to an oil painting of a handsome black man dressed in a military costume. The painter had emphasized the heroic features. A little brass-shaded light cast a glow that made the black skin look like satin.

"Yes."

"My parents idolized Paul Robeson, his voice, his acting, his politics. That's him in *Othello* in the picture. When I was a kid, Robeson was a god to the Old Left."

"So your friend was a fan?"

"According to Marianna, Robeson was her lover."

"What?"

"Yeah, she said he helped her get to the U.S. She met him in Moscow around 1960, when she was in her early twenties, and he was on one of his trips to the USSR. She said she seduced him. She had a lot of pictures of Robeson. She kept some in her storage room in the basement."

"You believed her?"

"I was a sucker for the stories," Lily said. "I never knew what to believe exactly. With Marianna it was always about the stories. She made the history so alive, I guess I was kind of enchanted; she'd play Robeson's records on her turntable, him singing opera and spirituals and Slavic folk songs, in that deep dark incredible voice. You know it, right? She told me her grandfather fought in the Russian Revolution. Marianna made her ghosts come alive." Lily put her hand on my arm. "Her ghosts. Maybe my own. She was like this wacked-out Scheherazade, suspended in her past. Once in a while I tried to pin her down—I'm a journalist, I'm supposed to care about the facts, but I didn't. The Russian stuff was like a delicious trap for me."

A trap for me, too, I thought. Without the honey. Somewhere deep down I knew the Russian thing would never let me go. I had almost made my peace with the whole fucking enterprise, until last summer, when Tolya's daughter died and I had to go to Moscow.

For now, because this was about Lily, if I had to, I'd deal with it one more time. I could do that. Suddenly, I knew what the dead woman's perfume reminded me of. It was a scent my grandmother used to wear: heavy, sweet, too ripe.

"You said she had a storage room. There's a key?"

"I have it," said Lily. "She asked me to get some things for her."

"When?"

"Yesterday."

"Did you?"

"I meant to but I was busy. I didn't even do that for her, I couldn't be bothered, and now she's dead."

"What things?"

"Russian Christmas decorations. She told me there was a special box she wanted me to have. She was big on presents, little surprises. She was always giving me those damn Russian dolls."

"I'll get the box for you if you want."

"Will you? Thank you." Lily burst into tears again. "Oh, God, I used her."

"How?"

"I made her tell me stories, even when she was sick, even when she didn't have much breath left. Then she died. She was only seventy. Artie?"

"What?"

"I taped her stories. Some of the time I didn't even tell her I had my voice recorder on. I figured she'd feel freer. Jesus, you become a journalist, a writer, you sell your soul for other people's stories. It's like a fucking addiction. The bigger the story, the more horrible the history, the more you crave it."

"It's what you do. It's who you are, and I don't think you used her. She probably loved it that you were interested," I said. "Can I ask you something?"

"Sure."

"She was OK last night, right? She was alive?"

"Yes."

"And this morning. What time did you come by this morning?"

Lily hesitated—it was only for a fraction of a second, an intake of breath, a faint sense that she was calculating her answer—and then said, "Just before I called you. Early. Around six."

"Did she usually leave the door unlocked?"

"No. I have keys."

"Only you?"

"She was paranoid about keys. I have one. The managing agent for the building has one, but he was always supposed to phone her unless she was away and there was a flood or something."

"Not the super?"

"She hated the super."

"She sounds like a demanding woman."

"So?"

"Everybody in the building knew her?"

"Yes," said Lily. "Especially on this floor. She'd been here a long time."

"Is everybody else in this building black?"

"What does that mean?"

"I'm just asking. It's a black neighborhood; she was white."

"You think somebody hurt Marianna?"

"I don't know. Just a gut thing."

"Because you're a cop?"

"Because you're so upset. I've never seen you like this."

"Maybe you weren't looking," said Lily. "I just failed Marianna, that's all. I'll go look for the doctor's number if you want," she added, but she clung to the little chair like a life raft. There was something she wasn't saying, or couldn't. "Is it such a big deal, this death certificate, Artie?"

"You just need one. You know that."

As if forcing herself back into reality, Lily jumped out of the chair. "I'll get the doctor's number," she said. "We should get moving now."

"What's the rush?"

"Marianna wanted a Jewish burial."

"She was wearing a cross."

"That was just jewelry. I remember I was here once, with Lionel, the doctor next door, and we were drinking vodka, and suddenly Marianna says, 'OK, I am born Jew, I die Jew.'" Lily imitated a Russian accent. "She says, 'I am not giving fuck about religion, but this Jew way, is fast, also they do not fry you like cremation,'" Lily added. "With Jews you're supposed to bury them fast, right, Artie? Isn't that right?"

I didn't ask Lily why she had suddenly seemed to remember that her friend wanted a Jewish burial when I mentioned the death certificate. I didn't tell her, not yet, that I was planning to call the Medical Examiner, or at least a friend in the ME's office.

I'd been in the building less than an hour, I'd come as a friend, but the cop in me was already in overdrive. Lily's behavior made me anxious. Something I couldn't put my finger on, something in this room, was wrong, out of sync.

If Simonova had wanted a Jewish burial, an autopsy would be a problem.

Jews don't like their dead in pieces. I don't care. I'm not religious. Dead is dead. But a pal of mine in Israel who knows this kind of thing once told me the Orthodox don't like anyone cutting up the dead. It makes it harder to put us back together in the afterlife. I remembered it was the law in Israel, after a bombing, the religious brigades would appear and gather up all the body parts to be buried together.

Lily was standing near the door, holding a pair of glasses. One lens was cracked.

"Hers?"

"Yes."

"Artie?"

"What?"

"I lied to you," she began, but before she could finish I realized somebody was knocking on the door.

CHAPTER 6

H e's here. Good," the guy in the doorway said to Lily. He meant me. "You must be Artie, good to meet you. I'm Virgil Radcliff," he added in a soft-spoken, easy way as he shook my hand. He was tall, rangy, and loose like an athlete, same kind of haircut as Obama, though he was darker.

Was skin color the first thing you noticed in Harlem? Was it always that way? Or was it me?

The guy was good looking. And young. In his hand was an iPhone, and he kept looking at it. It rang. He turned it off, then put it back on, examined it for messages.

"Sorry, I've got a lot going on," he said.

"Virgil's a detective," said Lily. "Like you."

"What do they call you," I said, "Mr. Tibbs?"

"What?" He looked puzzled.

"Forget it." He had no idea it was a crappy joke. I was hoping Lily, who seemed preoccupied, hadn't noticed.

"I saw you lecture once at John Jay, Artie, when I did my masters there. You were talking about radioactive material, that case of yours, the little suitcase nukes. It was really interesting," said Radcliff. "Are you OK, Lily? I'm sorry I took so long getting back."

"Artie wants me to call Marianna's doctor. I was just going to get the number. I have it at my place." She started out to the hall. I followed her. I closed the door behind me, leaving Radcliff in Simonova's apartment.

"Who's he?"

"He's a friend."

"I got that."

"He's a detective, I told you. He knows about Marianna." She looked nervously down the hallway, the strip of dark red carpet over the tiled floors, the walls papered in silver stripes. Somewhere a dog yapped. From outside came the siren of an ambulance.

"So what did you need me for? You don't trust him?"

"Of course, I trust him. It's just different."

"He was with you when you found her?"

"Sort of."

"What's that mean?"

"Virgil was in the building. I found her first, then I got him to come in to look at her."

"He was in this building at six this morning? Where exactly?"

"Don't do this, not right now," she said. "I found her, I was so upset I didn't know what to do. I couldn't really even talk. Virgil said maybe I should call you. He said, 'Maybe Artie Cohen can help,' and I thought, right, Artie will understand."

"How does he know about me? Other than that lecture he mentioned?"

"He said somebody where he works was talking about you recently. Look, I need to get the doctor's number and I need to put on some clothes, OK? Can you just go back and wait with Virgil for me? He's a good guy, Artie."

"So he heard about me from somebody at his precinct?"

"Yeah, there's that. Also," she said, "I talk about you."

When I got back inside Marianna Simonova's apartment, I saw Radcliff leaning against the mantelpiece, using his iPhone, waiting. He looked familiar.

Where had I seen him before? Then I remembered: election night. They had been dancing together. Him and Lily.

He wasn't more than thirty-seven, thirty-eight. I felt old. I felt jealous.

"You OK?" He looked up from his phone. "It's good you're here, Artie. Lily needs you."

"Why's that? She has you. One detective's not enough?"

He let it roll off him, just looked at the dead woman on the sofa and back at me.

I went and leaned against the mantel alongside Radcliff. He wore a thick black sweater, a heavy leather jacket, jeans, Timberland boots.

"Lily seems pretty upset." I toned down the sarcasm. I didn't like the sound of myself going for him.

"You're right, Artie. I don't get it. You've known her a long time; I thought you could help." He got a pack of smokes out of his pocket and offered them to me.

"I quit, but what the hell." I took one, lit it with some matches I had in my pocket, handed them to Radcliff, and gestured at the dead woman. "You knew her?"

"I didn't like her, Artie, since you're asking. She was damn demanding, she was imperious, she used Lily, if you ask me, and the more Lily did for her, the more she wanted. I think she played on some kind of guilt Lily has."

"What else?"

"Everybody in this building paid court to Simonova. It was like she had something on them."

"You were surprised when she died?"

He shrugged.

"It was pretty sudden."

"Yeah," said Radcliff.

"But you didn't call the ME? You didn't feel like doing that?"

"I didn't see a reason to call. The old woman was sick, she died. You have a problem with that?"

"Better to do it by the book, if it turns out there was a problem. Better for Lily."

"What for? She was sick, she died."

"There's no reason not to call," I said. "Is there?" I got out my phone.

"Since you're asking, Artie, I'm just telling you we shouldn't call. Trust me. It's a bad idea." He put his hand out as if to take my phone away, then withdrew it. "Listen to me, Artie, there's no damn reason to call. This wasn't violent, it wasn't a crime, or suicide; this woman was sick, and she's been seen by doctors. No need at all for the ME to determine cause of death. OK? You with me?"

"You been reading up on this, or you just remember it all from the academy?"

"Sure, if you want," he said.

"How come you're so fucking sure there was no cause? And I wasn't asking your permission about the ME. I'm just fucking doing it."

"I'm saying it's a bad idea, Artie. We can get Dr. Hutchison from next door to sign the death certificate. Let Lily be done with it."

I punched some numbers into my phone.

"Don't do that," said Radcliff.

"Fuck you."

"You call it in, you make it a case," he said. "They take the body, seal the apartment, if there's a will, it goes into probate, the thing goes on and on. You know that, Artie, you've been there. Lily's pretty fragile about this right now."

Radcliff had an annoying way of saying my name every few sentences: Maybe he figured it for good manners, or to reassure me he was paying attention. I didn't like his reluctance to deal with the death the right way. Something was wrong.

"You want to open a window on this for me, like they say? Just tell me what's going on," I said.

Radcliff's iPhone rang again. He took the call, walking across the room, speaking softly. He seemed somehow shifty. He wasn't coming clean. I didn't like it.

I was so pissed off that when I went and stubbed my cigarette out into the glass ashtray on the bedside table, I knocked it down. It shattered into a million pieces. I heard Radcliff finish his call. His phone rang again and I said, "Turn it off."

"Excuse me?"

"We need to talk."

"Right." He walked toward me.

"Look, I'm going to call. You understand?" I held up my own phone.

"Don't."

"Hey, fuck off, man."

"Please." He looked for a place to put out his own smoke and saw the broken ashtray. He stubbed the cigarette out against his boot and put the butt in his pocket. "Please. For Lily's sake. Please, Artie, just listen to me."

He was worried about Lily's connection with the woman's death. I saw that now. Did he think she had been involved?

"Then level with me."

"Sure, Artie. Of course," said Radcliff. "If it becomes a case, it will go to my station house, and my ex-partner, who's the senior homicide guy, is an old-fashioned by-the-book kind of cop. He doesn't let up. The pressure will be on Lily and I don't think she could handle it right now."

"But you don't feel right about the woman's death, either, do you?"

"I don't know, since you're asking. I took a pretty good look around the apartment, and everything looks OK. It looks fine. But I don't know."

"What about her fingertip?"

"The ring finger?"

"Yeah."

"I asked Lily; she didn't seem to know."

"At least I want Simonova's own doctor to sign off, so we have that," I said.

"Fine."

"What else?"

"You know that feeling you get on a case there's something you can't grab hold of, some piece of evidence you didn't see even if you were looking?" said Radcliff. "To me, first glance, it felt like the woman was sick, she died. Natural causes. The oxygen was on; there were no signs I could see of anything else. Except for one thing."

"Yeah?"

"She looks posed," said Radcliff. "You look at her, hands crossed, all tidied up, lying there like something in a church. Like somebody found her looking fucked up and put her right. It's too neat." He looked at me. "You thought that, too, didn't you, Artie?"

"Maybe. You told Lily?"

"I tried, but she started crying. I don't know. I don't understand, and I've known her most of a year . . . You ever see her like this?"

The way he acted, doing the right thing for Lily, even saying she needed me, made him seem like a guy who knew his relationship was so solid he could ask her ex-boyfriend for help.

He turned his phone back on, looked at the screen.

"I have to go," he said. "I'll get back as soon as I can. So we're on the same page, right, Artie?"

I looked at the door. "Where the hell is Lily?"

CHAPTER 7

After Radcliff left, I went across the hall and rang Lily's bell. Nobody answered.

A couple, tall, thin people—from their height and their looks, I figured them for Ethiopian or Somali—hurried along down the hall toward the elevator. They looked at me briefly and moved on. From the apartment next to Simonova's a dog barked, then the door opened a crack. The face of a very old woman—dark skin, little yellow silk cap fitted down tight on her head—looked out. She stared at me for a second or two, then shut the door. In another apartment music played, but I couldn't make out what the song was, and then I looked at my watch. It was ten past eight.

I got out my cell and called Lily and she said she was in the shower, she was changing her clothes, said for me to wait in Simonova's apartment. She seemed obsessed with the idea somebody had to be with the body.

"I called Dr. Bernard, OK? I called like you wanted me to," Lily said. In the background I could hear water running and I tried not to think about how she looked in the shower. She hung up and I went back to Simonova's apartment.

I felt it again when I looked at the body, something visceral, one of those flickers of intuition that's mostly physical, that runs up your neck and makes you shiver, pressing your brain into action. In the apartment there was something I couldn't see right, something I didn't understand.

Virgil Radcliff was gone, but the idea I might call the ME had worried him plenty. He didn't want this made official in any way.

Did he know something he wasn't telling me? Did he sense Lily was somehow involved and was trying to protect her?

I took the shawl off Simonova's face. It seemed grotesque that the cannula was still hooked in her nose, the oxygen tank still breathing for a dead woman. I removed it carefully. She had hairy nostrils, which reminded me of Stalin, of what my father told me he had felt when he saw Stalin lying in state in the Hall of Columns in Moscow. Hairy nostrils.

Years after we left Russia, my father told me how terrible he had felt back then when, looking at the great man, he saw only the huge hairy nostrils.

After I covered Simonova up again, I pushed the oxygen tank into a closet and noticed a small pile of Christmas presents under a scrawny tree hung with red tinsel draped on the branches. I looked at the tags, saw there was a present from Lily, another from somebody named Carver. I stopped what I was doing then, because for the second time that morning, I heard water dripping. It wasn't in the living room.

I looked around the rest of the apartment. In one of the bedrooms, there was water running in from the roof onto the heavy plastic sheeting that shrouded everything—bed, dresser, chairs, clothes racks.

The room was a mess. Water had stained the yellow paint, and in places, slabs of plaster had come loose and dripped down the wall like candle wax. In one corner, there was mold that had grown down the wall in long fingers. More mold was on pictures that lay on the floor. It had somehow encroached on the images behind glass, making strange frames for them. One was a photo of a group of Russians near a dacha, five people in shabby clothes. In the 1950s, I guessed. The other was of Lenin.

I fixed the plastic sheets as best I could, shut a window that had been left open a couple of inches, and tried to call Lily on my cell. She didn't answer.

I needed air. In the living room, I got my jacket and went out onto the terrace. I had only been in the building for a few hours, but I already felt trapped in it.

Snow was falling harder, big flakes, blown by a hard wind across the city. It fell onto the terrace where I was standing now. From my pocket I got out a wool hat and jammed it on my head.

I gulped some cold air, then I leaned out and looked at the street below.

From the terrace, which wrapped around the end of the building, I could see in almost every direction. The Armstrong was the tallest building in the area, fourteen floors of yellow brick at the northern end of Harlem. Up here I had a spectacular view of the city, even though it was blurred by the curtains of snow.

At the back of the building was a parking area enclosed by wire fencing. There was a row of garbage cans chained together. In front was Edgecombe Avenue and Jackie Robinson Park, trees bare, and the Harlem River. Beyond it was the tangle of highways, the Bronx, Yankee Stadium. It would be gone soon. Torn down to make way for some new stadium without any history.

I had loved the days and nights I'd spent at the Stadium ever since I got to New York; loved the games, the crowds, the noise, the singing, the players, the beer and dogs. Loved the camaraderie, the way you met other fans over and over, got to know them and their kids. I loved the playing of "New York, New York" when we won, the whole corny ball of wax. My New York.

North and west were the Hudson River and the George Washington Bridge, shadows through the snow. To the south, all of Harlem, stretching to 110th Street and Central Park and down to the sky line—the Empire State, the Chrysler Building, but these, too, were only phantoms today. Here up on Sugar Hill, the rest of the city felt far away.

I once got to know a musician at Bradley's downtown—it's long gone now—who had lived his whole life in Harlem. One night, he'd said: "Black America, Artie? It's another country. And Harlem is black America." He's been dead a while now, and I can't remember his name.

If you live downtown like I do, Harlem feels like a different planet, low-lying, wide, spacious boulevards, trees. Harlem had barely mattered economically for so long that no one bothered to tear most of it down. It's remained, for better and worse, suspended in its own past.

A decade ago, maybe, as city real estate prices soared, fear of losing out on a piece of the pie made Harlem a tasty prospect. A lot of it was broken down, some of the buildings condemned. But there were the great apartment houses like the Armstrong, there were the fabulous brownstones on Strivers' Row; you saw ads in the *Times* for Harlem alongside those for Central Park West, Soho, the Village.

Houses went on the market for a million bucks. Developers talked about Harlem as if it were the Promised Land. All that housing stock, they'd say, practically licking their lips. And people moved. The New Harlem, they called it. A few bistros opened for business. Somebody set up a supper club and charged big bucks for a membership. A guy in real estate I sometimes play a little ball with used to tell me about all this, salivating. I told him I love where I live. Anyhow, I'm always broke.

Earlier, I'd noticed the date on the Armstrong: BUILT 1919. It must have been named later. In 1919, Louis Armstrong was only eighteen.

As soon as I'd arrived, I'd seen the building notices stuck to the beveled glass in the heavy front door. In the lobby there were ladders, cans of paint, part of the floor covered with a drop cloth. I wondered whether the crunch of the last months would stop the New Harlem dead, how much would sink in the financial shit storm.

From Simonova's terrace, I could see the whole of Manhattan. Long and narrow, only partly visible in the snow, it looked like a great transatlantic ship that had hit an iceberg and was starting to slip down into the dark, cold water.

Suddenly, I heard the sound of water and a voice cursing.

"Goddamn this son-of-a-bitch raggedy-ass geranium plant! Damn it."

I looked over the low wall that separated Simonova's terrace from the one next door.

The man on the other side, tea kettle in hand, unlit cigarette in his mouth, was pouring steaming water into flower pots. He put the kettle down on a little table next to a coffee mug and turned to me.

"Hello there, sorry to bother you with my carry-on over here." He had a deep, polished voice. "But it's these damn plants just froze up on me. You don't have a light, do you?"

I got the matches out of my pocket, gave them to him, he lit up, took a deep drag with a look of relief and deep satisfaction.

"Thanks."

He was at least eighty, I guessed, but tall and lean with a full head of white hair. A purple birthmark stained his left cheek. His skin was medium brown, like milk chocolate, he had a thin mustache like old-time musicians often sported—he reminded me of Billy Eckstine—and he wore a good tweed jacket, a blue shirt, red sweater, gray flannels. On his feet were embroidered velvet slippers. He was a dapper guy.

"My wife doesn't let me smoke in the house," he confided. "She takes away all the matches, says I can't even smoke out here, it gets in her drapes when the terrace door is open, but I sneak one now and again," he said. "She says it will kill me. I tell her it's my one remaining pleasure. I don't mind about dying, only about pain. I usually go up on the roof to smoke, but it was iced over bad this morning." He let out a long curl of smoke with a satisfied sigh. "How do you do? I'm Lionel Hutchison. Are you a friend of Marianna's?"

I introduced myself. I said I was a friend of Lily's, that I was visiting and she had asked me to look at a leak in Simonova's ceiling. The lies came easy; they almost always do.

"Oh, dear, yes, well, it's an old building, leaks like a bastard in bad weather. It's even older than I am, but it's sound, you know. There's just a lot of foolishness about fancifying it. They rip stuff up, they run out of money, nothing gets finished, you know? You get used to it, though, or maybe I've just been here too long. I was only ten years old when we came here."

He was clearly enjoying both his smoke and his own words.

Glad for company, too, I thought. Not surprised to see me or hear I was a friend of Lily's.

"When we came here, I was just five years old. My mother wanted to live there." He pointed to the roof of the building next door. It was maybe ten feet below us. "Number 409 Edgecombe. Everybody lived there: Mr. Supreme Court Justice Thurgood Marshall, Mr. W. E. B. Du Bois, the Duke—lived in a seven-room apartment done up all in white. When it came to building the Armstrong—they didn't call it that until later—ours had to be just a little taller, a little grander. Built by the same brothers back in the day, built for white folk, and those two brothers, architects both of them, they went at it, raising the ante, each of them, one putting on more fancy touches than the other." He took another puff, holding the cigarette between his thumb and forefinger like old guys sometimes do. He chuckled. "Still, we never did have anyone throw a prostitute out our building, you know, not like over there—it did happen, yes, from the roof, I believe, or out the window, over at 409. We don't let them forget about it. You cold?" He picked up his coffee and sipped at it.

"It's pretty cold," I said.

"I love the winter, the snow, the cold. Always seems to me to clean up everything in the city."

"You're a friend of Mrs. Simonova?"

"Good friends," he said, but he didn't ask how she was and I got the feeling he already knew. Cigarette in hand, Hutchison leaned his elbows on the wall between us, and settled in for some more talk.

"You interested in history? I like to think I'm a kind of local historian. This building, see, we had the nine-room apartments right from the beginning, with electric refrigeration, lovely wooden floors, high ceilings, terraces. You know about this part of town we call Sugar Hill? Everything that was sweet and expensive, so they said, and it ran right up here from 145th Street. See that building?" He pointed at Edgecombe Avenue. "Billie Holiday lived over there. We had musicians and athletes. The Polo Grounds, you heard of the Giants? Greatest baseball club of all time. They let us play there as kids. I was a boy, I played stickball with Sidney Poitier and

Harry Belafonte in the street, I was here when Joe Louis beat Max Schmeling and when Ray Robinson took the crown. All of Harlem just walked down to 125th Street to celebrate. You have to picture it, thousands of people, all dressed up in the best they had walking together. I used to hang out at Ray Robinson's club, later on." He looked at me. "Sorry, I got to catch myself when I start rambling," he said. "It's the curse of the old, and in this building, we're almost all of us old now. We feed off our memories, you see." He smoked his cigarette, the end of it glowing hot and red, then tossed the butt into an empty pail. He seemed oblivious to the cold and snow. "One young man comes along, wants to buy my apartment. He says to me, 'Dr. Hutchison, the myth lingers on here in Sugar Hill, like smoke, or sweet perfume; I want to be part of it,' he says, a nice young Negro fellow, excuse me, African American, lawyer, very polite, and I have to bite my lip to keep from laughing because this young man, with all his expensive clothes, is about as sweet as a cheap cigar."

I laughed.

"Right? It's just so much, how shall I put it delicately, horseshit," said Dr. Hutchison. "Did you know this here, this little hilly area, this is Coogan's Bluff? Same as the film by that name with Mr. Clint Eastwood?"

"What about Armstrong?" I said. "Did he ever live in the building?"

"You a fan of jazz music?"

"Yes."

"For a short time, yes, I believe he did, just for a few months, but it was before we moved in. I knew his Lucille. I knew her well enough they invited us to the house in Corona over in Queens for Thanksgiving once."

I was hanging on Dr. Hutchison's story. Armstrong is one of my heroes.

"Louis used to hand out Swiss Kris laxative to everyone, he had a deal to represent it. He was a kind man, and he was a genius, but he was sometimes sad. Sometimes you'd catch him looking out a window, a cigarette in his hand, and a faraway look on his face.

You could hear it when he played sometimes. Most of the time, he just wanted everybody happy," Hutchison said.

I thought about the house in Queens where Armstrong finally settled. It's a little museum now where everything—the dishes, the furniture, Louis's horn—remains just as it was when he shared it with Lucille.

For some reason, seeing it, the modest house in Corona where he had been happy, made me want to cry. All the musicians I love are long gone. I still have the music, though.

Hutchison looked over at me. "Marianna's doing all right? Do you want to tell her I'll come by a little later?"

"Sure," I said.

"It's the pain that's the problem, of course. So unnecessary, so inhuman. Suffering, they say it's good for you, tests your character. Such foolishness, but it's as if some kind of fake stoicism has become our religion. Brave, they call it, when somebody's terminal, but what choice do they have? Being brave is about choice. Pain leaves you no choice," Dr. Hutchison said angrily.

"Do you still practice?"

"Only when I'm needed. I keep up my license, always have. I graduated Harvard Medical School, class of fifty-four. Thought I could change the world," he said, and then, under his breath, he added, "Sure done faked myself out on that one."

"You look after Mrs. Simonova?"

"Just help out. She has her own doctor. Matter of fact, I sent her to Lucille Bernard. She's a lung specialist. One of the best, yes, indeed."

"So you see Mrs. Simonova most days?"

"Some," he said warily.

"Recently?"

An insistent voice interrupted us, calling out to Hutchison from the doorway to his terrace.

"Lionel?" It was the little woman in the yellow cap I'd seen earlier. "What's going on out there? You talking to that damn woman? For heaven's sake, you'll catch your death. Now tell her to go back into her own apartment and you come home, stop your rambling

on about the damn past and killing yourself with those cigarettes."
She paused briefly. "She calls you, you just jump, don't you, boy."
Sticking her head farther out of the door, the woman saw me and
said, "Who are you?"

"My wife, Celestina," said Hutchison. He picked up the kettle,
tossed the remains over one of the plants, where it hissed and
steamed, and retreated into his apartment.

I had the feeling Lionel Hutchison had seen Marianna Simonova
recently. I had the feeling he already knew she was dead. He had
engaged me in a lot of talk to see what I knew. It had been a fishing
expedition.

CHAPTER 8

Lily found me in the dead woman's apartment looking at a photograph on the mantelpiece.

"Good shower?" I said.

"Great." She had changed her clothes and fixed her hair. She wore a deep, soft green turtleneck, skinny black jeans, ankle boots, gold hoops in her ears, an old stainless Rolex she had been left by an uncle. I had always coveted the watch. I'll leave it to you, she'd always said jokingly. Though I plan to live forever, she would add. In those days, when we were first together, she was unstoppable, optimistic, full of life.

Lily was the best looking woman I had met in New York, or any other place. I always remember the first time I saw her: It was a hot summer night. She was tall, almost as tall as me, long legs, red hair, blue-green eyes. Sexy. Husky voice. Smart as hell. She was a grown-up. I had never liked girls, not really. I knew right away, but for once I had let things take a little time, time for us to listen to music, go for a walk, laugh. We laughed a lot.

"You look nice," I said.

"Thank you." She was composed, almost disengaged. The feverish look had gone, as if she'd taken something to make her calm. When I looked at her, I couldn't see anything in her eyes—not what she was feeling or what she knew—as if in putting on lipstick she had pulled down the shades.

She held up a little Russian doll made of painted wood. "Here," she said.

"What is it?"

Lilly pulled the wooden doll apart and took out a key. "Marianna's storage room. You said you'd go look for the stuff she said she left me."

"Did I?"

"I think you did, Artie," she said. "Where's Virgil?" She put the doll on a table. "Marianna loved these things. They give me the creeps," Lily added. "Where is he? Virgil, I mean."

"He said he had to go, said he'd be back soon," I said. "You have the doctor's number?"

She nodded. "I called Dr. Bernard. It's fine."

"She's coming?"

"Soon, Artie, OK? Said she'd be here soon as she could get by. Relax."

I picked up a framed photograph. The picture had been copied from a newspaper clipping and it was faded now. It showed a little girl handing a bunch of flowers to Stalin. I could barely make out the girl's face.

"Who's this?" I said, and Lily crossed the room and looked at the picture in my hand.

"It's Marianna. She was a gymnast when she was a little girl, a little star."

"Jesus. She met Stalin?"

In another photograph, this one in a leather frame, was a young woman I could just make out as Simonova; it was only her profile. Behind her was the Statue of Liberty. She held a kid's hand, a little boy of about three, his back to the camera as he stared in the direction of the statue. He wore a tiny dark suit; he looked small and somehow lonely.

"Did she have a child?"

Lily picked up the photograph. "Marianna wouldn't say. I got the sense this was her little boy, and I got the feeling he had died. She wouldn't talk about it."

"Do you want to wait here until the doctor comes?"

"You don't need to stay," she said. "I'm fine now."

"I'll stay with you," I said.

"Thanks," said Lily. "The pictures are pretty amazing, right?"

She watched me. Somewhere in the building—maybe next door—I heard footsteps on old wooden floorboards, and the sound of people yelling at each other. No words came through, but the sounds were from the direction of the old doctor—Hutchison's—apartment.

"Yeah."

"Marianna kept everything, pictures, diaries, letters she liked to surround herself with it all, she told me," said Lily.

I looked at more photographs crammed on the marble ledge: Simonova in a striped summer dress on a beach near a river; Simonova in Red Square with Paul Robeson; Robeson alone in front of Lenin's Tomb, wearing an overcoat with a fur collar and a Karakul hat. There was a tumble of digital snaps, too, piled on the mantel and some of them were recent, I could see by Simonova's face. In one, she was playing a guitar. In another she posed, mugging for the camera with Lily and Dr. Hutchison.

"I met the doctor from next door," I said. "Hutchison."

Lily looked up from the picture she held. "How come?"

"He was out on the terrace smoking."

Lily laughed briefly. "He does that. His wife doesn't like it. Celestina is ninety, and she rules that roost. Poor Lionel. She keeps him on a tight leash. This building, most of them are old. Most of them never leave. Until they die."

"I got the feeling that Dr. Hutchison already knew about Simonova."

"I don't think so," Lily said. "Why?"

"You tell me. When's Simonova's doctor coming?"

"I told you, I called. She'll be here."

"When?"

"As soon as she can, OK? I left a message." Lily hesitated. "Listen to me, I thought about this while I was in the shower." Her voice was low now, almost a whisper.

"What is it?"

"I feel I have to tell you something."

"Go on. It's fine. Whatever it is."

"It was me, Artie."

"What do you mean?"

"I killed her. Marianna. Give me a minute." Lily turned her back to me, walked across the room, opened the door and disappeared onto the terrace.

Lily's face was red with cold and there was snow in her hair when she came back inside. "I think I can tell you now," she said. "I need to sit."

There was a small couch on one side of the room. It was covered with a blue plaid blanket. Lily sat on the edge. I sat next to her.

"Whatever it is, I'm here," I said.

"Yes."

"You said you killed her. Lily?"

"I made her tell me those stories over and over, sometimes she could hardly breathe and I would say, 'Go on, just finish,' so I could tape it. I thought I could write a book. I killed her. I murdered this woman who was my friend, I made her tell me all her stories and I killed her."

"For her stories?"

"You don't think people kill for that?"

I put my arm around Lily's shoulder, but she shrugged it off. "I didn't check on the meds, either. I was supposed to check. I forgot."

I waited.

"Last night I went out to a party and I forgot. This morning I counted the pills, like I always do, and she had missed a dose."

"Which meds?"

Lily was rattled. "I'm not sure, I think the bottle's in the bathroom."

"Look. Look at me." I got hold of Lily's hand. "Simonova's doctor will tell you she didn't die because she missed a pill. It doesn't work like that. Dr. Bernard, that's her name? At Presbyterian?"

"I already told you it was her name."

"It'll be fine. You didn't kill her, Lily. You didn't do anything. You were her friend, isn't that right?"

Lily didn't answer. I could hear the second hand on my watch. I waited.

And then, Lily just jumped up. Looked at me. "That's right, Artie, you're right, of course," she said. "Dr. Bernard will explain it. Of course. Anyway, I have to go now. I have things to do." Lily was brisk now, her mood changing again.

"What things?"

"Errands. Christmas. Things," she said. "You don't mind, do you? I won't be long. You can wait over in my place if you want. Yeah, that'd be good, you can wait for Dr. Bernard. Or whatever."

"Don't you want somebody here with Mrs. Simonova?"

"What for?" said Lily. "She's not going anywhere," she added. "Wait at my place. I made coffee."

"I should move my car first. It's in the driveway. I don't want to get towed," I said. We were both lying now.

"That's a really good idea." She kissed my cheek. "You do think it's OK to leave Marianna for a little while?"

"Will anybody come in?"

"Nobody else has her keys," said Lily. "I told you. I'll call you when I hear back from Dr. Bernard, Artie, and I can always get Lionel to call her. Lucille Bernard was his protégée, he told me once. I'll do that. I'll ask him. They worked together. He was her teacher."

"I see."

"I'll call you, Artie, and you have my cell. It's the same number, you know that, right?"

"Lily, listen to me, you didn't do anything wrong, OK?"

"Sure, Artie. Right."

She went to the TV set, picked up a remote, and pressed a button. A woman appeared on the screen. It was Marianna Simonova.

"Lily."

"Just watch."

"Hello, Lily darling, this is what you want? You are certain you want this old woman she sings for you?" Simonova paused, smiling and smiling, then she spoke again, her blue eyes shining, as she spoke into the camera.

Her face was alive, her voice clear. She wore a red sweater; gold silk scarf wrapped around her head. "I sing for you old folk song from my country," she said, and raised her hand. She was holding a wine glass. I couldn't see if the finger was intact. "When I shall be gone, my darling, you toss away stupid video, yes? So nobody see how bad I am singing." She reached down, picked up a guitar. "OK, I sing famous song everybody know, so if you want you can also sing," she said, as if there were an audience.

She sang "Moscow Nights." She sang it simply, no melodrama, just a voice that was surprisingly young and clear, singing the familiar song about the river and the silver moon and the dawn and Moscow evenings. Behind me I could hear Lily humming along very softly.

Watching Marianna Simonova so alive on the dusty screen, I could understand why Lily had been seduced. Simonova finished the song. Lily picked up the remote and froze the picture. Simonova remained on the screen.

Hands in her lap now, back straight, staring at the woman on the TV, Lily sat so still she made me think of a little girl waiting for her punishment. "I killed her," she said again.

CHAPTER 9

"Well, I'm off," said Celestina Hutchison as she emerged from her apartment. She was wrapped in a mink coat. In one gloved hand was a leash, a black Lab at the end of it. "You all been visiting with Miss Marianna?"

We had just left Simonova's apartment when Mrs. Hutchison appeared, popping out of her apartment like a jack-in-the-box, as if she had heard us. Lily stroked the dog's nose. Then she introduced me.

"How do you do," Mrs. Hutchison said. "And this is Ed, Ed for Edward 'Duke' Ellington, you know." She tugged at the Lab on the leash. "Lionel's idea. Ed's name. I don't care for jazz music. I must go now; my sister is expecting me. She always so looks forward to a little visit with Ed." She said, turning to lock her door. "I always have to lock up when Lionel is home alone.

"Lily, dear, you know how he just wanders about, going out on the terrace or up on that damn roof for a smoke. It's fine for him, but what about me? What am I to do if he drops dead from smoking? What if he just falls down dead from being out in the cold? Such selfishness."

Moving toward the elevator, with Lily and me in tow, this tiny woman—she wasn't five feet tall—was an imperious figure. She pressed the button, holding her dog tight on its leash.

"Are you just visiting?" she said to me.

"Yes."

"I believe I saw you talking to Lionel earlier, you were on Marianna's terrace. Isn't that right? You had something to say to each other?"

"Lily asked me to fix a leak in Mrs. Simonova's apartment."

"It takes some gall the way that woman gets other folk to do her chores. I think she believes she's some kind of aristocrat and we were all put upon this Earth to serve her," said Mrs. Hutchison. "I guess I should ask how she is feeling, her being so sick, or so she claims," she added. "Damn elevator appears to be stuck on the third floor. You'd think those people could just walk instead of holding the elevator so long."

"Why don't you sit down," said Lily indicating a chair near the elevator. "I'll hold Ed while you rest."

"Thank you, dear girl." She gave Ed's leash to Lily, then snapped open her black leather purse and pulled out a little bottle of hand lotion, removed her gloves, and began to rub it into her hands.

"Jergens lotion," said Mrs. Hutchison. "I have always favored it over the more expensive brands, like all performers back when Walter Winchell's radio show was sponsored by Jergens, and his sign-off line was 'With Lotions of Love.' I enjoyed that: lotions of love, and I always did relish the cherry-almondy scent. Lotions of love," she said again. "Nothing like it for dry skin, I have even made Lionel use it in the winter. Would you like some, Lily dear?"

The elevator arrived, finally. In it was the doorman I'd seen when I first arrived at the building. He wore a North Face jacket and a fancy peaked cap with gold braid on it. His name tag read Diaz.

"How very nice," said Mrs. Hutchison. "We have an elevator man at long last."

Ignoring the sarcasm, Diaz held out a stack of mail to her.

"Oh, dear, Lily, take the mail for me, won't you please?" Mrs. Hutchison took the dog's leash and stepped into the elevator.

Before he pressed the button to shut the door, Diaz looked at me and said, "That Caddy, that belong to you, man?"

"Right," I said.

"You blocking the front drive, man, you wanna move it?"

"Soon as I can."

"How about now?" said Diaz as the door slid shut.

* * *

"Poor Celestina," Lily said, after the elevator had gone. "All she wants is to sell her 'damn apartment,' as she calls it, and go somewhere warm. She's always in that ratty old mink."

"Why doesn't she?"

"Lionel won't move." Lily held out the stack of letters she had taken from Diaz. "Artie, I have to go get my purse. Can you put these under the Hutchisons' door, the one next to Marianna's?"

"You know everybody around here."

"They're old. I listen."

"Mrs. Hutchison didn't like Simonova. What was that about?"

"She hated Marianna. She decided Lionel was having an affair with her, if you can imagine."

"Was he?"

"What do you think?" she said, and I took the mail from Lily, who went into her own apartment and shut the door.

Before I put the mail under the Hutchisons' door, I glanced through it. Habit.

There were what looked like Christmas cards. A few bills. A letter from a real estate agency in Florida.

The last envelope was addressed to Dr. L. R. N. Hutchison. Idly at first, I looked at the return address. Then I opened it, carefully as I could. Inside was a letter indicating that Hutchison was a founding member of an organization promoting assisted suicide, along with a flyer announcing a new edition of a book called *Final Exit*.

From somewhere a radiator clanged.

From one of the apartments—I couldn't tell which—the radio blared out an all-news station.

A toilet flushed.

Somewhere else, Ella Fitzgerald sang "Give It Back to Indians." The words ran in my head on a loop after that—"Broadway's turning into Coney / Champagne Charlie's drinking gin"—and I couldn't make it stop.

From Lily's place I could hear the sound of a vacuum cleaner.

Behind the door of apartment 14C, a dead woman, Marianna Simonova, lay on the sofa in a freezing room.

As I got into the elevator, I looked at my watch. It was ten a.m. I'd been in the building, what was it, three hours? Four?

I felt enclosed, almost suffocated: the building, its faded grandeur, the leaking rooms and cracked plaster, the dead Russian, the Hutchisons who would never leave. Who else lived in this fortress on Sugar Hill where gargoyles guarded the door? There were signs somebody was fixing the place up, all the notices on the front door, the paint and ladders. The wallpaper on the fourteenth floor was new. And there was Lily's behavior, febrile, scared, moody. Her claim she had killed Simonova. Had killed her friend.

There was a small window at the end of the hallway, and when I looked out, I saw the city was socked in now by snow, ice, and fog. Sleet battered the window. People in the street below were like smudges on a Japanese print.

"You thinking of moving that car or something?" said Diaz the doorman, confronting me in the lobby.

"Sure," I said. I could see the guy was looking to assert his authority, and I wasn't giving him any. Still, I didn't show him my badge. I didn't want him thinking I was here on a case, so I kept my temper. "You want to tell me where's a good place to park?"

"Yeah, OK, I can show you," he said. Spotting somebody at the front door, he adjusted his fancy cap and rushed to let the man in.

Black cashmere overcoat, handmade shoes, yellow scarf, the man stopped to talk to Diaz, who practically saluted. I waited.

It was Saturday morning and the Armstrong lobby was busy with people, some collecting packages from a long table near the mailbox, others lugging suitcases out of the elevator as they headed off for the weekend, or tried to. The airports were shutting down fast that day, I figured. Maybe trains, too. The city would be cut off.

A group of elderly people, two in wheelchairs, one leaning on a walker, had gathered near the fireplace; they chatted and laughed. A woman cajoled two little boys, twins, it looked like, burdened by violin cases. Saturday morning. Music lessons. The majority of people I saw that morning, though, were old. The lobby was their village green.

The old tiled floor, inset with strips of marble, was partly covered with worn Persian rugs, blue, red, pink. Dark, heavy oak furniture stood in front of the fireplace, where real logs burned. On the walls were lamps with ruffled glass shades, one of them cracked, one missing a bulb. Near the elevator was a large Obama poster. HOPE, it read.

Heavy blue velvet drapes and silky swags framed the windows, which looked out on a courtyard. Snow fell on a terrified city watching its money go down the drain. Money was New York's blood and marrow.

I waited in the lobby for Diaz. Louis Armstrong was singing "Winter Wonderland." The speakers were by the fireplace. The lyrics took hold of my brain. Only Louis could have made it sound OK. In this fucking festive season, the whole city was a mess of noise, too much traffic, too many tourists, and, God help me, the music.

I wanted to get out of here. Diaz was still with the cashmere coat. The man glanced at me, then asked Diaz something and slipped a bill into his hand.

Every building in New York has its own system, but it's a seasonal thing, the Christmas cash, the yuletide tip. Leaning against the wall, I saw people dropping envelopes on Diaz, pushing money into his hand. Any way you looked at it, this was the annual payoff, this was how you got your packages faster, your cabs sooner, your kids looked after, your late night activities—parties too loud, people too strange—ignored.

New York, unlike any place on Earth, lives in its buildings as if they're minute city-states. The people who service them have real power; without them, nothing works.

"Carver Lennox," said the guy who had been talking to Diaz. "You're Artie Cohen. Lily's mentioned you," he added, though I knew it was Diaz who'd given him my name. "Welcome to the building. Anything you need?" He was plenty self-confident. I figured him for his late thirties.

"Thanks," I said.

"Christmas party tonight," he said. "Whole building coming over. Sugar Hill Club. You'd be welcome. Lily can give you the address."

"I know where it is."

"Good for you." He nodded slightly and moved on toward the long hall off the lobby.

Diaz finally strolled over in my direction and said, "Right, I'll show you the parking spot, man."

"Just tell me."

"You won't find it without me."

"You only have one elevator here?" I put my hand in my pocket. Diaz watched me get out my wallet. His tone changed.

"Three," he said. "Two for residents, one for service—we call that one the prayer elevator." He laughed without much humor. "You gotta say a prayer when you get in it. Just like there's two sets of stairs, main one, and they got another one back by the garbage chute that's on every floor." He paused. "Saw you with Mr. Lennox."

I waited.

"President of the co-op board," he said.

"Right." I knew Diaz would retail anything I said. He was the kind of guy who made a living off gossip. "Can we walk? The elevator looks like it's stuck." I extracted a twenty and gave it to him.

"Sure," said Diaz.

"Where you from?" I asked.

"Cuba," he said.

Diaz pulled open a heavy door that led to a stairwell. I followed him to the basement.

"You work here every day?"

"I live here, man, or I'm supposed to, down in the basement where they got what they call an apartment. It's a shit hole. Usually I leave one of the other guys in charge, he don't mind much, ain't got nowhere else to go."

"Who's that?"

"They call him Goofy, the Goof, 'cause he don't have all his marbles, you know? He help out. Do some maintenance work." He grinned. "He's OK unless you let him play around with them fuse boxes."

CHAPTER 10

Bare bulbs overhead lit the basement with a creepy glow. The walls were clammy. I could hear water falling somewhere. I was lost.

Diaz had left me in the basement, pointed in the direction of the parking lot beyond the back door and told me to check but if there was a space, then move my car from the front. After that, he turned, went back through the door, and disappeared.

I tried to get my bearings. I found myself in a subterranean maze with only a few windows, high up in the walls and barred with black metal. I tried to trace my steps back to the stairs. I was lost.

"Hello?" I called out. My voice echoed back at me.

I looked into what turned out to be a vast laundry room, with modern washing machines and a couple of ironing boards. Nobody around. Beyond it was another space lined with huge metal racks. Old-fashioned drying racks, rusted now, each with the number of an apartment and underneath a gas heater. Looked like nobody had used them for decades. I slid one out; it rattled with age.

I backed up, opened another door. In front of me was a boiler room the size of a basketball court. Machines clanked and hissed. The door of one of the boilers was open. Inside was the orange flicker of flames.

Another room was full of electrical stuff, skeins of wiring, fuse boxes, weird pieces of equipment, some obviously broken. Next door was space for maintenance equipment, all left helter skelter on the floor—cans of paint, stepladders, tool kits, a pair of work boots splattered with pink paint.

"Hello?"

The whole basement was like the guts of some ancient ocean liner, the *Titanic* gone to seed, the crew absent.

It was freezing. I could just hear the sound of traffic over my head. I must be under the street, I thought. There were sounds coming from every direction, the clank of machinery, voices, animals—I heard a dog yap—all echoing through the long halls.

I passed a row of doors, each one marked with an apartment number. I rattled a few of the doorknobs, and when one opened, I almost fell into the long narrow space onto something that looked, in the dim light, like a body before I realized it was only a dressmaker's dummy.

I reeled back, stumbled to my feet, and laughed at myself. I was a cop with a gun and I was scared of a dummy. Heard the walls laugh back. As I backed out, voices came from the next room, voices arguing, but when I banged on the wall there was only silence.

Storage rooms, I thought. Servants quarters, maybe, once upon a time.

When I got back to the main corridor, there was only a faint oyster-colored light that came through those windows with the bars like a prison. There was no way out as far as I could see.

And then, suddenly, from the corner of my eye, I saw something scamper away down the corridor, something small and hunched and wearing red. It could have been an animal, but what was the red? Was it red? A rat in a coat? A cat in a hat? Was it Diaz? The Goof?

There was somebody down here who didn't belong, somebody living in this basement, someone, or something, who ran like an animal, ran when I got near.

My cell phone didn't work in the basement.

I was confused. I went into a room and realized somebody lived there—there was a cot, pile of clothes, jeans, dirty T-shirts, a jacket. Plastic sheets were hung under the ceiling. Water dripped. Something scampered on the floor again; this time it was a rat, a rat that ran over my shoe, brushed my ankle, and ran under the bed.

Was I hallucinating? On edge because of Lily, because she was somehow convinced she'd killed an old Russian on the fourteenth floor? Because of an old doctor who had been friends with the dead woman and who believed in assisted suicide? Call it assisted suicide. Call it killing people.

Lily seemed to know them all, seemed to have made a life in the building with them. In the snapshots on the dead woman's mantel, there had been three that included Lily: Lily with the old doctor, Lily with Simonova, the dead Russian, Lily with the young cop—Radcliff—his arm around her.

I don't like closed spaces. I couldn't see a way out. Was I losing my mind in this basement in Harlem?

"Hello?" I started to jog down the long hallway. "Hello?"

There had been times the past year when I'd thought I was losing it. After Valentina was murdered; after I went to Moscow to find her father, my best friend, Tolya; after I made a deal with a bunch of creeps to get him free; after I got him home and thought he was going to die from a massive heart attack.

During the summer, I'd thought I was going crazy. I had found myself laughing at the wrong things, and more than once I just burst into tears. It was July, maybe August, when I'd started coming uptown, sitting drinking at the Sugar Hill Club, listening to the music and hoping Lily might show up. But she never had, not until election night.

Now, suddenly, there was a faint, long, low howl in the basement, or was it just a noise from the laundry room, one of the machines giving up the ghost?

I began to laugh again—nerves, fear—and then I started to run, chasing the thing, jogging toward it as it receded, running faster and faster until it was out of sight. I ran until I almost crashed into a young woman. She was picking up laundry she had spilled all over the concrete floor.

"Thank you," she said when I helped her stuff the damp clothes into the yellow plastic basket she was holding. She thanked me, but she looked nervous. Her skin was very black, she wore a white shirt, a pink sweater, and jeans.

"I'll take your stuff upstairs if you want."

"It's fine, thank you again," she said. She had a French accent.

Somewhere a dog barked. She cringed.

"What is it?"

"There are djinn in this building and they take this form, of black dogs."

"What?"

"Djinn," she said again. "What you call evil spirits," she explained, just as Virgil Radcliff appeared. He greeted the woman in French; she hurried away. "Marie Louise," he said. "She's from Mali."

"She believes that stuff?"

"You think it's stranger than believing, say, that Jesus was the result of virgin birth, then turned up again after he was dead? I mean, come on, Artie, religion, witchcraft, whatever. All the same."

"What are you doing here?"

"I parked out back. Easier to get in through the basement. I left something upstairs."

"At Lily's?"

"Right."

"The woman from Mali lives here?"

"Marie Louise cleans here for several of the inmates," he said. "Did I say inmates? Residents, I mean, since you were asking. And you, Artie, you're down here why, exactly?"

"You want to show me where you park?"

"Sure," he said. "You got lost, right? Happened to me; it's like an underground maze here. Even a cop can scare the shit out of himself, Artie, if he doesn't know his way around."

As we walked, Radcliff talked pretty much nonstop, telling me about the building as we passed spaces that had once housed shops, a cafeteria. One of the huge spaces had an empty swimming pool with blue-tiled walls.

He told me there'd been a hair salon where the owner ran a numbers racket. "You hear his ghost still hangs out down here," said Radcliff.

"Squatters down here?"

"Probably. You can get in through the courtyard." Suddenly Radcliff stopped. He looked up. So I did, too. Carver Lennox was coming toward us carrying a large rectangular box.

"Virgil, good to see you, my brother," said Carver, stopping so he could put out his hand, which Radcliff shook briefly. He wore round horn-rim glasses. His mouth was full of expensive pearly veneers. He was an ugly young man, but he'd had himself polished and buffed, and he dressed with style. "Came down to get some wine out of my cellar. I keep a nice little wine fridge in my storage room," he added. "Hello again," he said to me. "You guys working on something here?"

"Just visiting," said Virgil.

"Hey, listen, can I show you something? I think you'll like this." Virgil shrugged.

From the box, Carver removed a heavy bronze plaque. He held it up with two hands. On it were the words: THE BARACK OBAMA APARTMENTS.

"Nice, right?" said Lennox. "Good name change, don't you think?"

"How do the residents feel?" said Virgil.

"A few of the older ones think we should keep the name as it is, that this is a landmarked building—it is, you know—and it's wrong to change, but they'll come around, you know? Most people think the president-elect is a little more important than a dead musician, don't you agree?"

Virgil kept quiet.

"I know you do, Virgil. Of course you do," he said, putting the plaque back in the box. "Yeah, and say hi to Lily," he added. The low, polished voice had a tinge of, what was it? Menace? No, it was just a sense that Carver wanted his way and always got it. That he knew everything that went on in the building and that he was in charge. "Well, don't forget the party tonight, Virgil." Lennox's voice was bland now, cool and smooth as pudding. "You, too, Artie. It will be a special occasion. Good food, plenty to drink."

"You must be doing well," said Radcliff.

"Surely, I'm a lucky man," he said with a cocky smile. "Well, then, see you, my brother, I have to get along to a party at the Princeton Club first."

"Goldman Sachs," said Radcliff after the guy had gone. Said it like it was a curse.

"What kind of name's Carver?"

"Named after George Washington Carver. Big African American hero. Revolutionized agriculture, cotton, back in the last century. He was like this Renaissance man, or so many people thought back in the day."

"You don't like it that he wants to change the building's name?"

"It's the high-handed way he just does what he wants. People here love Obama, of course they do, but they're old, Artie, since you're asking, and they don't like change."

"What's Lennox's deal with this building?"

"Says he wants to return the place to its former glory, which is why he's trying to get his hands on as many apartments as he can, however he can."

"Where does he live?"

"Up on the fourteenth floor, one of the big penthouse apartments up there with Mrs. Simonova, the Hutchisons, Lily." Radcliff's phone rang. "Give me a minute," he said and wandered away to the other side of the hall, his back to me, talking into his phone. He turned. He had a cigarette in his mouth. He looked up at a No Smoking sign and shrugged.

When he finished his call, Radcliff led me toward the back door of the building.

"I was wondering, how come nobody knows Simonova is dead yet?" I said. "How come nobody stopped by her apartment if they're all so cozy?"

"Yeah, I was asking myself the same damn thing, Artie. Usually, they're all on the job, you know, checking up on each other, and if one of them even gets a cold, Lionel Hutchison is right there." He paused. "It's like Grand Central station up on that floor," said

Radcliff. "Everybody in everybody's business. They visit, they listen for each other, soon as they hear footsteps in the hall, they pop out of their doors, you know? You stand there waiting for the elevator and somebody opens the door and leans out and says, 'Oh, hello, I was just looking for my cat.' There are no cats on the fourteenth floor," Radcliff said. "Yak yak yak in the hall. The building's their life. They can talk your fucking ear off." It was the most pissed off I'd seen Radcliff yet.

"You've been in all the apartments?"

"I got asked by the Hutchisons for coffee and cake a few times, and every time Celestina Hutchison would mention they were expecting a visit from a niece or a granddaughter, and I knew she made me for a good catch, and she's thinking, What's he doing with that white woman who's older than him?"

"Lily."

"Your business is their gossip, Artie, since you were asking."

"They make you nervous?"

"Cranky," said Radcliff. "The only thing you need to know is if anyone dies, Carver Lennox will be waiting to snap up the apartment. He wants the building; he wants to run it. He wants it for the money he can make and for the power. Fucking Goldman Sachs." He came to a heavy door and pushed it open.

"Where are we going?"

"Place to park, isn't that what you wanted?"

"Right."

"Out back," said Radcliff. "It's for the help."

CHAPTER 11

C hristmas." Virgil Radcliff looked at a party supply truck with a pink elephant on it parked out back of the Armstrong. "I wish it was over already," he said.

"Why's that?"

"Doesn't matter. Listen, you can park out here." He gestured to an area surrounded by eight-foot metal fencing topped with barbed wire, where half a dozen cars were parked. It was cold as hell, snow falling hard.

"Where's your car, Artie?"

"By the front door."

"Come on, I'll go with you, help you with the wrath of Diaz. He probably already called the precinct to give you a ticket. He's a creep. He has another guy he hangs with, sometimes helps him out."

"This guy he calls the Goof?"

"No, that's just some poor kid who hangs around. The other guy is his pal from Cuba. Name of Fidel Castro, named for El Jefe. They spend most of their time nosing around the tenants, or playing cards in the basement and planning how they'll go back when things change in Cuba, and how the Mets are gonna win next year."

"Fat chance." I wondered why Radcliff was being so accommodating. Maybe he was trying to make up for his having Lily instead of me.

We headed for the street, went past a gas station and around toward the front of the building.

"I've been thinking, Artie, we're both a little uneasy about Simonova, right? So why don't you take another look, if you feel like. You have the time?"

"Sure. But how come? You suddenly don't buy she just died?"

"You want to look around, I'm with you, I'll back you up," was all he said. "I won't get in your face if you want to do that."

"What about you?"

"I'm up to my eyeballs. We got one homicide, dead white guy, somebody dumped him over at the Church of the Intercession, right there on West 155th. It's got the look of some kind of mob hit, but which mob?" Radcliff groaned. "It's too fucking much, especially when we already have another possible homicide. On Convent Avenue, in a brownstone, guy knifed bad, left in a closet to bleed out. About a month ago." Radcliff walked fast. I kept up. "They don't like this kind of thing around here. We've got a record to live up to, you know, murder down, crime down. My boss wants to keep up his image these days."

"I'll check out the Simonova thing."

"That'd be good. Thank you. I know you'll keep it between us, if possible," said Radcliff. "Yeah, I'd be grateful. I'm trying to get out of town by Wednesday. Visit my grandfather."

"Where does he live?"

"California," he said. "Berkeley."

I was suddenly angry. He was playing games with me. "Is that why you didn't want me to just call the ME in? You're too busy, and you figured you might catch this case and fuck up your holiday plans?"

"That's not why," Radcliff said.

Radcliff looked at my car when we got to the front of the building. "Nice," he said as I opened the door and got in. "Nice paint job." He got in next to me.

"You're interested in paint?"

"Just paying a compliment."

"Whatever." I looked straight ahead, stepped on the gas.

"Is this about Lily?" Radcliff's voice was quiet and he chose his words carefully. "You need to talk to her about it, Artie. I mean, you're gone a year, you show up, and you're pissed off at me big-time, even when you're not saying it right out, so talk to her. We've been having a nice time together, since you were asking." It was a verbal tic with him, that phrase. It was driving me nuts. "OK? We're all grown-ups, and I like her a lot, and I think she likes me," said Radcliff. "I'm not planning on voluntarily giving her up just because you showed up, unless that's what she wants, and I'm not under the impression she does. So there it is."

I didn't answer. I knew he was waiting for me to say something. He was Lily's boyfriend, and he was smart, good looking, young, and hard to hate. I drove around to the back of the building. Radcliff whistled softly "Spring is Here," a favorite song of mine, and I wondered if Lily had played it for him.

"You want to make that right turn, by the gas station," he said.

"How come you know this building so well?"

"I've been coming here since I was a kid. My parents always had friends here. I had an uncle who lived here for a while. I knew some of the kids. We sometimes played up on the roof in the summer. We called it Tar Beach."

"So you all know each other?"

"What 'we all,' Artie?" he said, but without attitude, and looked at his watch, an old Omega on a soft pigskin strap he might have inherited from a grandfather. "You mean us black people? We African Americans? You can pull in over there, next to mine," he added as we reached the lot. He pointed at a burgundy Crown Vic. It surprised me. I'd had figured him for something more stylish than the standard-issue cop car.

I parked. Radcliff made to get out, then handed me a card with his phone number. "So you'll keep in touch, Artie? We're on the same page about Simonova, right?" His tone was cool.

"What do they usually call you? Radcliff? Virgil?" I said, by way of minor apology.

He hesitated, one hand on the car door.

"So, since you ask, Artie, yeah. At Harvard, I got some of the guys to call me Rad. It didn't stick. It never fucking stuck," he said. "I was back to being Virgil. Jesus. When it comes to names, I'm fucked. Everybody in my family is trapped in the past. My father teaches classics. My mother writes scholarly books about nineteenth-century literature. I had to lie to my grandmother about being a cop. She thinks I'm a lawyer."

"You have a middle name?"

"Worse," he said. "Darcy. My mom's idea. Never mind."

"You think because I'm a cop I never heard of Jane Austen?"

"Sorry about that. But just since you are interested, there's been occasions when some of the time, in certain places, especially with some of my fellow officers, they call me nigger."

That word coming from him startled me. I hear the word plenty. There's white cops who use it plenty. There's black detectives on the squad down at One PP where I normally work who use it between themselves. Rappers, too, of course; teenagers on the street. But coming from Radcliff—and I was guessing he didn't use it often and not in front of Lily—it had a different kind of power.

"You think I'm a soft, naïve guy, don't you, Artie?" said Virgil Radcliff, who didn't wait for an answer. He looked at his watch again. "I have to get back to work, you want to look into this unofficially, fine, but do it fast. Easier for Lily. Easier for everybody."

"What's your house?"

"The Three-O. Captain's name is Wagner. Why, you want to check up on me?" He smiled. His tone was cool. I didn't see anything else on his face.

"Jimmy Wagner?"

"You know him?"

"Yeah, I do."

"I'm not surprised," said Virgil, and got out of my car.

I'm not surprised, Virgil Radcliff had said. Was it race? Did he think about me the same way he thought about Jimmy Wagner, a white Irish guy from Staten Island?

I've been in New York thirty years now, and I've worked with plenty of cops who are brutal racists; it goes with the territory. Same with the rest of the population. Nothing like the fucking Russians, though. I wondered if Radcliff knew from Lily I was one of them. A Russian.

Maybe Paul Robeson had been idolized by the whole Soviet Union back when, but it didn't stop the Russians from being the racist bastards they always were. Still are.

The asshole Commies had lured African students over, said they'd educate them, put them in dorms like Patrice Lumumba House in Moscow, told everyone, Look, we're not racists, we're not like the imperialist fucks in the west, we're good to the peoples of the world whatever their color, our system is free from racism.

Ironic, how we were taught as little snot-nosed Soviet kids to love and honor black people; the Negro race, according to our teachers, was dignified and even under imperialism, noble. It didn't stop anyone, kids, grown-ups, from being racists. Peoples of the world! It was horseshit.

It never ends. Never. Just goes on and on, and now there are a lot of poor Africans stranded in Russia, just flotsam left over from before, the detritus of a dead system, the way people see it, if they see it at all.

Those poor African bastards are the worst victims of the Soviet fallout. It was lousy then; it's worse now: in Russia, if you're black, you get the shit beat out of you. I was there.

I'm in Moscow, July of '08, and I see it everywhere: people spitting at Africans, swearing at them, beating on them. One day I'm near the Pushkin Museum, some ugly acne-scarred Russian creeps, three of them, pin a skinny black guy up against the wall of a building. Start punching his face. They kick him, screaming insults. The poor guy covers his head, but they yank his arms away and hit him in the face some more.

And I lose it. I start yelling, and when they don't stop, I push one of them on the ground, tell him I'm official, flash my badge. I manage to scare the bastards. When I walk the black guy back to his hostel, I ask if he wants me to call the cops. No point, he says, and thanks me.

There've always been two kinds of people in Russia. The first want to beat up all black people or just make them disappear. Then there are a few of us, like me, maybe my dad in his time, who have always sentimentalized black Americans, because of the music.

For me it was always the music. Jazz had transformed my miserable little pimply Soviet being, even when I was a good young pioneer singing the praises of Vladimir Ilyich.

I listened to Willis Conover's Jazz Hour on the Voice of America under the covers. When every other kid was secretly listening to Beatles bootlegs, if they could get an illicit disc, I was listening to jazz. I listened with my father on our big Grundig in the dacha; it was safer in the countryside.

But race has everybody fucked up. When Obama was elected it had been as if, for a second, it was all over, all the ugly stuff. It didn't last.

Now I was in Harlem, sitting in my car, an outsider.

What was Radcliff's game? Did he have one? Was it only Lily he was worried about? He knew the building, he knew the people in it. He thought Simonova's body had been posed, fixed up after she died, but he didn't want me calling the ME.

It was Jimmy Wagner who had called Sonny looking for me. Wanting me to translate the piece of paper left on the dead guy, skewered into his heart. And it was Wagner who turned out to be Virgil Radcliff's chief.

I'm not surprised, Radcliff had said when I told him I knew Wagner.

Is everything always about race? What the hell did I know? With this stuff there were no reliable witnesses, not anywhere. I stepped on the gas.

CHAPTER 12

*J*ingle *bell, jingle bell, jingle bell rock . . ."*
    In the station house, the sergeant at the front desk was field-
ing calls. He waved at me to wait while he finished. On his tiny
hand, little and strange like a dwarf's, was a school ring with a
huge blue glass stone. The man's name tag said he was Edigio Russomano. He was small. After a minute, I realized he was sitting on
a stack of phone books.

    Near the front desk, his back to me, was a guy in a black jacket
and gray hoodie, the hood up. Big guy. Meaty shoulders.

    "What's your name?" said Russomano to me after he hung up
the phone.

    I told him.

    He asked again. "I'm getting deaf," he said. "Doc told me my
hearing's shot. Yeah, right, Detective Artie Cohen, that's it, glad a
meetcha. Chief made me look for your number earlier. He had some
Russian thing he wanted you to look at. You Russian or something?
Cohen? That a Russian name? Why don't you grab a pew over there,
and I'll get the chief."

    I got the feeling the guy in the black jacket had been listening all
the time Russomano was talking to me. The little sergeant turned
to him. "I thought you was on your way out. You need something
or you just got nothing better to do than hang around here?"

    Without saying a word, the guy stuffed his hands in his pockets
and bolted from the station house, through the doors, into the street.

    "Who was that?" I said to Russomano.

    "What?"

"That guy who just left."

"You have to ask the chief. I ain't been around last couple days; I only just came on like a few minutes before you got here," Russomano said.

I sat on a chair near the door. It was warm in the precinct. I unzipped my jacket, got out my cell, looking for calls from Lily.

I'd heard the stories about the Thirtieth. In the early nineties, this had been a station house that dealt big-time in narcotics, mostly cocaine. It had been so famous for the corruption, they'd made movies about it. Back in the day. Not anymore.

I was impatient. All I wanted from Jimmy Wagner was some input on the Armstrong—there was stuff going on there I didn't understand. There was Virgil Radcliff—I didn't like his insistence we work the case ourselves, if there was a case. He'd been holding back.

I looked around, hoping I wouldn't find Radcliff still at the house so I could talk to Wagner about him. Was Radcliff still at the Armstrong where I'd left him in the parking lot? With Lily? Had she really gone out to do errands?

"*Dancing and prancing in Jingle Bell Square, in the frosty air . . .*" The song played. I tried Lily on my cell. No answer.

I sat on an orange plastic chair opposite Russomano's desk. A drunk who had wandered in and was yelling incoherently, inserting the word *motherfucker* between every syllable he uttered, was followed by a couple of kids, boys, maybe ten years old. Their jeans hung low on their skinny asses. They told Russomano somebody had stolen their sneakers. He told them to sit. They took the chairs next to mine.

"Hey, yo, what up, man?" the first boy said to the second.

"Jes chillin'."

"You comin' down J's party? I tell you, It's goin' down right there, man. We gonna tear it up, I mean this gonna be stoopid tonight, you know what I'm saying?"

The boys kept it up, looking at the sergeant and me, making sure they had an audience, turning up the volume. They reminded me of those comic characters in Shakespeare who show up in the middle of the action. The little boys had high, childish voices. I tried not to laugh. I didn't want to humiliate them.

The first little boy started talking trash again. He was a sweet-faced boy, he reminded me of my nephew Billy, when Billy was little and I used to take him fishing. Like the kid at the police station, he thought if he talked big, it would make him seem grown up, but it only made him seem younger. Billy was dead now, and I missed him.

"Shut up," the sergeant called out to the kids.

I was laughing now, couldn't help it.

"*Jingle bell . . .*"

"Detective Cohen?"

A uniform—a black guy with Coke-bottle glasses—finally appeared and showed me to Wagner's office. I passed dozens of cops bent over their desks, shooting the breeze, yakking into the phone, or worrying about money.

Mix of black, white, and Latino cops, a lot of joking around. It was almost Christmas, and in spite of all the shit in the city—money, crime, real estate—people could get it up a little for a holiday.

A lot of people probably think a station house is a lousy place to work—the smells, the noise. I realized how much I missed it, missed the community. It was probably too late for me now. I'd taken the promotions. I'd gone for special assignments. Special squads. But working at Police Plaza was like operating inside a corporation. I had been spending most of my days, until recently, reading official documents about Russian banks, at least until I caught the pigeon killer.

Maybe if I'd stayed the regular course, I could have been a captain like Jimmy Wagner. Anyway, it was too late.

"Artie Cohen? Hey, man, how you doing? What a fucking pleasure. It's good to see you, man."

"You, too, Jimmy," I said, as he came from behind the desk

where he had been sitting and gave me one of those man-hugs. I was glad to see him.

"Sit. You want coffee?"

"I'm fine."

"And thanks, man, for getting that translation, Artie. I didn't have a current number for you so I went through Sonny Lippert."

"Sure. You need anything else, Jim?"

"Hey, you didn't need to come all the way uptown, but I appreciate the thought. You still living in that crazy loft down there off Broadway?"

"Still there, Jimmy, same phone number. In case you need me again. You?"

"Yeah, sure, but I guess you heard I mighta croaked." He laughed.

We'd met a couple of days after 9/11. Wagner was one of the heroic cops who worked on the pile without any protection, for weeks. Digging out bodies, then pieces of bodies, then tiny fragments that only the DNA people could ID. They did it so people would know, so they could mourn, so the families would have something to bury.

I'd been out on the pile, too, but I didn't have anything like Wagner's obsession. He and a lot of other guys had worked it for months. I knew Wagner had been there until the end. He'd told me he was sure one of his pals was under the rubble; he kept digging in his crazy way.

Guys who'd been on the pile still have a bond. If you had worked with somebody like Wagner there, he was your friend for life.

White skin, freckles, reddish hair going gray, a fireman's mustache, Wagner had once been very big and very tough. Now, he was thinner and racked with a gritty cough.

"So how you doing on the case with the dead guy they stuck the Russian document on?"

"We just had to let a suspect go," Wagner said. "I was even hoping I could also get him for another homicide we had, what, almost a month ago, over on the West Side a brownstone, one of them fixer-uppers, some gay guy bought it, then he goes in the first day and finds somebody in his closet. Be funny if it wasn't so fucked up."

"Jesus." I took a piece of candy from a dish on Wagner's desk. Must be the case Radcliff had mentioned.

"Whoever the killer is, he is one vicious fuck," Wagner said. "He cuts up the brownstone guy, then he locks him in a closet, listens to him yell, waits until he don't yell no more."

"How'd you figure that?"

"ME figured it that way. You feel this coulda been some kind of Russki sadist mob muscle? You dealt with creeps like this before, guys who like making people suffer."

I thought of the last case I had worked, the girl bound head to toe with duct tape and left, still alive, to suffocate. "Yeah," I said. "The dead guy was white?"

"Right. Then we get the second vic, covered up with earth in a cemetery, paper skewered into his heart—paper you did that translation on—same kind of knife; we had to figure it for the same killer. And both vics was white, and looked Slav," said Wagner.

"I thought the Russians were in Brooklyn. I thought uptown was all Latino."

"You and me both," Wagner said. "I mean, this was close to Washington Heights that once was Russian, right, but now, geez, if we're getting more of them, that's gonna be a fucker. I mean, you get Russian gangs and Latino gangs, you get a shit storm. We got the lowest murder rate any place in this city, and this precinct is one of the best, so I could really do without this." He sneezed, fumbled in his desk for a Kleenex, blew his nose. "Fucking cold," he said, then hit his head with the flat of his hand. "Shit," he said. "Oh my God!"

"What?"

"The guy, the suspect I just let go—we held him as long as we could, couldn't get a thing, nada, nothing on him—we let him go"—he looked at his watch—"ten minutes ago? Fifteen? Around the time you got here. Shit, man, I coulda got you to talk to him in Russian."

"Big guy? Black jacket? hoodie?"

"You know him?"

"I saw somebody leaving the building while I was waiting for you—he was Russian? I figured he was black," I said. "I couldn't see his face."

"Fuck," said Wagner. "Fuck, fuck, fuck. Everything's timing." He groaned. "But, I still don't think it was him. We grilled him good, he was polite, he talked excellent English, he had a green card, a job downtown in a bank, so not your usual creepola."

"He had a name?"

Wagner snorted. "Ivan Ivanov. You fucking believe it? But there it was on his driver's license, social security, the green card, all of it, plus I called his home number and a nice lady answered and said she was his mother. Out in Queens."

"Right."

"I mean, so what could I hold him on, Artie? He had a few tats, but I couldn't hold a guy for some body ink, could I? He didn't have no dirt on his shoes that matched the cemetery where we found the victim."

"You got good people working homicide here, Jimmy?"

"Yeah. One of the best there is. Let me see if he's around." He left the office. I figured he'd reappear with Radcliff. Instead, Wagner returned and said to me, "Dawes is coming in to say hi."

"Anybody I ever met?"

"I doubt it. He's good. Julius Dawes, straight up by the book. Too methodical for some of the younger guys. You know, they watch TV, they want to solve a crime in an hour, not including commercials, so they take stupid chances and then we can't indict."

The cop in uniform who had brought me in passed, and Wagner bellowed out, "You got smokes?"

The uniform nodded, went away and returned with a crumpled pack and Jimmy lit up, coughed until I thought he was going to puke his lungs out, then leaned back and took another drag on his cigarette.

"I hate this fucking weather," he said. "If the snow gets worse, it'll be bad. We don't have enough guys, we already got a pileup over on the West Side Highway. No money in the city, more homeless."

"Listen, Jimmy, I hate to bother you, with everything you got going on, but I was wondering if you knew anything about a building called the Louis Armstrong Apartments. Friend of mine looking at a place there." It was an easy lie.

"Sure," said Wagner, then stopped and looked at his office door. "Hey, Dawes, come meet my pal, Artie Cohen," he said to the middle-aged black detective. Wagner told Dawes I'd done the translation. We shook hands.

"Artie's been asking about the Armstrong."

"I can't stop long," said Dawes. "Got to get over to my daughter's place in Riverdale. But what's your interest in the Armstrong?" he said, putting on his overcoat. Medium height, compact, about fifty, Dawes wore his gray hair short and had a small, trim beard.

"I have a friend who's thinking of getting a place there."

"I didn't think they ever sold those apartments at the Armstrong, unless somebody dies," said Dawes. "My aunt lived over there for quite a while. Who's your friend, then, detective?" He was polite but distant. I got the feeling he knew I was lying, or maybe he was just in a hurry.

"Just someone I know," I said. "Looks like you're busy."

"I have to get going now," Dawes said. "But if I can help you out, Detective Cohen, please be in touch. Tell your friend if they're thinking of moving in to the Armstrong, make sure they know what they're doing."

"How do you mean?"

"Great building. Definitively one of the finest. Built to show off Sugar Hill. But a lot of tension over there, old folks wanting to keep it like it is, younger people wanting to fix it up, raise the maintenance, don't care about who gets turned out on the street. No reason not to take it if your friend can get in, but just make sure the contract's solid," he said. "So, if I can help, you can get my number from Captain Wagner. That your red Caddy outside, by the way?"

"Yes."

"Nice paint job," he said, and I suddenly knew Dawes had intended to ask me about the car from the moment he saw me.

"Thanks," I said, as Dawes took a green peppermint out of the bowl on Wagner's desk and left the office.

"Man, I wish he wasn't taking off right now," said Wagner. "He's the best I got, but he planned this break with his family for almost nine months, ever since his oldest girl got pregnant."

"He's been here a while?"

"Long time. Before me. What's with this Armstrong business?"

"Just looking for enlightenment."

"Dawes is your guy. He's like us; he came up through the ranks. He walked a beat down around 125th Street in the worst fucking times, late eighties, crack fucking dealers in every door. He's good and he's straight, and even in the bad times at this house I don't think he ever took so much as a free cup of coffee from anyone. He's got cast-iron morality stamped on his soul, that guy."

"Thanks."

"So that's what you wanted, this thing about the Armstrong?" Wagner looked at his watch.

I didn't move.

"Artie?"

"Yeah?"

"You wanna tell me what this is really about?"

CHAPTER 13

I told Wagner a string of little lies, just knit them together the way an old aunt of mine used to knit the hideous brown wool scarves I had to wear as a kid. "I've been hearing this area is really good now—they call it the New Harlem," I said to Wagner.

He shrugged. "Lot of people coming uptown, buying in, before the crash, I mean. Nobody's buying nothing with this subprime shit, with those bastard fucks downtown on Wall Street. I know a lot of good cops gonna lose their houses. All they care about, those fuckers like Madoff and the others, sharks, you know, bastards, is money. I'd fry them if I could, motherfucking bastards," he said, echoing the fury of working guys all over town. "They just pocket the bonuses and leave us all swinging in the wind." Crushing out his smoke, lighting up a fresh one, he leaned back in his chair, told me his guys had been told to give the Armstrong special attention, in case I wanted to tell my friend.

"Who told you?"

"Somebody on the City Council, far as I recall. But the Armstrong residents usually call the firehouse anyway. People don't like calling cops, you know, Artie, not in Harlem; no love lost, right? I hear people say, 'Well, the fire guys always show up if you're stuck in an elevator.' There's people around here that still think of us as pigs, you know? I can't help it if we have other things to take care of, like homicides, instead of getting a cat out of a tree."

"They got cats in trees in Harlem?"

"Metaphorically, man. I mean, some old lady needs help because she got locked out, you know, Artie?" Wagner was irritated. "Me, I don't understand if you got the dough and you could buy a house,

79

why would you want an apartment? Everybody stacked up in boxes, one under the other, like those graves where they stick in extra people when they run out of space," he said. "Manhattan! Well, whatever, maybe I'm just a suburban asshole that likes my privacy. My house on Staten Island is free and clear. It took me thirty years to pay it off," he said. Wagner's cell phone rang. He picked it up, turned to me and said, "Excuse me a sec, Artie. I got something to take care of."

After Wagner left his office, I noticed a picture of the Twin Towers on the back wall of the office. Beside it was one of George W. Bush. Frank Sinatra was up there, the heavyset Sinatra with the rug on his head, and his signature in white. I'd seen it on a lot of walls. Also there was a color picture of Jesus with a bleeding heart, same as I always see on the wall over at Pino's, the butcher on Sullivan Street. Finally, there was a photograph of a pair of basketball players, signed and framed. In between them stood Jimmy Wagner.

I got up and looked at it closer. The players were Earl Monroe and Amahl Washington. Both black. Both a lot taller than Jimmy.

I was interested in it because I'd always been a fan of Monroe, at least from what I read, because I never saw him play.

"She white? If you don't mind my asking," said Wagner returning to his office.

"Who?"

"Your friend that wants to buy into the Armstrong."

"Yeah. Is that a problem?"

"She'll be fine," Wagner said. "There's always been white people this part of Harlem, a few now, a few more came in the housing boom, you know, fixing up stuff, designer types, actors, like that."

"I didn't really think about color when I asked about the building."

"No? Well, you should always think about it, man, no matter who we elect president, and don't get me wrong, I like Obama, OK? But no matter how many brownstones are on the market for a mill, or how many gay guys fix them up, or how many celebrities once lived on Sugar Hill, it is what it is," he said. "This is Harlem."

I knew that some of Wagner's views had been formed by his time in Crown Heights, back when the Hassidic Jews and local blacks decided to try and kill each other. Back in the day, back in Brooklyn.

"You manage OK here, even with those young guys you mentioned, the kind that want to solve a homicide in a TV hour?"

"Yeah, sure, and I got at least one that's smart as hell." Wagner looked at me. He had an old cop's instincts. "Maybe you know him."

"What?

"Yeah, well, I mentioned you to him, in fact, when was it, yesterday, I was trying to get hold of you to translate that Russian thing, and he said he met you once. Name's Radcliff. Virgil. Black guy. Very educated. It rings a bell, Artie?"

I paused, pretending to try to place Radcliff. "I don't know, maybe I met him over at John Jay when I gave some lecture."

"He partnered with Dawes for a while. It didn't work out. Dawes said he wanted to work solo."

"How come?"

"You'd have to ask him. He just said he didn't want to work with Radcliff, and I let it lay because Dawes earned a right to what he wants." Wagner was clearly itching to get back to work now. I asked for a cigarette. I stalled.

"So go on," I said.

Jimmy looked at me as he tossed over a pack of smokes and I lit up. "Listen, Radcliff, he's a good cop that joined up right after 9/11, worked like a dog, walked the beat. Dawes just doesn't think Radcliff will stick around long. Probably go to law school or become DA. No sense of humor," said Wagner whose phone rang again. He picked it up, listened, grunted, set it down.

"How's that?"

"First time I met him, he tells me his name is Virgil and I say, 'So what do they call you, do they call you Mr. Tibbs?' From that movie. He just looks at me like I'm some weird racist motherfucker or something and says, 'I don't know what you mean.' In that real nice voice, no acrimony, but I got the picture. I was just kidding around, no disrespect, you know? Gives you an idea how things go up here."

"So, if you're white, people figure you for a racist?"

"What do you think, Artie?" said Wagner, looking toward his half-open door, where a Latino detective in a suit was waiting. "I have to go."

I got up.

"Anything else you need, Art, you know, just let me know," Wagner said.

"Thanks. By the way, I was looking at that picture on your wall. You know, I used to read about Earl Monroe. You knew him?"

"I was a big fan when I was younger—I mean huge. I'm telling you, I never saw anything like him. Earl the Pearl, they used to call him, or Black Magic. The crowds would just go silent, and you could hear them gasp when he was on the court.

"Who's the other one?"

Was there a slight pause?

"Amahl Washington, played on the same team as Earl. Amahl—it was his real name. He was a gent. Matter of fact, he lived over at the Armstrong."

"Lived?"

"He passed."

I was interested now. "When?"

"Six months, seven."

"What did he die of?"

"Lungs. Then liver. Cancer spread everywhere, but I never knew how sick he was. I felt really bad. But you know how us cops are, crybabies about stuff when we care. You know that, Artie. 'You cops are such bleeding-heart liberals some of the time,' Well, anyhow, Jesus, I hope they just give me a shot and put me out of my misery when the time comes. Poor Amahl. I really loved that guy. What a fucking talent!"

"So it seemed sudden?"

"I don't know, these things go real fast some of the time."

"Can you get me the name of Washington's doctor?"

Wagner looked surprised. "Sure," he said. "I sent some money for us over to the hospital when they set up a fund, so yeah, I got it some place. I'll call you. What's this about, man?"

"I'll let you know."

I stood out by the front door of the station house and tried to get my bearings. My car was parked at the curb. Again, I wondered vaguely why Julius Dawes had taken an interest in it, but I had something else on my mind.

Amahl Washington had died in the Armstrong from lung disease. Jimmy Wagner had been surprised he went so fast. Lily had already been in the building when it happened. She had never mentioned it. I was zipping my jacket when somebody tapped me on the shoulder. I jumped.

"You OK, man?" said Wagner, and I turned. He had a piece of paper in his hand. "I got it for you, Artie. To tell the truth, the whole thing with Amahl, it all stuck in my craw. I didn't fucking like it, the way he went so fast. It gave me pause, you could say," Wagner added. "Still, there was no evidence of nothing, not so far as I could see."

"But it bugged you?"

"Maybe I just didn't want to believe it, end of an era."

"So it was the cancer that finally killed him?"

"They said it was his heart gave out; he couldn't breathe."

"But there was something else?"

"I saw him one day, it's a Sunday when I go over, and he's OK. I mean, he's sick, but he's walking and talking, and the next day, that Monday, I get a call that Amahl passed. Fuck. You get older, it happens," he said. "You wanted the doc's name, I found a thank-you letter she sent us when we gave some money in Amahl's name."

"Thanks, Jimmy."

"Name's Lucille Bernard. Dr. Bernard. That help you out, Artie? That works for you?"

CHAPTER 14

In my hand was a hot pretzel with yellow mustard I bought from a guy on the corner near the hospital. I was hungry as hell. I hadn't eaten all day. I sat in my car and ate, and tried to process what Jimmy Wagner had told me. The pretzel tasted fantastic. I washed it down with a Coke.

Lucille Bernard was Marianna Simonova's doctor. She had treated Amahl Washington. Both of them died at the Armstrong.

As soon as I'd left the precinct, I'd tried to call Lily, see if Dr Bernard had been over to sign the death certificate. No answer. Bernard didn't answer her phone, either. I finished the pretzel, wiped my hands on a Kleenex, and got out of my car.

Two patients stood outside the main door at Presbyterian, leaning on walkers, coats over their hospital gowns, smoking. The overhang of the roof kept the snow off them. Out for a smoke. One of them, a young woman with red hair, waved a hand at me as she saw me looking. I waved back.

Who could blame them? What else did you have by the time you were in the hospital for Christmas and needed a walker to get around? By the time you were falling apart, all you had were cigarettes. Maybe music.

Lucille Bernard's office in the hospital was empty except for a distracted woman in jeans who told me she was gone for the day. It took me a while to find somebody else, an Indian doctor, who said Dr. Bernard was in a conference in the other building, where I went, only to discover nobody knew anything about a conference. I called Bernard again. I left another message. I got hold of a secretary and told her it was urgent. She gave me directions.

I had to double back twice, had to cross a bridge between two buildings. Everything looked the same, everyone was in a hurry, doctors, nurses, visitors. The elevators were packed, the halls blocked by people pushing the sick on gurneys. Only the patients were still, staring at the ceiling as somebody pushed them, like trays of meat, to another part of the hospital, to surgery, or who knew where, maybe to die.

Come on!

Finally, back at Bernard's office, I bullied a young guy, an intern, maybe, into getting her home address for me. Either my badge impressed him, or he didn't care, and he simply walked into her office and looked in her Rolodex, and as he came out, I noticed a woman with little piggy eyes and a pinched mouth watching us. I didn't care. At least I got a smile and a cookie in the shape of a Christmas tree from a small, sexy nurse. I ate the cookie. It had red sugar on it.

When I got into my car and looked in the rear view, I saw red sprinkles all over my mouth and I laughed at myself, first time that day, then wiped it off with a Kleenex I found in the glove compartment, put a CD into the slot, and listened to Louis Armstrong. "West End Blues" cheered me up even more than the cookie.

Twenty minutes later, I was on 139th Street in front of Dr. Bernard's house. The traffic was jammed up because of the weather and hard pellets of ice hit my windshield.

"Yes?" Her voice through the door was pitched low. I knew she was looking at me through a peephole. I gave her my name and waited, looking at the beautiful brass knocker and knob, polished up to shine. The door opened a crack.

"Yes?"

I showed her my badge, and she opened the door wider to let me in. She was a tall, handsome woman of about forty. She didn't like me the minute she saw me.

Wearing a gray suit, her hair caught back with a velvet headband, she had an impatient face.

"You better come inside," she said, looking at the wet snow on my jacket.

The heels of her boots rang on the dark wood floors of the long hall, and I followed her, keeping up as she walked faster and faster. It was a beautiful, high-ceilinged town house that must have dated back to the turn of the twentieth century. I said so. "Stanford White designed this house," she said. I said I had read *Ragtime*, in which the architect had featured. She seemed faintly surprised that I'd read a book.

On the deep red walls of the hall were photographs, sepia studies of Harlem in the early twentieth century, as well as a framed poster of Angela Davis.

Bernard saw me looking.

"You know who that is?"

"Yes."

It was the second time that day somebody had quizzed me on my knowledge of famous black Americans—first Robeson, now Davis. Angela Davis had visited the USSR. She had been a member of the American Communist Party and was much admired. She was also stunning and articulate. People in Moscow were charmed by her. "She speaks such nice French and is so kind," my mother, an obsessive Francophile, had said after she met Davis at a party. There were plenty of places where the Soviet Union and black America had once intersected.

I didn't want to risk crossing Dr. Bernard when I needed information from her about Marianna Simonova, so I just nodded again and said, "Yes. I know."

"Please sit down," said Dr. Bernard when we got to a small study. There was a red and blue kilim on the floor, the walls were lined with books. On a shelf some antique surgical tools were displayed. The windows, old-fashioned wooden shutters folded back, looked out onto a courtyard, where there was already half a foot of snow.

Bernard sat down at her antique rolltop desk.

"Right," she said. "What can I do for you? I only came back to my house to get some paperwork I need. I haven't much time, and to tell the truth I only let you in so you'll stop bullying my people at the hospital. Don't do that again. Now, what is it you need me for?"

"I just wanted to see when you're coming to Marianna Simonova's place. I could give you a ride," I said, keeping my temper.

"Excuse me? What are you talking about?"

"Didn't Lily Hanes call you?"

"Who?"

"Lily Hanes. She called you this morning about your patient Mrs. Simonova."

"No, she didn't," said Bernard.

"Can you check your messages?"

Bernard picked up her cell phone, then listened to her voice mail on the landline. She called the hospital. She turned to me.

"You're satisfied? Now what's the problem with Mrs. Simonova?" she said.

Bernard leaned back slightly in her chair. On the credenza behind her was a large Mac. On the screen was a picture of a tall, pretty girl of about fourteen with Dr. Bernard beside her. Bernard was wearing a yellow sleeveless summer dress and high-heeled sandals.

"Simonova is your patient, though?"

Bernard glanced at me. "Yes, of course," she said. "I've been treating Mrs. Simonova for COPD for a while now. That's emphysema to you."

"Was it your opinion she was terminal?"

"Why?" Her head snapped up. Clearly, Lily had not called the doctor. She had lied to me.

"I'm simply asking."

"What's happened?"

"Can you give me some background?"

"Why don't you tell me what's going on," she said. "I'm busy, and unless you tell me why you're here and why you've been calling me, there's no way that I'm going to share privileged information." She reached for the phone as if to indicate she was finished with me.

"Look, I'm sorry," I said. "Let's start again. Marianna Simonova died earlier, probably sometime this morning."

"What?"

"You're surprised?"

"Yes. She was in only Wednesday, I think. I thought she was a bit better. Her saturation level was better. We'd been worried," said Bernard. "It's not impossible, of course; she was pretty sick. This cold weather is terrible for anyone with lung problems, though she was tough. Still, she hadn't followed my instructions. I know she continued to smoke."

"Did anyone come with her, bring her to your office?"

Bernard looked up. "Yes, a woman came with her the last few months. A white woman."

"Lily Hanes," I said.

"I think that's right. Tall woman? She was a bit of a stickler, taking notes, wanting to know everything about Marianna's condition, what medication she needed, everything. Well, she was meticulous, I'll say that for her. Thank you for letting me know about Marianna," said Bernard. "But what's your interest?"

"I know some of her friends."

"You mean this Hanes woman?"

"Yes. She suggested her neighbor—Dr. Hutchison—could sign the death certificate, because it would speed things up. Apparently Mrs. Simonova wanted a Jewish burial. It requires a pretty quick turnaround, so to speak."

"I know that. I have Jewish patients," said Bernard. "Was Marianna Jewish?" She gathered up her purse and some folders from her desk. "I'd prefer to sign the death certificate myself. I'll get there as soon as I can."

"You know Dr. Hutchison?"

"Yes. He's a good doctor. He's certainly got all his marbles in spite of his age. He is past eighty, you know. But Lionel's problems are with his ideas. I am fond of him, though."

"But you'd still rather sign the death certificate yourself?"

"We disagree on certain things."

I thought about the euthanasia book. "Ethical things?" She nodded. "But you trust Lionel Hutchison? In spite of the ethical issues?"

"Yes, of course." She hesitated. "I'd just like to see Marianna. You're a cop. Is there something about this that bothers you? Is that why you're really here?"

"Could I have a glass of water?" I was stalling for time.

She couldn't refuse the water, especially since I faked a hacking cough. And while she was in the kitchen getting it, I managed to glance at her desk. I had seen her scribble a name while we were talking.

"You were stalling for time?" Bernard had a portable phone in one hand. In the other was the glass of water, which she gave me, and I drank it while she sat down on a chair opposite mine and crossed her legs.

In the long black boots, her legs were spectacular, and I had to force myself not to stare. Sometimes I think I must be sick, looking at a woman's legs at the same time I was inquiring about dead people. Maybe all guys are like me. I don't know.

I put the glass on the desk. "Thank you."

"I've just spoken to Lionel Hutchison," said Bernard. "We went through everything together. He assures me that it was Marianna's lungs, that it was the disease that killed her. He said she had been in pain the past few days. But I told him not to do anything until I got there."

"Like what? What can you do now that Simonova is dead?"

"I want to see her. That's all. I'll make my way over this afternoon, as soon as I can."

While I was putting on my jacket, it hit me: Lionel Hutchison really had known Marianna Simonova was dead all along. He had entered the apartment through the terrace, or he had a set of keys Lily didn't know about. Or Lily had told him.

"I have to go."

"I must get back to the hospital," said Bernard.

"You were close, you and Dr. Hutchison?"

"Once. Yes. He was my teacher, but I'm a Roman Catholic. Lionel has views, as I've told you—he has his reasons, but I can't condone them," she said. "I'll see you out. I have patients this afternoon, then I'll make my way over." She took a card from the desk. "All my numbers are here."

She got up, went to the front of the house, put her camel-colored coat on, fastened the belt.

"One more thing."

"Yes?"

"Amahl Washington. You were his doctor, too?"

"I was his doctor, but how is that your business?"

"I'm interested."

"Be that as it may, I can't talk to you about Mr. Washington," said Bernard. "And by the way, detective, you didn't have to read my memo pad; you could simply ask. You saw something that interested you?"

"Carver Lennox."

"He's my husband," she said. "But anyone could have told you that."

"You don't live together?"

"We're separated. I don't believe in divorce." She opened the front door. We went outside.

"He lives at the Armstrong."

"Yes," Bernard took her keys out of her bag. "Last I heard he was trying to transform the building. Buying up the apartments, making the place grand again. That bloody building. Carver was obsessed. How he loves money and all it can buy. Eventually all he talked about was money. Maybe it makes him feel that white men will let him into their playground," she said softly, locked her door, went to the curb, got in her dark blue Audi, and drove away.

* * *

Lily had lied to me about calling Dr. Bernard. How was she involved in Simonova's death? I killed her, Lily had said. Had she really screwed up the meds? If Simonova's death became a case, would it count as involuntary manslaughter? Could they indict Lily if she had been negligent? Is that what Radcliff thought and wouldn't tell me?

Leaning against Lucille Bernard's front door, I got out my phone. "Where are you?" I said when Lily answered.

"Doing some errands," she said. "I told you."

"What kind? You've been out a long time just doing errands."

"I'm just at the drugstore, for chrissake, Artie. Please."

"Which drugstore? I'll come meet you."

"Don't do that, Artie. I'm just getting lady stuff, you know, makeup, things," she said. "I'm going back to the apartment as soon as I'm done," she added. "Please, Artie, just do whatever you're doing and meet me up at my place, right? OK? I love that you worry about me, but I'm fine now."

"Which drugstore?"

"Stop being a pain in the ass. I'm getting you a little Christmas present, OK? So stop bothering me right now." Her words ran on, her voice was stilted. I didn't believe her.

"I love you," I said without meaning to.

"I'll see you in an hour or so?"

"Sooner."

"Fine. I'll be back soon. It's just Christmas shopping," she said lightly. "And her pills."

"What?"

"Marianna's pills. I wanted to make sure her prescription was filled, you know?"

"What are you talking about?" I said, but the line cut out, or Lily hung up. What was she talking about? My car was parked by the curb. I got in. I was shivering.

This was what terror felt like. I'd worked cases where they'd killed and frozen babies in food lockers, cases where a man was poisoned with radioactive shit he had been carrying around in his own suitcase. I'd seen things done to women that gave me an ulcer. I'd been beaten up. This was worse.

Watching Lily, listening to her, feeling she might be cracking up, losing her mind. I was terrified. Literally. I didn't know if I could help her. If she had lost her mind, I'd stay. I told myself I'd always stay. But what was she doing getting meds for a dead woman?

CHAPTER 15

Diaz, cigarette hanging from his lips, was out back of the Armstrong, talking to a man in a black winter jacket, hood over his head. As soon as Diaz saw me pull up in my car, he said something to the man, who nodded, then jogged away. I realized it could have been the guy from the station house, the Russian Jimmy Wagner said was named Ivan Ivanov.

What was he doing here? Had he been following me? Was it even him, after all? Lot of guys wear black North Face jackets with hoods. I got out of my car, and crossed the bleak backyard to where Diaz stood.

"Who was that?" I said.

"Some guy." Diaz sucked on his cigarette.

"You looked pretty cozy."

"Whatever."

"He was asking about me?"

"I didn't understand him that well. He had some kind of accent."

"Russian?"

"I have to get back to work," Diaz said.

The underground smells in the Armstrong basement, the noises from the floor above, the footsteps, the sound of a mouse, or a rat, made me edgy. In the basement you heard pipes clang; the ancient boiler roared. It was very cold. Before the signal went out on my phone, I tried Lily, left a message saying I was in the basement and I'd stop by Simonova's storage room to get the Christmas ornaments she had asked me to find.

"I'll be upstairs in a few minutes," I said on Lily's voice mail.

When I tried Lucille Bernard, she answered. Said she'd be over in an hour, two, tops. Just wait, she said. I'd wait. Anyway, I'd been itching to get into Simonova's storage room since early that morning when Lily had given me the key.

From the laundry room came the sound of machines going around and around. Somebody in there was singing. I made a detour.

"Did I startle you?" said a voice.

I squinted into the room lit only by a couple of dim overhead bulbs. The voice belonged to a woman who looked about sixty-five, dark skin, carefully curled silvery hair, bright blue apron over her sweater and slacks. She was short, a little stout, and she was sitting on a plastic chair, arms resting on the washing machine. She removed the ear buds from her MP3 player. She got up slowly.

"Can I help?"

"I was looking for the storage rooms."

"Turn to your left, then left again, you'll find them fine," she said. "Any room in particular?"

"Mrs. Simonova's. You know her?"

"We live on the same floor," she said. "You couldn't say we were friends or nothing, I don't think she liked my playing my music."

"What were you listening to?"

"Ella Fitzgerald," she said.

"Which song?"

"Are you a fan?"

"Big-time."

"It's a nice one for sure. Called 'Skylark,' Hoagy Carmichael and Johnny Mercer. I met Mr. Mercer several times," she said with a smile that revealed a gap between her front teeth, then offered me one of the ear buds so I could listen with her.

The music flowed into my head. We stood in the dank laundry room, the washing machine vibrating, and listened. I remembered something my father told me.

He had been in America as a very young KGB agent, his assignment to learn his way around American culture, and he fell for the music. For jazz, most of all, and of all the jazz he loved, Ella Fitzgerald was his favorite, his saint, if he'd had a religion. He once said to me, very quietly, "In New York, I felt that my good Communist soul was being sucked out, Artyom. Not by material goods, or by the American way of life, but by the music, especially by Ella Fitzgerald."

"Do you know this?" said the woman and fiddled with her MP3 player. "This is a nice old Decca one, just Ella and Ellis Larkins on the piano. I always did love it."

"You knew her?"

She removed her earpiece.

"Oh, yes, sir. I grew up in Yonkers where Miss Ella, she was an orphan living with some relatives, my ma lived next door, I was just a girl. She grew up, then she began to sing, nobody ever did hear a voice like that, a pure instrument, you see, like God singing right into that girl's head and out of her mouth. Never could find a man, though, after Ray Brown broke her heart."

"Please, go on."

"I met her in the nineteen fifties. There wasn't no work around, so I offered to help her out. She liked to iron her own clothes, and I'd say to her, 'That's not right; you're a star,' and I went to help her out at her house in Queens, Murdock Avenue, Addisleigh Park, they were all there, all the musicians were there, and Count Basie, he was a fine, lovely man and we all liked him. Then Ella went to California. I did go out there for a little when she was so sick. We stayed in touch all of her life. After she died I wasn't any good to anybody for a long time, I missed her so bad. But she made sure I had a nice place to live. My name is Regina McGee."

I told her I was visiting Lily. "Good girl, that Lily. She is kind to everybody," she said, as the washing machine finished its cycle and beeped. She opened the door and extracted a pile of wet towels. "Thank God I still got that little apartment."

"You know the people here well?"

"Yes, sure do, I been here most of the time since nineteen fifty-seven. Come by my place if you want, and I'll show my pictures of Ella. I have pictures from times we shared in New York when we were just lonely girls together around town."

"I'd like that," I said. "You must have been very young when you knew her."

"Oh, not so young. I'm eighty years old today."

I wished her happy birthday.

"Can I come see you a little later?" I asked.

"Not going anywhere," she said. "Not even if that Mr. Lennox makes me an offer I can't refuse."

"What's that?"

"Well, he wants my place, wants to break through the wall and connect it to some other apartment, make a big old space out of it, he says."

"He pressures you?"

"Honey, I have been pressured by the best. I was born in North Carolina. Grew up by the tracks in Yonkers. I done slept on the New York City streets. Ain't selling to nobody, 'specially not to Mr. Carver Lennox. You know, he puts me in mind of Stumpy Brown. You know who that was?"

I shook my head.

"Not the height, but the way he has. Stump was a little guy, big-time numbers runner up here, lived right next door at 409. Tiny little man, small like Chick Webb—you know, the band leader that gave Miss Ella her big break—and Stump, he lived in this building a while. He worked for Madame St. Clair at the end of her days. She ran that gang they called Forty Thieves. Extorted from everyone. Stump wore flashy clothes, and he would flash a wad of cash. He was arrogant and he was slick, and he always got what he wanted. Like these fellows, what you call them? Hedge fund? De-riv-i-tives. Yeah. Like Carver Lennox, only he ain't so short. Just short in his soul."

I nodded.

"You're interested?"

"Yes."

"You were up in Miss Marianna's place?"

"You know that?"

"Honey! We all know everything. She was quite a person, that

Russian lady. Her and Carver, always talking together. I was surprised to hear she passed."

"Why's that?"

"Don't know, I saw her day before yesterday; she look all right to me," said Regina McGee, pausing. I knew she was making up her mind about something. "You're a detective, that right?"

"I've been one a long time," I said.

"I like you," she said. "My son was a detective, a good one, too. Got killed by some junkies down by 116th Street back when crack cocaine ruled these streets."

"I'm sorry."

"Maybe it's time I told somebody," she said finally, glancing in the direction of the door. "You want to keep this to yourself, but you ask if I was surprised about Mrs. Simonova passing, well, indeed I was, just like I was surprised when somebody else in the building passed a while back."

"Who was that?"

McGee moved a little closer to me. "Mr. Amahl Washington," she said.

"You knew him?"

"I did. He was a sweet man, and for a while we were what they used to call stepping out, but he got sick and his friends were just buzzing around, specially that Carver Lennox, making like he cared so much, and by the end I didn't hardly see Amahl at all." She paused, nervous. "I still think about it sometimes. I ask myself, How did he pass so suddenly? Now it happens with Mrs. Simonova, and I'm thinking you get sick in this building, you die, but maybe that's just my sadness speaking."

She looked at a little gold watch set with diamonds. "Gift from Miss Ella," she said. "It's getting late. Make sure you come by and visit me."

CHAPTER 16

Hello?" I had Marianna Simonova's storage room door half open. I called out again, but what did I expect, some fucking ghost? It was pitch black in the room, and I fumbled on the wall for a switch. The light came on—a low-watt lousy overhead bulb.

I moved inside. Left the door open a crack. I didn't want anyone to see me poking around, but I hate tight spaces. Hate them. Already I could feel the walls closing in.

On the wall near the light switch was a half-peeled sticker with the Atomic symbol. This had been a nuclear fallout shelter once, back when Americans figured Russia was going to bomb us. We thought the same thing when I was a kid. I'd wake up at night sweating, thinking America was going to nuke us and we'd fry in our beds, our faces oozing off.

The room was about eight by fourteen, long, narrow, the old paint on the walls scabby and falling off. It was jammed all the way back and halfway to the ceiling with furniture, chairs, dressers, rugs, tables all piled on top of each other.

A crummy metal rack to the right held rows of pictures, most in fake gold frames. I slid one out. It was an oil painting of some happy workers on a pig farm. From the 1950s. But there were also Chagall prints and what looked like a Rodchenko poster. Not an original, I figured.

Something about Simonova had made me feel she'd been playing a part. All the right props. Maybe I was just pissed off at her for dying and making Lily sad. Making me spend time in a dark little room that felt like a coffin. On a shelf to the right were about a hundred wooden dolls, all sizes, all kinds, an endless row of wooden dollies. Gave me the creeps. I ran my flashlight over the room.

I had no idea where the Christmas decorations would be. Boxes on top of boxes, some so precarious I figured they were going to fall on me, topple over, bury me under tons of stuff. Books were stuck into the crevices between pieces of furniture, little gilt tables with legs missing, cracked mirrors, a samovar, varnished boxes in plastic bags. It was like a souvenir stall, a bazaar, a flea market. What the hell did she need all this crap for?

Close to where I stood was a pile of cushions, red, gold, green, velvet and satin, fabric frayed. The stink of damp came off them. I could hear water drip. A few drops fell on my head. I brushed them away. I reached out for the wall; the cement blocks were moist. There were newspapers tied up like bales of hay and a baby stroller with a wheel missing.

Again, I heard a rat, maybe the same rat I'd heard that morning. All New York buildings have rats. There had been rats on Sutton Place when I worked a crime at the Middlemarch, a huge fancy building, rich people, swimming pool, and rats. Fat ones. Well fed. Too fat to run. Fat people. Fat rats.

Here, I was shut up with the rats, and I could hear one, maybe more, scratching at the walls. I'd give it five more minutes, I said to myself. I found a cardboard box that was half open. When I scrabbled inside, it made me gag—mothballs, old newspaper, something I couldn't identify that smelled like a dead animal. It was a fur hat.

There was a huge rusting metal trunk, the lettering—Simonova's name—was in English and Russian. It was easy to get to, so I opened it.

Start at the top, I thought. I found a thick folder with papers in it, official stuff, old and yellow, and I set it aside. Maybe a will, I thought, maybe something important about the woman's life.

It was like an archaeological dig, everything packed in layers. On top were two winter coats and boots with labels from Macy's. There were copies of the *New Yorker* that dated back ten years. Underneath were books, huge tomes in Russian on socialism, economics, history.

Then more clothes. Fancy dress-up clothes, evening things, stuff she might have worn to go out, and hats, and shawls. Beneath these were some stage costumes—Robeson's, I wondered?

I dug further. There were military uniforms, heavy rough pieces, brown, khaki, scratchy fabric, stiff with age, and with them thick leather belts and broken boots. Maybe her father had been in the war. I even found a Young Pioneer's outfit, complete with shirt, shorts, red scarf, stinking of ancient kiddie sweat. I'd had one like it that I'd hated. In a cardboard hatbox, I found a little nest of children's clothes with American labels. A little boy's clothes.

At the bottom of the trunk were old Soviet magazines, including the famous issue of *Soviet Life* with the bear on the cover, along with copies of *Pravda, Komsomolskaya Pravda, Izvestia.*

I took out one brittle yellow paper and it crumbled into my hand. It was from October of 1962, the year of the Cuban Missile Crisis, when my own father, a young KGB agent, was stuck in New York. I had read his diary. In one of the newspapers now, mesmerized by the style of the propaganda, I read an article about Cuba. Russians loved their little socialist brother, the author had written. How stylish and handsome and brave were its *barbudos,* the bearded ones, how wonderful the music. That year, the top hit in Moscow was "Cuba My Love."

I used my flashlight to read the papers. There were stories about Paul Robeson's visit to Moscow, about the wild party in 1961, about his alleged suicide attempt and the CIA's efforts to silence him.

There was more. Programs from Robeson's performances, articles about his part in the Spanish Civil War, a thousand-page biography. It was as if Simonova had been trying to piece together his life, as if she had been an actress preparing for the part of his lover. I wondered if she had made it all up, a story she retailed to make herself important, a tale that had ensnared Lily.

Finally, I found a shoe box—BONWIT TELLER, the logo said—and I rummaged through it. There were glass baubles, red velvet flowers, gold bows. There was a small, flat box addressed to Lily. I put it in my pocket. Ready to leave, I turned off my flashlight.

Something hit me hard on the back of the neck. The pain was so intense I wanted to vomit. I could hear somebody behind me in the storage room breathing hard. I kicked out as hard as I could. I kicked again and again, fumbling at the same time for my gun. Remembered I'd left it in my car when I went into the hospital.

In my pocket was a Swiss Army knife. Getting it out, I cut my own hand on the corkscrew. My hand started to bleed. I dropped the knife. Just then I thought I heard the man behind me swear in Russian. I couldn't be sure. I was frantic. It was pitch black in the little room. Then he hit me with the butt of a gun. I waited for the next blow; it would kill me.

Suddenly from someplace out in the basement came the sound of voices. The creep backed out. Then the door slammed. It was locked from outside.

My hand was still bleeding. I found an old shirt and wound it around the red gash. I thought: this is where I'm going to end up, suffocating in a basement room in Harlem full of stinking Russian clothes and newspapers. All around me was the detritus of the Soviet Union—Simonova's past, my own. I'd never escape.

If I get out, I said to myself, I'll quit. I'll quit being a cop. I'll teach school, or take my pension, or work for Tolya tending bar—he was always asking me to go into business with him. The rest of the time, I'll take care of Lily. I'll lie around and watch baseball and listen to Ella Fitzgerald and Stan Getz, like a New York Oblomov.

I didn't believe I'd get out, and the feeling of loss and pain, the thought that Lily was just upstairs, made me crazy. This was where I was going to die.

How long did I stay in the room? I must have passed out. When I came to, I looked at my watch. It had been almost an hour.

I'd told Lily I was going to the storage room. Where was she?

Maybe she had slipped on the ice when she was out, or got hit by a car in a skid. Why didn't she come looking for me or call some-body, call Virgil Radcliff? Where was she?

I banged on the door, yelling, but there was no reply. I'm going to die in this room. I'm going to bleed and die.

Minutes went by.

Animals scampered past.

Footsteps passed overhead.

Somebody playing Ella, improbable, my hallucination. Ella sing-ing "Manhattan."

My finger bleeding through the scrap of white cloth.

Me, gagging on my past.

CHAPTER **17**

W hat happened?"
　 I sat in Tolya Sverdloff's SUV, trying not to cry from the pain. My head hurt so bad I had to close my eyes. Leaned back. Tried not to whimper. Floaters cruised the air in front of my face, bubbles of light and the pain that I couldn't stop. Again, I tried to open my eyes. It was really Tolya sitting beside me. We were parked on Edgecombe Avenue opposite the Armstrong. He handed me a bottle of water. My hand was neatly bandaged.

"You did this?" I said to him.

"Sure," he said. "You recall I have been medic in Russian army. So we are going to see my doctor, Artyom. I made this appointment already. I pay. No emergency room, no quacks, nobody on police health insurance plan."

Somebody tapped on the car window. Still squinting through a fog of pain, I saw Carver Lennox. I opened the window. Lennox leaned in.

"How you doing, Artie?" He looked worried.

"I'm OK," I said.

"Carver is who finds you, Artie," said Tolya.

"What?"

"Lily calls you on cell, says you told her you'd be at her place in ten minutes, that you're in the basement of the building, but she can't reach you, can't reach this guy, Virgil. She calls me. I call Carver."

"Thanks," I said. "Yeah, thank you." I didn't like it that I owed him now.

"I was worried as hell," said Lennox. "You must have been in that storage room an hour. More."

"You have any idea who did it? You think it was somebody who works in the building?" I said to Lennox.

"I can't see why," he said. "They didn't take anything off you, did they?"

I checked my pockets. My wallet was intact, my phone, too.

"Nothing."

"You been hassling any of the guys that work here?" said Lennox. "They get pissed off. Not that a few of them couldn't do with a wake-up call."

"Why would I?"

"You're a cop, aren't you? But listen, I'm sorry. I'm getting in some real security. I don't want this kind of shit going down in my building," he said, referring to the building as his own. I thanked him again and otherwise kept my mouth shut.

"Don't mention it," he said. "I have to go now, but call if you need anything. Artie. Tolya." With a nod, he left and went into the building, the black coat flapping behind him in the cold wind.

"How the hell did you know to call Lennox?" I said to Tolya.

"Everybody in Harlem knows him. If you want real estate you must know him. So I know him. Drink some more." He gave me a second bottle of water.

Wearing a black suit and red shoes, the Gucci loafers he has made for him out of the skins of weird reptiles, six six, three hundred pounds, Tolya was looking good. The heart surgery he had during the summer had worked out. He was happy running his club, Pravda2, in the West Village. He bought good wines for it; he traveled to France regularly.

Tolya has been my best friend for a long time. I met him fifteen years back, more even, and, as they say in Russian, we've shared more than one sack of salt.

Last summer, when some creeps snatched Tolya off a Moscow street, they asked me for the promise of a favor. I told them I'd do whatever they wanted if they let Tolya go. Anything. It had been my fault that his daughter Valentina was murdered. He had never blamed me.

We got the creep who did it, but I'd never figured out who had fingered Valentina in the first place. I never knew who had discovered where she lived in New York, where she went, who she went with. I knew if I ever did, I would kill him. I loved Val a lot.

The promise I had made in exchange for Tolya was to the FSB, the new version of the KGB. These guys were tough, and they were corrupt. So far they hadn't asked me for anything, but it would come.

"Artyom?" Tolya was watching me, looking worried.

"I have to go," I said. "I have to get to Lily. Tolya, listen to me, I think whoever beat me up spoke Russian. What are you doing here, anyway?"

"I told you, Lily calls me, she's worried, I don't know if she's crazy or this is for real, so I call Lennox, like I tell you. I was not far away."

"I mean what were you doing uptown?

"I have business."

"What business?"

"You recall from election night? I said I love this Harlem, and so I will buy a house, I said this to you, and I have bought."

"You bought a house?"

"Sure. Maybe I buy nice little club, you can run, you can employ jazz musicians instead of getting beat up, Artyom. Maybe I buy Minton's Playhouse for you if you want. Is enough already, being a cop."

"Where? The house?"

"Strivers' Row, you tell me I am striver, so I buy lovely, lovely brownstone. I am striver, no?"

"I thought you were done with business, with deals, all that shit."

"Oh, but Artyom, one lovely brownstone is not deals. You will come. Tonight, you can stay with me."

"You're living there already?"

"Sure. Cash deal. No problem."

"You're fucking crazy."

"Yes."

I put up my hand as if to catch one of the floaters in front of my eyes, a long gold and purple flash, like an exotic insect.

Tolya handed me some pills. "Take this," said Tolya, in Russian now, the beautiful, elegant Russian he had learned from his parents, who had been actors. They had taken him with them to France and England when they performed. They were pretty upset when Tolya became a rocker. He had been arrested back in the day, when rock was illegal in the USSR.

He speaks four, five languages, if you include Ukrainian, and his English is great, except when he's drunk, or when he's putting me on, dropping articles, speaking his make-believe Brighton Beach English.

"I have to go," I said again.

"Not yet."

"Listen to me, I need to finish this case, I really do. Give me some more of those pills, OK?" I climbed out of the SUV and held onto the door handle. Tolya followed me.

"I'll come with you, in that case."

"What for?" Shivering, I realized my jacket had disappeared in the storage room.

"In case you pass out," he said. "You look like crap. Put this on." He reached in the back of the SUV and handed me a black sweater. Cashmere. Triple X. I pulled it over my head.

As we went into the lobby of the Armstrong, I spoke softly to him in Russian. "There've been a couple of murders not far from here." I described the guy with the tats killed in the cemetery, the paper skewered to his heart.

"Your cases?"

"No."

"You are interested, why?"

"Somebody beats me up, there's creeps out there killing people, I get interested."

"Russians?" Tolya said.

"Probably. Gangs, maybe. I need your help."

"You never ask me before," he said. "What do you want?"

"I'll let you know. I have to see Lily now."

"Be good to her," said Tolya.

I nodded.

"You will try to win her back?"

I pressed the elevator button. "I have to."

CHAPTER 18

I have an old woman's feet, Artie. I have ugly, wrinkled old feet now," Lily said. Sitting on a white leather stool at the kitchen counter in her apartment at the Armstrong, she looked down at her bare feet. Her soggy winter boots were on the floor. I was opposite her. "How do you feel?"

We had been sitting like that for a little while. Lily had helped me wash the blood off my face and put some clean bandages on my hand.

"I'm OK now. And your feet are OK. I like your feet," I said.

She didn't answer, just pulled herself off the stool and crossed the kitchen to make coffee.

The apartment had cream-colored curtains and sofas. A milky pink glass vase filled with orange roses was on the granite kitchen counter. The living room, this kitchen, had been renovated— stainless steel appliances, sleek wood floors and cupboards, a blue-and-white-striped kilim. Unlike Simonova's apartment, no water dripped from the ceiling; no plaster cascaded down the walls; the paint was fresh. Glossy magazines were artfully arranged on a black glass coffee table.

Lily put two mugs on the counter. "Do you want something to eat?"

I shook my head and glanced at the old clock that hung on the kitchen wall.

"What is it?" she said.

"I was wondering if Dr. Bernard had stopped by. She said she'd come. I was stuck in the fucking storage room." I rubbed my head.

"Don't touch it," said Lily, handing me a dishcloth. "There's blood on your head, Artie. You need to see someone. You need them to check for concussion. I mean it." For a moment, Lily's bossy, practical side took her over, and it made me smile. For a moment.

"So what about Dr. Bernard?"

"What? I think you should eat something." Lily, fussing in the kitchen, opening the fridge, pulling out plates, slicing bread. She put it all on the counter and began to make sandwiches. As she unwrapped hard-boiled eggs, the smell got to me and I felt sick.

"Dr. Bernard was coming to sign Simonova's death certificate," I said. "You remember?"

"Oh, that. Right," said Lily, placing salami on a slab of bread and spreading it with mustard. "Sure, but it's done, Artie. I took care of it. It's just fine. We don't have to bother Dr. Bernard after all."

I went to the sink and ran the water, drank from the tap, washed my face, and dried it off with some paper towels. I turned around and leaned against the sink so I could see her.

"Lily?"

"What?"

"What's going on? Why were you getting meds for a woman you know is dead?" I looked at her. "You have to tell me. It doesn't add up."

"Yes, yes, sure, Artie, I'm behaving like an idiot, I know we need to get this sorted, of course." She picked up a plastic bottle, took out a pill, put it in her mouth, washed it down with some coffee.

"What are you taking?"

She didn't answer.

I went to the window and looked out. It was dark now. Still snowing.

"Lily?"

"Come and sit down. I can't talk to your back," she said. I went to the counter and sat down again on the stool.

"What is it?" Lily said.

"I went to see Dr. Bernard. She said you didn't call her at all today."

"Maybe the messages didn't get through. I tried her. I told you."

"She said she didn't get any. I don't think she's the kind of woman who loses her messages," I said.

"You shouldn't have done that without telling me."

Lily looked down at her feet again. "I'll go get Lionel," she said.

"You didn't call Dr. Bernard at all, did you?" I asked her. "What else is there you didn't tell me?"

"Her number was busy, OK?" Lily was angry now. She got up abruptly, left the apartment, and slammed the door.

"Lily tells me you've had a bit of a rough time. May I look at that gash on your forehead?" Dr. Hutchison inspected my head. "Can I fix those bandages for you?"

Lily hovered close by. She had slammed out of the apartment, then reappeared, Hutchison in tow.

"Not now." I looked at my watch. "Where the hell is she?"

"Who?" Lily said.

"Dr. Bernard. It's getting late."

"No need to worry," Hutchison said. "I just called Lucille, we talked earlier, as you know, detective, but I called again and I persuaded her that everything had been arranged properly. Lily, would you make me a cup of coffee, please?"

I was surprised. Lucille Bernard didn't seem like a woman who would change her mind easily. "You mean she's not coming?"

"I told her I had examined Marianna and I had signed the death certificate."

"Where did you get it?"

"It's not that difficult, please believe me. In any case, I told Lucille I had called Riverside Chapel, which is a Jewish funeral home. I knew, as I believe Lily explained to you, that Marianna was of the Jewish persuasion and wanted a Jewish funeral."

"She told you."

"Oh, yes, we discussed these things many times, as old people will." He adjusted his lapel, as if to play for time while he considered his words. "You see, the good people from Riverside came over and took Marianna."

"What?"

"The burial will be tomorrow," Hutchison said.

"I told you all this, Artie," Lily said. "I'm sure Marianna even wrote it somewhere. Wasn't that what you thought, Lionel, that she had specifically put it down that she wanted the Jewish thing?"

"Did she have surviving family?" I said.

"No," said Hutchison. "Absolutely not."

I got out my phone.

"Who are you calling?" Lily said.

"Just checking for messages," I said, hoping Bernard had called me. But there were none.

"You really don't have to call anyone," Lily said. "Or don't you trust Lionel? Or me?"

"I know you're concerned, detective, but it's just fine," Hutchison said. "I have my license; I've been a doctor a very long time, and I can certainly sign a death certificate. The law says that if the deceased was in the care of a particular doctor in the period preceding death, it's acceptable."

"So she was in your care?"

"In mine, in the sense that I saw her most days. In Lucille Bernard's as well. I was often in touch with Lucille on the subject. I saw Marianna, I saw her frequently. Of course," he said. "I warned her against drinking too much of that vodka she loved. I said to her, 'Marianna, dear, you can't drink like that in your condition.' She didn't listen. She was full of life."

"When he called Riverside, Lionel discovered that Marianna had arranged everything in advance—her funeral, her casket, all of it. She had even paid for it. Didn't you?" said Lily to Hutchison.

"How did you discover it?" I said.

"I spoke with the director from Riverside Memorial. Marianna had also purchased a plot in a cemetery on Long Island," Hutchison said. "They've arranged for her to be buried early tomorrow, first thing, to keep within twenty-four hours, which is what is preferred for people of the Jewish faith."

"I thought it had to be right away," I said.

"Unless it's the Jewish Sabbath, and today is Saturday, of course," said the doctor. "We've acceded to all of Marianna's wishes. That makes me feel good. We were very close, you know."

"You signed the death certificate. What was the time of death?"

"Three seventeen this morning."

"You know that?"

Hutchison looked at me. "Yes."

"How?"

"You'll have to trust me," he said.

"Cause of death? According to you."

"Her heart gave out."

"And how did you manage to see her this morning? I gather your wife locks your door."

He laughed without humor. "It's our little game. She likes to think I wander in my sleep and she protects me." He grunted. "Naturally, I have my own keys."

"So you saw Mrs. Simonova earlier this morning? Before Lily found her? At say, three seventeen a.m.? I had the feeling when you asked me for matches out on the terrace, you already knew."

"Yes, detective. I knew that she had already passed as I just told you. In any case, I was meaning to raise it with you when my wife called me back into the apartment."

"She didn't know?"

"She didn't know that I often dropped in on Marianna early in the morning."

"Lily told me she's the only one who had Simonova's keys."

"Things change."

"And anyway you can go from your terrace to Simonova's, isn't that right?"

"Yes. I'm in quite good shape, as you see. I can climb over that foolish little wall that divides us."

"When were you planning to tell your wife?" I felt like I was being played.

"Why are you badgering Lionel?" Lily said.

"Detective Cohen asks good questions," said Hutchison. "It's his habit. Deduction. A bit like Sherlock Holmes, perhaps, wouldn't you say? Or would it be that doctor on TV, that Dr. House?" In his sharp eyes was a hint of almost joyful malice. He'd had enough of me, and he let it show.

Hutchison had been used to his power in his own world, and he resented my questions. As a doctor, he was used to giving orders, used to people who obeyed them.

"So you knew from early this morning."

"Yes."

"That she was dead."

"That is correct," he said.

"But you waited to mention it."

"It was very early. I often take my coffee out on the terrace, take my coffee, juice, the damn pills I have to take. That way I could see if there was a light on in Marianna's."

"So you could visit. And was there a light?"

"Candles," he said. "I was going to talk to Lily as soon as I could manage it out of my wife's hearing."

"What did you think when you saw Simonova?"

"I am a doctor. I knew she was at the end. I waited until she passed. She was not alone."

I thought of the way the dead body had seemed posed.

"You touched her, you arranged the body in any way?"

"I don't know what you mean," said Hutchison.

"But you didn't tell your wife."

"Celestina is a silly old woman. She did not like Marianna."

"Anything between you?"

"I am eighty-two years old, detective, but Madame Seminova had bad breath and, well, if you were asking, she was not my type." He gave a small measured smile. "We were good friends. We had things in common. I loved her."

"What kind of things?"

"Politics," said Hutchison. "Poetry. We discussed literature. We'd laugh about how I had to sneak cigarettes past Celestina. We played cards. Marianna told me her bridge set had been given to her by Anatoly Dobrynin when he was Soviet ambassador. She called him Toli. We discussed international affairs. She played her wonderful old records for me. We both loved this building. That was a bond too." He looked at his watch. "I must go. You're satisfied now, detective?"

"When you talked to Dr. Bernard, did she say anything else?"

"She said you seemed rather decent, for a cop, which coming from Lucille Bernard is quite a compliment. In any case, I must get back," he said.

"You didn't want her to suffer, of course. Simonova, that is?" I said to him.

"Yes."

"Had she been in pain?"

"Surely."

"What kind of pain?"

"Stop it," said Lily. "Please, Artie, this is hard enough without you playing detective."

"One more thing," I said.

"Of course."

"Amahl Washington."

Suddenly, it was as though everything slowed down; no one spoke. Dr. Hutchison, who had said he was in a hurry, took his time selecting a chocolate cookie from a plate Lily had placed on the kitchen counter. He picked it up and ate a small bite. He didn't answer me about Amahl Washington, not then; I saw he was waiting for me to challenge him in some way; Lily was on his side. Then the doorbell rang. Lily hurried to answer it, shut the door, returned carrying a casserole dish covered with a yellow cloth.

"Who was it?"

"Regina McGee, lady who lives down the hall. To see if she could help out with the funeral arrangements."

"So everybody knows."

"Of course, they know," said Lily. "People saw the funeral home take Marianna away. In a black bag, Artie. Like garbage. On a gurney. Garbage on a gurney, that's what it was like." Lily pushed her hair back. "They'll all be ringing the doorbell, they'll all be wanting to talk about it. Wanting a funeral, a memorial, something. I'm not sure I can do this."

"Why you?" I said to Lily.

"They know we were friends."

Hutchison was on his feet. "I'll talk to them." He kissed Lily on the cheek. "I'm around if you need me," he said and started for the door, then stopped suddenly and turned around.

"I don't know who I'll be able to talk to ever again, you know," he said. "Most everyone is dying off. You have a best friend like Marianna, you get that thing only once in a long while. She was different; she knew the world. Crazy as she was." He smiled. "Oh, we laughed. We were an odd pair for certain, but she never talked foolishness. That was what I liked. You sure you don't need me to stitch that up?" he asked, looking at my forehead.

"I'm OK."

"You have something for it?"

"Yes. Thank you."

"Let me know if there are any side effects. Rest if you can. You must be feeling pretty raggedy. Call me and we can talk."

"What kind of pain?" I said again.

"What's that?"

"Mrs. Simonova. What kind of pain?"

Hutchison's voice was steady, but his eyes teared up. "The kind of pain that makes it not worth living, the kind that comes when you can't breathe," he said.

CHAPTER 19

|t's over now," Lily said in a flat voice when Hutchison had gone.
On the kitchen counter was her laptop. It was open. She began
tapping at it.

"Is there anything else you want to tell me?" I said. "What are
you working on?"

"Just checking e-mails," she said. "It's over. I told you."

"You're sure?" I closed my eyes for a few seconds as the pain
sliced against my eyeballs and reached for the pills I had in my
pocket.

"Don't," said Lily. "It's too much. I'll get you some aspirin."

"I'm OK."

"Who beat you up, Artie? Do you think somebody wanted you
to stop asking questions about Marianna?"

"Do you?"

"Do I what?"

"Want me to stop asking? Lily, did you ever know Amahl
Washington?"

"I met him," she said. "I didn't get to know him."

"He died. Six months ago."

"He was old," she said. "Almost everybody here is old. They live
in the past. They live in this building like a little village, as if it's all
that keeps them going, keeps them safe. It contains their history,
you can see that? Artie," she added, "I'm getting old. Maybe it's the
building. Or my feet."

"You're not old."

"Older than you," she said. "Years and years older."

"I never cared."

"I never really talked to Mr. Washington," she said. "I remember Celestina Hutchison was pretty sniffy about him. A basketball player, she'd say. She's such a snob."

"Lucille Bernard was his doctor, too."

"She was?" Lily stared at her computer. "Well, she's a lung specialist, so why not?"

"Was he friends with Lionel Hutchison?"

"How would I know?" she said sharply. She got up, found a bottle of Scotch in one of the cupboards, got two glasses, and poured some for both of us. She gulped at hers. "Please, let it be, Artie," she said. "Can't we just trust Lionel? I want us to trust him, I want it to be over, I want to go to the funeral tomorrow morning and let it all end."

"I'll go with you."

"No. My friend, my job."

"What about Hutchison? Won't he want to go with you? To the funeral?"

"I'll talk to him. His wife will make a stink, though. So we can do that, right? We can let it be."

We sat and talked across the counter now like two polite acquaintances, people who had just met, who found themselves next to each other in a coffee shop or a theater. We sat for a while, and were nice to each other, and sipped our drinks, and I was OK with it, I was with her.

I looked at the Obama poster taped to the fridge, other Obama stuff spread out on the kitchen counter, a stack of campaign leaflets. I picked one up.

"Election night was really something wasn't it, honey?" I said. "You worked hard on the campaign."

"I really loved it," she said softly. "I worked with such good people, you know. And I love this man. I think he's put his neck out in a way no politician I remember ever has. He tells the truth. He speaks brilliantly. We all wanted it so badly. It's been such shit for so long with Bush, and suddenly this hope, and you could taste it. Remember election night? Funny that I ended up at the Sugar Hill

Club. I was on my way down to 125th Street with the people I was working with, and somebody said, Let's stop for a drink, and then, I don't know. I was really happy I got to see you. Even cops like Obama, right?" She laughed a little.

"Even cops. Or this cop, anyhow."

"Of course, it will change," said Lily. "We think he's some kind of superman who will fix everything the way we want, and in fact, he's a good, American, middle-of-the-road guy who will probably have to toe the line plenty. I know that. I don't care. Did you read his book, Artie? About his father?"

I said I would read it.

"That was how I got to know Marianna. At first I'd just go over and drink vodka with her, and I'd think, What the hell am I doing here, and then suddenly, one day, she gives me money for Obama. A lot, like five hundred bucks, and she says, in that ridiculous accent, 'This is wonderful man, this Mr. Obama. If I am younger, I fall big-time for him.' She was very, very gung ho. She held those debate-watching parties, she served up Russian stuff she bought at some Russian grocery. She was something."

"Go on."

"There was something epic about her, Artie," Lily said, sipping her drink, wanting to talk now. I didn't stop her.

I still wanted to know why she had been buying medication for a dead woman, but it could wait a little while. I'd find out why she had gone to the drugstore, I'd find out why she had really called me in the first place, but only if I let her talk.

Rubbing my head, I discovered a lump like a walnut on the back.

"She must have had a rough time growing up in the USSR," I said.

Lily looked at me. "I'm glad you understand, Artie. Of all people, I knew you'd get it. It's one of the reasons I wanted you here. Marianna had survived everything—the war, the Cold War, the whole fucking thing," said Lily. "How come novels about women are hardly ever epic? It's always about, I don't know, domestic shit. About the little things, about marriage and babies and shopping for food at Trader Joe's, or nannies, or living in Park Fucking Slope, or some other shit, and it's the men who write the big books, even the big books about women, like *Anna Karenina*, and all she ever did was moon around about some bastard and then kill herself. Men go into space; we just go to the grocery store."

I reached over the counter for the Scotch, poured a little more in our glasses.

"I wanted to go to the moon, Artie. Or some place big. But I settled for other people's lives, their stories. Marianna's was the best; I told you I made her talk into a tape recorder. 'What this is for, Lily? You plan to reveal my secrets, you tell everything to world?' She would say stuff like that—and it was half serious, half a joke."

"Where is it?"

"I have my voice recorder in the bedroom," said Lily. "Sometimes I used it. Sometimes she did her own recording on a cassette player I got her. She didn't understand digital stuff that well."

"Where are the tapes?"

"She kept some. I have some. A lot of what she said was in Russian. I'd ask the questions in English, but she said she could only think and talk properly in her own language."

"I can translate for you. Do you want me to do that?"

Lily ignored my question.

"She was still a believer, of course. The Communist Party," said Lily. "She gets to the U.S., she joins the Party here. I can't believe she's dead, just like that."

"I know you feel guilty about her meds or something, but it wasn't your fault. I tried to tell you this morning."

"How do you know?" Lily looked at me desperately.

"Tell me about the meds. How come you were at the drugstore?"

"I was just tying up loose ends, you know, closing Marianna's account, stuff like that."

"You said you were getting meds for her?"

"Did I? I must have been out of my mind. I feel I could be going nuts, you know, Artie?"

I held her hand.

"I don't want to talk about it anymore. Do you mind? Is that OK," said Lily. "I'm just so tired."

I stood up. "Fine," I said. "Sure. Whatever you want." I was tired, too, tired of the deceptions.

"You can't let it go, can you?" she said. "Even when Lionel was here, you had to know, you had to keep asking him questions like he was a suspect."

"Why didn't he tell me he knew she was dead early this morning, when I saw him out on his terrace? Why didn't you tell me?"

"For God's sake, you don't think Lionel's involved, do you? He was her friend."

"I'll let it go if you want me to."

"Let what go? What is there to let go?" she said. "You need to let go of being a cop, but you can't, can you—it's like it's in your genes, asking questions, finding the place where it matters. Just like your dad," she added. "Like in the KGB."

I felt like I'd been punched in the stomach. I kept my mouth shut.

"But that's your genius, the way you get people to talk to you, isn't it?" Lily said. "Isn't that your thing?"

I turned away and walked across the room to the window again. The pane was cold. After a minute or two, Lily came and stood beside me. She put her hand on my arm.

"Artie? I didn't mean to be cruel," she said. "It's a talent, asking questions, getting the answers you want. I know. I have it, too. It's what reporters do. Same as you. Sometimes I hate myself for it— you just keep on asking and asking, pushing at people, and sometimes it's when they're hurting."

"Was it the cop stuff that got in the way with us? I know it bothered you. I know you hated the stuff I had to do."

She was silent.

"But he's a cop. Radcliff."

"Who you are is a cop; right at the very core of your being you're a New York detective. It's what you wanted and you got it, and it's who you are," said Lily, both of us standing at the window, our faces pressed against the glass, looking out at the snow.

"And him?"

"It's something he wanted to do. But he'll get it out of his system and then he'll go on to something else."

"I see."

"I feel happy with Virgil right now." She looked at me. "Shit, I'm sorry. You know I could never lie to you. I'm sorry."

"Didn't you feel happy with me?"

"It was different," said Lily. "It was a different kind of being happy. With you and me it had to be the whole thing. We were too connected. We both spent some of our lives in hellish places seeing horrible things. We shared that. You brought it home. So did I."

"We shared other things," I said. "We shared music, and the city, and trips to Montana, and friends. For a long time, almost fifteen years," I said. "What happened to us?"

CHAPTER 20

Fifteen years since the hot summer night outside St. Vincent's, where I'd first met Lily. I'd been waiting for somebody to die. There had been a shooting and I was on the corner of Twelfth Street and Seventh Avenue, staring up at the hospital and smoking. It was after midnight, a sultry New York night. Lily was waiting, too. She asked for a light, or maybe I asked her for one.

That night, we smoked and waited. She'd pointed out the school across the street, where she'd gone when she was a little girl. There had been something about her—hair, eyes, voice—that made me want her bad right then. Our first date, we went to Bradley's to hear music. She already loved my music, Miles, Ella, Stan Getz. I taught her to love Louis Armstrong.

I knew right away, but for once I had let things take a little time, time for us to listen to music some more, time to go for a walk, stop for a drink, or dinner. It was a week, maybe two, before we'd gone to bed together. It was so good.

Lily had been born in New York and still lived in the apartment on Tenth Street where she grew up. I had fallen in love with the city as soon as I got off the plane, or maybe before. I think I was in love with New York before I ever saw it. As soon as I met Lily, I'd felt she was New York. With her, I felt I had come home.

That summer, we walked over the Brooklyn Bridge, we took picnics to Central Park, and rode the Staten Island Ferry late at night. She came to ball games with me at the stadium and cheered like a crazy person. We haunted the city's bookstores.

Reading was Lily's obsession. She read everything—she had five, six books on the go at one time, novels, history, whatever she could get her hands on, and she could read a book in an evening. She told me she had once had a dream, a half-awake kind of dream, that she could eat books, and that if she could she would be able to read everything; one of her worries was that she'd never get through them all, all the books that remained, the ones she hadn't read, the ones she had to read again. She read like a hungry woman.

Lying there on my sofa, she'd devour the book in her hand, still glancing up at the TV to comment on a ball game.

She had learned how to fish for my sake, though our first time out on the Yellowstone River in Montana she cast her hook into my neck. We couldn't stop laughing. She was a lousy cook—she said so, and didn't care, so long as we could get some decent takeout, Chinese, Thai, Indian—and her driving was worse, though she thought she was a hot-shot behind the wheel. When she drove, I held my breath or just looked out the window as if the scenery interested me.

Lily had worked on TV, for newspapers and magazines. She had covered wars, she had been to the Soviet Union—she understood the place I had left, and why. She had taken on tough stuff like the sex trade, and she had a do-good streak a mile wide, which she admitted, but she could laugh at herself. If there was a guy begging on the street, she'd give him money and ask how she could help. She was particularly fond of a guy on my block who used to panhandle for "The United Negro Pastrami Fund."

"Anybody who makes me laugh gets an extra five bucks," she always said.

Of everybody I knew, had ever known, she was the most generous. She gave more than she could afford, she bought presents for people, she found them jobs, she helped their kids. And then forgot about it. Oh, did I do that? she'd say, astonished and pleased.

Restless as she was, her friends were the most important thing in her life; it was sacred to her, this friendship thing. It mattered more than any belief system or politics or job. You were Lily's friend, it was forever, for good. The only time I ever saw her cry was when one of her oldest friends simply disappeared from her life and never told her why, though I would have liked to kill the bastard for hurting her.

I had proposed to Lily once, one New Year's Eve, but she'd refused. I never knew if it was my job, or because she wanted her freedom, as she saw it. We both, Lily and me, let other people get in the way, but it was mostly my fault, I had fucked it up. I'd been a jerk. I didn't know if I could get her back, now or ever.

Lily believed you could make the world better. Anyhow, she made me better than I was, than I am. I couldn't remember a time when I hadn't known Lily. Long time now.

"Lily?"

She was at the kitchen counter, now, head down. I couldn't tell if she was asleep or crying. I wanted to hold her, take her away. I had never felt I wanted to do anything so much. I stayed where I was.

"I'm sorry I was such an asshole with Dr. Hutchison. Honest, I am," I said.

She looked up. "I was just resting my eyes." Lily went to the stereo. She pressed a button. "Listen."

It was Stan Getz's *People Time*, an album I had given her.

"You play this a lot?"

"Yes."

"For Radcliff?"

"Come over here." Lily sat on the gray sofa. I sat next to her. "You can't just go on hating him," she said.

I laughed. "Why not?"

"Because he's my friend, and I like him."

"More than a friend."

"Yes."

"Somebody you spend nights with."

"You weren't around, Artie."

"You either."

"I know that, but you married somebody else."

"Because you wouldn't marry me. Because we couldn't make it work. Not that my marriage worked." I shrugged. "Maybe I can't make anything work."

"I think about you," she said.

"Me, too."

"But Virgil's good for me. He's a good guy and he's around and I like him."

I didn't say anything.

"I heard you were seeing Valentina Sverdloff. Before she died."

I had been waiting for her to say it.

"I wasn't seeing her."

"But you loved her."

"Who told you?"

"Tolya. Your friend, but mine, too. We always keep in touch, you know? Tolya and me. He told me he knew you'd loved his daughter, and he told you he'd kill you if you went near her—Val was half your age. But after she was gone, after she was murdered, he was sorry he didn't let it happen; he knew you had loved her and that she felt the same way about you."

"I'm sorry."

"Things happen. It was hard for me, too," said Lily. "Val was a fantastic girl. She was like the little sister I never had."

"I don't know what to say."

"It's not just Val."

"What else?"

"I just want to be happy, or at least content, if I can," Lily said. "I can't just drop Virgil. I don't want to."

I wanted to say, Are you in love with him? but I was too scared to ask. "Do you?"

"Do I what?"

"Play that album for him?"

"No." Lily leaned over and kissed my cheek, and I saw she still liked me, I saw it in her face, and I thought, right then, that maybe I still had a chance.

This was as close as I'd been to her for a long time. I remembered the times we had spent together, places we'd gone.

We used to love bars, all kinds, fancy bars, low-life bars, music clubs. It was one of the things we did, drinking, eating, wandering around the city, the boroughs.

Not getting drunk, just drinking. We drank in jazz clubs, at funny

Korean cocktail lounges where they brought the booze in a watermelon. We'd gone to Brazilian joints where there were pineapple caipirinhas; to Beatrice's place, where we knocked back bottles of Nebbiolo; to Fanelli's for beers. Sometimes we had consumed silly cocktails in small, slightly seedy hotels, old places on Madison and Lex, places no one we knew went to.

We'd hang out in booths, half hidden, sipping our drinks, making out, laughing, desperate to run out, grab a cab, and go home to bed. We used to make out in the cabs, too, and in the elevators, all the way up to her place or mine.

Sitting on the sofa in the Armstrong apartment, I just took Lily's hand and put it against my face.

"You're right," I said. "Dr. Hutchison signed off; I'm OK. I really am. I mean it. This is over."

"Thank you." She patted my cheek and took her hand back. Lily seemed to have reclaimed her usual self. As if now that Simonova's funeral had been arranged, she could cope.

All I wanted now was for Simonova to be buried. I didn't ask again why Lily had lied about calling Dr. Bernard. I didn't want to know. I tried to forget I'd been hit on the head in the storage room. That Lionel Hutchison was covering up something and Lucille Bernard had been Amahl Washington's doctor around the time he died.

I could do it. I could forget. My time as a cop was almost over. I didn't want the life any more. Had I always brought the work home? It had fucked us up, me and Lily. Maybe Virgil Radcliff could do the job right; maybe it was his time.

When Lily had said to me about Simonova "I killed her," I knew she'd made a mistake, or was covering for somebody. She couldn't have hurt the woman who'd been her friend.

But what if she had? Would I lie for her? Run with her? I began to sweat, cold, dank sweat that dripped down the middle of my back. I pushed it all away.

Twelve hours, give or take, it would be done. Sunday morning,

Simonova would be buried. I wanted to make Lily feel better. I wanted to tell her again, "You didn't do it. You couldn't do it. Not to your friend."

I got up. "Come with me," I said.

"Where?"

I held out my hand. She took it.

CHAPTER 21

So far as I could tell, nothing had been touched in Simonova's apartment except the sofa where I'd first seen her body. It was rumpled now. The shawl that had covered her was on the floor; the funeral home guys who lifted her onto a gurney must have dropped it.

I made my way around the room while Lily waited near the door. I picked up bits of paper from the desk, I went into the bedroom, and looked briefly through Simonova's clothes. It would take days to search the whole place.

In the living room, Lily was kneeling at the little table by the sofa, looking at the pills.

"Which ones do you think you screwed up?"

Lily picked up a plastic box, the days marked on it, and opened the lid.

"This one," she said. "I think I forgot this one." She poured the remaining capsules onto her palm. "I always counted. There's one more than there should be."

"Show me."

I took the capsule, read what was marked on it.

"Why are you smiling?" Lily said.

"Because these are ACE inhibitors, blood pressure medication, Lily, honey. And it's a low dosage. And you couldn't kill a mouse if you forgot one, or probably ten or a hundred. Why didn't you tell me this earlier?"

"I was scared. How do you know, anyway?"

"Tolya takes this stuff. He says it interferes with his eating grapefruit, and I tell him to eat caviar instead. I tell him he's an ass.

It's fine, honey." Putting my arm around her, "Is that why you went to the drugstore?"

She nodded. "I was trying to figure out if Marianna had another prescription, if there were meds I didn't know about that I forgot to get, or she forgot. She sometimes got confused, especially when her breathing was very bad. It took all her will to concentrate."

"Who would have prescribed something for her that you didn't know about?"

"I don't know. But there wasn't anything. At the drugstore, anyway," said Lily. "I'm sorry I've been so crazy. God, I'm so glad you're here. I was sure I had done something awful." She reached out for my hand. "Thank you."

"It's OK."

"You know what?"

"What, honey?"

"I miss Tolya. Let's call him and tell him to come over or something. Come on, I'll make some coffee. I'll get out some wine. Let's go back to my place." Lily made for the door. "You know, if I hadn't seen you on election night, I might not have had the guts to call you this morning."

"I'd always come," I said. "You're OK now? About the meds? You believe me now, that you didn't have anything to do with her death?"

"I guess. Yes. I do. I'm going to believe you."

I looked at the portrait of Paul Robeson on the wall.

"What is it?" Lily said.

"My mother got her gold earrings to see Robeson perform in Moscow. Whenever he came to Moscow to perform, everybody dressed up, some even in evening clothes, the kind that were normally forbidden in the 'people's paradise,'" I said. "My father got tickets once and my mother says, 'What will I wear, Maxim? I haven't got anything nice enough.' So he takes her out and buys her a blue silk dress and gold earrings with little diamonds, the kind every Soviet woman wanted back then, and it costs him two months' salary, but she's so happy. Afterwards, they sit up all night in the kitchen discussing the concert and how heroic Robeson is. My mother told me." I looked at Robeson's portrait again. "It must have been like coming home for you in some ways," I said to Lily. "And for Simonova, too."

As if a dam had burst, Lily began to talk. About her childhood in Greenwich Village, her stiff-necked father who preferred his politics and his atheism to his kid—they never celebrated Christmas or anything else. Her mother had catered to him; he came first. Lily was an only child, left to fend for herself.

Still, when she grew up, after college, after her parents had died, she went back to the family apartment on Tenth Street. Maybe it was all she had in the way of a past that she could love.

Sitting in Simonova's apartment now, she looked around her.

"I have all this culture in my bones. My father with his Robeson records," she said. "His politics, the Civil Rights Movement, all that, it formed me, the good part; at least, I hope it's only the good part," she added. "God, my father loved the workers, he loved the whole world, but his own kid, that was something else." Lily picked up Marianna's shawl and wrapped it around her shoulders.

When she was little, Lily's father had given her a copy of *Das Kapital*, but he had forbidden her the girls' magazines she wanted; he had been horrified when he found her and her friends playing with their Barbies. On Sundays, he drove her around Harlem so she could see how poor people lived. Afterward, he would stop off at the Plaza Hotel.

"He always drank exactly two Gibsons, never more, that was it, and he smoked two cigarettes, and that was our so-called quality time together. I was ten. He loved books, too, good books, and movies. He did that for me. We went to the movies together," said Lily. "Sometimes he'd let me pick a movie, and even if it was something stupid with Doris Day, he would secretly enjoy it. He adored the movies, and I guess there was a little softness in him those times, a feel for just pure pleasure." Lily smiled. "Not like my Uncle Lenny, my mother's brother, my dad's best friend; he was obsessed.

He gave up his law practice to organize the Mohawk Indians who built the Verrazano bridge. Joe McCarthy's ghouls hunted Lenny down—he really was a Communist—but he wouldn't talk and he went to jail. My cousin Nancy was in love with a Russian boy for a while. They were really happy, but it didn't last. She was a lot older than me. She was a real Red Diaper baby."

"What happened to her?"

"I don't know. She disappeared. I haven't heard from Nancy for twenty years."

"Maybe that's why Simonova trusted you, because you understood."

"Maybe. God, the stories. She told me she had slept with Che when he visited the Soviet Union, stuff like that," said Lily. "Was it true? I don't know. I didn't care. The stories, the folk music, the endless talk about politics." Lily got up. "You remember that time I got drunk and got up on the table and sang old Union songs?"

"Do I ever. Something about, what was it, *'the vaults are made of marble with a guard at every door,'* and then I forget."

"*'And the mines are stuffed with silver that the miners sweated for.'*" Lily laughed. "You want me to sing some more?"

"No, thanks."

"Did you know my dad's last wife was black? Fourth wife. Long after I left home. It validated him, and Virginia, that was her name, was very good to him, self-obsessed bastard that he was. We were raised to love and admire and understand what black people did and had endured. It was important. It was a cause, something to fight, to win."

"Obama gave you that back?"

"In a way. Those days. Long time." She looked at me. "Artie, I know you want to look around, so go ahead. I'll wait here. I'll sit on Marianna's sofa one last time."

A few things were slightly out of place in the apartment, things I hadn't noticed before. I had a sense that papers on the desk were not where they had been this morning. A drinking glass that had been on the table near the sofa was gone. Even the smell in the room was somehow different.

"I noticed you left a present for her," I said to Lily, gesturing to the Christmas tree I'd seen earlier. Alongside the gifts for Simonova, was a pile of stuff still unwrapped. "What's all this?"

"She bought stuff for everyone," Lily crossed to the tree. "She was planning to wrap them today. She had already written the cards."

There were liqueur chocolates in a Russian lacquered box for Regina McGee; for Lionel Hutchison there were Russian cigarettes and a fancy lighter. A Russian box had a muscle man on the label and the words "Elixir of Life." On the card, Simonova had written "To Lionel, who is the elixir of life."

For Carver Lennox there was a fancy silver samovar. Draped over a chair were green velour Christmas stockings full of Alenka chocolates, addressed to Allison and Thomas Lennox. In the stockings were also crisp hundred-dollar bills, one each.

"Who are these people?"

"Carver Lennox's kids," said Lily.

"Simonova knew them? They were important enough to her to give them money?"

"I don't know," Lily said.

I picked up one of the chocolate bars.

I'd grown up on Alenka chocolate, from the Red October factory; it never failed to take me back to my childhood, the chocolate bars with the picture of a little girl in a headscarf, a baby babushka, that too-sweet chocolate we thought the best thing on earth.

"Where did she get all this Russian stuff? Brighton Beach?"

"Shop in Washington Heights," said Lily. "I went with her once."

"What about you?" I said to Lily. "What did she give you."

"A necklace her mother gave her," she said. "And a biography of Robeson, and a nicely bound copy of *Das Kapital*, a really good edition."

I looked through the presents again. "There's something else for you here." I picked up a small red-foil envelope.

"You open it, Artie. Or let's take it with us. I want to get out of here."

"Sure."

"I want to go get dressed for the party," Lily said. "I've had enough of the past. They're all dead, my parents, their friends, their ideals. Marianna was my last connection to all that." Lily pushed her hair back. "She remembered, she knew some of them, she had even heard of my Uncle Lenny. Another world. God. Now she's dead. They're all dead." Lily looked around Simonova's apartment. "I won't come back here. I don't want to be here again."

I knew I would come back. I knew there was something here that I had missed. I couldn't stay away.

CHAPTER 22

The Hutchisons' dog was barking. In the hallway, as we crossed to Lily's place, Marie Louise was cowering against the wall.

"What's wrong?" Lily asked her.

"It's that dog. I was coming from the elevator, and the dog begins to bark. Lily, please, make the dog stay away."

"It's OK," said Lily. "He's inside the apartment."

In basement light, I hadn't really seen how beautiful Marie Louise was. She wasn't more than thirty-five. She wore jeans and a white sweater, over one arm was a beige down coat, over her other shoulder a fake Vuitton purse. She was terrified. Again, the dog barked, and she moved in closer to Lily.

"It's just Ed, the Hutchisons' old pooch," said Lily. "He really won't hurt you. Artie, this is Marie Louise Semake." When I shook her hand, it was cold with fear. "She works for several people on this floor," Lily added and asked if she was OK.

"I think so," she said. "But, Lily, please, tell me, what is the matter with Madame Simonova? I've been trying to phone to her for many hours. I was supposed to prepare supper for her today, but there is no answer, and I have no keys. I tried you earlier, but you did not respond."

"I'm sorry," said Lily. "I probably missed your call."

"Something bad has happened? I feel this," said the woman. "Is she worse?"

"Yes," said Lily, then, leaning forward, spoke very softly to Marie Louise, who put her hand over her mouth.

Carver Lennox appeared in the hallway, suddenly, as if he had heard our voices. His horn-rim glasses were pushed up on top of his head, and he seemed to be in a hurry.

"Good, you're here; I can use some help," he said to her. "Marie, can you help me out?"

The dog barked again. A look of sheer terror crossed Marie Louise's face.

"You tell me this is just an old dog, Lily, but this black dog that belongs to Mrs. Hutchison. In my country, this is how evil spirits reveal themselves, in this shape, as a black dog."

"Marie?" Lennox was impatient. "Are you coming? I can't wait all night." He held the door open to let her in. She hurried inside as if nothing could be worse than the sound of the dog.

"Bastard," said Lily when we got inside her apartment.

"Lennox?"

"Yeah," said Lily when we were back in her apartment. "He treats Marie Louise like a servant. She was a doctor, Artie. In her country she's a doctor. Here, she cleans up other people's shit to support her kids—she has two little boys. She puts up with it, but Lennox is a real prick."

"Not your favorite guy?"

"He's on the make all the time."

"Women?"

"Money."

"A bastard how?"

"He already has a job downtown, but he develops real estate in his spare time."

"And the others?"

"What others?"

"In the building."

"They're OK. And a lot of them are just old, old and wanting something to do, somebody to talk to. You want to meet them all?"

"Yes."

"Come to the party tonight?"

"The weather's lousy." I didn't want to drive all the way home in the stinking weather. I had once skidded on the FDR and almost gone into the half-frozen river. I told Lily.

"You don't have to go all the way home," she said. "You can stay."

I was pathetic, eager, desperate. I wondered what she'd do if I kissed her. I couldn't make a bad move, not this time. "I'll stay, if you're sure that's OK."

"Great. I'll call Sugar Hill Inn—it's a nice B&B—I'll fix a room for you there. That way you won't have to drive downtown later."

"Because Virgil will be staying with you?"

"It's not your business now. I'm not asking you to stay here with me because, yeah, I'm sort of involved with Virgil, OK? We've been through this. I can't do this all over again," said Lily. "I can only think about what's happened here, Artie. Please. Just help me."

"I'll help you."

"I don't want you to feel I'm using you, but I'm scared, Artie, and there's nobody I can tell except you, and it's probably wrong of me, I know that. Virgil is a good person, and a nice guy, and I like him. But it's different."

"Don't." I pushed a strand of hair out of her eyes, as gently as I could. "Don't apologize."

"You'd help me even if it had been my fault, wouldn't you? Even if I screwed up the meds, right? Even if I had killed her, you'd have covered for me, wouldn't you? Artie?"

"Yes."

She looked at me. "You would, wouldn't you?"

"Yes."

"Right," said Lily, a grin on her face now. "Anything?"

"Yes."

"Would you listen to Springsteen for me?" she said. "You never would before."

"I'd buy all his albums."

"Would you go to his concerts with me?"

"I'd learn all the words to all the songs, and we would drink beer from plastic cups at the Garden and dance around like all the other middle-aged white people there." I got up, went to Lily's CD player, shuffled through the discs, found *Born in the U.S.A.*, put it on, turned it up loud. Then I got up off the sofa and sang:

> *You can't start a fire,*
> *you can't start a fire without a spark.*
> *This gun's for hire,*
> *even if we're just dancing in the dark*

"How's that?" I said, collapsing back onto the couch.

"That's lovely. Thank you. You sing just like Bruce."

"You're welcome."

"How come you know the words?"

"I learned them all for you."

"How'd you do that?"

"I got them off a record cover," I said. "You feel a little better?"

"I think so, yes. You cheered me up, you really did. You're a good friend," she said, and then, out of the blue, she reached over, and put her arms around me, and kissed me on the mouth. Kissed me for a while, her body against mine.

Lily was in the bathroom. I got out the present Simonova had left for her under the Christmas tree. I opened it, found a letter inside. I read it quickly and put it back.

"What's that?" said Lily emerging from the bathroom, retrieving her glass, pouring herself more Scotch.

"It's a letter Simonova left for you. In the box under the **tree**."

"One of her games?"

"I don't know."

"Read it to me."

"You sure?"

"Of course." She downed the Scotch.

I put on my glasses and Lily laughed.

"How come everybody laughs at my glasses?"

"Who's everybody?"

"I saw Sonny this morning?"

"How is he?"

"Lonely."

"We're old now, Artie. We'll be old people soon."

"I plan to be old Russian guy, I drink borscht, I play chess on beach," I said, putting off reading the letter that I knew would scare her.

"Russia," she said. "You still feel it, Artie? You still can't let go." She put her arms around me. "Go on with the letter," Lily added. "You already read it, right?"

"Yes."

"Then go on."

I read. "'My dear Lily, You have been more kind to me than any-one I know in this country. You are a true comrade.' You want me to read all the flourishes? All the ways you helped her and how you are a true revolutionary sister?"

"Not right now," Lily said.

"So, let's see, she just adds again that you understood her, you understood the cause."

"I know you're holding back. Can we cut to the chase?"

"OK. First of all, she left you a lot of stuff in the storage room, including the Christmas ornaments I found there."

"That's nice," said Lily. "I don't think that's why you look so weird, though, Artie."

"'Comrade, Lily'—this is how she now addresses you," I said. "'I leave to you all my money, and my jewelry. I have not had the moment to make this legal, but so I write letter to you. There are jewelry of my mother in apartment, also money in bank box.' Then there's a lot more stuff about you, how grateful she was, stuff like that. There's one more thing."

"What?"

"She left you her apartment. Free and clear." I took my glasses off and held out the letter. Lily backed away.

"No."

"What do you mean?"

"I don't want her fucking stuff. What's the date on the letter?"

I looked at it. "There isn't a date."

"Good, that's good. It can't be legal then."

"I don't know."

Lily was shaking. Her mood had changed again. She was frightened.

"I don't understand."

"I don't want the place where Marianna died. There's a will anyway, you'll see. It will be different. This is just some old woman trying to be nice. Or playing a trick on me."

"You think there's a will?"

"I know there is. I know it. She mentioned it."

"Did she have a safe-deposit box?"

"She had an account at a bank on 125th Street. I went with her once."

"She gave you a key to the box?"

"Yes. You can fix this, anyway, can't you? You can get in her box somehow. Tomorrow? Even if it's Sunday? We can do it tomorrow, OK, Artie?"

"I'll try."

"Just tear up the letter, OK?"

"I'll keep it for you."

"Right, keep it. Keep the money, the apartment, whatever."

"You can sell it," I said. "You can give the money to something you care about. Sell it to Carver Lennox."

"I wouldn't give him the satisfaction," she said. "He nagged Marianna all the time. 'Sell it to me, dear,' he'd say to her, and it upset her; it was her home. Hers is one of the biggest apartments on the floor, and he's been desperate to get it."

"How does he act with you?"

"Who?"

"Lennox?"

"He's fine with me; I'm the kind of yuppie, as he sees it, he wants here. You know—Vassar grad, good job, fancy friends. He once says to me in the elevator, 'What a marvelous coat, Lily.' Asshole. I mean, I played along because I live here for now. Also he gave a truckload of money to Obama."

"So he's been harassing people?"

"In his very cool way. I heard someone say it killed Mr. Washington back then."

"What did? You didn't mention that."

"The idea of losing his apartment. I think he just gave up."

"Who owns it now?"

"His estate. Some kind of probate problem was involved. Lennox is crazy to get it."

"Is that why you don't want Simonova's apartment? You're worried about Lennox?"

"Of course not. I just don't want anything from her. Just wait," said Lily, and disappeared into the bathroom. When she came back—it must have been at least five minutes—she was calmer. Maybe she had taken something.

"Is Washington's apartment empty?"

"Yes."

"Which floor?"

"The ninth floor," said Lily, as her phone rang.

When she walked away from me, phone in hand, I knew Radcliff was on the other end, and from what I could tell, he was on his way over to see her.

"Come downtown with me," I said to Lily when she had finished her call. "You'll feel better away from here."

"No, Artie. I can't do that," she said. "What? You think somebody will find out Marianna left me her apartment and they'll do something bad to me to get it? Lennox isn't that crazy." She straightened up. "To hell with it. I'm tired of feeling scared. I'm going to change for the party. I want to look nice. It's been a long day. I just need a little time, clear my head. I'll meet you at the party later."

"One more thing."

"Not now, Artie," she said, as the doorbell rang and she went to answer it.

It was Virgil Radcliff. He shed his jacket, and accepted a drink from Lily.

"That tastes great," he said. "Everything OK?"

"Yes," said Lily. "It's fine."

"Thanks, Artie, for being here," said Virgil. "Thank you."

He'll be gone Wednesday, I thought. He'll be in California. Just fuck off.

As I went to the door, I noticed the way Radcliff put his hand lightly on Lily's sleeve. The way she looked at him. They were connected. They were a couple.

CHAPTER 23

"What the hell are you doing?" I said to Diaz, who was on the floor outside Simonova's apartment.

Diaz had the ferret-like look of a man who had been waiting for somebody, for me, for Lily, a man who, as soon as he heard the door open, probably got down on his knees, pretending to fix a piece of loose carpet. I didn't know what he was up to, but he gave me a queasy feeling. He reminded me of a low-level KGB hood, the kind who used to wait for kids outside Moscow schools to check if our hair was too long. Diaz probably made a career of watching out for the main chance, a way to make a little cash. He knew his way around the Armstrong, and he used it.

He wore workman's pants and a shirt with the Armstrong's logo on it. His heavy boots had left a trail of wet snow on the carpet.

"Where were you?" I pointed to the snow.

"On the roof," he said. "The old woman is dead?"

"You probably know that."

He grunted.

"You didn't like her?"

He hauled himself to his feet and leaned back against the wall, putting his hand on the wallpaper. "Right."

"Why's that?"

"Why? Because she was a Communist."

"So?"

"I'm Cuban, man, you get it?"

I took a twenty out of my pocket and folded it. "*Feliz Navidad*," I said to Diaz, handing him the money.

"What you want to know?" He wasn't coy. It was the money he had been waiting for.

"What was she like?"

"Russian," he said. "Communist." He snorted. "Well, not now, she's dead now, gone to be with Marx, like they used to say. Bastards."

"How did she treat people in the building? The people who work here?"

"Like shit," he said. "Except for the old doctor. I think they were doing it," he said making a dirty gesture, and then made as if to puke.

"What about Carver Lennox?"

"OK. Yeah, he's OK. He treats me good. Maybe one day he helps me get good apartment." He looked at me.

"Here?"

"Shit, no. He has buildings in Queens."

"So you're friends with him?"

"No. Not friends."

"But friendly?"

"Sure."

"Simonova was lousy to you?" I said it again. I wanted more out of him.

"I already say, she treats people bad, and me, I hate the Commies. She doesn't like this. Even when I tell her I got here on a fucking raft."

"You were in her place?"

"Why?"

"Listen, why not just tell me straight? I can be generous," I said, putting my hand back in my pocket.

Diaz sized me up. "OK, I was in."

"Just now?"

"Before I go on the roof."

"You have a key?"

"Passkey. I got one for all the apartments. Listen, I went inside with the funeral home guys, OK, and that's it—I go with them, I leave with them. You ask the old doctor, he was there, OK? I didn't take one fucking thing. I wouldn't touch her shit."

"So you were in Simonova's place other times? Maybe fixing something?"

"Sure. When she asks me. I change light bulbs for her."

"Right. She seemed sick to you?"

"Yeah. I have to get to work."

"You like the building?"

"Doesn't matter. It's good job."

"So about the roof? What were you doing up there?"

"I check things is all. Doors is locked, stuff like that."

He picked up his work gloves from the floor. From around the corner came the sound of voices, and Carver Lennox looked out into the hall. He smiled at me but didn't seem to notice Diaz, or didn't care, and retreated back into his apartment.

"People always treat you like that, don't even say hello," I said to Diaz, in a conspiratorial voice. I figured that and another twenty might put him in a confiding mood. I gave him the twenty and waited.

"Whatever," he said.

"I thought you said you were friendly with Mr. Lennox."

"If he gets me apartment, I'm friendly."

"What were you in Cuba?"

"Engineer."

"It's hard here."

"We do it for the kids. I go downstairs now, to sit at the front door in a stupid hat."

"I'll ride with you."

"Sure," he said. "Maybe I show you something," he added as we got into the elevator.

"What's that?"

"Something in the basement."

Between the seventh and eighth floor, Diaz pushed a button on the panel and the elevator stopped. He leaned against the wall. I kept my mouth shut. I knew it was his way of showing he was in control, that he could stop the elevator, that he had some kind of power in the building.

144

When he spoke again, he lowered his voice, and I knew he was preparing to deliver some information.

"So, you know about somebody threw this woman off the roof."

"When? What woman?"

"I don't know. I hear."

"While you've been working here?"

"No."

"How long have you been here?"

"Six years," he said.

"So this thing happened before that?"

"Sure, but I hear. I hear she is fucking whore, and this guy is some pimp, and he throws her from roof."

"Maybe it was a long time ago. Maybe it's just a story."

"No."

"Anybody who still lives here involved?"

"I don't know."

"So, listen," I said, extracting a third bill from my wallet. "Did you know Mr. Washington?"

"Sure. I do things for him, fix stuff, sometimes he say to me, 'Diaz,' he calls on my cell phone, he say, 'my hands are trembling, man. Can you turn the valve on the oxygen?' OK? He is always real polite, and I say to myself, Why not Miss Regina McGee, who is girlfriend of Mr. Washington, but he wants me. One time I go, and he is all confused and puking up. I help him. He is grateful. *Demasiado*."

"What's that mean?"

"Too much."

"What happened to it?"

"What?"

"The oxygen machine."

"I take it away. I want to return to the rental company. Maybe I forget."

"Where the fuck is it?"

"I can look," he said, backing away from me.

"Did somebody tamper with it?"

"What's it mean 'tamper'?"

"Did somebody mess with it?"

"So many people go visit Mr. Washington, his friend, Miss McGee, who lives on fourteenth floor and runs down to nine to say hello, or bring food. The Russian bitch, too."

"What did she have to do with him?"

"In this building, who knows?"

"What else did you do for Simonova?"

"For money. I told you, I changed her light bulbs, I cleaned up her terrace. She is Russian, she loves Russia, she loves the Soviet system, she has all the books, she tries to tell me, 'Join union, join Party.' Who in fuck is joining Communist Party now? She likes giving orders. Like all of them. Communists," he said. "I grow up with this shit in Cuba, where for all my father's life they shit on his head. But he says, 'Fidel is good, Cubans is happy. Society is just.' I come to America to escape that shit."

"And Mr. Washington?"

"He is OK. This one I like, this Mr. Washington, sure. He is a gentleman to me. I even go to his funeral."

"Who's in his apartment now?"

"Nobody. Nice one. They call it classic seven. Somebody lucky will get it."

"Do you think somebody hurt him?"

"You mean did somebody off Mr. Washington?"

"Yes."

He shrugged. "It's not my business," Diaz said.

"Can you show me? His apartment?"

"Sometime. Now I have to work."

"Start the fucking elevator," I said to him, and he just grinned. Then he hit the button. I noticed he wore a ring with his initials: UD.

"What's the U for?"

He laughed. "Usnavi. You know what that is? My mami, she sees the sign near Guantanamo, U.S. NAVY, and she thinks if she gives me this name, it makes me American," he said.

"Let's get going, if you really have something to show me."

＊　＊　＊

Diaz led me down a hall, and as we passed the basement storage rooms, he glanced at Simonova's, sealed up with yellow police tape now, and grinned.

Was it Diaz who beat me up?

A few minutes later, he turned a corner, led me into a room. He got a key from his pocket and unlocked it. "Here," he said.

Inside was medical equipment. Wheelchairs folded and stacked. A few walkers propped against the wall. At the back were two oxygen tanks, cubes on wheels that looked like R2-D2. "You stole this shit?" I saw one of the oxygen tanks that looked like the one I'd put into Simonova's closet earlier. Diaz must have swiped it. I tried to push past him. Diaz held his ground.

"My stuff. My shit," he said. "I got other stuff I can show you, I got information. Maybe we can talk more some time." He looked at his watch. "Right now I gotta go back up to the lobby."

"Yeah? What's that?"

"Gotta go," he said, edging me out of the room. He locked the door behind us jogged to the elevator. Punched the button and got in. I followed. Then I pushed him against the wall. I'd had it with the smug look on his face.

"What stuff? You want more money, that it?" I was furious. "You want to tell me what you were really doing on the roof? What about your pal, Carver Lennox—you work extra jobs for him?"

He shrank back from me but he managed to push the button. A few seconds later, when the doors opened on the ground floor, people waiting saw that I had a guy with dark skin pinned to the back of the elevator.

CHAPTER 24

Y ou can watch the moon rise right over there, nights when the sky is clear," said Lionel Hutchison, when I found him on the Armstrong roof. I asked him if he'd seen Diaz.

"You think he's up to something?"

"He said he'd been on the roof checking something."

"Didn't see him."

"You know him well?"

Hutchison shook his head. "No need. Don't like the fellow much, I admit."

"Isn't it cold, even for you, doctor?"

"Good for the health," he replied. "And please do call me Lionel. You know, I used to belong to the Polar Bear Club. They swim out at Coney Island every year on New Year's Day. Terrific," he said. "I enjoy it here. I come on up mornings, before everybody is around, sometimes bring my coffee. You look cold, Artie. I'll tell you what, see that toolshed? It's not much in the way of shelter, but we can sit in there for a minute if you like."

In the wooden lean-to, cigarettes in hand, Lionel offered me one, and I took it. He sat on a rough bench and I sat next to him. He got out his old Zippo, lit his smoke and mine. "Got this old lighter when I was in the service, back in the war," he said. "I was just a kid, but did kill a few Nazis," he added with satisfaction. "You wanted to ask me anything else about Diaz, Artie? Or you're wanting to ask me some things now we're out of Lily's hearing?"

"Yes."

"What is it you really want to know, then?"

"You knew Amahl Washington?"

"Of course I knew him. He lived here. He was the local councilman, as well, a very decent good man. What's this about?"

"Did he die unexpectedly?"

"Yes, but he was a sick man, he had been ill for a long, long time. I see the connection you're making. I'm not unaware."

"Did you treat him?"

"I helped him out from time to time."

"You come up here a lot?"

"Detective, just ask me your questions. You don't have to make small talk."

"When did Amahl Washington die?"

"I would say approximately six months ago. Let me see. It's December. That was June. Died from his heart giving up the fight. Still, it was lung cancer that made it all happen," said Hutchison. "I watched him suffer. Suffering is not noble, you know. Pain cripples our best selves and makes us hopeless at best, at worst evil," he added. "Do you know how Marianna lost the tip of her finger?"

"Tell me."

"She was in such pain at one time she bit it so hard it had to be amputated. As for Amahl, I believe it was mainly his own doctor who tended to him."

"His own doctor being Dr. Lucille Bernard?"

"He had several doctors, I believe. Lucille was called in toward the end."

"She was married to Carver Lennox?"

"Still is. Lucille's a wonderful doctor, but she believes in all that Roman Catholic foolishness, like my wife, in fact." He leaned back comfortably against the wall of the shed. "Do you know what the best thing about this neighborhood was?"

"What's that?"

"The real advantage of growing up on Edgecombe Avenue was that you had a sense of possibility. Couldn't not. You knew people, your parents knew people, who had made something of themselves. This building was like a fort where we were protected from even the worst times in Harlem. A lot of people thought we were snobs, of course, and that we looked down on them. Living here gave us a sense of ourselves, especially as kids. It empowered us, we thought we could do anything, even back in what I like to think of as the dark ages, back in the thirties, forties, you know?" He paused. "We met all kinds of people, of course. One of the profits of segregation, I guess you might say was that even in buildings like the Armstrong, we were all thrown together eventually. As time went on, it wasn't just professionals, there were people who worked as maids downtown. The oldest fellow in the building used to run the elevators. Pullman porters. Doctors like me. All kinds."

"What year did you move here?"

"I moved in with my mother and daddy in, what was it, 1931, and except for school and my military service, I've lived here all these years, had my medical practice in an office right downstairs for a long time. Couldn't get a job at any hospital in my specialty— hematology. Couldn't hardly get a job in any hospital at all in New York," he said. "So I set up in general practice right here on the ground floor. Graduated Harvard Medical School. Couldn't get a job in a New York hospital. Felt like the whole of America was an alternate universe for us. Sepia universe," he said. "I stayed on here. By then times had got bad, and after that it got worse and worse; even the Armstrong wasn't completely immune to it—the murders, the heroin, the poverty, the crack cocaine, the landlords and real estate people who sucked the place dry, the corrupt police force. Whole big areas of Harlem just a burnt-out case. My parents died; I married Celestina. Couldn't do it until Mother passed, though."

"How come?"

"Hold on, I just need to light up afresh." He used the butt of his smoke to light another one. "Calms me down. Must be my blood pressure's up again." He laughed. "Old age."

"Please go on."

"You like a good story, is that it?"

"Yes."

"Mother didn't like Celestina. She's older than I, and she had worked as a dancer at the Savoy Ballroom as a teenager. Didn't have much education. Her parents had come from Trinidad. Always was a tension between folk from the islands and the rest of us. They felt themselves to be superior. My mother didn't agree. Celestina was also quite dark-skinned, to my mother's way of thinking."

I didn't know what to say.

"You're surprised by all this foolishness about skin color and class?"

"Yes."

"Where my folks grew up, Artie, in South Carolina, in one of the churches—a black church, mind you—they hung a comb in the entryway. If you couldn't pull it through your hair easily, you were not acceptable, you were not allowed in," he said. "'Important to have good hair,' many of the church ladies whispered. Same ladies that would inspect a baby's ear, see what color the child would darken up to. Claimed the ear would tell you. That kind of thing goes on to this day."

"But you married Celestina."

"When my mother had passed, only then. Mother had her eye on a nice lady doctor I knew. 'Blood will tell, Lionel, dear,' Mother always said to me. When I was little, I thought she meant it could actually speak. People didn't talk about good genes back then, they talked about blood. 'Blood counts, dear,' she'd say, and it turned out she was right in a way she couldn't have expected. My little brother had sickle-cell anemia, the worst form. Not enough treatments back then. He went blind, his organs failed. He died in agony when he was twenty. I was already in medical school, so I decided I'd study the blood." He looked at me. "I decided I wasn't going to watch anybody suffer like that, either. Maybe that's why I never wanted children—married a woman too old for it. Maybe that's so," he said. "I knew I was a carrier." Lionel pulled casually on his cigarette, but his eyes watered. "Guess I've about told you every-thing. But you didn't come on up here for that, did you?" Hutchison tossed his cigarette onto the ground and took out a worn leather notebook and a fountain pen. "It's the pen my father gave me when I finished medical school."

It was the same kind of ancient Parker my father had, the one he had used until he died.

"What's that you're writing?"

He looked up. "Just the name of a song I've been thinking about. We better go inside now. You look cold. You're feeling pain from that blow to the head you received?" He got up and opened the door to the shed. "Get some rest, Artie. And if you need anything, come on by. I'm a pretty good doctor. Come sometime when Celestina is out, and I'll play you a record. Lily says you like jazz music, is that right?"

"Yes."

He held up his notebook. "Tune called 'Blood Count.' Billy Strayhorn, last thing he wrote when he was dying. Ellington recorded it. I met Strayhorn right over at the Hospital for Joint Diseases around that time. Friend of mine worked there—when was it? It must have been '67—and he told me about the tune. Tell Lily to play it for you. I gave her a copy," he said.

"I'd like that."

He tapped his cigarette pack. It was empty. "I better go get myself some smokes before Celestina decides she has to lock me in again. Silly woman. Bitter. But you're not interested in my domestic arrangements are you, Artie?" Hutchison left the shed and I followed him outside, where he crossed the roof toward the door to the building. He paused, turning to look at me. "What you're really after is knowing if I killed Marianna Simonova, isn't that right?"

CHAPTER 25

Around the perimeter of the roof was a yellow-brick wall about four feet high. One area was damaged, bricks missing. KEEP AWAY read a handwritten sign. Plastic sheets marked the area. There was snow on the roof. I saw my own footsteps in it

Hutchison had gone downstairs now. I was alone on the roof. I went and looked at the work area and my foot slipped on the wet plastic. I backed off. I was dizzy. It would be easy to topple over, fall from the roof, land in front of the Armstrong on Edgecombe Avenue where there was snow thick in the bare branches of the trees. I crossed the roof, found more broken wall, looked out, this time over the parking lot back of the building. You'd go over, and just fall, fucking splat, a mess of broken bones, dead.

My head hurt like hell. The Oxycontin I'd taken for the pain was making me wired, out of control. I needed more. I hated the side effects. What the fuck did Hutchison spend his time up here for?

I liked the old man. I didn't believe he had killed Simonova, no matter what he'd said. But he had been with her when she died. He'd been in her apartment.

I went back to the shed, looked around, but there wasn't anything, no sign Hutchison had been here except for a few cigarette butts on the ground. I reached in my pocket for the painkillers. Put the bottle back. Realized I still had Lionel Hutchison's lighter.

Regina McGee was lying on a gurney when I got to the fourteenth floor. I'd emerged from the stairwell, and she was there, lying on the thing, medics pushing her toward the elevator. She half opened her eyes, saw me, and tried to smile, but couldn't. She was trying to tell me something, and I leaned over, but she couldn't speak. She looked frightened.

"Hold the door, will you, man?" said one of the medics, gesturing at the elevator.

"What's wrong with her?"

He shook his head. "She's old, man."

"Trouble breathing," said the other medic. "We got her on oxygen."

I looked down the hall. Nobody was around. I looked at McGee. Was somebody else going to die here, die from lack of oxygen, die from something nobody could quite pinpoint?

"Lady said she had chest pains, couldn't breathe, we gotta respond," said the first medic as the elevator door opened and I held the button for them. "You a friend?"

"Yes."

He leaned closer. "Ask me, it's just dehydration, but better safe than sorry, you know?"

As they maneuvered her into the elevator, I looked around again, surprised nobody was in the hall. People on this floor were always alert to new sounds, movement, people coming and going. Now, nothing. The elevator door slid shut. Again, I wondered: Was Regina McGee another victim? But what of? Of living in the Armstrong?

When Mrs. Hutchison answered her door, she looked at me, my hair and clothes wet from snow, with disdain. Or was it contempt?

"She was wearing a heavy tweed jacket, a man's jacket, too big for her. Around her neck was a woolen scarf, and on her head, the same yellow cap I'd seen her in before. The jacket had a button missing.

"I have your husband's lighter," I held out the Zippo.

"Do you?" said Mrs. Hutchison. "You shouldn't encourage him." She didn't offer to take the lighter. I held on to it for the time being and stood in the doorway, hoping she'd invite me in. I wanted a look at the Hutchison place. I gave her my best smile.

"Cold today," I said by way of small talk. "Is the doctor here?"

"He's gone out. He came back from his smoking—with you, I imagine—and said he had to nip out. Cigarettes, I'm sure. I don't like it the way he wanders about. Just do not like it, but never you mind," she said. "Will you come in? I haven't much time. I only came back from my sister's to change my clothes for the party this evening. I must remember to pack my little bag, as I shall stay over with my sister afterwards," she added. "Well, don't just stand there, come in."

I went into the hall, which was lit by a huge hanging chandelier, half the bulbs missing.

"Can I offer you some sweet tea?" said Mrs. Hutchison.

Taking off the yellow cap, she smoothed the few remaining strands of hair on her bald head, then put it back on. Her face was small, the skin taut and deep brown. The dark eyes peered at me, they took in everything, but they also held a barely suppressed fury.

I followed her into the living room, hardwood floors, old Turkish rugs, the same high ceilings and moldings as Simonova's. The ancient floorboards were scrubbed and polished. The place smelled of pine oil. There was a small Christmas tree on a grand piano. The piano keys were yellow and broken.

The dog bounded in from another room.

"Ed, say hello to Detective Cohen," said Mrs. Hutchison. "Do you know that silly girl, Marie Louise, is frightened of him? Who would be frightened of my lovely Ed? She had the gall to tell me he is possessed by some kind of evil spirit. She's a backward one, that girl, but that's Africa for you." Mrs. Hutchison played with the dog's ears. "Now your Lily, she's a lovely girl. She appreciates my Ed. Very caring, that girl, at least so far as it goes. Interested in us old folk up here. You were her boyfriend." It wasn't a question. Clearly, there were no secrets in the Armstrong. "You should marry her, Detective Cohen."

I kept my mouth shut.

"I know she's been seeing the Radcliff boy, but he's too damn young for her, and if you ask me, like should marry like. Wouldn't you say? You think I'm blunt, well, as one of my sisters says,

'Celestina, she takes no prisoners.' What about that tea? Or would you prefer some whiskey?"

I said I'd like the tea. I called her Mrs. Hutchison, but she said to call her Miss Cellie. I wanted to get under her skin, but it was tight, that old skin, and hard to get under.

"Come with me," she said.

It was a very big apartment. Like Simonova's, it appeared pretty grand at first. There was old furniture in the big rooms and wood floors. When I looked hard, I saw that, same as Simonova's, some of it was very shabby—windows loose and rattling in the frames, a musty smell emanating from behind closed doors that opened off the long hallway. I had the feeling some of those rooms hadn't been used for a long time.

On the walls were framed black-and-white photographs. All of them included Celestina Hutchison as a very young girl—I could just make her out—with some of the greats: Duke Ellington, Lena Horne, Bill "Bojangles" Robinson. It occurred to me that she'd hung them on her wall to represent a better past, in the way Marianna Simonova kept pictures of herself with Stalin. Neither woman could escape the past, or wanted to.

"You must know Regina McGee," I said. "The lady who lives down the hall and worked for Ella Fitzgerald."

"I knew Ella, naturally, but Regina was only a maid," said Celestina. "I may have run into her once at some time, but we didn't move in the same circles. But are you interested in stories of old times?" said Mrs. Hutchison, turning to me. "Did you know that Mr. Carl Van Vechten took that photograph of me?" She gestured to a picture of herself in a dress, hat, and white gloves. "He was quite a prominent figure. Me, I don't care much for jazz music or the performing world; I did it because it was all I could do. But Lionel, he's what he likes to call an aficionado." Her tone was bitter. "He keeps those pictures up on the wall."

"I see."

She pointed to a picture of herself and another black woman.

"You know who that is?"

"No."

"That is Miss Hattie McDaniel. She won the right to live in a nice section of L.A. they called Sugar Hill, another Sugar Hill out west. It was a big court case, and I knew her. I was in that house," Celestina Hutchison said. "I met Hattie. She won the Oscar for *Gone With the Wind*, played Mammy, even got me an audition for the part of Prissy. People criticized her, but she said, 'I'd rather play a maid for seven hundred dollars than be one for seven dollars.' She was my friend. If you look right next to it, you will see Miss Bette Davis, now she was a lady. She joined with Hattie and Lena Horne and Miss Ethel Waters, with a black acting troupe, to perform for black regiments in 1942. I did meet them all. I even met Mr. Clark Gable." She looked at me. "Otherwise, I had my fill of the entertainment world. I danced. I lived with another girl, Gladys Mae Jagger was her name, but we couldn't get many jobs. We wanted to dance at the Cotton Club, but she was too fat and I was too black. We were out of work and no place to stay. We lived from hand to mouth. Sometimes we found a room, sometimes we sat up in a movie theater all night, or out on the street. I was fifteen then."

I listened.

"Are you in a hurry, Mr. Cohen? I notice you look at your watch quite frequently."

In the large old-fashioned kitchen—the appliances must have been fifty years old—she put a pitcher of iced tea on the table and poured some into a couple of glass tumblers. I thanked her, addressed her as Miss Cellie. She lightened up when I did, and now, as she spoke, it was like something out of a play.

"You put me in mind of my friend Becky Cohen. We played together as little children. My mamma worked for her people, such lovely lovely people, Southern Jews, you see, not at all pushy like those in New York. You've seen *Driving Miss Daisy*, with Morgan Freeman?" she asked.

For a while longer, she sat at her side of the old table, sipping her tea, and watched me as if inspecting a specimen in a cage.

"What can I do for you?" she said.

I put Lionel's lighter on the table. "I told you, I just wanted to return this," I said.

She examined it. "That old Zippo. He goes on about it and the war as if General Eisenhower himself gave it to him. I mean, after all, Lionel was just an old foot soldier. Wasn't like he flew with the Tuskegee Airmen, not like my cousin Cecil."

"I thought he might want it."

"What do you really want?" she asked bluntly, as if she'd made a decision to put the charm to one side along with the lighter.

"I was wondering when you last saw Mrs. Simonova?"

She shrugged. "A few days ago, I expect," she said. It certainly didn't matter to her if I stopped by; I only did it out of courtesy, which is something that was foreign to that woman. Once upon a time we exchanged little gifts at this season. I made an effort; she gave me those same ridiculous Russian dolls every year." Mrs. Hutchison looked at me. "I didn't like her. That's what you're asking? I didn't visit much. He went every day."

"Dr. Hutchison?"

"And don't think he was there for the doctoring." Celestina Hutchison snorted. "God knows what he saw in her, so ugly. Big raw bones, that woman, ugly as sin." She drank more tea. "That help you, detective?"

The bitterness was so virulent you could smell it.

When I didn't answer, she shifted the topic. "Will you attend the party tonight?"

"I'll try."

"Dear Carver always does it up nicely. He tries so hard." She slipped back into her ladylike manners. "He has so many troubles with this wretched building. I wish him well. I do. Most of the other old folk don't like him. They're so set in their ways."

"Why's that?"

"Carver tries to give good advice, tells us that should we decide to sell up, he'll help us out, buy the apartments for top dollar. He already owns quite a few of the apartments, but I do hope he's not in financial trouble." She giggled. "It's not only the Jewish people like Mr. Madoff who play this game, no, indeed." She stood up. "What else do you want to know?"

"What else is there?"

"We're like characters in a play up here on the top floor. Relics. Like those Southern characters out of Lillian Hellman or Mr. Tennessee Williams—you ever see those plays? That's us, except we're black." She paused. "What a thought. And Carver wants this particular attic cleared out of all us old people. We're worth a fortune to him. We have the grand apartments—seven rooms, nine rooms. All he has to do is clean them up, do over the lobby, then sell for a bundle. Well, for my part, he can buy this one. I would retire to the sunshine faster than you can say Jack Robinson. But Lionel is so damn stubborn."

"You know a lot about Carver Lennox."

"He has nice manners. When he came to the building, quite some years ago now, he introduced himself. I have to say I really established him in the building, talked him up, helped him get on the board. He was always grateful. I wanted him to feel right at home, and the building is, as you see, a little village."

"I see."

"Do you? Carver never knew his mother—he was adopted—and he saw me as the family he never had."

"Right. And your husband? He'll be at the party?"

"He won't be up to it. I'll leave something in the oven for his supper. I always make sure he's safe and sound before I go out."

"You just lock him in."

"Well, he's a bad, bad boy, you see, and I never know what he'll get up to with all his ideas. I can't trust him."

In her imagination, Lionel was old, forgetful, unconnected to reality. It made her feel she was the powerful half of the couple.

I finished the tea and asked if I could use the bathroom. She gestured to the hall.

* * *

The bathroom had cracks in the plaster and broken tiles. I washed my hands with soap that smelled of almonds then left and went along the hall into a small office, where the shelves were full of CDs, old LPs, medical books, and volumes of poetry.

On the desk was a laptop as well as a portable typewriter. Hurriedly I looked through some of the drawers, listening for Mrs. Hutchison.

In one drawer I found some mail addressed to Lionel. Hearing footsteps, I stuffed them in my pockets, took a brochure from the desk, and pretended to study it.

"You found what you wanted? Your snooping around produced something for you?" said Celestina.

I held out the button I'd taken from Simonova's dead hand.

"You found that in here?" Mrs. Hutchison asked. "It's from this jacket I'm wearing. My husband's, of course."

"I found it in Mrs. Simonova's hand this morning," I said.

"So he *was* there. Yes. I thought so." Anger crossed her face. For a moment she was silent, staring at something on the desk. It was the brochure I had been looking at.

"This interested you?" She picked it up. "Why is that?" she said. "It's just some of Lionel's nonsense. He joins all these silly societies." She took the brochure from the desk and tore it in four, tossed the pieces in the wastebasket. "That sad old man I'm married to, all he thinks about is death, and just because his little brother had some pain sixty years ago. Ridiculous. I don't understand him anymore," she said, almost to herself. Then she smiled brightly, arranged her yellow cap, and added, "Well, I guess we are all entitled to our beliefs."

I didn't answer her.

"I always say life is life, after all. Don't you agree?" She let out a humorless little laugh.

I held out the button again. She shook her head.

"Keep it," she said. "Perhaps it will lead you to something. Perhaps it will help you find Marianna's killer." She paused. "Ha ha, of course I'm joking. Can't believe old Lionel would do that. But you, detective, isn't that what you do? Find the killers?"

CHAPTER 26

Virgil Radcliff caught up with me as I was leaning on a railing across from the Armstrong overlooking Jackie Robinson Park, trying to catch my breath, get some air.

"Hey." Virgil leaned next to me and lit up a cigarette.

"Where've you been?"

"Upstairs," he said. "I got my car out back, and when I was pulling onto Edgecombe Avenue, I saw you. What's going on?"

All the time I had been on the roof, then with Celestina Hutchison, he had been with Lily.

"I thought you had a bunch of fucking cases to work?" I said.

"I had to take a break. I'm going to be on all night," said Virgil. He looked up. The snow had finally stopped; the temperature had dropped. "Jesus, it's cold."

I didn't know if Lily had told him about Simonova's letter, that the Russian had left her everything. I didn't feel like sharing, not then.

"How do you think Lily is doing," said Virgil.

"I don't know. You?"

"I think she'll be fine once the funeral is over. Tomorrow, it'll be better," he said and then I knew she hadn't told him, not about the letter, and I wondered why.

"I have to go," said Virgil. "You have my numbers if you need me, right? Listen, Artie, you should go the party with Lily. I'll probably be working all night."

Nice to have the boyfriend's permission, I thought.

"If you drive, take it easy. Lot of black ice under the snow."

"Right." I knew he wanted something.

"Streets up here can be bad. Hills, inclines can deceive you. Weirdest damn thing happened on election night, you know? Just a few blocks south."

"What's that?"

"So, there was this van that was parked on that street, and some asshole left the hand brake off, and it just slid down the street, and around the corner."

I didn't say anything.

"There was nobody in it. Nobody. It was just this empty silver van."

"So?"

"I think we caught most of the event on camera. Not usually a lot of cameras up around here, nobody bothered for a long time, but that night there were plenty. We think some film crew caught it—they were passing, filming on their way to 125th street, and they caught it."

"I have to go." I was going home to change for the party, to look good for Lily.

I looked at Radcliff. He'd mentioned the silver van casually, brought it up almost as an afterthought. But why? Did he know I'd been there? Was my red Caddy—you couldn't miss it—on a piece of tape, caught by some passing film crew by chance on election night? I'd half forgotten the fucking thing, out of control, passing me like some crazy ghost van.

Did Radcliff want me to know he knew, without actually saying it? Why? To put me on edge? Was he fishing? Was it just conversation?

"No kidding," I said. "Yeah, weird, right, so see you."

"Worse, Artie. I was telling Julius Dawes over at my house the other day you know, we were talking about it, how this van just keeps going, gets up speed, turns the corner and pins a young guy against a lamp-post."

Dawes, I thought. Dawes had mentioned my car, the paint on my car.

"And?" I turned up my collar, tried to stay cool, though I could see in Radcliff's face something bad was coming, some piece of news I didn't want to hear.

"It kills him," said Radcliff. "Even if it was an accident, even if it was just some fool left a hand brake off, or a drunk in another car who nudged the van out of place and set it rolling, we're into vehicular homicide. Either way, I mean, that's jail time, Artie, isn't it?"

CHAPTER 27

There was already a crowd when I got to the Sugar Hill Club at ten, people looking for a good time. In the corner was a tall Christmas tree, blue and white lights looped through the branches, a silver star on top. Last time I'd been here was election night, six weeks ago. It seemed like years, but hard to forget—the joy, the celebration, and Lily.

I leaned on the bar, ate some peanuts from a bowl, and listened to the conversations swirl around me.

"Fucking Madoff. They should crucify him."

"You saved anything when the shit came down?"

"*So* not, but I'm stacking cheese like crazy now. Gotta save it."

I needed a drink. I called out to Axel, the bartender, who crossed to me and said, "You wanna hear the one about the guy goes into a bar and drops dead . . . ?"

"Zip it, man," somebody shouted. "We heard that one already a hundred times. Enough!"

With his big soft shoulders, Axel was a chunky young guy built like a rugby player gone to seed. German mother, black GI dad, a crew cut dyed platinum, a red and white bandanna around his forehead, he was working on his routine as a stand-up comic. "So the other guy goes into the bar—Oh, fuck, I forgot the end," Axel said. "What are you drinking, Artie? Man it is cold out there. Cold as you-know-what, witch's tit in a brass bra—my old man used to say that in Berlin when I was a kid. He hated that weather. He wasn't crazy about the Germans, either." He laughed. "Have one on me, Artie."

I asked for a beer. Axel set a bottle and a frosty glass on the bar.

"Ain't seen you since, what was it, election night? I'm glad you brought your ass over here. It's good to see you, man."

I drank, looking at the door. I was waiting for Lily.

On the sound system Oscar Peterson was playing his elegant version of Christmas music, an album Lily once gave me. The six-piece combo played "I'll Be Home for Christmas" as such a lovely piece of music, it made me believe for a minute in the whole holiday thing.

I had a second beer. Somebody switched the sound system off and a guy went to the piano, and started to play. I'd heard him the summer before when I'd been at the club.

He was probably seventy at least, but when he played "You Took Advantage," he ran through it like a virile young man, smiling, singing to himself.

I signaled to Axel. I wanted to know the piano player's name, but a familiar voice interrupted.

"Martini please, Hendricks gin, straight up, very dry, with a twist. Make it a double." It was Virgil Radcliff.

Radcliff, who'd said he'd be working all night, was sitting with Carver Lennox, the two of them talking and laughing. I was pretty surprised. Radcliff had told me he didn't like the guy.

"Artie, come join us," Lennox called. He held up his glass, a smoky, golden single malt in it, and offered me one.

The whiskey was good. Radcliff wore the clothes he'd been wearing all day, but Lennox had on a beautiful black custom-made suit, the wool as fine as silk, and a pristine white shirt, open at the neck. On the bar was a red Santa hat.

After a minute or two of "how you doing" talk—we talked malt whiskey—Radcliff got up. "I have to go. Thanks for the drink, Cal."

"Not at all, Virgil. Please, Artie, have another one. I had better do some circulating; there's a big group coming on later."

"Not everyone's from the Armstrong?"

"From the Armstrong, plus other friends," said Lennox, who picked up his Santa hat! "I'm hoping the mayor will show. He's been so good to us up here, he's a man that understands development. Helps out, attends the black churches. He gets it."

"You want to walk me out, Artie?" said Radcliff.

"I thought you were working?"

"I'm on my way," he said, as we made our way through the crowd. "I just checked up on Ms. McGee at the hospital, by the way; it was dehydration, heat got turned up so high in her place she passed out, wasn't drinking enough water. They'll have her home in a few hours."

"Good. What's with the 'Cal' business? I thought you didn't like Lennox."

"Friends call him Cal. Name's Carver Antoine Lennox. Sometimes you need to make friends with the enemy, right?"

"He's the enemy?"

"I'm speaking metaphorically. More or less," Radcliff said. "Can you do me a favor? I mean, no reason you should, Artie, but I would like to ask you to do something for me." He was hesitant, formal.

He was going back to work. Lily was on her way to the club. I felt generous.

"Sure."

"My dad will probably stop by. I asked him to come before I knew I had to work tonight, and I can't get hold of him. Can you just make sure he gets a drink or something?"

"There's something else you want, isn't there?" I saw it in his face.

"Since you were asking, Artie, yeah. You could tell my dad being a cop is OK. Maybe if he meets you, he'll stop getting on me to quit and go back to grad school."

"Why don't you tell him?"

I saw that Virgil was nervous about his father. He was fearful, not that his dad would beat him or ignore him, but of the pressure. I knew about that. I remembered my own father pushing me at school, wanting to turn me into a linguist or a scientist, something important, useful, something that would aid the socialist cause we believed in—or that he did. He was dead before I became a cop, so it didn't matter.

"You know what I'm talking about, don't you?" Virgil said. "Ever since I was a kid, I did stuff they didn't approve of, couldn't even fathom. My idea of connecting with what my dad called 'my people' was wearing big satin basketball shorts and gold chains that made my parents go nuts, I mean, their Virgil, in bling? And us living in Cambridge when he taught at Harvard, and then on Riverside Drive? God, were they disappointed in me," he said, lighting up a cigarette as we reached the door of the club. "Christ, I shouldn't have had that drink with Lennox, not when I'm working."

He was on a roll. I was guessing he'd had more than one drink. Told me that as a kid, he had been crazy about basketball and Tupac, and his parents always saying, "Can't you find something that doesn't involve criminals or ball players?" and he thought to himself he needed some culture and started listening to MC Solaar.

"I can imagine."

"Yeah? My dad dragged me around Harlem as a kid; he showed me the old buildings, the Jumel Mansion, that kind of thing, and eventually I fell in love with them. I guess he knew me better than I knew myself. So I majored in the history of architecture, and I figured afterward I'd get a degree in architecture, which I did, and then I was going for one in urban planning because by then I realized my big love was New York City, the city itself. Still is. Still love it, the good, the bad, the ugly. Then it was 9/11," said Virgil. "I was on the subway. I was heading to the Trade Center to get some air tickets, going over to Italy to look at old buildings. I made it out of the train just in time." He paused. "I saw them jump. The smoke made me blind, I fell over, got up, thought I was somehow in a pile of cattle, legs all sticking up, you know?"

"Yes."

"I realized it was people. They were all dead. I couldn't shake that," said Radcliff. "I had to do something. You worked the pile, didn't you?"

Yeah, I said. Yes. I knew where he was coming from. I couldn't help it but I was getting to like him. Virgil. I'd stop calling him Radcliff. I didn't want to look like a jealous old man, not with this guy who was one of our own, who had done the thing.

"Man, you guys were the heroes," he said. "They wouldn't let me on, so I worked night shifts at some of the shelters the cops and fire guys used. I served meals and whatever else they let me do. I didn't have any other skills. I was useless. I thought, Fuck architecture, I want to do something, and I got myself into the police academy. I guess they were happy to have a black guy with a college degree."

The club was packed now. The mix of music, laughter, chatter, made it hard to talk. We were standing near the door, and now Virgil said, "Let's go outside. I need a smoke. It's suffocating in here."

I followed him into the street, he lit up a smoke, offered me one. I shook my head. He glanced up and down St. Nicholas Avenue where the club was, a few doors down from St. Nick's Pub, a few blocks from the Armstrong.

"You know, Artie, I've only been in Harlem a couple of years. I feel like a fish out of water some of the time," said Virgil. "You should hear me trying to talk with some of my 'homies.' People piss themselves laughing, or they get mad. White men can't jump; black men don't talk good English. Right? Never mind," he added. "My dad went nuts. 'You're gonna be a cop?' he said, and I said, 'Listen, it's that or I'm going into the military, OK?' First time in my life I went up against him that way, you know, Artie? He blew his top. The idea of me going into the military was too much."

"Why's that?"

"I don't know. Had something else in mind for me I guess. I better get going." He looked at the street. "Maybe he's not coming. But if you see him, say it's OK, will you? And you can talk jazz with him. He loves that music. You guys can talk the talk."

"Listen, there's something else," I said. "What do you know about Lionel Hutchison and his obsession with suffering? That stuff about euthanasia?"

"He had a brother who died young, I know that," said Virgil. "Can we talk about it tomorrow? I'm gonna be dead meat if I don't get back to the station house soon."

"Right."

"By the way, Artie, I have something for you." From his pocket he took a small package wrapped in red tissue paper and tossed it to me.

"What's that?"

"Consider it a Christmas present. I mean, Merry Christmas." He zipped his jacket.

"Wait."

"What?"

I'd been holding back. I wanted to tell him I thought Lionel Hutchison had—what? Killed Marianna Simonova? Released her from her pain? That maybe Lily had helped him? Did Virgil know?

"Can it wait?" Virgil asked, seeing my hesitation.

"Sure," I said.

CHAPTER 28

I ripped the paper off the package Virgil had given me. It was a DVD. *In the Heat of the Night,* the movie where the Southern sheriff played by Rod Steiger says to Virgil Tibbs, the northern black detective, "So what do they call you, boy?" And Sidney Poitier, young, dazzling, tall, superior, looks down on this redneck and says, in his own particular Philadelphia don't-mess-with-me way, "They call me Mr. Tibbs."

He knew. Virgil knew all along. He played me for a fool. Worse, I had deserved it.

Where was Lily?

People were streaming into the club, some I recognized from the Armstrong lobby. A group of women in down coats went through the door; behind them a quartet, the two men black, white haired, distinguished, both in suits as if they'd been to a board meeting, their while wives in for coats. Behind them, a crowd of younger people, guys in Sean Johns, the long-legged girls in tiny skirts, denim jackets, huge earrings, high heels, expensive bags. Almost all of them were black. I followed them in. I was freezing.

The pianist swung into a great version of "Take the 'A' Train," as if by way of welcome to the new cluster of guests.

At the bar, Axel was filling an order from a piece of paper, mixing cocktails, glancing again at the paper, making things that were pink and green, and placing the glasses on the tray a waiter held. He manipulated bottles and shakers and crushed ice like a juggler at a circus, stirring, mixing, pouring, adding cherries, lemon peel, slices of pineapple and lime.

I climbed on an empty bar stool. A white man in a black turtle-neck with light hair climbed up next to me. He nodded pleasantly.

He had an expensive haircut. He was around forty. He kept quiet, just drank, finishing one vodka, ordering another, and listened to the music, and from time to time pulled his sleeve down, as if to hide some defect, eczema, a scar, a wound. It was the kind of tic you noticed.

"You like the music?" I said.

"Yes, good stuff," he said, and we made some small talk about jazz. I noticed the accent.

"Where are you from?" I said.

"Excuse me?" He seemed not to have heard me.

"Where are you from, originally, I mean?"

"Oh, from St. Petersburg, but a very long time ago." He laughed. "The music wasn't nearly as good as this."

We raised our glasses to the music. It was Christmas, after all.

In the mirror behind the bar we both looked pale as ghosts in the dim light, like guys who spend too much time indoors. But he liked the music; he was tapping his foot on the bar rail and nodding his head. As I got up and started for the door, cell phone in hand, about to call Lily, the Russian guy turned to look at me. He smiled slightly and raised his glass again.

Half an hour later I was beginning to worry. No Lily. No call. Instead of leaving her another message—she'd be furious if I bugged her—I left one for Tolya. Send one of your guys, I said; tell him to stick around the Armstrong. See if Lily's OK. Tolya always has guys to help out; guys with muscle, if necessary.

I stayed outside, I wanted some air. My head hurt. I reached into my pocket. I changed my mind. The painkillers made me crazy.

At the curb, along St. Nicholas Avenue, a guy was dragging a shopping cart. The snow had stopped, but it was cold and on impulse I went over and shoved five bucks into his hand.

The bright lights, the party, the successful people at the club were real enough, but most of Harlem stretched out for miles, hidden, back streets, rough avenues, dark, poor, cold, shabby at best.

Cars pulled up, people got out, patted their hair or their clothes, and went into the club. I noticed when an old Mercedes 380 SL, lovely dark blue, pulled up; because it was a car I had always wanted. The headlights went off, the door opened, a tall man, white guy, unfolded himself from the seat, got out, locked the car, looked around as if he wasn't sure of his surroundings.

"Is this the Sugar Hill Club?" he said

"Yes."

"Thanks," he said, and went inside, and a few minutes later, because it was cold as hell, I went in, too. I saw the guy looking around, looking a little lost.

"I'm just looking for somebody," he said.

"Can I help?" I said.

"It's my son," the man said.

"What's his name?"

"Virgil Radcliff."

I did a double take and tried not to let it show. This guy was white as me. I picked up my drink. "He just left," I said. "He asked me to tell you he tried to reach you on your cell, and that he had to go. He's working tonight."

The man reached in his pocket for his phone, "You're right, he sent me one of those text things. I never looked. Damn," he said, but it seemed to cheer him up that Virgil hadn't lied about the message. "You're a friend of his? I'm Joe Radcliff."

I introduced myself. Asked if I could get him a drink, and he thanked me and said he'd like a glass of red, a cab, if they had any.

I asked if he was OK at the bar or wanted to go into the next room, where there was food. He said he'd like to eat something.

In a room off the bar, Marie Louise stood behind a long table heaving with platters of food. She nodded at me, asked Mr. Radcliff what he wanted, served him turkey and salad.

"Shall we sit?" he said.

We crossed to a small table. I put down my drink.

"You're surprised by my color? I really am Virgil's father," he said. "My parents were much darker than I, my siblings, too, my children. Genes are a funny thing. My ancestors came from Nova Scotia, there were plenty of Scots and Irish there. I always could pass, you see, as white I mean, but I didn't want to be white, my family are not white, my children aren't white, so it's always been complicated, you might say. I couldn't go around with a sign, a letter on my forehead, could I?" He smiled slightly. "How to tell the world you're a black man. It's an odd problem, wouldn't you say?"

I wasn't sure how to answer him.

He asked what I did. I told him I was a detective.

"Like my son, then?"

"Yes."

"Do you believe my son has a chance, as an African American, as a black man, of making a real career in the police department?" He looked at me. "For me, the police were always the enemy, you see, never on our side. Maybe I've lived too long in the distant past—the classics, that's what I've always loved. Poor Virgil, he always hated his name. I suppose it could have been worse—he could have been Achilles." He chuckled to himself.

I asked if he wanted another drink, and he thanked me. It gave me a chance to go back to the bar, but Lily wasn't there. I tried to call her on my cell, but the signal in the bar was lousy.

"Do you think I'm just out of touch?" Mr. Radcliff asked me when I came back with the drinks. "Can I tell you a story, Artie?"

He leaned forward a little, elbows on the table, glass in one hand.

"I was the only black boy in my dorm at Columbia. There were a few Jewish boys I could hang out with," he said. "Steve Middleberg, who is still my great friend, a dean down at NYU, we both became academics and stayed close. Virgil still calls him Uncle Steve. And Max Zwerling. Next door was Jackie Finkel and a Southern boy in the room beside his. Name of Billy Wilkes. He was from North Carolina. Like you, I suppose, he assumed I was white." He leaned forward a little more, finished his wine, and went on.

"One night we were all in Billy's room, and he asked what we were doing that Friday night. Jackie says he'd be studying, and Billy told him studying was for fags and weekdays," said Mr. Radcliff. "Then Billy said he had come to New York for its cultural delights, and I could see Jackie thought he meant museums, but Billy said he was speaking of dark flesh." Joe Radcliff looked at me. "Poor Jackie. I think he thought that meant some kind of chicken dish. But what Billy had in mind was some black women who would initiate us boys. He told us Southern boys understood these things, understood about a certain intensity in the ways of love. He meant rape, of course. Paid for, but rape."

Mr. Radcliff paused.

"Anyway, it was chilly in those Columbia dorms, and Billy Wilkes saw we were cold. He got out some sweaters, and Jackie, who was next to the closet, saw something and asked what it was. Wilkes said, 'It's not for you boys,' then looked right at me. Jackie wanted to know. Wilkes turned to the closet, slipped on the garment, and turned to us. It was a sheet with a hood and those familiar eyeholes. 'This is something every Southern gentleman is proud to be part of,' Wilkes said. 'That's right, boys, the Ku Klux Klan.'"

I finished my drink and was silent.

"I never knew for sure if Wilkes had figured out I was black until a few days later, when I told him and punched him out," said Joe Radcliff. "I should go now. Thank you for listening, Artie. I must sound like the Ancient Mariner. I'm sorry. Maybe I'm wrong about Virgil. Maybe being a cop is just what he wants, and he's entitled to that. I can't believe it's the best he can do, but it's his choice now. Please ask him to call me when you see him."

"Of course."

"And give him my love."

I said I would.

And then Lily arrived.

CHAPTER 29

Y ou look beautiful," I said.

"Thanks," she said. "Sorry I'm so late, couldn't decide what to wear. You look nice, too. New jacket, right?"

Her red hair was up, diamond earrings—I had given them to her a long time ago. She wore a plain black dress, and the skirt swayed when she walked. It had a low back and long, tight sleeves. Around her neck was a gold necklace I didn't recognize.

In high heels, Lily was as tall as me. I put my arm around her waist. She didn't push me away, only leaned against me slightly.

By now a band had replaced the pianist. They were good, playing standards, new stuff, Latin tunes. A few people danced. Waiters swooped through the crowd like birds, with trays of champagne and eggnog. Lily and I talked, laughed, drank. For a little while it was as if we were back where we had once been.

Then I saw Carver Lennox signal the band, there was a little drumroll, he put a rectangular package on the bar, and started to talk.

He made a speech about community and Christmas and how he planned to return Sugar Hill to its former greatness, listing the greats who had lived here, how the Armstrong would be the center of it—and 409 Edgecombe, of course, he added, acknowledging those of its residents who were present. He talked about how hard various organizations had worked to bring in supermarkets, and drugstores, how over the last few years everybody in the city had realized what great housing stock Harlem had, and how it was time to honor the past, but also to move on, to stop living in the 1920s, and celebrate a New Harlem Renaissance. He wished everyone a good holiday, and singled out some of the famous and the nearly famous in the room.

He was persuasive; it would have been hard to guess there had been a financial meltdown, that everybody was scared of the coming year. Finally, Lennox picked up the package from the bar, unwrapped it, and held a bronze plaque up over his head, like a trophy. It was the plaque he'd showed me earlier.

"Our new name, to honor our new president," he said. "We are now the Barack Obama Apartments."

There was some applause, but a few people turned away.

Somebody behind me said in a low voice, "I heard Lennox is in trouble."

"Money?" someone asked.

"What else?"

"I heard if he doesn't turn the Armstrong around before the end of the year, he's fucked. He'll have to sell those apartments."

"He'll find a way."

"No, seriously, he is fucked, man. He's running out of cash."

"He thinks he's in with Bloomberg, thinks the mayor will bail him out."

"Mayor only interested in those church guys, the ones who own big pieces of Harlem, you know? He's always going to church around here—I mean, Jesus, man, the guy is Jewish."

When I turned around, I saw it was two elderly guys I didn't recognize, leaning together, holding drinks.

"Why should we change our building's name?" one said.

"For Barack," said the other one.

"I love that man, sure I do, but we've had our name too long to change. I don't like Carver Lennox, the way he just takes hold of everything, the way he just bought his way in, got himself elected president of the Armstrong board, members are all his people," said one of the old men. "Says it's to restore the building to his glory days. Truth is, that fellow's just waiting for us to die."

"Let's go eat," his friend said.

* * *

"You're having fun, Artie?" Lily put her hand on my arm.

"Yes."

"Me, too."

As if she'd finally left behind the business with Marianna Simonova, Lily looked happy.

I was guessing she'd had some wine before she came out, and she was lit up. She knew everybody in the room and was flushed with the attention, the way people greeted her, kissed her, shook her hand, beamed at her. She stood near me for a while and kept up a running commentary. "You know who that is, right Artie?" she said, pointing out S. Epatha Merkerson, the police lieutenant on *Law and Order*.

"So you watch cop shows behind my back?" I said.

"Only once in a while," she said, turning to greet somebody else.

"You love it up here."

"Yes, I love the history," said Lily. But I knew what she had fallen for was a sense of community.

We could live here, I almost said. We could move uptown together. Have a life. Be part of it. Live in a brownstone, on a pretty street with trees. A dog, if you want—Lily's always wanted a dog. But I kept my mouth shut. I didn't want to scare her.

"Merry Christmas, Lily," said a familiar voice, a man's voice with a Southern accent. I watched as she turned and was embraced by a tall white man in a very good suit, a white man with silver hair and blue eyes like flashbulbs.

"Merry Christmas, Mr. President," said Lily, flushed with pleasure.

When I spotted her, Celestina Hutchison was crossing the room with Carver Lennox at her side. He showed her to a table as if she were royalty, and she lapped it up.

I went over, admired her silver dress, which was covered with sequins. On her head was a red satin hat, a jeweled Christmas tree pinned to it. People flocked to her, fussed about her.

"Is your husband with you?" I heard somebody ask.

"Lionel? He's asleep. He was not feeling well. You see, he hasn't my stamina," she said, turning away to greet a young woman who came over to kiss her cheek as if paying homage to a grandee. I thought the girl might curtsy. Celestina was holding court now, and I moved away.

Among the crowd I saw more people from the Armstrong. Lily introduced me to a couple from her floor. Massimo, an Italian, was a designer, his partner Sam Cowan, was black, a plastic surgeon. Standing with them was Jeff Smith, a guy with a pleasant face, a goatee, and a big afro, the kind they'd worn in movies like *Shaft*. He was tall and thin and wore a slim cut brown suit with high lapels. He told me he taught semiotics at City College, something to do with French rap, or Algerian rap, something like that.

Lily told me he'd been a serious radical once, had called himself Jeffrey X. I got the feeling she admired him for it, or once had. Jeff's Moroccan wife, Amelie, joined us, and so did their two teenage boys, who looked desperate to get away from the grown-ups and were eyeing the other kids bopping around between tables.

"God, I love this city, Artie," said Lily. "I love the crazy mix of people. I've had a lot to drink, you know."

"Me, too," I said, and she pulled me along with her as she went to greet still more people.

Earlier in the day, I'd spent as much time as I could talking to people in the Armstrong, people I saw in the elevator or the lobby. The building itself was a favorite source of gossip, complaints, ambition—for a new washing machine, repairs to the roof, irritation at a neighbor's dog or child. Kids make the best spies; they were always happy to talk. I glanced at the Smith boys, but they had finally crossed the floor to join some other teenagers.

Not everybody in the Armstrong was as prosperous as Carver Lennox, far from it. I recognized a guy from the third floor who was a retired subway worker, a guy named Bassey. I'd run into him in the little parking area out back of the building. Now he told me he was waiting for his girlfriend, a nurse called Shirley. Apparently Mr. Bassey proposed to her regularly. She could be Shirley Bassey, he always said.

Others in the crowd simply hung back, watching. Some made repeated trips to the buffet table, and I saw one elderly woman slip dinner rolls into her handbag.

Latinos, a few Asians, a few whites, and from the chatter you could hear some had been to an opening party at the Studio Museum. Art dealers. Lily pointed out DJ Spooky, a trio of drop-dead-gorgeous girls hanging off his arm.

We giggled, and eavesdropped. Lily had always loved sitting in bars and cafes, listening to people talk. We had confessed to each other a little guiltily that we preferred it to visiting museums or galleries. I'd always thought that some day we'd visit cities I longed to see—Rome, Venice, Rio—and spend all our time sitting in cafes. Or in bed.

Around midnight, Lucille Bernard stopped by with her daughter. In a red dress, Bernard looked fabulous. Younger people streamed in, including one dazzling girl in a jean jacket, a big skirt, and lime green stilettos.

"You're staring at her," said Lily, laughing, leaning closer to me. I could feel her breath. I didn't want anything else.

A short white man in a leather jacket and a tie with vertical stripes, a white soul patch on his raddled elderly face, wandered by, holding hands with a woman who wore a lot of stuff she must have gotten in India—big paisley shawl with glitter on the fringe, hanging gold earrings, some kind of pink silk top. The guy knew everyone, talked loud, used the lingo, dropped the names of musicians, some dead, some still alive. After the next number, he looked at the pianist and said, "Smokin'!"

One of these days I'd find myself jiggling my head and my foot, eyes closed, thinking "Smokin'!" or, worse, saying it out loud. I'd be a finger-poppin' daddy-o, an old white guy wanting to listen to this music and to be with Lily and not much else.

"He really likes to run the show, doesn't he?" Lily was looking at Carver Lennox, who seemed to be everywhere, greeting people, seeing them off, dancing with the little girls, pressing flesh. I saw him talk to Jimmy Wagner, who had dropped by. I saw him with Lucille and their daughter. The girl put her arms around both her parents, as if she were the grown-up.

"Are we drinking too much?" said Lily.

"Yes," I said. "Let's have some more."

"Did you see that weird guy?" She took another glass of champagne from Axel.

"What guy?"

"He wished me Merry Christmas, which is why I noticed, and he had such light hair, he looked like an albino. He kept looking at you."

"I talked to him earlier. He told me he liked the music."

CHAPTER 30

The Russian with the light hair was by the door, and I saw him look at me. He looked at me then looked away, leaned down to talk to a short woman in a white dress. When he had finished, he glanced up again—and I saw his face, saw something on it I couldn't read—or maybe it was just the distance between us, and the crowd and the booze. I lost sight of him. I was distracted by Tolya's arrival.

It was some arrival. He wore the huge black fur coat I'd seen him in once before. On his head was a sable hat. As he moved through the club to the bar, he swept the coat off to reveal he was wearing a bright red silk jacket, a Nehru jacket, and in one hand was the wine case he always carried with him. As he got closer, I could see the large emerald in his ear.

The dimples in his face deepened when he saw Lily. He set his hat and the wine on the bar, tossed the coat over a stool, pushed the black hair from his forehead, leaned over and kissed her. Then he kissed me three times, Russian style.

"Merry Christmas, Artyom" he said. "You're feeling better?" His face was pink, his eyes were glistening, he'd been drinking, and drinking plenty. Softly, in Russian, he added, "You noticed this guy with pale hair, black sweater?"

"Yes. Why?"

"He was going out when I arrived, he wished me good evening in Russian, I didn't recognize him, but he seemed to know me, I don't know. I'm not sure. Also, I saw him say something to Carver Lennox, and Carver, something suddenly makes him nervous."

"The guy seemed OK," I said. "We talked about music earlier. Lily said he was looking at me."

"Maybe he's gay," Tolya said. "Maybe he liked your looks."

"Fuck off," I said, and we both laughed, and then Tolya extracted his cigar case from his pocket, the solid gold case with a cigar engraved on it, a large ruby for the glowing tip.

"You can't smoke in here, darling," said Lily.

He put the cigar case back.

"Let's drink my wine, then." He set a pair of bottles on the bar and asked Axel for glasses.

Everybody in the club was looking at Tolya as if Santa Claus himself had arrived.

"Château Lynch-Bages, 1982." Axel whistled. "Fuck me, man."

"Please, help yourself to glass," said Tolya. "And serve this to my friends, please."

"You're nuts," I said.

"You look so beautiful, Lily," he said to her and then described the house he'd bought.

"You're nuts," I said again.

"That's so nice," said Lily.

"OK, so I give you house if you like, for Christmas present, or I buy you one same as mine."

"Thank you, darling," said Lily.

There had been a time when I'd thought they might get together. Tolya would take care of Lily; she would be loyal. It never happened.

"Please, Lily, you will introduce me to these nice people, now I am neighbor?" Tolya took her arm.

"Of course," she said, and they made their way into the crowd. I saw Tolya talking to a tall black woman with short hair and a great face. She was almost as tall as he was, and they looked good together. Lily left them and came back to me.

"What are you thinking about, Artie, darling?" she said.

I was thinking about my father.

The music he had learned to love during his year in New York had saved him, had made him human even though he was a KGB agent, a man who was famous for interrogations.

* * *

I missed him. He was a wonderful father. Even after I understood what his job was, that he spent some of his time interrogating suspects in the Lubyanka—no, not interrogating, not just asking questions, something probably much worse; even now I couldn't bear to imagine that about my dashing father.

I still loved him. With me, and with my mother, he had remained sweet and gentle and full of interesting stories. He gave me his jazz records. We listened together to anything we could, on records, on illegal radio stations. There had been some jazz musicians in Russia, and he took me to see them all.

In Israel, too. After we were kicked out of the USSR—my mother had become a refusenik by then, my father had lost his job—we listened in Israel, where you could get all the music you wanted.

How many hours did we sit in his tiny study in our apartment in Tel Aviv, listening to his Blue Note albums? He listened to other jazz, too, taught me to love the earlier stuff: Armstrong's Hot Five and Hot Seven; Benny Goodman; Ben Webster; Lester Young. We listened to Ellington and Artie Shaw, Sinatra and Ella, Sarah Vaughan, and Billie Holiday. My dad had listened to Ella every single day of his life.

I can remember us sitting in that room, him in a big secondhand armchair covered in some nubby green fabric, and me on the floor, sprawled out, both of us drinking beer and smoking. It was the best time with my father, those years.

One morning he calls to my mother that he's going out. I'm at home working for an exam; my mother is trying to cook something out of her French cookbook, and the smell is of wine and butter, which is all wrong on the hot semitropical day, but she's happy.

And he goes. He buys his records in the best jazz store in town, on Dizengoff Street, and then seeing he's late for dinner, catches the wrong bus, intending to walk the extra mile home when he gets off. Then a bomb goes off on the bus.

"And that was it," I said to Lily

"You never told me that," said Lily.

"Why can't we be together?"

I was outside the club with Tolya who was smoking a cigar at one in the morning. The city looked slick, asphalt gleaming, ice on the sidewalks alight with the reflection from neon.

Just then, Marie Louise appeared, lugging a shopping bag.

"Can I get you a cab?" I said.

"I will find a bus," she said. "Mr. Lennox gave me so many nice presents for my children, merry Christmas."

"It is late, one o'clock. I will give you a ride," said Tolya. He took the woman's bags, handed them to his driver, who was waiting, and escorted Marie Louise to the big SUV.

"What's wrong, Artyom?" Tolya said. "Something is up. I see your face when you come out of the club."

"Nothing." I didn't want to ruin the evening.

"Time to go home," he said.

"In a while."

"I go home," he said. "I go to new lovely new house."

"I'll call you."

"Sure. I like this uptown, Artie. Maybe I'll open restaurant or bar or little jazz club for you. You will quit this cop nonsense and make a life."

"My God. You mean it."

"Yes, this is me, I am God." He kissed me on both cheeks three times.

"Tolya?"

"What is it?"

"You have one of your guys available?"

"Always."

"That man with the very light hair? Now I keep thinking about him! See if one of your guys can find him, maybe hang out close by."

Tolya held out his iPhone. "I already take little picture."

"How come?"

"Why not? I don't feel good about him, so nice to have a picture," said Tolya, switching to Russian. "Goodnight, Artyom. I wait for you at my new house on 139th Street. Unless you are perhaps staying with Lily?"

"Send me the picture, to my phone."

"I already did."

CHAPTER 31

W hat did he want?" I said to Carver Lennox.

"Who?"

"The guy with light hair, a Russian? Tolya said he made you nervous."

"It's nothing. He was interested in an apartment, I said they weren't for sale, it pissed him off a little, but it was no big deal," he said. "Nice of you to ask. He had too much booze is all, and everybody's getting crazy about the financial meltdown, now people think we're screwed, and they think I know something. If I knew something, I'd do something, my brother." He looked around the club. People were beginning to leave the party. "I don't know, man, most of last century, black people lived in an alternate universe in this country. We had our own schools, clubs, neighborhoods, everything, you know, and whatever was going on in America, it had its mirror image in black America, banking, baseball, all of it. So if it's bad for the country now, it's worse for Harlem. I thought we were on our way; we even got a Starbucks," he said, not without irony. "We were keeping those real estate companies like Pinnacle out and putting in our own people, and now, who the fuck knows? I'm sorry. I think I had too much to drink."

"How are things with you, speaking of the financial fuck up?"

"You want the truth? They could be better. I lost a ton in the market. I'm just moving fast as I can to get things right with the Armstrong. Thanks for caring, man," said Lennox. "Glad you could come, glad your pal Sverdloff made it. I like this dude, you know that? He's your pal, right?"

"Yeah."

"Good party, right?"

"Very good."

"You met my little girl?"

"I saw her with her mother."

"Lucille is great with the kids, I'll give her that. Did you know that Alex, my daughter, she's getting straight A's at Brearley. Best high school in the city. And beautiful, too, right?"

"She looks like a great kid." I thought I might need his help, so I dropped compliments, and, anyhow, his kid probably was great. "What about your wife, you and her still friendly?"

"Why?"

"A matter of interest. A guy thing."

"I don't know," said Lennox. "She gets on my nerves. She was always wanting to know where we were at, and I used to say we're at this particular place, we're married, we're making great money, we have fabulous kids, you enjoy cutting up people over at Presbyterian, you run a free clinic for people who can't afford you to cut them up otherwise, you do good work, what else is there? 'That's what I'm asking,' she used to say; Lucille would say that. She was never content, you know?"

"I get it."

"Glad to see you're with your lady, by the way," he said. "Couple of times we met by the elevator, and Lily kept saying Artie this and Artie that, and I said, who's this Artie dude?"

I didn't say anything.

"You're thinking about her and Virgil? He's a nice guy, but he's not right for her."

I called over the bar for another drink.

"On me," he said, and I knew he was pretty boozed up. "You can't pay anyway. The whole night's on me. Christmas party. What do you feel like?"

I said I'd have what he was having, and he got a couple of malt whiskeys and we sat at a little table for a while and toasted some musicians I discovered we both liked.

"Lily was very sad about old Mrs. Simonova, I know," Lennox said.

"You can get hold of her apartment, now, right?"

He shrugged. "I do what I do for the neighborhood. I grew up here when the whole of Harlem was desolate—crack and cronyism, murders, rapes, gangs, old ladies who couldn't leave their houses at night, no investment, no jobs, white cops who went home before dark, rats in the schools—now we're pulling ourselves up; we're doing it. I found out at Princeton there's a different way to do things, there," he said. "I met with President Clinton, you know, when he first moved to his office down on 125th Street, and he says to me, 'Carver, I like your approach.' This is a year to celebrate, don't you think, now we have President-elect Obama," said Lennox.

"And you see yourself in his footsteps."

He didn't rise to the bait easily; he was a cool customer. Raising his glass, he just smiled. "Drink your whiskey, Artie. This is an excellent one I got over in Scotland, one of those glens, Glenfiddich, Glenallen. What about we brew up some Glensugarhill or something—We got glens, right?" He went on making up names for whiskey, and I drank. "I knew an old guy said once upon a time back in the day, him and a couple friends made wine in Harlem." He laughed.

I drank. He gave me a guy hug, thumped my back, did a knuckle bump as a follow-up, let me know I was OK. "Good to have you on our side, my brother. Isn't that right? Hello, Lily," he said, as she came up alongside me and took my glass and drank from it.

I put my arm around her.

"Lionel Hutchison's here," she said.

CHAPTER 32

I have to hurry," said Lionel Hutchison. He wasn't wearing an overcoat, and he still had his velvet slippers on his feet. "Is Celestina here?"

"She left earlier. Said she was going to her sister's place."

"Thank God. But I have to hurry. She might come back to the apartment and find me out. The dog is all alone. She wouldn't like that. Celestina, I mean," he said.

I tried to get him to sit down. I tried to get him to drink something, but he was distracted. Something was wrong. He was agitated and almost incoherent. I asked what the matter was. He looked around the room, frantic. Had to hurry, he said. Had something to tell me, but he had to get back, the dog was alone, he said over and over. Celestina would be mad that he left Ed, the dog, alone.

Lionel started to talk about ghosts. Ghosts in the building, he said. He was shivering. A waiter got him a cup of hot coffee. He held it between his hands, and for the second time he said he had to talk to me. Ghosts, he said. Pale faces.

I got him to sit down. The club was emptying out fast now.

"It's not right," he said. "It wasn't right."

"What wasn't?"

"What he did."

"Who?"

"I have to go." He put his coffee on the bar. "Sorry about this."

"Did you take anything before you left?"

"I don't remember. Sleeping pill. Maybe. Not sure." He was rambling.

"You need some warm clothes," I said.

"I like the cold," he said, but he was shaking now. "Like it."

"I'll take you home."

"Something to tell you."

"I'll take you home and we can talk on the way."

He looked around the club and saw Carver Lennox who waved. Hutchison shrank back. He seemed afraid.

"What is it?"

"I'll tell you when we leave here. It's important," Hutchison said. "There's something I have to tell you."

"About the ghosts?"

"About Marianna Simonova. I have to tell you something about her. Nobody knows. I know. Only I. I knew her in a way nobody else did."

"I understand."

"You don't understand," he said. "Damn dog. I can't wait. I have to go back for the blasted damn dog. Son of a bitch. Literally."

"Or I could come in the morning? I could put you in a taxi and come over in the morning. Lionel?"

It was a mistake. I saw he wouldn't ask again, wouldn't beg for my time.

"Just wait here," I said. "I'll get my car keys."

As I went to find my coat and my car keys, I knew I was too drunk to drive, and all I really wanted was to stay with Lily. Be with her. Dance with her. But Lionel had looked dazed. Maybe his wife had been right; maybe he did wander in his sleep.

I got my coat, went to look for Lily, told her I'd be back as fast as I could, and then discovered that Lionel had already gone. Axel said that one of the guests who was leaving, said he'd give Lionel a lift home. "Which guest?"

Axel didn't know. "How did he seem?" I said.

"He seemed a little nuts at first, then he was calm. He seemed fine when he left," Axel said.

I found Lily, I told her a little about Lionel, but not all. Just told her he had dropped by and somebody had driven him home. We got another drink and went to listen to the pianist who had resumed playing after the band left. He was playing "Someone to Watch Over Me." It was the first song I'd heard with Lily, at Bradley's.

So we danced in the almost empty club, for an hour—I lost all sense of time—then sat and whispered and danced some more together. I didn't want to let go of her. I thought if I held on, she'd stay forever.

I forgot about Lionel Hutchison. I would spend real time with him in the morning, I told myself, I'd sit in the freezing cold, if he wanted, smoke with him, hear him out, but for now I just let myself forget. I didn't think about him again, not for hours, two, three, four hours, there wasn't much sleeping that night, so I didn't think about him again until after I woke up in Lily's bed.

SUNDAY

CHAPTER 33

It was a beautiful, bitter-cold morning, clear black sky, an icy slice of moon, the stars still out just before dawn. I could see them from Lily's window. I could see the faraway lights downtown on the skyscrapers. On the dark, quiet streets closer to the Armstrong, there was only a solitary figure coming in the back door with a big, shaggy dog, somebody who couldn't sleep, somebody whose pooch had begged for an early walk. Something else caught my eye, but I was distracted by Lily; dressed in a black skirt and jacket, green shawl over her shoulders, she was rummaging in her bag for her gloves.

"I have to go," she said, picking up her coat. She kissed my cheek and rubbed off some lipstick.

I said I wanted to go to the cemetery with her. She said no.

"Just wait for me, will you? Please?"

I said I'd wait. As soon as she closed the door behind her, I looked out of the window again. My car, a slick of white ice over the red, was parked in the lot surrounded by wire fencing. On the ground a figure sprawled, face down.

I shoved the old sash window up and leaned out as far as I could, looked down, saw the row of gray metal garbage cans, one on its side, maybe knocked over by the wind, or by somebody falling. And the man, spread-eagled, black blood already pooling on the crusts of snow and ice. He was hurt bad, or dead, and then I recognized the Harris tweed jacket.

I didn't want to believe what I was seeing, figured from fourteen stories up maybe I was wrong. I yanked on my clothes and, not waiting for the elevator, ran down the fourteen stories to the basement, hurried along the endless corridors, banged through the heavy metal door that led outside.

On the ground, face down, Lionel Hutchison was still wearing the jacket he'd had on when he came to the club a few hours earlier. It looked, first glance, like he'd skidded on black ice, fallen over a garbage can, collapsed on the ground, maybe had a heart attack, a stroke. I knelt down beside him. The light over the back door spilled a pool of white light over the body.

The garbage can was on its side, rolling back and forth in the stiff wind. Cigarettes, the Lucky Strikes I'd seen Hutchison smoke, were scattered on the ground. One of his velvet slippers lay on top of a ridge of dirty snow. There was no blood on it.

I got down and put my hand against his neck, and right then I suddenly felt somebody was watching me.

Hutchison was dead. There was no pulse. But there was too much damage to have come from a simple fall, too much broken for a man who had simply tripped on a garbage can. His limbs were skewed in strange positions, at least one arm and one leg looked broken.

I stood up fast because, again, I had the feeling somebody was watching, that I wasn't alone out by the garbage cans with a dead man on the ice. I should have come back to the Armstrong with Hutchison last night, I thought, I should have paid more attention when he came to the club. But I'd been all wrapped up in Lily.

By now, I was dialing Virgil Radcliff on my phone, trying to get through, then finally reaching him, waking him up. He said he was at his apartment, a couple of blocks away over on 145th Street. He had just climbed into bed, but as soon as he could throw on some clothes he'd get to the Armstrong. I knew he'd been working most of the night.

When Virgil arrived, he found me crouched by Lionel Hutchison's body. It was still dark.

"Christ, Artie," he said, clutching two cups of Starbucks coffee, handing me one. "It's Dr. Hutchison, isn't it? Jesus, Artie. Shit. I liked the guy so much. Is he gone?"

"Yeah. I called for an ambulance."

Virgil crouched near the body, his phone already out. At the bottom of his jeans, green flannel pajamas hung out over his boots. He looked like a little kid.

Gently he put two fingers alongside Hutchison's neck, the way I had done.

"Fuck," Virgil said. He gulped the coffee. "You're thinking what?"

"He liked coming out for a smoke. I don't know."

"Heart attack?"

"What about all the blood?"

"Where's Celestina?" said Virgil.

"Last I talked to her, at the party, she was going over to stay at her sister's. You know where that is?"

He punched something into his iPhone. "I can find out. What time did you see her?"

"Midnight? I'm not sure. Poor bastard. We should check in case she came home. Somebody should go up to the apartment."

Virgil got up. "I'll go."

"I was thinking it looks like he fell from somewhere high up. His bones look all broken."

"Old people break easily," said Virgil. "You don't have to fall off anything, all you need is to trip."

"You're an expert?"

"Yeah, if you want to know. My grandmother broke her hip last year. Lionel's age, you can break bones if you just trip and fall over, stumble on the ice, slip. It happens. But does that give you a stroke? Does it make you bleed like that?"

"No. Listen, I saw your father," I said as Virgil started for the door.

"He told me."

"Yeah?"

"He called. He liked you. I guess he told you his story. He tells everyone."

"Those were lousy times when he was in college."

"Hard to imagine, for us, I mean. These guys, my dad's age, they suffered such fucking absolute segregation. Guys like Lionel Hutchison. Jesus, Artie. This is bad. I'll go up."

"You called your house?"

"Yeah, and I also managed to get through to the chief at home," said Virgil. "Soon as I got your call."

I'd been expecting Virgil to ask about the party. He didn't, not about the party or about Lily. Maybe he knew not to. Maybe he was preoccupied with Lionel Hutchison. I felt guilty about Lily and me, but I didn't sleep with her to get at him. I wanted her. Needed her. Maybe for her, it had been a one-time thing, a party, the booze and music. I didn't want to think that.

I just leaned against a garbage can and waited for the ambulance, the cops, the whole gang of assorted characters who would arrive, each with a different part to play, a traveling troupe of death.

The first cops to arrive, a couple of uniforms in a cop car, unreeled a spool of yellow CRIME SCENE tape, marking off the area, as if it was their stage.

A few minutes later, the ambulance came. Somebody from the ME's office followed. She was young; she looked like a kid in her purple parka.

A yellow cab pulled up and a couple of detectives climbed out—there's plenty of detectives these days who use customized yellow taxis. It's useful in neighborhoods where a four-door sedan would stick out like a sore thumb.

From the back door of the building, Diaz emerged, alerted by the noise of the sirens. He stood, looking down, his back against the wall. With him was a teenager, tall, gangly, head too big for his body. Goofy, Diaz said. The Goof.

"Hey, Goof, help the detective if he asks you, right?" He tapped the boy on the back.

"I'm fine," I hurried to the other side of the parking lot.

"Celestina wasn't home," said Virgil. "I went upstairs, no one answered the door. I'll try her sister. They took the body?"

"Yes."

"Go find out what they're doing with it," said Virgil to a young detective, who looked at me because I was obviously the senior guy.

"Just do it," I said, then turned back to Virgil. "What about that damn dog," I said. "Lionel said he had to get back to the building because of the dog."

"When was this?"

"He came to the party looking for me around two in the morning. He said he needed to talk."

"Yeah, and?"

"He looked cold and tired, he was confused, he rambled on about something, and then I asked him to wait so I could take him home and I left the room for a minute, and when I got back I discovered he'd just gone. Bartender said he had pulled himself together and left."

"Then you can't be feeling too good."

"I'm not," I said. "So you went inside the apartment?"

"I called, I buzzed, I yelled and hammered on the door. Loud enough to wake the dead, since you're asking. If the dog was there, it would have heard. I would have heard it. You want me to just go on in, Artie?"

"What about keys?"

"I can find a way without keys."

"It's your call."

"You found him," said Virgil. "You want me to check out whoever gave Lionel a ride home?"

"I think the apartment comes first. Virgil?"

"What's that, Artie?"

"You want me to try to work this with you? Or not. Just spit it out. This is your part of town, you work homicides here. It's your call."

"Thanks for asking," said Virgil. "Yeah, I could use your help. If Wagner agrees," he added. "You think it is a case? You don't think Lionel could have just fallen over?"

"Do you? Lionel Hutchison was in good shape. Looks like a case to me. First Simonova, now Lionel. Lot of dying, wouldn't you say? Listen, you get along OK with Jimmy Wagner?"

"He treats me OK, but I don't think he likes me," Virgil said. "He thinks I'm a cocky overeducated son of a bitch, and I'm black, which doesn't help if you're from the captain's background. No offense, but Wagner is old school. He can't help it."

"Right. I'll talk to him," I said.

CHAPTER 34

B undled up in a North Face jacket, Jimmy Wagner pumped my hand. "I'm really glad to see you, Artie, man. But how come you're here?"

I said I'd been visiting somebody. To Radcliff he said, "What the fuck's going on?"

Virgil told him what had happened.

"Poor bastard," said Wagner. "I met the old man once or twice at community meetings. He was a pistol. He didn't put up with no shit whatsoever. He fought for his community. I liked him. You think he just slipped, Artie?"

"I have no fucking idea, Jimmy. I had a good look at the area around the garbage can, that stuff, but we'll need the ME to figure it. Hutchison was old, maybe bad heart, he smoked like a chimney, the ground was icy."

"You believe that, Artie?"

"I don't know."

"Did you meet him before?"

"Yeah. Couple times."

"You got a lot of interest in this building, that right, man? Some friend of yours was wanting to buy an apartment, something like that?" Wagner said. "You got a lady here or something? Nice girl?"

Radcliff looked at me.

I kept my mouth shut.

The woman from the ME got up from beside the body, came over to talk to Wagner, told him her preliminary thinking. Then Wagner huddled with some of his guys—a detective, a couple uniforms, the women from the ME's office. It was hard not to notice most of them were white except for Virgil.

Some people who had emerged from the building, wrapped in sweaters and jackets, stopped to watch. Then I saw Wagner motion for Radcliff to join his group. I waited. A few minutes later, he turned to me. "I'm gonna need you, man," he said. "Radcliff is cool with it. He'll work it with you. I'll call whoever it takes to get you the time off."

I told him not to bother. It was Sunday morning early, and what was the point of waking people up. I told him I was mostly on fraud cases these days, Russian stuff; nobody went in on Sundays for that. He didn't need to call anybody.

"But if I work with Radcliff, it's his case, right? His precinct?" I said.

"For chrissake, man, yeah, fine, all them fucking niceties, man," said Wagner. "Also, I only just heard an old lady died in the building Friday night. You knew about this?"

"I heard."

"You didn't bother to tell me?"

"It wasn't my business. You want my help, Jimmy? I'm happy to do it."

He said he wanted it. "We got cars sliding around crazy, on icy roads, like *Dancing with the Stars*," Wagner said. "Not to mention our other homicides. So you're cool with Virgil Radcliff. You asked me about him when you came by yesterday, right? He's good, man, he is really good, very sharp, does his work." Wagner glanced at Radcliff, who was talking to the ME. "He also likes to fly by the seat of his pants, so keep an eye on him, see that he don't fucking reinvent the rules."

By now, more people had come out of the Armstrong's back door and others from around the front. They'd heard the sirens. News was spreading. Some pretended to walk their dogs.

From across the street, still more onlookers stopped by, the cops fending them off, or swearing at them for hanging around, for gawking at the dead, or trying to. One kid held up his phone to take a picture and a cop gave him an earful. Made me remember, for some reason, the time I was down at Ground Zero, after 9/11, and fucking tourists were taking pictures. Dust was everywhere. One cop got so crazy, he just looked at some tourist assholes and yelled, "You know what that is? That's people."

"So you're on it," said Wagner, obviously nervous as fuck about this incident.

"I told you, Jimmy. Yes. Sure."

"Thanks, man, I owe you."

"It's fine."

"Listen, Artie, the old man had a wife, right?"

"She's at her sister's. Radcliff's going."

"I'll go," said a voice. I looked up to see Carver Lennox in a thick orange silk bathrobe, his bare feet stuck in a pair of driving mocs, staring at the body. He was crying.

"Where is she?"

"Her sister Vanessa lives over at the Hurston—it's a new condo on Broadhurst," Lennox said. "Let me go." He took my arm. "Please let me go. We're close. Celestina helped me out when I first got here. She was like my mom, swear to God. How did this happen?"

"Fine," I said. "Listen, you knew Amahl Washington?"

"What? Sure. You asking me that now? Why?"

"Never mind."

"That's it?"

"For now. Give me your number," I said, and I got out my phone and punched it in.

"Artie?"

"Yeah, Jimmy."

"That girl from the ME says she can't say until she looks at X-rays and they start the autopsy if the old guy just toppled over by the garbage cans or what. Jesus, you can't even say girl—I mean officer," said Wagner. "She says her guess is he fell off some-thing high up, the way the body was splayed out on the ground. I don't know, a terrace, or the roof, the building could be liable and then we have a shitstorm coming down." He wheezed and began coughing.

"Or he was pushed."

Wagner looked up at the building. "Christ, no, not another homicide. You think? Shit, man." He hacked again, turned his head, spit into a big handkerchief, and I saw there was blood on it.

"Take it easy."

"The cold weather stinks," said Jimmy. His big face, the reddish hair going gray under his black wool watch cap, the veins in his nose, the way he gulped at the air once in a while, he was a very sick guy. He pulled his jacket tight around his bulky body and turned up the collar. "This sucks," he said. "Christmas coming, an old man dead, one of the best buildings. Fuck."

"Don't ask me exactly why right now, but can you get me Amahl Washington's medical records? I need to know if he really just passed, if that was all."

"I ain't asking why, but I'm asking why, Art."

"Personal favor."

"Then consider it done."

"If Lennox is going over to find the wife at her sister's, I want to go up to the apartment with Radcliff, take a little look before anyone else goes up. You can do that, Jim? I need twenty minutes. Thirty. Tell your guys to hang on down here, or let them canvass the building or whatever."

"You got it," he said. "One more thing, there's a time component."

"How's that?"

"It's Sunday. Things are quiet. Come tomorrow morning, maybe before, I'm going to have officials on the phone. Hutchison was a big deal in the community, and I'm not even sure one of them churches doesn't own part of the land the Armstrong is on. They'll all be on me, the preachers, the rest, Christ, for all I know, Al fucking Sharpton will show. You hear me?" He coughed some more. "I'll feel a whole fucking lot better when Dawes gets back on Wednesday."

"I'm ready, Artie," said Virgil, who had been talking to the medic. Next to Jimmy Wagner, Virgil looked tall, young, and easy. It was like looking at Obama and McCain. I think Jimmy Wagner saw it, too. He shuffled away to join the other cops, then he turned around.

"Tomorrow," Wagner called out. "You hear me?"

CHAPTER 35

"He was pushed," said Virgil, trying the door to the Hutchison apartment.

"I thought that, but tell me how you figure it?"

"You were with Wagner, I was talking to the ME, and she was saying it looked to her like Hutchison hit the ground from some-place high up, you heard that, right? So I get to thinking, Artie, since you're asking, I mean how's he going to just fall?" He got some keys from his pocket.

"Where'd you get those?"

"I sweet-talked Mr. Diaz," said Virgil, opening the door.

"Let's go. I want a good look before the rest of them get here."

"Right," said Virgil, pushing open the door.

"Jesus."

"What's that, Artie?" Virgil flipped on a light in the hall of the apartment, surveying the room.

"He went up there a lot to smoke, right? Maybe something hap-pened. His wife didn't like him going up there. They played this game that she locked him in the apartment. What do you think her game really was?"

"Humiliation."

"Right. Yeah."

"What did Wagner mean when he said 'tomorrow'?" asked Virgil.

"Wagner wants this, whatever it is, wrapped by tomorrow. Says on Monday people will start to make noise, officials, people who want a piece of the publicity."

"What else?"

"Says he'll be glad when Dawes is back. I met him over at your station house."

Virgil was silent.

"Wagner told me Dawes was your partner."

"We split up. He didn't like the way I do things, he thought I was some kind of loose cannon," said Virgil. "Don't get me wrong; Dawes is a good man, but it's like working for your censorious uncle," he added. "Listen, Artie, maybe Lionel could have had a heart attack and then fallen?" He had changed the subject.

"He was healthy as a horse. He told me he swam off Coney Island every winter."

"Told me, too."

"Listen, Virgil, you OK here by yourself for a couple minutes?"

"Sure."

"See if you can find any of Hutchison's notes. He kept a little notebook, maybe he wrote stuff down about people he treated," I said. "Or helped."

"You talking about his interest in euthanasia? I'd want my grandparents to go out easy," Virgil said. "Wouldn't you, Artie?"

I thought about my mother.

"I guess. Anyway, see if you can find the fucking dog too; maybe it crawled under something and fell asleep. This apartment has about nine rooms, from what I saw. I'm going on the roof."

"What for?"

"Can you just do this? We only have twenty minutes until there's cops all over this place."

"Be careful up there."

The wind whipped at my face. There was snow on the roof. The sun was coming up, and the sky was bright and slashed with color.

There were footprints in the snow that led from the door to the low brick wall.

Had Lionel come up here to smoke again? Had somebody else been here? Somebody who had pushed him? The footprints looked fresh, but it was hard to tell.

From the street I heard the sirens. From somewhere on the roof came the banging of a radiator, a generator, the noisy innards of an ancient building. The wind howled.

At the edge of the roof was the plastic sheet I'd seen the day before, some cans of paint, a ladder. The wall here was broken, and I could look over and see the cracked back of one of the stone figures—a gargoyle—that faced the street.

In spite of the fancy marble fireplace in the lobby, the high ceiling, the old chandeliers, restored now, the doormen in their caps with the gold braid, this was no fairy-tale castle on a hill. It had, like most of the great old buildings in the city, a secret life, all the histories buried in the apartments, in the basement rooms, in the people who had lived here on and on for decades.

A building was like a village, enclosed, wrapped up in its own life, with its own class system and a ruling caste—the co-op board. These were people who had power—it might be power to decide who got in, or just what kind of decorations went on the Christmas tree.

I had once worked a case where potential owners were so desperate to get into a co-op, they had their dogs' voice boxes removed so they wouldn't bark. Couldn't get into a good co-op if your dog was noisy. I had worked another co-op downtown on Eleventh Street where one owner hated the color of paint in the lobby so much that, after a lot of martinis, he went for the board president with a sushi knife. Cut the tip of his nose off.

Easy at the Armstrong to get people talking, kids, old people, guys working around the place, guests at the party the night before. It was a talkative group, and they talked about the building, the Armstrong, its past, its problems, its glories. It was one of the building pastimes, like villagers in Russia might talk about the potato crop.

What I'd found out was that the Armstrong had fallen on bad times in the fifties and sixties. The landlord let it go, didn't pay taxes or fix the plumbing, so the city took it over. Bad times— heroin, cocaine, Harlem in the toilet. Then in the eighties, the tenants go it together to take it back, formed their own co-operative, kept the maintenance prices same as their rentals had been. Low.

So people stayed on. Some had been here sixty years. A few new people bought in when there were apartments on the market—usually when somebody died. I figured what Carver wanted was to turn it around, make it into the usual kind of New York City co-op—fix it up, raise the maintenance from five hundred to five thousand. Sell off the apartments that were empty. He'd been buying them up, warehousing them. Telling people he'd buy them out.

He got himself on the co-op board, became its president, the rest of the members are his people. I'd heard one old man say at the party the night before, "Lennox says it's to restore the Armstrong to its former grandeur, the glory days, but if it happens, the residents will just get moved on. Lennox? That fellow just waiting for us to die."

I went to the other side of the roof. When I leaned out, I was right over the back lot where I'd found Hutchison's body. There were still a few cops, but the ambulance had gone. I leaned out as far as I could, lost my footing, and gasped for breath.

For a split second I felt myself dangle in the cold space, the wind pushing at me; for a second I wondered if someone had pushed me from behind, or if it was an accident.

A voice from behind startled me, and I crashed back onto the roof, my foot twisted under me. Pain rattled my brain.

"Jesus, man, you OK?" A hand reached down to help me. It was Carver Lennox.

I stumbled to my feet. He asked if I wanted a doctor. I said I was OK and hobbled a couple of feet back from the edge of the roof.

"You almost killed yourself—you sure you're OK? I could call somebody."

I said I was fine. I asked if he'd talked to Mrs. Hutchison, and he said he'd called her over at her sister's, but the sister said she wasn't there, and was trying to find her. The sister thought she might be at church but wasn't sure if she was attending her usual Catholic mass or was over at the Abyssinian Baptist, where she sometimes went with a friend.

"I want to tell her about Lionel myself," he said. "I want to be with her. She's going to take this hard, you know; I mean, fifty, sixty years or something like that, they were married. You have anything at all on this? I talked to Captain Wagner, but he didn't have any idea. He said you and Radcliff are working it." Lennox looked at me. "How the fuck did Lionel fall? Celestina used to tell me she locked him in because he walked in his sleep."

"She has quite a few stories."

"Yes, and I never got the impression Lionel Hutchison listened to anything she said; he just humored her."

I headed for the door and he followed, not touching me, but holding an arm out as if to catch me in case I fell. My ankle was throbbing like somebody had stuck it with nails. Lennox opened the door to the stairs and held it for me.

"You were close to them, weren't you?"

"Yes."

"So you wanted them to stay here."

"Of course," he said. "Even though Celestina never stopped telling me she wanted to sell—even last night at the party. She wanted to go somewhere warm."

"I thought you were anxious to get hold of the apartments."

"You think I'd just buy them out and not help them? I've offered to re-house all of them, anywhere they like—brand-new apartments in midtown so they can go hear music or go to the theater, or in lovely assisted-living facilities up in Westchester, or Queens, just a stone's throw from here, lovely gardens. Many have already told me they'd like to move somewhere warm—Hawaii, the islands. I can enable that. Did you think I would just kick them out into the street?" he said. "Well, how would that look to prospective buyers? As for the Hutchisons, I told Celestina I'd be real sad if they were to go. They're part of the history. I see this building as a fusion of past and future."

"I see," I said, walking painfully down the stairs from the roof.

"You don't believe me, do you?"

"What about Simonova? Was she was part of your glorious plan?"

Lennox didn't answer, not until we got to the fourteenth floor. In the light of the hallway I saw his face, saw a change in his expression.

"You were saying. About Simonova?" I looked at him.

"I wasn't saying anything." He removed his thick tweed coat and looked at it. "Where did I get this old thing? I can't remember."

"You didn't like Simonova, did you?"

"I didn't have a view about Marianna Simonova," he said, and I knew he was lying. "She was a little crazy, but she was part of the Armstrong family, so attention was paid. I'll go to Celestina now."

"What the hell were you doing on the roof, by the way?" I said.

"Saving your ass, it looks like," said Lennox, and hurried into his apartment.

Carver Lennox was fucked up over Hutchison's death, but it felt like grief he might have borrowed from some TV talk show, public grief, standard clichés. What really worried him, was that the death would give the building a bad rep.

Or maybe I was wrong. There were things about Lennox I didn't get. I had met guys like him, bankers, lawyers, hedge-fund guys on the make, had met them in restaurants, at parties. But Lennox was black. There weren't a lot of black guys like him on Wall Street, and I wasn't sure I'd read him right.

There was plenty I didn't understand about the building, too, about what I'd seen and heard: the decent old doctor, as limber and healthy as somebody twenty years younger, who believed in euthanasia, was sharp as hell, talked about status and light skin and dark, laughed about New Harlem, had loved Marianna Simonova; the African woman who thought the place was haunted by evil spirits in the shape of black dogs; Celestina Hutchison's bitterness; the stiff-necked Dr. Bernard; Virgil Radcliff, the young detective who didn't play by the book, whose father looked like a white man.

It was more than that. I was a white cop in a black neighborhood—I had felt the tensions between Jimmy Wagner and his black detectives. I was an outsider. For all my love of black music, I didn't belong. I should have been used to it. I'd been an outsider as a kid at school in Moscow, a nonbeliever, with a mother who became a refusenik and a father who was kicked out of the KGB; I'd been an outsider in Israel, where I spent most of my time hanging with peaceniks or Arab kids or lolling on the beach with sexy Sabra drop-outs, girls who liked smoking dope better than fighting wars.

New York, too, those first years, when I still had an accent, and got lost in the subway, and later at the academy, where I tried to be a tough cop.

Finally, I had found a place I could belong. When I lost my accent, ditched my past, became a real New Yorker, it seemed right. For a long time now, I'd been at home here, along with all the millions of foreigners and outsiders.

But now, I felt it again, that disconnect, the sense of being on the outside that made me wonder if I understood anything.

Am I getting anything right? I kept thinking. Is it just I'm so focused on Lily, or did the beating I got in the storage room fuck me up in some way I couldn't determine? Was I tone deaf in a different country? A code I couldn't quite catch, or hear, or translate? I thought of the bebop guys back when they invented music so fast, so complex, almost nobody got it at first, and how, in a sense, they did it to outfox whitey.

In the Soviet Union, we had done the same thing, though without the genius. Ways of dealing with the system. You left home, you stepped out the door, you took on a different role—at school, at work, any place where you pretended to listen, pretended to follow the party line, at least until you got home where you could take off your mask, sit at the kitchen table, curse the bosses.

Maybe it had always been that way in Harlem, for black people. Maybe it still was. Maybe no matter if you were a doctor or a teacher, you had to toe the line when you were outside, when you went to work or school in white America, or were confronted with white people, cops especially. Were you always somebody else? Even in 2008? Even after Obama's election, after that one dazzling night in November?

Did Carver Lennox feel that I threatened his empire? When he'd suddenly come up behind me on the roof, had he been planning to help me, or push me over?

CHAPTER 36

Virgil was looking through a pile of mail in the Hutchison apartment when I told him about Lennox, and the roof, and he just nodded then examined his iPhone as if it would give up the answers to everything. I figured it was the way he did his thinking.

"Sorry." He put his phone away. "You find anything up there?"

"Hutchison didn't just fall off the roof. He wasn't a fool. You have to make a big effort even to lean over the edge of that fucking roof," I said. "He'd have to get up over a wall, and why the hell would he do that?"

"What are you saying, Artie? He was pushed?"

"I'm not sure about anything. There's stuff on the roof, that's for sure, prints in the snow, indicates it's not impossible. There's only one set, far as I could see. Lionel could have gone off the roof, but not by himself. Where the fuck is that dog?"

"I don't know. Did you talk to Lennox much at the party last night?"

"Talked my fucking ear off, most of it about the building, said he wanted what was best for everybody. He was like a politician. In between the lines I got the feeling he had money troubles."

"What about Celestina?" said Virgil.

"She was there. Holding court."

"She left before Lionel?"

"Before he got there. I don't think she pushed him though, do you? She weighs about ninety pounds, I'm guessing."

"Maybe she convinced Lionel to off himself," said Virgil. "Maybe he was sick and only she knew, and she went on at him about his believing in euthanasia. Maybe she played on him, made him feel guilty."

"Doesn't sound right," I said. "Lionel didn't seem like a guy to feel guilt about his beliefs, and if he was sick, he'd have used pills or something."

"I'll get some more input from the ME, then." Virgil looked around the living room. "Sad room," he said.

"You see it like that?"

"I do, Artie. There's something about it, like it's a shabby old museum piece. Suspended in time. People can't stand change, some of them." He tossed the mail on the table. "Nothing here except some real estate brochures from the islands. Maybe that was it," Virgil said. "From what I heard, Celestina couldn't stand Lionel, and she wanted to sell up here and move south," he added. "She was jealous of him and the Russian."

"Enough to kill him? How jealous could a ninety-year-old woman be?"

"Oh, Artie, man, you just have not met a lot of old folks," said Virgil. "They are just like us, only more, a lot more. You think old people don't have sex? Trust me."

"You're an expert?"

"I have a grandfather who's ninety-five out in California; my great-granddad died at one hundred and five; my own father is going up to seventy."

"Fine. Meanwhile, we need to talk to Celestina Hutchison."

"You have a plan?" Virgil said.

"I want to see her here, with Hutchison's things. I want to see her reaction. Tell her if she wants any of her clothes, anything like that, they're gonna seal the apartment up tight as a drum until the ME releases Hutchison's body and the will goes to probate, at least that long. Lennox said he thought she might be at some church. Get her here. Can you do that?"

He was already on his phone. "Right," he said. "Fine."

"I need the keys to Simonova's place," I said.

"I already borrowed them from Lily's place." He gave me the keys. "You have any idea when Lily's coming back?"

I looked at my watch. "It's a long way to the cemetery. It's out on Long Island some place. She said she had to go by herself, some kind of duty thing."

"Simonova exploited Lily," Virgil said. "I told you I thought that. She made Lily listen to her stories, do her errands. Lily has some kind of liberal guilt, so she just did it." Virgil got a set of keys out of his pocket and gave them to me. "You going into Simonova's place, Artie?"

"I want a look at her terrace."

He held up his phone. "I'll keep on Celestina. I can do more on the phone than running around now. I got guys out there in cars spread out everywhere. Anyway, I want more time in this apartment OK? Try to keep Wagner's other guys out, if you can. Buy me a little time, Artie."

"Check in with the ME, too," I said. "What about that dog?"

"I have a really fucking bad feeling, Artie. About that dog, I mean," said Virgil.

"Keep me posted." I left the apartment, and went over to Simonova's place. Something was nagging at me.

CHAPTER 37

For twenty-four hours now, more, I'd been in this strange capsule that was the Armstrong. Now it was Sunday. It was 8:45 and Jimmy Wagner was in a hurry. He wanted Hutchison's case wrapped up fast. You have until Monday, he'd said. Get on it.

I was hungover, my head hurt, so did my ankle. The Oxycontin, the lack of sleep, the night I'd spent in Lily's bed, it was all making me nuts.

I couldn't stop thinking about Lily, the hours we'd been together. Where we were going—if we were going anywhere. Neither of us had said anything this morning; she had been on her way to Simonova's funeral, and I didn't want to ask. I got out my phone now. I hadn't heard from her since she left.

In Simonova's apartment, prowling from one room to the other, I was desperate. Again and again I had come back to this place with its endless rooms and books and old smells. Maybe it was the Russian thing. I knew I'd missed something. But what?

I tried to get my bearings. I knew Hutchison had been here often. Knew he had been the last to see her, that she had somehow grabbed at the button on his jacket and it had stayed in her hand where I'd found it; the dead hand curled around it.

He had loved this woman, one way or another. He would not have let her suffer. Did he come in to give her something to release her from her pain? Did he come back to clean up after himself?

Suffering is not noble, he had said; pain cripples our best selves and makes us at best hopeless, at worst evil, he had said.

I thought about Hutchison his sense of history, of hardship, his humor, the intellectual rigor. Maybe he was also a zealot, a believer, obsessed with a mission.

I knew about zealots, all kinds, religious, political—I'd met them all my life. Hutchison didn't seem to fill the bill—he had been too lively, he told jokes, had seen the comic side.

Marianna Simonova was something else. This was a woman who kept a hammer and sickle for a paperweight, and a picture of herself with Stalin. It was still on the mantelpiece: Marianna as a girl handing Stalin a bouquet.

Something was missing.

I saw it as soon as I looked at the row of photographs. One of the pictures I had seen earlier was gone. I looked everywhere. Where was it?

I couldn't find the picture of Marianna Simonova with a little boy, his face turned away to look at the Statue of Liberty, his suit too big. Why would anybody have taken it?

I went through Simonova's papers in her desk fast as I could. There was a small leather address book with phone numbers and notes in her tiny writing crammed onto the pages.

From the notes, I saw she had Russian connections, some in New York, some in Moscow, even a few in Miami and Los Angeles.

But who was she working for? She had been a devout Communist, and there were the names of sympathetic organizations. But the pages with their details were old and brittle and I knew most of the groups must be defunct.

I put the book in my pocket. There was something going on, but I needed time.

Nobody would notice the missing address book. As far as the world was concerned Simonova had died of disease, and the only people who would look at her things were her heirs.

On the table by the sofa were her pills. I grabbed the three vials, read the labels, put them back, then pocketed one of them and ran out, locked the door, went into the Hutchison apartment. Virgil was combing through the dresser drawers in a bedroom.

"Did you get anything?" he said. The day before he had been combative. I had been an ass. We were both on the same side. I could work with this guy. He was good.

"I have to find Lionel Hutchison's meds. You got anything?"

"Artie, you notice anyone weird hanging around down there, at the scene?"

"What kind of weird?'

"I don't know, somebody watching. I was pulling up in my car, and I just saw this guy kind of half hiding behind a truck."

"There's always wacko sightseers who show up at a scene," I said, but my stomach turned over. I had felt somebody watching, too. "What'd he look like?"

"Hard to say. North Face jacket. Hood up. Saw me and beat it."

"Black?"

Virgil looked up at me. "No."

"You felt he was connected to the case?"

"I just thought, What the fuck's he doing here so early in the morning? He didn't look local, he wasn't walking a dog, so I thought, yeah, in my gut, I felt it was connected. You mentioned Lionel's meds? What's that about?"

Everything in the bathroom seemed to have belonged to Celestina—there was no razor, no shaving cream. I pushed aside the hand lotions, the shampoos, the soaps. She favored, as she'd said in the hallway the day before, Jergens lotion. You could smell it everywhere—vanilla, almonds, cherries. It made me want to gag.

I yanked open a drawer in the vanity and found Lionel's stuff—shaving brush, bottles of herbal remedies, most of them in capsule form. The only prescription medication I could find was in a single vial. On it was her name. The doctor who had prescribed the pills was Lionel Hutchison himself. But so what? She might have run out, he would have written her the prescription.

I took the vial.

"Artie?" Virgil came into the bathroom. "They've located Celestina Hutchison, Artie. You want me to go or you want to do it? I also heard from the chief and he's sending up more people, forensics included."

"Give me the address where Celestina is."

"Yeah, sure. Say your prayers, Artie, my friend."

"Who called you?"

"Carver Lennox."

I drove over to the drugstore on 145th Street. In my pocket were two bottles of pills. They looked the same, but I wasn't sure. Simonova's was labeled Altace. Hutchison's was Ramipril.

At the local Duane Reade, I pushed past a woman waiting at the counter and got hold of the pharmacist, an Indian guy, name on his tag read Ravi. I him asked what the hell Ramipril was.

"Generic name for something that also goes under Altace," he said.

"What's it for?" I asked, even though I knew. Tolya took the stuff but I had to be sure.

"High blood pressure," said the pharmacist. "People who've already had a heart attack, a lot of docs prescribe it for them."

Can you overdose, I wanted to say, and then the woman I'd pushed past got impatient and yelled at me. I didn't wait

I got in my car, and drove as fast as I could over to the church. "Say your prayers, Artie," Virgil had said, when he told me where to find Celestina Hutchison.

CHAPTER 38

In the strange light I squinted to adjust my eyes to the dusky church interior, tried to work out what was going on, and if I could spot Celestina Hutchison.

A cold New York winter sun streamed in through the colored glass, and the sound of people mumbling rose up inside the old Gothic church on 141st Street. Christmas greenery surrounded the altar. The sound of people praying was what I heard first, then the organ music began, and singing.

I had never been inside a church until I got to New York. Not a lot of churchgoing in Moscow when I was a kid, not a lot in Israel. Before I saw the inside of a church, I was twenty years old.

"I thought they did this stuff in Latin," I whispered to a young cop standing at the back, leaning against the church wall.

"Not usually. Only Our Lady of Mount Carmel down on 116th Street still does the Tridentine mass," he told me.

"Got it," I said. I didn't.

His name was Alvin. Officer Alvin. I had seen him at the Armstrong. Asked him if he had been assigned to the Hutchison case. He nodded. Said Virgil Radcliff was heading it up. Alvin knew my name.

In the rows of pews, people, a lot of them old, including Celestina, some on their knees, worked at their beads, or stared at the priest up front, at least from what I could see. To me, it was a scene from *The Godfather*, except these old people were black, not Italian. So I stood in the back and waited for the service to end, and waited for Celestina Hutchison to finish praying.

Religion wasn't something I knew much about. Didn't care. Maybe the way I was raised. I had tried to understand once or twice. Had visited a few churches in the city.

I'd dated a girl once who made me go to a synagogue on the Lower East Side. She told me she wanted to connect with her roots. Somebody had played a guitar during the service. It made us laugh. We'd tried a few other synagogues, including one where the women sat separate from the men.

I'd been new to the city then, and it was all fine by me, the music, the holidays, the celebrating, I was OK with it. The girl, I was crazy about her; she was beautiful and funny. Once she'd said wistfully, "I like the idea of community. I like feeling Jewish. I just wish I could find a synagogue without God or pixies." She married an Indian guy in the end.

Suddenly, as if she knew I was looking, Celestina turned, half raised herself from her seat, and stared at me. She was in a pew surrounded by other women—her sisters, friends, hard to say—all in black, half hidden by their hats. She whispered to them, and they all turned to look at me.

I started toward her, but somebody put a hand on my arm. It was Carver Lennox.

"You told her."

"Yes," he said. "Let her finish here, please."

"I locked the windows, locked the doors. I tried to keep him in, I tried to keep him safe, but I had to go to my sister's, she was not well, and poor Lionel, whatever did he do to himself, jumping like that?" said Celestina, when she reached the back of the church after the service, speaking to me in her high, small voice. "I do believe he was finished with this life, but then he must have suffered terrible guilt," she added, adjusting her black felt hat. She handed her mink coat to Carver.

"What for?"

"For all the killing, of course," she said. "His idea of helping people. Fifty-three years I lived with a man who was a murderer. Thank you, Carver, dear," she said as he helped her into her coat, then took her hand in his.

"Is that what you think?" I said to her. "That he killed himself?"

"It is what I know," she said with fury, her head snapping up so that I could see her eyes. "It served his purpose, fulfilled his belief, in a sense, it assuaged his guilt. I know for a fact he felt guilty about those poor, sick people he hurried to their deaths. Surely, for that, and to spite me," she added. "He knew in my view that suicide is a terrible sin. What do you think, then, Detective Cohen?" She raised her eyebrows, as if actually inviting me to comment, and put her free hand on her hat.

Was this what Lionel had wanted to tell me at the party the night before? Had he planned to tell me he had helped Simonova die? Amahl Washington, too?

I started to ask Celestina where she herself had gone after the party the night before. Quickly, the women who had been sitting with her gathered. Murmuring comforting words, they surrounded her like a palace guard and forced me outside the circle.

At the back of the group of women was Lucille Bernard. She wore a belted black coat with a fur collar, high-heeled boots, and a small hat with a little brim.

She saw me and gestured for me to meet her out on the steps of the church. In the bright, hard light I saw she had circles so deep under her eyes they looked as if they had been engraved into her skin.

"I'm sorry," I said. "Dr. Hutchison was important to you."

"Yes, he was, and I feel I should have been more tolerant," said Bernard. "I didn't see enough of him because I didn't want to argue with him, and now he's gone."

"How did you find out?"

"Carver called me and asked me to meet him so we could tell Celestina together," she said.

"You're close to her?"

"I knew her through Lionel, of course. She's a very old woman now; I'll do what I can for her." There wasn't much warmth in her voice.

"You don't like her?"

"What does it matter?"

"I'm interested."

"Is it, detective, that you're interested in us like some kind of so-ciological study? Is that what you're saying? You have a soft spot for black folk? You like our music or something?"

"Lionel Hutchison is dead. I found him. This is a case I'm working."

"You think this is a case?"

"It is now. The police are involved. There's an autopsy going on. At first when I saw him, I thought he just fell over, but the ME doesn't think so."

"You mean, fell over suddenly, like Marianna Simonova, for instance?"

"For instance."

"He wasn't sick," Bernard said.

"He seemed pretty vital to me. Unless he was sick and didn't want anyone to know."

"Sick and thinking of indulging in suicide? He would not have jumped. He would have used an easier way. We argued about it. I felt he'd used his skills as a doctor to kill people." She took a deep breath. "I guess we're both aware that this makes three people who have died at that damn building recently."

"Yes. You knew them all?"

"You think I was involved? Do you want to question me? Is that why you're here?"

"Only for what you can tell me about the two who were your patients—Marianna Simonova, and Amahl Washington," I said quickly. "Can we go somewhere and talk?"

"Let me see," she said, adding that on Sundays, the ladies often had breakfast together after mass, usually at somebody's apartment. Today they would go to Celestina's sister's, it would do Celestina good to eat, give her strength to prepare. She would have to iden-tify the body.

"There are plenty of others who can do that."

"Celestina will want to do it. If necessary, I'll go with her," Bernard said.

At the edge of the sidewalk was a girl, maybe fifteen, sixteen, and she was high on some shit. Singing to herself, she was dancing around a fire hydrant, stepping down to the gutter, back up on the sidewalk, pulling up her shirt—a dirty yellow T-shirt with silver glitter on it—pulling it back, playing with her hair, giggling, jiggling, calling out curses. Her hair was dirty, her eyes vacant, and over and over, she did her little dance, prancing out into the street as cars passed by, propositioning the drivers.

From the church steps, the women stared at her, and at least one made to go over, to help her, another pulled a sweater out of her bag and tried to put it over the girl, but she just jerked away, taunting the women, and continuing her dance.

The sun was bright but cold. I saw Alvin, the young officer, head for the girl. I told him to back off and stick around with the ladies. I told him to keep with Mrs. Hutchison when she went to breakfast and then to the morgue, to act polite, as if the department had assigned him to drive the woman officially. He nodded, and up close I saw he was just a kid, maybe twenty-two, glasses, short hair, skinny.

"Wait for me here," said Bernard, sounding imperious but weary. She walked down the street a few yards, returned with Carver Lennox by her side.

"Carver will go with the ladies. He can go with Celestina to the morgue. That way you and I can talk," she said to me.

"Just so long as Celestina isn't bothered anymore, I'll be happy to help out," said Lennox. "She's very agitated, not being home for Lionel, being at the Christmas party and then at her sister's all night." Then, quickly, offhand, as if it were a matter of course, he gave me an accounting of Celestina's time over the past twelve hours, even before I asked for it.

I leaned close to Lennox and said, softly, because I wanted to see his reaction before he heard it from anyone else, "I think Dr. Hutchison was pushed."

He was silent.

"Pushed from behind, maybe from the roof, or hit first, so by the time he was pushed he was either dead, in which case he wouldn't bleed, far as I know. Isn't that right?" I said to Bernard.

"Most likely."

"Or had a heart attack from the trauma when he hit the ice. Or maybe not. Maybe he lay there on the ground dying slowly."

Lennox looked at me. "My God," he said. "What should I do?"

I told him to take care of Mrs. Hutchison, just keep her calm, and I'd get back to him.

He lowered his voice, and there was fear on his face. "You believe whoever killed Lionel, if somebody did, had a hand in Simonova's death, don't you? Isn't that right?" said Lennox, and without waiting for an answer, followed the women to breakfast.

While I waited for Lucille Bernard, I called Jimmy Wagner. Told him even though it was Sunday, I needed access to a safe-deposit box at a bank on 125th Street.

I'd found a charge for a safe-deposit box on Simonova's bank statement earlier, and I had the address of the bank. If there was a box, maybe there was a will.

Wagner told me he'd do what he could, sounding harried. "Just find me somebody I can nail for this one," he said. "This was an old guy, pillar of the community, Christmas is coming, it's the best building in the neighborhood. Just get me something."

I told him about possible prints on the Armstrong roof. I asked him to let me know what the ME came up with, if there was anything unusual in Hutchison's system when they cut him open.

"That woman that died in the building, the one I only heard about this morning, you think we should check on that, get the ME to look at her, do a tox screen?"

"It's too late."

CHAPTER 39

L ionel was murdered," said Lucille Bernard.

"How do you know?"

"I can read you, detective. It's what you think. And whatever else you may be, you're not stupid."

"What do you think?" I held the door of my car open and she slid in to the front seat. I got in, too, and closed the door.

"Thank you," she said. "It's cold out there."

"Go on."

"I've been thinking about Lionel. He was a tough old bird, and he was strong. I would have known if he was sick."

"How?"

"He would have come to me. We disagreed, but he knew I could keep any secret. He taught me well."

"Right."

"Whatever his beliefs, this was a man who loved life," Bernard said. "He held on to his misconceived ideas, such as they were, because he felt they enhanced life; the avoidance of pain, the avoidance of suffering at the end, was worth it." Her voice wavered. "He so enjoyed himself. When he was younger, my God, I remember when I was in med school, and I saw him much more often, he would invite students over, and I don't think we'd ever met anybody who was more involved in his subject, but who also experienced so much joy in life." She took a deep breath. "Once in a while, even these last few years, he would call me, and we would go out and eat and talk until all hours, about music and medicine and Yeats—he loved poetry. He loved Langston Hughes, and Yeats, and Whitman. He would always gossip about the building—he adored that bloody place—and now somebody has killed him in it."

"Can you ride with me, I have to pick something up at the Armstrong."

"Yes. That would be better," she said. "I don't want the ladies from the church telling Celestina I'm talking to you, and I was thinking it might be useful for me to look at Lionel's apartment, see if there's anything that helps me understand this."

"The apartment is sealed," I said.

"I'm sure you can manage something," said Bernard. "I got so damn fed up with that building when I lived there." She took off her hat and arranged her hair.

I asked why, as I started the car, heading north to the Armstrong.

"When I lived there with Carver, everybody wanted help. I didn't mind. I'm a doctor. But for every scratch, every sore throat, I was on call. They considered me not just their in-house doctor but their shrink. They'd come around, tell me their problems. I felt like telling them to watch *Oprah* instead. Or that Dr. Oz."

I drove carefully. The streets were slick with ice. Harlem was quiet that Sunday morning. I still hadn't heard from Lily. I was jittery as hell. Tell me some more, I thought, glancing sideways at Lucille Bernard.

"You ever run into a woman named Marie Louise? She cleaned for the Russian, Mrs. Simonova," I said, not quite sure why I was asking. The idea just floated into my head.

"How come you're asking?" said Bernard. "Sure, I know her. "African girl, French accent, right? She cleans several apartments at the Armstrong. Works for Carver some of the time. I think she used to bring Simonova for appointments before Lily Hanes took over."

"What do you think of her?"

She shrugged. "I don't get her. I'm sure she has a hard time in America, but she has these strange ideas about Western medicine. She said she had been a doctor back in wherever—Senegal?"

"Mali."

"Yes, Mali. She's an MD, but she often gave Mrs. Simonova

crazy potions, stuff she bought down on 116th Street. She told me about them. I said they wouldn't help, so she just clammed up. She was scared of me. I guess she's illegal."

"Anything else?"

"Why?"

"I'm asking you."

"You can't believe she killed Marianna, and then Lionel? Why would she?"

"I didn't know you thought anybody killed Marianna Simonova."

"But it's what you're after, isn't it? I mean, if you were sure she died from the emphysema, you wouldn't have been all over this even before Lionel died, you and that Virgil Radcliff."

"You don't like Virgil?" I pulled up in front of the Armstrong.

"I don't know him," said Lucille. "I've met him a few times at fund-raisers. I don't understand why he's a cop."

"You mean he's too smart?"

"I apologize for that, but yes. I do."

"Or because he's dating Lily?"

"That, too, if you want to know. I suppose there aren't enough nice black women for him," she said sarcastically. "Look, just forget the sociology. I want to see Lionel's apartment."

Lucille Bernard began, very softly, to weep, as we got to the Hutchison apartment.

A cop in uniform was on his hands and knees, looking at the carpet, peering at fiber. When he got up, I asked him to leave Lucille Bernard and me alone in the living room.

Sitting on the edge of a chair, she said, "I loved Lionel. He was good to me, he was a mentor when I was very young. He got me into the City College program. He helped me. God, I spent so much time in this apartment when we lived here."

"When you were married to Lennox?"

"We're not divorced. I think you knew that," she said.

"You don't believe in divorce."

"That's right. Can I ask you something?"

"Sure."

Lucille Bernard sat up. Her eyes wet, she looked like a very young woman, young, vulnerable, and very pretty. She was tough and I liked her. I called her Dr. Bernard, though. She had never asked me to use her first name.

From her purse she took a handkerchief and wiped her face. "I think Carver's in big trouble," she said.

"It matters to you." I called her Dr. Bernard. She had never asked to use her first name.

"He's the father of my kids."

"What kind of trouble would it be?"

"Money."

She told me that she and Carver had split up because of his business. It consumed him, she said. There was no room for anything else. He was generous, though, she added. Paid for the kids, the teenage girl, her younger brother. He spent time with them. Had offered Lucille money to buy her house.

According to Bernard, Lennox had made a ton of dough in the years before the crash. Hedge fund, she said. Derivatives. Whatever. But lately he had been erratic, she knew he was losing money. His obsession with the Armstrong, fixing it up, selling it off, had become his only subject. The kids told her he talked about it all the time.

"So he's in serious financial trouble, right?"

"Yes. The market tanked, and Carver got scared. He was heavily invested in this building and others—he has other property—and then the real estate market turned bad. I think somebody's getting ready to call in his debts. I think he's on the verge of losing his job. I saw him at the Christmas party and I saw panic in his eyes."

"How much panic?"

"Enough," she said. "He wanted too much. It's not healthy." Bernard got up. "I want to look at Mrs. Simonova's medication."

"I looked," I said. I took the bottles out of my pocket, gave them to her. She slid on a pair of glasses.

"This is what you found?"

"There was other stuff in Simonova's place, but all of it was prescribed by you. The only interesting thing was that there were the same pills in her apartment and Hutchison's." I held out a vial of blue capsules.

"This is only blood pressure medication," said Bernard.

I was on the verge of asking, of saying, Can you get these pills checked? I stopped myself. Better to ask a friend, to keep any evidence until it was needed. Use it. Ignore it.

"You let me come up here because you wanted to see my reaction to being in Lionel's apartment?" asked Lucille Bernard. "Is that it?"

"Yes."

"Thank you for being straight with me," she said, and left the apartment.

CHAPTER 40

Gloria Lopez picked up on the second ring. In the background I could hear a radio and a little kid chattering. "Hey, Artie, good to hear from you," said Gloria, who's been a friend since we'd met on a case out in Red Hook. She was a detective, but when she got married and had a kid, she'd gone into forensics. After she divorced her miserable husband, she and her boy went to live with her mother up in Washington Heights.

Gloria had a network of friends all over town, people at the ME's, people with the Feds. Gloria always returned favors, and she was a really good woman. We had spent some time together. She was funny and sexy. We'd had a lot of fun and I knew she wanted more from me. I could hear the expectation in her voice when she asked if I wanted to come over for dinner or go out later in the week.

I hesitated. I didn't want to be a jerk with women any more, if I could help it.

"You're back with Lily Hanes, or is it somebody else?"

"What makes you say that?"

"You think I can't read you, Artie?" She softened her tone. "What is it you need?"

I told her I had some pills I wanted looked at. She said she'd do her best and I told her I'd get them to her.

"You can still come for dinner one night," she said. "My mother is crazy about you." I sent her mother good wishes and hung up, then I called Officer Alvin, who said he would deliver the pills to Gloria, then I went to 125th and Seventh to wait for the bank manager.

Jimmy Wagner had called to say the manager at Simonova's

branch would meet me there. Gave me the guy's number. His name was Mr. Cash. Hard to believe. I looked at my watch. I called Mr. Cash. He sounded pissed off. It was Sunday, and he lived in Corona in Queens, but he said he was on his way.

I walked, trying to get warm. It was late Sunday morning, and in spite of the cold, a few of the stalls were setting up, owners putting out their goods, the incense sticks and cheap aromatherapy oils, black romances and vampire novels, portraits of Cleopatra painted on velvet, photographs of Malcolm X, Martin Luther King Jr., Michael Jackson. Most of all, there were pictures of Obama.

The discount stores were full of people looking for cheap Christmas presents and tree ornaments, but the shops with the fancier duds, the leather and fur, the stage outfits, were empty. There were some chains, Starbucks, other signs of progress, but there were also plenty of empty storefronts. For all the tales of Sugar Hill and the promise of real estate deals and fabulous money, the financial meltdown was hitting hard.

The bottom was falling out of the market, all markets, and housing was in deep shit. Houses that had been under renovation were still covered in scaffolding, but work had stopped. A year earlier, they would have gone for at least a million.

Carver Lennox was in trouble. I thought about the incident at the party the night before when the guy with the strange, pale hair had stopped to talk to him. Remembered how scared Lennox had looked. I wondered what kind of debts Lennox had, and who he owed.

In the doorway of a boarded-up building was an old man, clutching his shopping cart full of scraps of old rugs. He was smoking the stub of a cigar.

A guy in jeans and a good leather jacket jogged past the old man, who tried to get his attention, get some change off him.

I turned a corner into a side street, looked up, and saw apartments with broken windows, and laundry hung over the sills, three pillowcases frozen solid. Kids were walking up and down the street, jeans hanging down low on their asses, one slapping a couple of pizza slices together to eat them doggie style.

There was nobody on the stoops, no open windows, no music. It was a bleak place on this frigid day.

I went to the bank. Where the fuck was Mr. Cash? I was getting impatient. I took out his number, I called, and again he said he was running late.

How late?

Coming in from Queens, he said. Bad roads.

I told him to step on it. I wanted to look in Simonova's safe-deposit box. I wanted to know if there was a will, and I wanted to know before Lily got back from the funeral. If, like the letter, the will named Lily, I had to know before anybody else. Simonova was the kind of woman—I was guessing—who had made a will.

"Excuse me," said a soft voice, and when I turned I saw Marie Louise.

Wrapped in the beige down coat that was too big for her, her head encased in a yellow wool shawl, the fake Vuitton purse over her shoulder, she stood as if deciding what to do.

"Can I help?"

"I don't know," she said so softly I could barely hear.

"I'm not from immigration. I don't need to know anything about you, but if there's something you want to tell me, we could talk," I said. "Something about Mrs. Simonova?"

"Yes, and about Dr. Hutchison."

"You know?"

"Yes. I went to the building this morning and I saw the policemen."

It occurred to me that Marie Louise had followed me from the Armstrong somehow. I didn't ask. She was already nervous enough, talking to a cop.

"Let's get some coffee," I said on impulse. "It's cold. Or lunch? Would you like to eat something?" I gestured to the restaurant across the street. Through the windows you could see people celebrating.

Marie Louise looked at the restaurant with longing, and unable to fight the desire, smiled and said she would like some coffee very much.

"Ten minutes only, before I must go," she said, and followed me inside Chez Lucienne.

The guy in charge came toward us. I figured him for the owner. He smiled and asked if we wanted a table. Marie Louise answered him in French, and he looked pleased and sat us at a table near the window.

The exchange made her smile. She agreed to a glass of wine and some cheese, and when it arrived, she seemed to sigh slightly as if she had entered a different world, seemed to relax into the woman she might have been when she was a doctor and had status and could speak her own language.

She removed her coat. Underneath it she was wearing jeans and a white turtleneck.

The restaurant was full of people lingering over brunch. People were exchanging gifts, and kissing, the place buzzing with life. Music played. It was as if we'd landed in some safe place, far from the Armstrong, out of the storm.

"Why don't you eat something else?" I said in French, thinking if I could keep her a while she'd talk. I put my phone on the table, waiting for the bank manager to call back.

She asked where I had learned French. I told her I had learned some back in Moscow, that my mother had loved the language.

"Do you have children?" she asked me.

I shook my head and ate some bread. I was hungry. I ordered a burger, urged Marie Louise to have something. She looked at the menu and asked for an omelette.

"What about you?" I said.

"Two nice boys," she said in French, and then switched to English. She probably figured my French was rusty. "I was just shopping for their presents."

"Their father is in your country?"

"I married an American, then he died. I don't want to talk about this."

"Your English is very good," I said to change the subject.

"Not very. I spent only one year at a school in England," she said. "Can I say something to you?"

"Of course."

"Madame Simonova? Sometimes I cleaned for her."

"She was sick for a long time?"

"I am not sure."

"You don't think she died just because she was sick, do you?"

"No." Marie Louise turned suddenly and stared as a customer came into the restaurant carrying a little black dog in her arms. "They should not allow that," she said.

"What?"

"A dog in a restaurant is not right."

"It's a little dog," I said. "You know? Nobody will care. Maybe it's too cold out for the dog." I was making idle conversation, trying to get her to relax.

"I do not like dogs."

"Do you think somebody hurt Mrs. Simonova?"

She looked at her hands, took a sip of wine, and put her hands together around the stem of the glass.

"I think so, yes." Her eyes darted toward the woman with the dog.

"What is it?"

"I am afraid of all dogs, but the black dog which belongs to Madame Hutchison is a very dangerous dog. Some times when I clean for her, I lock the dog in the bathroom."

"I see."

"You think I am a little bit crazy?"

"No."

"Thank you."

"It's nothing. Something worries you?" I said. "Something else?"

She nodded. "Can I mention a name here, do you think?"

"Nobody's listening. Somebody at the Armstrong?"

"Yes. He is living there."

"On the fourteenth floor?"

"Yes," she said, looking around, lowering her voice. "I need the job, but Mr. Lennox is a strange person."

"Strange in what way?"

"He wants all those big apartments. I hear him talking sometimes on the phone. He doesn't bother hiding it. He thinks because I do not speak very good English, I have no brain."

"OK, so this guy wants the apartments, so he squeezes people. But would he kill them for it? Some of them are old anyway. Why doesn't he wait?"

"This is a very impatient man. And there is something else."

"What?"

"He has guns."

"Guns?"

"Yes. I clean drawers, I find guns."

"How many?"

"Four, five, I do not remember, but there are many guns. I know in this country you often keep guns, but why so many? He is always very polite with me, very correct, he pays me on time, he does not shout at me. Still, I am scared. I feel that I wait for something to happen."

I watched her, and I drank my wine. Neither death had involved guns, but I was interested in the information that Lennox kept them.

"He has a temper?"

"Never with me," she said.

"But with others?"

The food came. We ate.

"This is very nice," said Marie Louise.

My phone rang. I picked up a message from the bank manager saying he'd be another forty minutes.

The burger tasted good, so did the fries. I ordered another glass of wine. The people at the next table finished their coffee and left.

"Do you want to talk to me about Mrs. Simonova," I said.

"I was inside her apartment last week, two evenings at least. She wasn't feeling well. She wanted me to help with the Christmas presents. Wrapping the gifts."

"You liked her?"

She shrugged. "She was ill. She needed help."

"Go on."

"I work for all of them on that floor, you see, they share me," she said. "Like a valuable property. It is not easy to get somebody to clean and cook at the drop of a hat—is that what you say?"

"Yes."

"Sometimes Madame Simonova asks me to spend the night when she is feeling very ill, as I have said, or Madame Hutchison asks if I will do her shopping."

"And Carver Lennox?"

"Yes."

"And you worked as a waitress for him at his Christmas party at the club?"

"For extra money, yes. It was a good job. I work for Lily some times, but that's different. She helps me. She tries to help me get papers. She is a very nice woman."

"I'm glad."

She looked at me. "She loves you," she said.

"What?"

"Lily. She loves you." Marie Louise smiled at me. "Perhaps this is why I feel I can trust you. I saw how she looked at you today, yesterday. Once I saw her staring at a photograph of you. Virgil Radcliff is nice, but it's different."

I was flustered. I wanted to hear more, much more. Instead, I just said, "Go on about Mrs. Simonova, please."

"Often people played cards at her apartment early on Friday evening, but this past week, she was feeling too ill. She asked me to stay late, and I was in the other room when Dr. Hutchison came to visit.

"What did they talk about?"

"I don't know. I didn't hear much, but I think he gave her some medicine, because later she asks me to return some pills to him. When I returned them, I saw the label had his name on the bottle. Miss Celestina took the bottle from me."

"Did you notice what color?"

"Blue," she said, and I thought of the Altace from the drugstore. "The same sort of pills she asked me to pick up a few days earlier."

"On 145th Street? At Duane Reade?"

"Yes. From this Ravi at the pharmacy. I always speak with him."

"Did anyone else visit Simonova Friday evening?"

"Sometimes, I heard Madame Simonova on the phone, but that evening, Friday, Mr. Lennox visited her, the second time during the week, or perhaps even the third. Almost every evening he would drop in, and each time the words became more and more angry."

"And he was there Friday, you're sure?"

"Yes."

"Before or after Dr. Hutchison?"

"After. Yes, definitely, I am sure. I was frightened to leave the kitchen, they were so angry, especially him. He was very angry."

"You hear anything?"

She shook her head. "Only their angry voices."

"Did anybody else come?"

"One woman. I don't know who she was," said Marie Louise, finishing her wine. "That was delicious," she said. "Thank you. I must go now," she added.

I paid, trying to absorb everything she'd told me without getting out a notebook. I didn't want her to stop talking. I didn't want to make it look official.

I excused myself and went into the bathroom and scribbled what I could on the receipt for lunch. I called Virgil, told him to stay with the building. I had to get back to the Armstrong. I almost called the bank manager—Mr. Cash—and told him to forget the meeting, it could wait, but he sent a text saying he was twenty minutes away now, no apology, but he was coming. Wait for me, he said.

"I'll drive you," I said to Marie Louise.

"Thank you. It is very cold. To 116th Street, please," she said. "Just for one minute to check at home, and then I will go to the Armstrong, where I have work to do."

My car was parked across the street from the restaurant and we got in. She settled back, smiling as if enjoying some unexpected luxury, and gave me directions. For a few minutes we drove silently through the icy day while Marie Louise closed her eyes.

At 116th Street, she asked me to pull up in front of a little shop. She got out, pulling her down coat around her.

"Is this where you live?"

"Yes," she said, and went through a narrow door next to the shop. I got out to look in the window.

It was a crummy storefront, the window jammed with bottles and boxes, dusty jars of dried herbs, and dusty jars with strange names, not in French, but some African language, I guessed. I got back in my car.

Marie Louise came back out of her apartment five minutes later and she turned into the shop. I could see her through the window, inspecting various items, turning over the bottles with fierce intensity.

"You often buy things in that store?" I asked when she got in the car.

"Yes." She indicated her purse. "Madame Simonova is dead, so I have purchased some things to try to help her."

"Help who?"

"Madame Simonova."

"But she's dead."

"In my country, we hold many things in our heads at the same time, old and new, do you understand? One day you may have a modern procedure at a clinic, the next day you visit a native doctor. In Bamako, our capital city and my home, we are known for our treatments for many things. Western doctors visit just to procure these, many from our baobab tree," she said, looking at me, and smiling. "This is what I explained to you about the black dog."

"I see."

"These djinn, these ghosts in the Armstrong, I try to make them disappear," she said. "This is difficult for Americans to understand."

"Yes."

"But many of them are so superstitious," she said. "Many of them give all their money to faith healers, to psychics, they believe God created the world in seven days, as in a film, rather than evolution, they believe in some heaven where God resembles a big black actor, isn't that right?"

I nodded, then I stopped short at a red light. "Are you OK?"

"Yes, fine," said Marie Louise. "You know, this is a strange, difficult country," she said. "Before I come, I read how many American people of color say they have roots in Africa, they admire Africa, yet here many look down on us. They think we are poor and backward, except perhaps for a few musicians."

"That's hard for you."

"Yes. It is ironic now that we are Africans in Harlem, from Nigeria, Ghana, Senegal, Mali, Cote d'Ivoire, but we are the lower classes." She paused, looking at me. "They say they are African Americans, but so many have never been to Africa, and know nothing. Many speak no foreign languages, and also they have a chip on their shoulder—is that what you say?"

"You can say that."

"I understand this, I married an American, and then he died, as I told you, and nobody believed I was married. I had lost the papers in Mali, where I married him. I went to see his family, his sister, but she was angry all the time, angry at me, angry at everybody," said Marie Louise. "She told me about slavery in the United States as if no one else has ever experienced this, even though she had a good job and a nice apartment." Marie Louise grinned. "I told them that it was black people, Africans, who sold her ancestors into slavery. She was quite unhappy with me."

"I'm sorry," I said.

"It's not your fault," said Marie Louise. "And your Lily has always been so nice, and also Dr. Hutchison, I admired this man so much. He asked me questions from time to time, as if to consult with a fellow doctor."

I was a block from the Armstrong now, and I stopped at a red light.

"I'll get out here, please," said Marie Louise.

"I'll take you to the door."

"Thank you, but no." She opened the car door.

"Did you follow me earlier? Did you follow me to 125th Street?" I said, but she just smiled, closed the door, and hurried away.

Mr. Cash—a grumpy, middle-aged man with a Jamaican accent in sweatpants and a brown down jacket—led me down to the basement of the bank and unlocked the door to the vault. He took the key I handed him—I'd found it at Lily's—opened the little door, and extracted a flat metal box from a wall of identical slots in the vault.

"Is that it?" he said. "Will you be long?"

"Yeah, that's fine," I said.

"I'll be next door in my office." He yawned.

Late night? I wanted to say. He knew I was a cop, he knew I was on business. I didn't like his attitude, but I just left him, went into one of the little rooms opposite the vault, turned on the light, shut the door, laid the flat box on the ledge, and sat down.

I keep my own stuff in a similar box at my bank downtown. When I got hold of my father's journals, I'd wanted them safe. I keep the journals in the box, along with cash for emergencies—I usually end up spending it when there's no emergency at all except my being broke—and a spare weapon and some ammo.

What for? I've got a second gun at home. There isn't any revolution coming. I just like knowing it's there. In the box I also keep my father's watch and the gold earrings he'd given my mother the night they went to see Paul Robeson.

I'd put on my glasses and opened the box when my phone beeped. I couldn't get a signal, but I could see from her text that Lily was back from the cemetery. She was upset as hell that nobody had called her about Dr. Hutchison.

From Simonova's box, I removed an assortment of little worn leather boxes containing old lockets, gold chains, earrings, a diamond ring, and a few Soviet medals, all tarnished now.

There was an envelope full of twenties—I was guessing around a couple grand—and a plastic bag. In it were vials of pills. Spare medication? But why keep it in the bank? I took the bag.

There was also a worn leather passport case. Inside were two passports, one American, the other Soviet, long out of date, a passport from a country that no longer existed. She had also kept her Communist Party card.

Finally, in a blue folder tied up with cotton string, there was a will.

At first, scanning it quickly, I was relieved. I didn't see Lily's name. She had gone crazy when she'd thought Simonova had left her the apartment at the Armstrong. But there was something else, and it hit me like a hammer.

I sat up straight, cleaned my glasses on my shirt, and kept reading. I was still feeling lousy from getting beat up in the basement of the Armstrong and I was taking too many painkillers. I shut my eyes for a moment and then reread the will. I didn't want to believe what I was reading. But it was there, legal, properly spelled out, signed by a lawyer. I took off my glasses, rubbed my eyes again, fumbled in my pocket for some aspirin, and ate them.

In that little room in the basement of the bank, I got up, sat down, picked up the paper again. I thought I must have been wrong the first couple of times I read the will, that my vision was blurred, that I was tired. I read it again carefully.

CHAPTER 41

In her will, Marianna Simonova had left almost everything to Marie Louise Semake. All of it: the apartment, furniture, clothes. She had also left her some cash. This was because Madame Semake was a worker and she, Marianna Simonova, in solidarity with the working class, had bestowed what was rightly hers upon the person who most deserved it. I looked at the date. The will had just been signed on Thursday, but when had she given the instructions to the lawyer? Who put it in the safe-deposit box? Had it been Lily who kept the key? Would she have done it without looking in the envelope? Lily had a fierce sense of what was right. She was obsessive about privacy.

The will had been executed by a woman lawyer from a midtown firm, signed and sealed and witnessed by somebody from the firm. The executor was named as Dr. Lionel Hutchison.

Had there been an earlier will?

The lawyer on the will was G. Neuwirth. She was listed. I left a message. Less than five minutes later, she called back.

Yes, said Ms. Neuwirth, she had been up to see Mrs. Simonova, along with her assistant, yes, on Thursday. She wasn't sure about earlier wills, and she wasn't in the city. She had picked up the message and called me back from her place in Montauk. No way she could get back today; nobody she could ask, either, not on Sunday. She'd do it first thing in the morning. What's more, said Ms. Neuwirth, the attorney who had looked after Mrs. Simonova for years had recently died, and she, Ms. Neuwirth, wasn't completely up to date with the previous material, at least not without looking at her files. She said she'd call first thing in the morning.

Mr. Cash was hovering now, cracking his knuckles. I didn't know if I should laugh or cry, I was so relieved Lily wasn't named in the will. The will would trump the letter.

But why the letter to Lily? Did Simonova find out something about Marie Louise she didn't like? Was she just out of her mind? One of those people who constantly rewrite their wills depending on the state of their relationships?

For a few minutes, I sat, the door closed, the overhead light making my hands yellow. Then I put the document back in the envelope, stuffed it in my canvas bag, along with the few other things I'd found. I returned the box to the bank manager and went upstairs, and by the time I left the bank it was already getting dark.

It was only four, but it was the shortest day of the year, and only a smudge of cold, bright color was left in the sky over the Hudson.

From my car, I called Lily. No answer. I tried Virgil. Nothing. I put in a call to an ex-cop I know who had gone to law school. I needed somebody who hadn't been involved in writing the will.

My pal had gone into estate law. Said she wanted a quiet life. Told me if the will was solid, Marie Louise Semake could inherit even if she was in the U.S. illegally.

Before I put the key in the ignition, I opened the document. Marie Louise's address was there, but it was in Mali. She wasn't illegal in Mali, she was a citizen. Maybe it was what she had told Simonova, that it was her permanent address. Maybe she had worried that if she was illegal, she wouldn't get the apartment.

Either way, Marie Louise had known. How else would Simonova's lawyer have had the Mali address?

The apartment, the money, would change Marie Louise's life. She could hire a good immigration lawyer, stay in America, send her kids to school. Or she could sell the apartment and go back to her country and open a clinic. There were a million ways it could change her life.

Suddenly, I wondered what time she had left the party the night before. Tolya had given Marie Louise a ride from the Sugar Hill Club. It had been my idea. I left him a message, then I called Jimmy Wagner and asked him to get me the time of Simonova's death. He put me on hold, came back, and said the ME made it for between two and three in the morning.

"One more thing, Artie?"

"Yeah, Jimmy?"

"For sure, he must have been pushed. The way the bones were broken, the angle, all the signs. I have people up on that roof right now looking. Are we getting someplace with this?"

I told him I was on it and hung up.

I married an American and then he died, Marie Louise had said. Was it true? If it was true, why did immigration scare her? If it was true, she was the widow of an American.

Immigrants get desperate. I'd met Chinese who had paid forty grand to get to America on ships where some of them died in sealed containers.

I didn't make Marie Louise for a killer. I liked her. But she had children. She was a doctor who worked scrubbing toilets for people at the Armstrong. Money would change everything.

Did she kill Simonova? Did she think Hutchison knew? He was the executor on the will. He knew Marie Louise would inherit. Did she kill him, too, to stop him talking? She could have pushed him. She had access to most of the apartments on the fourteenth floor. She was young. Strong.

My phone rang.

"Tolya. Listen, you remember the woman you gave a ride to last night?"

"Sure, Marie Louise. Lovely young lady, sure."

"What time did you drop her off at home, you remember at all?" I felt safer talking to him in Russian.

"I didn't," he said.

"What?"

"She said she felt bad making us go out of the way, that she preferred it if we went to my house on 139th Street first, and then the car could take her to 116th. I think I got to my place around one fifteen. I can ask Janet."

"Who?"

"Nice lady I met at the party."

"She went home with you, this Janet?"

"None of your business," he said, sounding pleased with himself.

"Can you ask your driver what time he dropped Marie Louise and if she went inside her building?"

"I'll try, Artyom. This guy who drove was not regular guy, just somebody I use on and off, and I think he's gone on vacation. I'll find him if it's important."

"It's important," I said. "I'll call you."

I turned my car around so fast, I almost crashed into the curb, but I wanted to see Marie Louise's apartment. I wanted to talk to her neighbors, see where she'd been the night before, where her children were, if anybody had ever seen an American husband. When I got to the building, I found her name on the buzzer. Somebody let me in.

The fear in that apartment made it worse than I'd expected.

CHAPTER 42

The face that looked out through a crack in the door belonged to a little kid. He was about six. I showed him my badge. He looked terrified. He let me in, then scrambled back to the chair where he had been watching an ancient black-and-white TV set perched on a shaky table.

I could see a bedroom through a partly open door. At one side of the main room was a kitchen, and another kid, a gangly teenager, was constructing sandwiches for himself and his younger brother. Both boys, skin dark like their mother, were polite, as if they had learned manners in some fancy school.

Putting a sandwich on a plate, pouring a cup of milk, the older kid gave them to his little brother and spoke softly to him, then stood and faced me and asked if he could help. He had a faint French accent. I tried speaking French with him. I gestured for him to sit down and eat while we talked.

He was thirteen, he told me, and he always took care of his little brother when their mother was at work. His name was Luc Semake, he told me, and his brother was Olivier Semake.

I knew Luc wanted his brother to see he wasn't afraid of me, though I knew he was scared and desperately shy. I tried to keep it short. I hated this.

"Where is your mother?" I said, gently as I could.

"She is at her work," said Luc, while Olivier just stared at the TV, his sandwich untouched.

"Do you know where she works?"

"Yes." He told me the address of the Armstrong. He asked if he should phone her. I said it wasn't a big deal.

"It must be hard taking care of Olivier by yourself," I said, and thought to myself: I'm not going to do this anymore. I don't want to be in a shabby apartment, making two kids tell me about their mother so I can get the goods on her. I don't want this.

"It's OK," said Luc. "It's fine. I can take care of him."

On a shelf were a row of medical books in French, a few magazines, a few albums, music from Mali, by Amadou and Mariam. I picked up a CD.

"You know this music?" said Luc.

"It's good," I said.

There were pictures of the kids near the CDs, and a photograph of a good-looking young guy, maybe thirty, in a T-shirt and a Yankees cap. Luc followed my gaze.

"This was our father," he said.

"I see."

"He was American."

"Where is he?"

"He is gone," he said. "Dead."

I got the feeling Marie Louise had maybe invented the American father so if anyone asked, the boys would say they were Americans.

As I asked questions, the kids were polite and attentive, and it made them seem even more lost, these two skinny boys alone in a room in Harlem on a freezing day when it was already dark outside at four in the afternoon and their mother was away cleaning apartments.

"So you visit Mali?"

"Yes," said Luc. "Soon we will go home, my mother says so. This morning she tells to me that we will go soon."

"Does that make you happy?"

He nodded.

"You don't like it here?"

"It is bad for Olivier. We are Muslim, and people here do not like us, and we are not permitted to pray at school."

"Why did your mother say that this morning?" I said.

"I don't know. She comes in very happy, she brings us a nice breakfast, and she says soon we will go."

I didn't want to ask. Olivier had been listening hard, and he came over to the kitchen. I was sitting on a stool, my jacket unzipped, my elbows on the counter, and the kid came over and leaned against me.

He was still a little boy. In my jacket pocket, I found a candy bar I'd forgotten about and offered it to him. The older boy just shook his head and refused politely, but Olivier leaned against me some more, maybe for the warmth or the safety or just because he was a friendly kid, and he took the candy.

"You take good care of your brother," I said to Luc. "I'm sure your mother works very hard."

"Yes. Sometimes she works all day and also in the night."

"That's rough," I said, seeing the kids were getting comfortable with me. "May I have a glass of water?"

Luc got the water. Olivier sat eating the candy bar. "Would you like to see a picture of our mother?" he asked.

"Yes."

He got a snapshot off the bookshelf and gave it to me. In it were Marie Louise and the two boys posing on the Staten Island Ferry, the city in the background. Just tourists for a day, they were smiling and mugging for the camera.

"She's nice," I said. "And she works really hard, I know. You said sometimes works in the night?"

"Sure," Luc said. "Sometimes she works as a babysitter for people."

"But you're OK to take care of Luc all night?"

"Yes. We have her phone number. I'm grown up," he said. "Last night, she was away so I made Olivier do his homework, and I made supper, and then when our mom comes in the morning, everything is nice for her."

"What time did you have breakfast today?" I said.

"I think eight."

"OK, well, if you just tell your mom I was here." I took my card out and put it on the counter. I wanted to do something, give them something, take back all the questions. But all I did was say goodbye and run down the stairs.

Marie Louise had been out all night. I had seen her leave the Sugar Hill Club party, but she wasn't home until morning.

Where was she during that time?

Plenty of time to get to the Armstrong and Lionel Hutchison.

Who could she have been babysitting for? Who?

At a local candy store, I scooped up candy bars, comics, and a box of chocolate, put it all in a bag, ran back to the apartment, went upstairs. I felt shitty about the stuff I bought—it was only a bribe after the fact—so I just left it by the Semakes' door. I didn't go in.

On my way back to 116th Street, my phone rang. It was Virgil.

"Where are you?" he said.

I told him.

"Can you get over here? The Armstrong."

"Soon as I can."

"No. Now. Just come." His voice was tense.

"Where are you?"

"I'm in the Armstrong, in the basement," said Virgil. "Please just hurry the fuck up, OK?"

"Where's Lily?"

"With me."

"What's going on? What happened?"

"I can't tell you over the phone," he said.

CHAPTER 43

The wet sheets, piled up in plastic baskets in the Armstrong's laundry room, were like crumpled ghosts. On a line stretched between hooks screwed into opposite walls, hung a newly washed pink cotton baby blanket, shedding water onto the floor. The acrid smell of bleach mixed with the wet laundry hit me as soon as I got to the entrance. A young guy in uniform tried to stop me going in. I showed him my badge.

All the overhead lights were on. A portable spotlight had also been set up. It was aimed at one of the washing machines, where Virgil was standing, looking down. Lily stood a few feet away, still wearing the green shawl she'd worn to Simonova's funeral that morning. Her arms were crossed. Diaz was there, too, along with a middle-aged woman in jeans, a yellow sweatshirt, and an apron. There was the low buzz of talk, people mumbling, hesitant.

"Over here," said Virgil. "Jesus, who the fuck does this kind of stuff?" He pointed at a mound covered by a green bath towel.

"What is it?"

"It's the dog," he said.

"What?"

"The Hutchisons' dog."

"Ed," Lily said.

"The black Lab?"

Virgil nodded. "Shirley found it," He nodded in the direction of the woman in the apron.

"The dog?"

"Yeah, somebody put him in the washing machine and ran it for a complete cycle," said Virgil. "Then they stuffed him into one of the old gas dryers and tried to light the mechanism under it. There was gas in there, it almost blew the place up. We're waiting for the ASPCA forensics truck. They can test on the spot, but there's no question what happened here. I've seen the shit people do to animals. I remember one case, we picked up some crush videos."

Lily looked at me questioningly.

"You don't want to know."

"Tell me," she said.

"Men use dogs to fight each other, you know that, but there are women who like to put on high heels and stick them in the dogs' flesh. They kick them to death."

She turned away.

All I could think of was Marie Louise and her fear of dogs. She'd been terrified of the Hutchisons' dog.

"First Lionel, now the dog," said Lily. "Virgil told me about Lionel. I can't believe it. He was fine. I should have done something."

"You couldn't."

"Virgil told me he was killed around three this morning."

"I know," I said.

She looked at me, and I knew what she was thinking. We had been at the club dancing, or fooling around in her apartment, when somebody killed Lionel Hutchison.

"Does Celestina know?" I asked Virgil.

"I told her."

"It must have hit hard."

"She said she brought the dog home from her sister's yesterday when she came to change for the party, and she left the dog with Lionel because her sister couldn't put up with Ed's yapping. She said Ed was especially nervy and barked a lot, so she left him with Lionel for the night."

Again I thought about Marie Louise. If she had been in the Hutchison apartment, if she went to get rid of Lionel, she would have found the dog. Did she, terrified, kill Ed? Did the dog yap at her? Was she also scared the neighbors would hear, would hear the dog and find her? But why like this? Was this some kind of awful exorcism?

I had seen the awful fear in her eyes, her fear of this black dog, a dog she'd told me had orange eyes and was an evil spirit. There had been plenty of time in the night for Marie Louise to stuff it in the washing machine. And she knew her way around the laundry room.

"Lily?"

"Yes?"

"Have you seen Marie Louise?"

"Why?"

Lily knew about Marie Louise and her fear of the black dog. "What do you want her for, Artie?" She was defensive.

I moved a few yards away from the washing machine and closer to the dog. Virgil pulled back the towel covering the animal. I wanted to puke.

"You found him?" I said to Shirley.

"Yes. I opened one of the old dryers. I saw something sticking out that made me open it. I found him. I put him there on that mat. I put the pieces there." She turned away suddenly, and covered her face.

"Lily?"

"I saw Marie Louise a little while ago, when I got back from the cemetery."

"Where was she?"

"She was on her way into Lennox's apartment. She had some cleaning to do, she said."

"On a Sunday?"

"Yeah, sometimes. If he needs extra stuff, ironing, shit like that. She works like . . . she works really hard," said Lily, and I knew she'd almost said "works like a dog" but caught herself.

"I know that."

"She works two, three, four jobs. She's determined to go back to her country and make a real life."

"I understand."

"I don't think you do, Artie."

"Where else does she work?"

"She does anything—cleaning, babysitting, she works at a local coffee shop. The job market sucks, you know that."

"Why don't we go upstairs."

"I don't see why you want to know about Marie Louise suddenly? You're doing a favor for a pal in immigration?"

"No."

All the time we were talking, Virgil stood back, phone in hand, watching us, his face expressionless. "I have to go," he said suddenly. "I'm going to leave a couple of guys here to wait for the animal people." Without another word to Lily or me, he left the room, and I could hear his footsteps as he went down the hall.

He knows, I thought. He knows Lily and I were together last night.

"Can you go see if Marie Louise is at Lennox's place?" I said to Lily when we got upstairs. "I don't want to bother her if I don't have to," I added. "You understand? But she cleaned for the Hutchisons and maybe she saw something, or someone, OK? I'll try to help her. If I can."

Lily nodded, handed me her keys, I went into her apartment as she walked across the hall. Less than a minute later, she was back.

"She's there," she said. "Marie Louise is at Carver's place. She said she'd stop by when she was done."

"That's good."

"I don't believe she did anything," said Lily. "I want a drink."

"Me too." I went to the kitchen, found the Scotch and some glasses, and poured the drinks.

Dropping her shawl onto the floor, Lily slumped onto a kitchen stool, took the glass, drank half the Scotch in one gulp.

"At least it's over. With Marianna. At least there's that," said Lily, who, in spite of Hutchison's death and the dead dog, seemed composed, as if the trip to the cemetery had helped steady her. Maybe she was relieved that her friend had been buried, that she, Lily, had done the right thing.

I put my hand on her shoulder. "What was it like?"

"Lonely," she said.

"I'm sorry."

She looked at me. "There was nobody except me and the guys making the grave, putting the coffin in like something in a bad Shakespeare production. I didn't know if I should laugh or cry—you know how I can get really stupid giggles at the wrong time?"

"I remember."

"So, I'm there alone in this cemetery, and there's only one other group, at a grave close by, and they're all in black. They look like something from a mafia movie, except I guess they're Jews, since it's a Jewish place, and there's me, and this skinny young rabbi. I guess they got him cheap. Or he's all they could get on a Sunday or something. Lionel Hutchison told the funeral home Marianna wanted a Jewish burial and they sent this rabbi, he looked about twelve, and he was Orthodox." Lily finished her drink. "Marianna would have hated it, and I was no good. I mean, my mother was Jewish, but she didn't have any religion, so what do I know?"

"You did what Marianna wanted. What Lionel Hutchison said she wanted, and we know she talked to him. They were close."

"I guess," said Lily. "I don't want to be buried like that, all alone. We didn't even call her friends."

Simonova's address book was still in my pocket. "There wasn't much time."

"Lionel told me she wouldn't want anybody there. But early this morning—you were still asleep—I decided I wanted him to go with me, that Marianna would have wanted him there. I knocked on his door, but nobody answered," Lily said. "I thought he was asleep. I guess he was already dead. My God, how did it happen? I don't understand."

"This is a bad time," I said, because I couldn't think of anything else.

"There was one bizarre thing," said Lily. "Carver called me."

"Why?"

"He called and said, was I at the cemetery, and I said yes, but I couldn't really talk, and he said, could they hold it, he wanted to come, and I said it was too late. They had already put Marianna in the ground, and he asked me to describe the scene and tell him the location of her grave, I think he was crying. Then he just hung up." Lily pushed her hair back and fastened it in a pony tail with a rubber band. "When I went by his place a few minutes ago, to find Marie Louise, he looked wrecked. I asked what it was. He just shook his head and didn't say anything."

"Listen, didn't Simonova have presents for him and his kids under the tree? She made up stockings for them, with money and chocolates, right? Maybe they were close."

"I guess." Lily leaned on the kitchen counter. "All the way home, I was thinking how lonely it was there, Marianna all alone. I don't want to be like that," she said. "Artie, tell me about Lionel."

I told her how I'd found him lying on the ground, that I figured it for an accident at first and then thought it might be suicide. I told Lily the ME was now sure Lionel Hutchison had been pushed.

"How sure?"

"When they find the spot where he was pushed, when they match some boot prints to the person who pushed him, when there's some decent forensic stuff, we'll know for sure. Meanwhile, pretty sure."

"Pushed from where?"

"The roof. I was up there. There's a broken wall."

Lily poured more Scotch for both of us.

"Talk to me, Artie."

"What should I tell you?"

"Everything. Anything. Whatever it is that's buzzing around in your cop's brain. I mean, who would fucking kill Lionel? Who would kill a dog like that?"

"I don't know. You want to know what's on my mind?"

"Sure." She drank a little more and pulled a plate of cookies across the counter. "If we're going to drink like this, we should eat something." She picked up a cookie, put it back. "I can't eat."

"How well did you know Amahl Washington?"

"Hardly at all, I told you," she said. "Why?"

"You must have figured out where I'm going with this. Lily? Right? I'm going to work this case, if it's OK with you," I said.

"What about Virgil?"

"With him. It's his case. I'll help."

"So it's been decided."

"The chief at the local house is going out of his mind. This is pretty high profile. I mean, Hutchison meant something in this community."

"And you think whatever happened to Lionel is connected to Amahl Washington?"

"Yes," I said.

"Artie?" She kicked off her boots. "The dog—you thought Marie Louise was involved, didn't you, as soon as you saw it?"

"Didn't you?"

Lily hesitated, and before she could answer, somebody knocked at the door. Lily opened it. It was Virgil.

"Celestina Hutchison is back," said Virgil. "She's asking for you, Artie. She says you'll understand."

"She knows about the dog?"

"They came, the animal forensics unit, and she wouldn't let them take the dog. It's in her apartment. Your phone's ringing, Artie."

It was a message from Gloria Lopez. I sent her a text saying I'd call soon. She sent me one back saying she'd have information by the next day, information on the pills I'd sent over to her.

CHAPTER 44

Celestina Hutchison was in her bedroom, packing a suitcase. On the floor near the bed near the suitcase were six pairs of shoes, tiny shoes with high heels, all highly polished.

In the room with her were Virgil, the young cop from the church—Officer Alvin—and Carver Lennox.

As soon as Lennox saw me, he whispered something to Celestina, nodded at me, and left the apartment. "The place should be sealed," I said so Celestina could hear me. I wanted to see her reaction, but she went on packing.

"I told her she could get some of her clothes before moving over to her sister's," Virgil said.

I lowered my voice. "Just so she doesn't take anything we might need."

"I hear you."

"And Lennox?"

"She says she needs him. Says he's helping her with the funeral plans. He's saying it should be a big, important funeral because Lionel was a big deal in the building."

"Where's the dog?"

"Bathroom," Virgil said. "I'll leave you with Celestina now."

"They killed my Ed," said Mrs. Hutchison when we were alone, as she folded a white silk blouse carefully and placing it in the suitcase.

"I'm sorry."

"I don't know that I can survive without him," she added. What about your husband, I wanted to say, but I kept my mouth shut.

"I really am sorry," I said.

"And no, detective, I did not kill Lionel, if that's what you're wondering. Or his friend either."

"Simonova, you mean?"

"Ugly woman that she was, ugly with stupid political ideas, and her theories about black people, black people and Communists, we were alike, she said, we understood one another, she said. Paul Robeson, my ass, if you'll forgive me, it's no more likely he cared for her than a pig can fly. But Lionel liked her. He said he wanted to help her. I was so furious yesterday with all his nonsense, I said to him, 'Well, did you kill her, dear? Did you, as you like to say, help your girlfriend on her way? Did you kill Amahl, too?' I said. 'Did you help them leave this life less painfully?'" Her tone was mocking. "He did not. I knew from his face. He didn't kill them, or himself. In point of truth, detective, I'm not sure he would have had the guts, if he himself was sick. Somebody else murdered him." Her face was blank, eyes filled with rage. "Killing is a sin," she added.

"Was he sick?"

"No, so long as he took his medication, he was fine. It was only his blood pressure, and that was under control, and he was very rigorous about it. He was an old man, of course, he had his aches and pains, but his illness was all in his head, his ridiculous ideas. He was a weak man. He could not bear to see even a little minor suffering but that he wanted to murder the patient. But this time, somebody murdered him."

"We know that now."

"Do you? Good." She looked around the room and said, "I hope this is the last time I ever see this place. I've been a prisoner here for too many years."

"Prisoner of what?"

"Of all the history," she said. "Now please ask nice young Officer Alvin to take me to my sister's. I've had enough of this for today."

"What was Carver Lennox doing here?"

"As I'm sure you were told, he is helping me plan the funeral. The last thing I will do for Lionel is to make sure he has a good funeral. Even if he was an atheist."

"At your church?"

"Of course." A faint vengeful smile on her face, she sat on the edge of the bed, removed her hat, ran her hand across her head. Her body sagged, as if she had let go for a minute. "I asked Carver because he is my friend. He wouldn't let them take Ed away. We're going to have a lovely funeral for Ed."

"I see."

"Mr. Diaz is coming to get him."

"Who?"

"Ed. To take him to the funeral home. It's in Brooklyn. Mr. Diaz can drive Ed to the All Pets Go to Heaven home in Brooklyn. They will prepare him. I've contacted them."

"Will Carver help with that, too?"

"Carver will do what I ask," she said. "With him, I don't have to pretend."

"Pretend what?"

"All of it. You wouldn't understand."

"Why's that?"

"Because you're white."

"I see."

"You don't see, detective, you can't see. It doesn't matter. I didn't kill Lionel, I don't believe in killing, and if you need to check, you'll find I was at my sister's house all night after I left the party, I can give you the receipt from the taxicab I took from the club to my sister's, if you like, and not only was she there but so were several of her friends. I shared the guest room with one of them. You can call her. Her name is Miss Sophia Roberts."

"I believe you."

"Do you? You seem mighty suspicious, especially about Carver." She put a yellow silk scarf around her neck. "He helped me out, as I said. I wanted to leave this place a long time ago. I wanted to leave this city. I wanted to live somewhere warm. I thought about Hawaii. Or a lovely condo in Sarasota, Florida, quite a few wealthy African American executives have retired down there, Carver tells me. Or perhaps I'll go to Trinidad. Every year, Carver has always purchased two tickets for me for one of the islands, though Lionel only ever accompanied me quite grudgingly. Said he didn't like the heat. One year I just went with my sister. I did like Barbardos, but not Jamaica. I would certainly not choose that island," she said with contempt. "Carver thought it would help persuade Lionel if he saw how nice life could be."

"What did Carver want?"

"He wanted us to sell him the apartment. I promised him that we would. I didn't care if it was a bribe; it was just lovely to have those two weeks to look forward to, and every year at this time, when it started turning cold, I'd say to Lionel, dear boy, I want to spend our remaining days near the sea, under the sun, and if we sell this apartment, we can live a really fine life with the money, and he refused me. Every year, he refused. He said his people were here. What people?" she asked. "Was I not his people? After all I had done for him?" She was enraged. "I was sick of it, of this city, of its memories. Oh, you think that I relish all this, the past, everything that's dead and dying? If you do, it's because you're still young. Because you don't know what it all meant, especially for women. To be colored and female," she said. "Never mind. I don't dwell on the past," she added. "He wouldn't leave. Lionel said the Armstrong was his life."

I looked at her carefully. "So there was good money if Lennox bought the apartment?"

"Yes, indeed. In fact, he has already given me some." She smiled. "As a sort of down payment."

"And the vacations?"

"Money, too, and little gifts to make life agreeable. I believe he did the same, or proposed it, to the others."

"What others?"

"Marianna, Amahl Washington, and Regina McGee, though I don't know that any of them was smart about it as I have been. I have put a little money into property here and there," she said.

"The apartment is in your husband's name, isn't it?"

"It was," she said, expressionless. "Until this morning."

"It's yours now."

"Naturally," said Celestina Hutchison. "Carver Lennox is the only real man in the building, the way he's helped us and put up with so much from so many silly old people."

"You can sell it to him now."

"Yes. But I won't have my Ed." She placed a photograph of the dog in her suitcase. "I'm going to say good-bye to him now. Will you come with me?"

In the mint green bathtub was a large wet bundle. It was the dog—or the pieces of the dog—wrapped, the sheets and blankets like a kind of shroud, blood on it. There was blood in the bathtub. The smell was bad.

Celestina went to the tub, looked down, kissed her fingers and placed them lightly on the bundle, nodded at me, and turned, and I followed her out.

In her room, I picked up the suitcase, and we went to the living room, where Alvin took it from me and escorted her to the door. He was a tall guy, and with her hand in his, she looked even smaller, small as a child.

At the door, Mrs. Hutchison turned to me.

"When will you arrest that woman for killing my Ed?"

"What woman?"

"That African," she said. "Marie Louise. She hated my Ed. She said he was a devil, not to my face, but I knew it was what she believed. Who could think my Ed was a devil?"

"When did you last see the dog?"

"I told you, for heaven's sake, or I told somebody, I came home from my sister's to change for the party last night. I left Ed with Lionel. I assume that woman came by to help out with the cleaning at Carver's. Perhaps she heard poor Ed crying, barking and crying, and she couldn't stand it. She's a crazy woman, but what can you expect? She's from Africa."

"How would she get in to your apartment?"

"Maybe Lionel let her in."

"I see."

"Maybe she killed Lionel, too," said Celestina Hutchison. She walked out of her apartment, Officer Alvin following her with her suitcase, and didn't look back.

CHAPTER 45

It's Marie Louise, isn't it?" Virgil was waiting at the back of the Armstrong when I went to get my car. "Fuck," he added. "I like her. Where is she?"

"Gone. I went to see if she was anywhere in the building, but she'd gone."

I was sure Lily had warned her. For all I knew, Lily had given Marie Louise money, told her to get her kids and leave the country. I knew Lily was capable of it. There was that side of her, the bleeding-heart liberal, that sometimes made me crazy. And she liked fixing things. I wasn't in the mood to make nice, but I didn't want to lose what little ground I'd gained with her. I hadn't stopped at her place, I just left the building.

"I figured it was her. Who else would do that to a dog? We should have paid attention when she told us she fucking believed in spirits and evil dogs. That damn dog was a sweet old pooch. I had a Lab all the time I was a kid," Virgil said. "I'll have Amahl Washington's medical records for you tomorrow. Wagner told me to get hold of them and give them to you."

"How'd you manage that?"

"I'm a detective, Artie."

I looked around. The lot in back of the building was empty except for Virgil's car and mine. The garbage cans were still on their sides. The yellow police tape that had marked out the scene, the place where I'd found Lionel, drooped on the ground. Just beyond the wire fencing, near the gas station, was a cop in uniform.

I told Virgil—I'd forgotten earlier—that Diaz had possibly packed away Simonova's oxygen tank in the basement, the way he had with Washington's. "He's also due to drive Ed to the pet funeral home in Brooklyn," I said. "Celestina apparently made a reservation with All Pets Go to Heaven."

"The what?" Virgil tried not to laugh.

"You heard me."

"All Pets Go to Heaven?" He bit his lip, but he couldn't hold it and he started laughing. I looked at him and I cracked up.

For a few seconds, in the desolate parking lot, the two of us stood, laughing like fucking crazy guys, repeating the name of the pet funeral home, laughing because of it, to release the lousy tension, to remind ourselves we were still alive.

"I'll get one of the uniforms on the oxygen tanks. I sometimes think Diaz feels about black people the way Marie Louise feels about black dogs. Cubans can be pretty fucking racist like everybody else," Virgil said. "I'll find some petty cash for him if I have to." I got out my car keys.

"I was on my way back to see Marie Louise," I said. "Now I'm thinking it would be better if you went. I'm probably already in deep shit with her. I doubt she'll talk to me."

"Why's that?"

"I went to see her kids."

"Without their mother?"

"Bad fucking idea. I know."

"You get anything?"

"They told me she didn't come home last night. They said she had a babysitting job. Who leaves two young kids alone all night for a crappy babysitting job?"

"It's what poor people do," said Virgil, and I wanted to say, How would you know, but I bit my tongue.

"Yeah, well, maybe, so you want to do this, Virgil? I mean, I got Jimmy Wagner on my case. He keeps calling to say what do we have."

"Me, too, since you mentioned it, Artie." Virgil looked at his watch. "I'm under the gun. He's got some bug up his ass about getting this done tomorrow. I mean, he's fucking nuts."

I told him about the will.

"Jesus," he said. "Then it really could be Marie Louise. I mean, there's those three truths, right? Follow the money, follow the woman." He tossed his cigarette on the dirty snow and ground it out with his foot.

"What's the third one?"

"I read it somewhere but I can't remember. Anyway, I'm thinking if we can get one more person to tell us Marie Louise didn't go home last night, and we can get somebody to say she showed up at the Armstrong, it's enough to take her in. At least we'll have something."

"Tolya Sverdloff's driver supposedly took her home, he's trying to get hold of the guy. What about a security camera, anything in the building that might have caught her? There's one over the front door, right? I saw it earlier."

"Maybe I'll get that kid Diaz calls the Goof. He seems willing," said Virgil. "Just find out what time your pal Sverdloff's driver dropped her home?"

"I'm on it, I just fucking told you." I was upset about Lily. "Wait a minute." I dialed Tolya. Come on, I said half out loud. Come on.

There was no answer.

"So, Artie, listen, with Marie Louise, are you happy for me to find a little pressure point?"

"What do you have in mind?"

"I have friends here and there, Artie, since you're asking, let's say hypothetically, like at the Justice Department. It's a Harvard thing, if you want to know," he said, heavy on the irony. "I got a few at Homeland Security, too. But not," he added "from Harvard."

"Your call," I said. "You're assuming Marie Louise is illegal. Why not Immigration?"

"They're overworked. Also, if she's from Mali, she's probably Muslim. Could be she's on somebody's watch list." His face was creased with ambivalence, but he had taken charge. He was working the case the best he knew how. "I'm going to make some calls."

"It's Sunday. You have home numbers for those people?"

"Yes."

"You don't mess around, do you?"

"Not when I'm on the job." He zipped up his jacket, set his face in a blank expression, and made for his ugly car, the burgundy Crown Vic. I started for mine, when the phone rang.

"Meet me," said Tolya.

"Soon as I can. What happened?"

"I can't get hold of this driver you wanted. Asshole should be grateful I give him work. The driver who took Marie Louise home? I'm sick of waiting. But I know where to find him. I'm going myself," he said. "Unless you meet me."

I didn't like the idea of Tolya running around trying to do things himself, or leaning on the guy so hard the evidence would be useless. I knew Tolya kept a gun in his glove compartment.

"I'll meet you."

"I'll pick you up," he said.

"Not here."

At the corner of 155th Street, Tolya pulled up. I got into his SUV.

"How's your head?"

I put my hand on the back of my head. "OK."

"I still want you to see my doctor."

"You told me. Where are we going?"

"Washington Heights."

"Why"

"Because this asshole driver, his name is Pavel, he lives there."

"I didn't know there were still Russians up there. I figured it was almost all Latino," I said, and remembered I'd promised to call Gloria Lopez. I dialed. Her mother answered. "Sorry," said Mrs. Lopez, "Gloria say to tell you she go out on a date."

"What is it?" Tolya said.

"Somebody telling me to fuck off," I said. "I deserved it." I knew Gloria would get me the information on the pills, though, she was a real pro when it came to work. "So, Tol, there are Russians around here?"

"A few. This guy, the driver, he has a brother with a grocery store, 180th, 182nd Street."

Tolya broke the speed limit. I ignored it. There wasn't any traffic on the streets, and we made the twenty-five blocks in ten minutes. Most of the signs were in Spanish. Tolya pulled up outside a small shop that was getting ready to close. Its name out front was in English and Russian.

"Come on," he said, getting out of the car.

A couple of guys, bundled in North Face jackets, were smoking on the street. One of them was Tolya's substitute driver. As soon as he saw Tolya jump out of the SUV, the guy, it was Pavel, tossed his smoke into the gutter, fussed with his jacket, and stood up straighter. I thought he might salute.

Adjusting the collar of his enormous black coat, Tolya looked at Pavel and asked, in Russian, why he had not returned his calls. Pavel looked plenty nervous.

"Good evening, Anatoly Anatolyvich," he said.

"I've been looking for you," said Tolya in a steely autocratic voice. Pavel apologized. He apologized again. The other guy, hearing Tolya's voice, wandered away into the dark night, cigarette clamped in his teeth.

"Please," Pavel said. "Please come inside the shop. Maybe you will see something you like."

The long counters in the shop, the glass cases and shelves, were full of Russian goods—cookies, pastries, chocolate, fish, cheese, cosmetics, folk remedies, Astrakhan hats, Russian dolls, samovars. It was a little brightly lit Russian island in the middle of a vast Hispanic ocean.

Pavel introduced us to his brother—his name was Goga—who was behind the counter. He offered us a drink and produced a bottle of good Georgian wine, and poured it into glasses. We toasted the holidays.

"Good," said Tolya, somehow decreeing with one word that the getting-to-know-you period, the toasting and smiles, was finished. "What time did you drop the lady off last night?" he said to Pavel.

"The African?"

"Yes."

"I didn't drop this one at home, no."

"I told you to take her home."

Pavel moved backwards, away from Tolya. "After I take you home, I tell her, 'Okay, lady, I will drop you,' but one block from her apartment, she says she needs air. I think maybe she is sick."

"You didn't wait?"

"It was late. I watch in rear view, see she's OK. I think she did not go home. I think she turns around to go in other direction."

"But you're not sure."

He hung his head as if expecting a blow, but Tolya didn't touch him, merely took a fifty from his money clip and handed it over.

"It's not your fault. Relax." He sipped his wine, turning to me, speaking English now. "Artyom? What this Pavel says, it helps you?"

"It helps." I was sorry Marie Louise had not gone home, sorry the evidence against her was piling up, but if she had killed Lionel Hutchison, and Marianna Simonova, I wanted her locked up fast.

I thanked Goga in Russian, thanked him for the drink, and complimented him on his shop. "Great place," I said and asked about the name. I had seen the sign out front, but I wanted to hear it from him, why he had used it. He'd be proud of it, he'd like me for asking. I might need Goga again, and he was a guy you could easily get to talk to you, like you, look forward to your visits, even. He tried to give me a free bottle of wine. I accepted. I rarely took shit from Russians, but this was different. "So the name?"

He lit up. He was a bald, short, fat man with a weary, cheerful face. He poured some more wine. He told me he had named his shop Tolstoy, for his favorite writer.

I remembered. It was the shop where Marianna Simonova had bought her Christmas presents, her ointments and creams, the wooden dolls, chocolates, the samovar. There had been silver stickers with the name on the packages.

I asked if Simonova was a customer.

"Many, many years," he said. "Of course. Very good customer."

"She came lately?"

"Once in a while. Sometimes with friends who help her."

"Which friends?"

"Black man. Old doctor, I think. She tries to persuade him Russian medicine is best."

Lionel Hutchison.

"Anything else?"

"Sometimes she stops here to talk to other customers in Russian, about this and that."

"What's this and that?"

"Politics? Who can say. She is still believer, believer in Communism, crazy, right? But she is good customer, so I listen politely."

"Artyom, time to go," said Tolya, softly now, still in English. "You OK with this, about the African lady, this information from my asshole driver?"

"Yes," I said. "Fine." I got the shop owner's card, and Pavel followed us out to the sidewalk to see us off and into Tolya's SUV. He looked relieved.

"Where do we go?" said Tolya.

"Drop me at the station house."

"Which?"

I gave him the address, and before Tolya started the car, he threw off his big black coat—it was warm in the SUV—and revealed that underneath, he was wearing a Santa costume.

CHAPTER 46

The ashtray on Jimmy Wagner's desk was heaped with butts when I got to him, around seven. He looked up.

"You have something?"

"I'll have something for you soon."

"How soon?" he said

"Before tomorrow. I think."

"You shitting me?"

"No."

"Thank fuck. Who is it, who do you make for Hutchison's killer?"

"I'm looking at a woman who worked in the Armstrong. Let me work it a little more, OK? I just wanted to put you in the loop, see if you had anything for me."

"I'm fucking grateful, man."

Before I said anything else, Julius Dawes walked into Wagner's office.

"I thought you were with your daughter," said Wagner. "How's she doing?"

"Good, good, left my wife there. I just forgot a few things in my locker," he said.

"I need you," said Wagner. "You know about Lionel Hutchison?"

"I heard," said Dawes, sitting on the edge of a chair. "Bad news. I'll be back tomorrow. I'll just take the one night. You OK with that Captain? I'm only just up in Riverdale. I can be here in half an hour."

"Thanks," Wagner said.

"I should get going," I said.

"I'll walk you out," said Dawes.

* * *

"That you over there, the red Caddy?"

He knew it was my car. He had mentioned it last time I'd met him at the station house. I waited.

"Listen, detective, if you have something on your mind, you want to spit it out?"

He shrugged. "I'll let you know," he said. "If I get to having anything on my mind." He didn't like me. I wasn't sure why. I didn't really know the guy.

"It might be better if you tell me now," I said.

"I'll be back tomorrow," said Dawes. "I'll be back to run the Hutchison case. I want you off it."

I didn't answer. Bit my tongue. Let him go on. I'd find out what was eating his liver later. For now all I wanted was to keep going. Pavel had given me enough to pick up Marie Louise.

"I didn't mention it to the chief because you're his pal," said Dawes. "But we don't need you freelancing on this," He shifted to his other foot, pulling his coat tight against the wind that had come up.

"It's Radcliff's case."

"You think that makes it better? He likes to work on the edge, he talks to people he shouldn't include in cases, he's a wise-ass."

"He's a good cop."

"You would think so, I imagine," said Dawes, and made for his own car, a battered green Ford Explorer.

Virgil was at Marie Louise's apartment when I got there. She was standing on the other side of the room with her two boys, her arms around them. She didn't look at me, just held on to her children.

I went over to Virgil, talked to him quiet as I could. "I have something," I said. "The driver didn't take her home. She didn't go home. I think we have enough."

He looked at me. "She didn't do it, Artie. She didn't do any of it. I found the people she said she was babysitting for, they confirmed it, but I also got the security tape off of Diaz. She never went into the building at all until we saw her heading for Carver Lennox's place."

"What did she say?"

"She's barely talked to me."

"Did you already call any of those friends at Homeland Security? Your Harvard houses?"

"I only talked to one guy, didn't give him many specifics, told him it was hypothetical."

"He believed you?"

"I don't know. I almost made the biggest fucking mistake of my life," he said, rubbing his eyes. "Christ. I hope it doesn't come back to bite me on the ass."

"You told him her name?"

Virgil didn't answer, and I crossed the room to Marie Louise. She answered my questions briefly, her face blank, her eyes full of disappointment. She had trusted me. I tried to say I was sorry and ask if I could help, but she turned her back on me. Her boys stayed close to her, providing protection for their mother.

We left, Virgil and me, and closed the door behind us.

"You think you can fix it for her?" I said to Virgil. "You think you can warn off whoever you talked to?"

"God knows I hope so," he said. "You get this stuff wrong, you can wreck a whole bunch of people. It's like some kind of fucking infection. I hope I can fix it."

In the dim, stinking hallway, Virgil added, "If Marie Louise didn't kill Hutchison, it doesn't say she didn't murder the dog, does it?"

"Why don't we concentrate on the people first? There's those people who deal with dog forensics; they'll come up with something."

"Right. You have to believe whoever killed Lionel killed Simonova, don't you?" said Virgil.

"It's how I make it."

"I'm going back to the Armstrong. I want to get the rest of those security tapes," said Virgil.

"I'll see you." I wanted time to make some calls. Wanted to do a little thinking. Wanted to call Lily.

Who killed Simonova and Hutchison, and the dog, and who's next? I wondered, thinking of poor Regina McGee. I wasn't convinced yet she'd been taken to the hospital because of dehydration, not yet, not at all.

CHAPTER 47

Cold so bad that night it got under your clothes, and into your skin, your soul, too, if you had one. The wind blew tiny slivers of ice, like glass shards, against my face. No one out on Edgecombe Avenue, except Virgil, staring up at the Armstrong, smoking, tip of his smoke glowing.

"You like it out here or something," I said.

"I know who it is, Artie." He looked triumphant. "Yeah, I was going to call you, just needed a cigarette."

I waited to hear, let him tell me about his victory in his own time. He turned to look down at the city. Dark night, ribbons of traffic, red and white lights streaming across the tangle of highway over in the Bronx, people trying to get home. I took a cigarette from the pack of smokes Virgil offered me.

"Diaz is now my pal, also that guy he hangs with."

"The Goof?"

"No, it's the other one, Fidel, you remember? Diaz's other crony?"

"What'd you get?"

"I got the building security tapes. Back and front doors. I got to look at some of them on a DVD player Diaz keeps in the basement. It's like fucking Best Buy down there. I think when people leave or die, he just helps himself to whatever he can get his hands on. TVs, computers, beds, whatever."

"What did you say to him?"

"You don't want to know, I'm not sure it's exactly kosher." Virgil tossed his cigarette away.

"So who is it?"

"It's Carver Lennox. I know it. In my gut."

"We'll need more than your gut."

"I made a timeline, and I think he fits, Artie."

"Go on."

"Lennox was in and out of the building a lot, yesterday, last night, after the party, but before Lionel Hutchison was murdered, according to the times I got from the ME. Lennox's daughter was with him. I saw them on a tape," said Virgil. "Made it look nice, him with his pretty teenage daughter."

"You think he'd use her that way?"

"Why not? He was first on the scene after you found Hutchison, right? Made it look like he was distraught. How did he know to show up?"

"I don't know."

"Also, he has a good motive, better than good. He wants those apartments."

Something struck me. "You were here last night?"

"I was working the other homicides, like I said, but I stopped by, just to see who I could see while most everyone was over at the club. People in the building, especially the help, feel more like talking when Lennox isn't around. I thought I might hear something about Simonova."

"Diaz?"

"Him. Others."

"You want to pick him up?" I said. "It's your case."

"Not yet," Virgil said, putting his notebook away. "I want it solid, Artie. I don't want any fancy lawyers finding a nice little well-greased legal loophole. I want to get Lennox in a place where we have the goods to lock him up for life. I know it's him. He has access to pretty much all of the building, the roof, the basement, all of it. I think he even fucking killed the dog."

"What for?"

"Maybe he did it to make Marie Louise look guilty. Everybody knew how scared she was of that dog."

"You want to take a look in his place?"

"Without a warrant?"

"You on for that?"

"It so happens that he's out with his daughter at this very time," said Virgil. "Nice, right?"

"You know that?"

"Not for nothing that I'm a detective," said Virgil. "I managed to have a pleasant conversation with Lennox about life and the holidays and children. I believe he thinks I'm up to his standard, thinks because he went to fucking Princeton and they let him join one of their eating clubs, he's somebody. But deep down he thinks I come from class while he only learned it. What an ass," Virgil said. "Snobs are such easy prey."

In spite of myself, I liked Virgil more and more. I liked working with him. He was smart. Sharp. He was a detective with balls, who didn't wait around for the bureaucrats to give him permission, and he had a brain and a sense of humor. I would like him even more if I got Lily away from him. Anyway, for now it looked like she didn't want either one of us.

Virgil had told her what had happened with Marie Louise, or most of it—I wasn't sure he'd told her about his pal in Homeland Security—and Lily was furious with both of us. I'd already had a couple of angry messages, her voice icy and unyielding. I'd called back. She didn't pick up.

"You must have loved hearing Lionel's stories about people who lived up here, all those jazz musicians, right?" said Virgil as we got to the Armstrong's front door.

"Sure. Not your music, though, is it?"

"Not really. More my father's thing." He held the front door open for me.

"I should tell you I sent some pills I found in Huchison's apartment to an old pal. Same type of meds as I found in Simonova's."

"What kind of pal?"

"A good friend in forensics. She knows people who can take a look at what's in them fast. It's just a hunch, OK? But I figured, what the hell. OK with you?"

"Your friend has a name?"

"Gloria Lopez."

"That's good for me, Artie. I know Gloria," he said, as we went into the lobby. "How long will she take to see if there's anything that shouldn't be there? I don't really make Carver Lennox for a guy who offs people with bad meds. You?"

"Gloria said by tomorrow. She can put the nicest kind of pressure on her contacts."

"Good. Listen, Artie, could you believe Carver beat you up in the basement?"

"No. If it went back to him, it must have been somebody he hired. I think I heard somebody speak Russian, or maybe he wanted me to think he was a fucking Russki."

"Or a Cuban who spoke some Russian? Carver could find himself a Cuban, right?" said Virgil, just as Diaz opened the inside door for us. Tipped his hat at Virgil. Looked at him nervously. Wished him *Feliz Navidad*.

CHAPTER 48

Y ou any good at picking locks?" I said to Virgil as he looked at
Carver Lennox's apartment door.

"You mean because of my bad black childhood in the mean
streets of Cambridge, and Greenwich Village?" He smiled. "Actually,
I am pretty fucking fine at it." He got down and inspected the lock.
From his jacket he took a Leatherman, one of those little tool kits.

The doors on the floor were all shut, but you could feel the people
inside, feel them waiting, alert, listening. People had heard the sirens
this morning. Some had gone downstairs to see what had happened, had seen the cops, and the body on the ground. They would
have seen the seal on the Hutchisons' door. The news about Lionel
Hutchison, and about Celestina's dog, would have traveled through
the building. Everyone on this floor would know by now.

Behind those doors, people were talking, making calls, angry at
the intrusions into their lives, sorry about the deaths, scared for
their own safety. There had been two deaths on this floor, not to
mention the dog. The little fortress high above the city had been
invaded.

I held my breath. I didn't want anyone to see us, least of all Lily.

"Virgil?"

"Just don't talk for a minute; I have to concentrate," he said,
working at the lock. A few seconds later, the door snapped open,
and we were in.

From Lennox's terrace came a noise, like somebody tapping on
glass. Instinctively, both of us reached for our guns. What we were

doing was illegal and probably dangerous. If Lennox had hired somebody to kill Hutchison and trash a dog, he probably had a thug on his payroll who would be happy to work over a couple of detectives like us.

"I'll go," I said.

Turned out the noise was only a piece of glass blowing around. But I saw how easy it would be to get from Lennox's terrace to the Hutchisons. The terraces were adjacent. Three in a row I thought: Simonova, Hutchison, Lennox.

"Anything?" I said to Virgil who was combing the apartment.

It was a rich man's apartment: the old oak floors, wide deep planks, covered with antique kilims; the furniture was 1950s; pictures on the wall so famous you had to blink, including an Andy Warhol silk screen of Mohammad Ali. The kind of place you see in a magazine.

As Virgil worked, he talked, softly, in a low voice, with plenty of irony. "The New Harlem, they call it." He snorted. "New and for rich people," Virgil said. "Who might not have any taste but sure know how to hire a decorator who has some. You know how old this prick Carver is?"

"Forty?"

"He's thirty-six, Artie, two years younger than me," said Virgil. "You know why I think he wants this building? I think he wants it for the history. He doesn't have any. He's the kind of guy who invents himself. I mean, I looked him up, it wasn't hard, he's been written up, young, black, hedge-fund guy, Goldman Sachs." Virgil took some art books from a shelf. "He's also a liar, even about his own past. He didn't come up from the streets like he tells people, didn't grow up in Harlem. His mom and dad are just middle-class folk who adopted him. He grew up in Queens, a bright, ugly suburban kid who made it to prep school and then Princeton on a scholarship. His mom was a secretary, his dad worked for Con Ed." Virgil put the books back.

"Not for Clinton?"

"Sure, maybe the dad helped on Clinton's campaign. But so what? Lennox didn't grow up rich, or poor. Ordinary. No story. So he's fixated on the Armstrong," said Virgil, flipping some silk pillows on a low sofa. "I've been thinking a lot the past day or so, you know, you can read the whole history of this part of the city in this building," he added. "First it was the glamorous heart of the Harlem Renaissance, then it went downhill in the Depression, got bad in the 1950s. By the seventies, it was a mess, the taxes hadn't been paid. Bad times all over Harlem, even up here on Sugar Hill. It was not sweet, not then. People stayed on of course. Most had no choice." Virgil examined an antique breakfront. "Marie Louise said Carver Lennox kept guns, right?" He opened the doors, peering inside. He pressed a strip of wood and a hidden drawer popped open. "Shit, Artie, look at this."

"What's that?"

"The guns."

"How many?"

"Six," he said. "But this is all collector's stuff. Old West shit, pearl-handled revolvers. Look."

The drawer was lined with velvet. The pistols were handmade, beautifully polished and cared for. These weren't weapons Carver killed with.

"Maybe Lennox sees himself as a cowboy," said Virgil. "*Blazing Saddles*, right?" He chuckled. "God, I love that movie. That scene with Count Basie always cracks me up."

"Let's see if there's any kind of documents, stuff we can nail him with."

"Right," said Virgil, following me to the study.

"Go on with what you were saying about Lennox." I began sifting through folders piled onto the steel and glass desk.

"So, in the 1980s, 1990s, middle-class black people start buying in to Harlem, some because they want a toehold on what they think is their culture—you ever see Spike Lee's *Jungle Fever*? Great, great film, Artie. Really, a great look at middle-class black families. Anyhow, the people who bought in then were smart. They bought in to some insanely good real estate, the brownstones, the big apartments," said Virgil. "My dad wanted us to move up from the Village, where we were at the time. My mother said, No way, it's dangerous and there's drugs, and they'd fight like crazy about it. He was pretty tough on her."

"What about you?"

"In my house, the kids did not have a choice, me and my sister," said Virgil, bent over a filing cabinet, looking at more of Lennox's papers. "I think my father wanted us to move because he felt he was raising kids who had no relationship with the black world. Maybe he was right; what the fuck do I know, Artie? Wait a minute." Virgil knelt down, spreading documents on the floor in front of him. He was excited.

"Artie, listen. It's all here. There's copies of tenancy agreements for most of the apartments in this building. Some of them are really half-assed, the kind any lawyer could challenge, agreements where the former tenants bought their apartments for next to nothing. Lennox, fucking predator that he is, knows it. He must have been putting pressure on," Virgil said, combing through the papers, picking up a document, scanning it. "Oh, man, this is priceless!"

"What?"

"He's been doing this for a long time, all over Harlem, before the Benneton rainbow nation, the Asians, yuppies, gays, got here, Carver Lennox was in the business, buying condemned buildings, apartments, town houses. He has mortgages you wouldn't believe."

"And the market is crashing around him."

Virgil laughed. "Yeah, with the help of people like him and his pals at Goldman. I don't think he can afford the mortgages on some of this," said Virgil. "I think he has to make a go of the Armstrong, which is the best property he has, the one where he bought apartments so cheap, even if he sells them for less than he could have a year ago, it'll go a long way toward solving some of his financial problems. Either he does that, or he'll be in very very very deep shit, Artie."

"How many apartments does he own here?"

"Ten, I think. He's been warehousing them." Virgil gathered up the papers and put them back in their original folders.

He went to the living room, and I followed. For a few seconds, he stared at the orange Warhol silk screen.

"Beautiful, isn't it?" he said, shifting it to one side, then placing it carefully on the floor. Behind it was a wall safe. "Presto."

"How'd you know?"

"For some crazy reason people always put the safe behind a big picture. I swear, it's true." Virgil was already spinning the dials on the safe. He looked up. "You think I only do locks? I also do safes, they're my specialty. I'm serious, Artie, when I was a kid I knew my parents kept walking-around cash in a little safe in their bedroom, behind a picture, and I got so I could steal from it really easy. My parents' safe was behind the picture by Romare Bearden, which was considered the family treasure. I always loved those English novels about gentlemen crooks, you know, real period stuff. I figured myself for a future in the business. Cary Grant in *To Catch a Thief*—you know it?"

"You're kidding."

"You don't have any fucking idea," he said, his ear to the wall as he moved the dial on the safe, peering into the near distance as if the numbers would show up out of thin air. The door to the safe sprang open. He looked in.

"Anything?"

Virgil took out a flashlight and looked inside. From the innards of the safe, he pulled out a shoe box, opened it to reveal a stack of envelopes.

"Cash," he said, "lots of cash. Envelopes with cash in them and names of people in the building on them, one for Celestina, another one for Regina McGee; there's some with names of people downstairs on other floors."

"Put it back," I said. "We need a warrant now."

While Virgil closed up the safe, I surveyed the room, made sure everything was in order. "You think he's still out with his daughter? You don't think he'll forget to come home, or just decide to take a vacation somewhere with no extradition?"

"Trust me, his ego is bigger than his brain. He's invested in this building, this apartment. He'll be here," said Virgil. "Anyhow, he thinks we think Marie Louise did it. He thinks the dog makes it credible."

"I'm not so sure."

Virgil stood up. "Well, Artie, I'm fucking sure, OK?" he said. "Sorry. But I know it's Lennox. I know he got to Simonova, then Lionel Hutchison, and maybe Amahl Washington. Right?"

"I'm going to see Lily. "

"Artie?"

"What?"

"We need to talk," Virgil said. "About Lily."

"What do you want, a duel?"

He smiled faintly. "I wish."

"Why, because you know how to fence?"

"I do, since you ask. Yeah, I did some very pretty fencing. I was on the team. Harvard," he said in a tone of self-mockery. "You don't believe me, do you? There's been black guys on that team for quite a while, cross my heart," he added. "Listen to me, I really like her, Artie."

"It's Lily's decision," I said. "Right?"

"Is it?"

"What do you think, that I'm going to hypnotize her or something?"

"You spent the night," Virgil said. It wasn't a question and I didn't answer, and for a few seconds, we were both silent. Then he held up a single piece of paper. "You should know I'm taking this, I found it in Lennox's files. It shows what he's been up to."

"It's no good without a warrant."

"I don't care. Carver Lennox is too connected. We might never get the fucking warrant. Don't push me on this one, Artie. I'm just doing it." He put his hand on the doorknob. "I'm going to get Lennox now," he said. "Please don't stop me."

CHAPTER 49

Have yourself a merry little Christmas," Sinatra was singing on Lily's stereo.

She looked up from a pile of presents she was wrapping on the floor of her apartment. "Where were you?"

"Can I sit down?"

"Let him talk," said Tolya, who, attired in his Santa suit, looked like an enormous red tomato. He sat on the floor near her and put his hand on Lily's arm. "OK?"

I looked at all the stuff on the floor. "What is all this?"

"I'll take it to some kids tomorrow," said Tolya. "Nice kids. Local school." He peered into an enormous canvas bag, handing a package to Lily. "I want to be part of this community."

Tolya's magic had worked on Lily. Lap full of ribbons, she sat near him. Being with Tolya made her feel safe. The place was littered with silver paper and gold and red ribbons and sparkly stuff, and stacks of greeting cards. There was a bottle of red wine on the floor, two glasses.

Lily asked if everything was OK with Marie Louise and I just nodded. I just said it was all fine now.

"Will you help her get a green card?"

"If I can, of course," I said. "Yes. You're not mad at me anymore?"

"Not very mad," she said.

Tolya handed Lily a toy truck, closed his eyes for a minute, listening to the music.

"It is toss-up, Artyom. Verdi, Sinatra. I should have been Italian."

I went to the kitchen to get some water and he followed. I swallowed a couple of aspirin.

"Artyom?"

"What?"

"I got a little information about some dead guys, dead Russians. It's all connected, Artyom, the guy in the cemetery, the one in the closet who bled out, maybe the old lady—Mrs. Simonova, even the doctor. Nothing solid, but I don't like it. You should be careful, you hear me? You will get beat up again. Bad. Worse."

"Get me more information."

"Soon," he said.

"You're worried about this. Is that why you're here with Lily?"

"Yes," he said.

"Artie? Sit with me," Lily called out and I went and sat on the rug near her.

"Are you OK?"

"I'm better," she said. "I'm sad, but better. I'm sad about Lionel. You'll find out who killed him, won't you?"

"Yes. Soon."

"Good. I remember you used to say there was a moment in a case when you felt it was coming to an end."

"You remember."

"Most things," said Lily, as I leaned over to kiss the top of her head. I got up off the floor. "Come back soon," she added.

At the door, I turned to look at her, at Lily on the floor, the bright paper and ribbon around her, a glass of wine in her hand, Tolya in the kitchen, the music. She suddenly looked up at me and smiled in a way that told me the night before hadn't been an accident, wasn't just the party and a late night and too much booze.

I closed the door behind me, I was already on my phone. I wanted to make sure Virgil was on his way to get the warrant. I wanted to see Lennox, and alone. Virgil was so angry, I figured he might blow it. I got him, he told me he was at the station house. Then, I left a message for Carver Lennox. Told him I wanted to meet. I suggested the Sugar Hill Club. I hung up, got in the elevator and went looking for Diaz.

* * *

Regina McGee stopped me in the lobby, and I got the feeling she'd been waiting for me. She was nervous, shifting from foot to foot, hands clasped.

"I thought you were in the hospital."

"They let me go. I got dehydrated. Stupid, I forgot to drink water. I felt a chill, I turn the heat up too high, must have done passed out. Sometimes I think I'm going soft in the head," she said. "I said to them, please, send me home, soon as they ran a couple tests. I begged. I don't hold with being in hospitals."

I said I was glad she was better. She said she had been looking for me.

"What do you need?"

"Please, can you come to my apartment? I don't want to talk here." She lowered her voice as she led me to the elevator, and, when it came, peered inside, as if to make sure we would be alone.

There was an alcove for her bed, and another for the kitchen. A door led to the bathroom. There were two windows that faced south over Manhattan. The apartment was very small, the whole room jammed with record albums, hundreds of them, some on makeshift shelves, others in cartons on the floor. There were photographs of Ella Fitzgerald on the walls.

On one side of the room was an elaborate stereo system, which Regina said Ella had given her. On the small table, there was a coffee pot and the remains of a meal. Books were piled up, most of them biographies of jazz musicians.

"I found this when I went to put the garbage out." She held up a dog's collar. "I heard about the Hutchisons' dog."

I took it from her. "You think it's his?"

"I know it," she said. "Celestina treated me like a maid, and I didn't take kindly to it, but I didn't mind walking Ed from time to time. So when I see there's fur in the garbage chute, I get the feeling somebody tried to push the dog down, and he wouldn't go, so they stuffed him in the washing machine. Who does this type of thing?" she said, clutching a Kleenex. "Can I offer you some tea?"

I shook my head. "There's something else, isn't there?"

Regina sat down on the edge of a chair, gestured to another. I sat.

"I can't sleep at night," she said. "All night I think about Amahl Washington and how fast they buried him—they didn't bury him, they cremated him before anybody could say good-bye. Then they held this big fancy funeral over to the Abyssinian. It wasn't Amahl's church. Why? I have asked myself over and over, and I can't make no sense of it."

"Who was in charge?"

"What do you mean?"

"Who organized his funeral?"

"He didn't have much real family, just the one niece from out of town, from up near Buffalo. He had a lot of friends and associates, so first I think to myself maybe this funeral been organized by somebody from his basketball days, or from his time on the City Council. But at the church I notice it's Carver Lennox running things. He gives the eulogy."

"What's happened to the apartment?"

"Do you want to see it?"

"Yes"

"It's on the ninth floor. Come on."

Amahl Washington's apartment sounded empty, that strange, faint noise a vacant place makes, when all you hear is the refrigerator and the heat.

"They changed the locks on Amahl's apartment after he died," Regina said. "But I kept a key to this here back door. Some of these apartments have a back door that leads into the kitchen. Nobody uses them much anymore. They were for folk who did the cooking and washing," she said, "I was counting on them forgetting about the back door, you know?"

Regina led me from room to room. The place was immaculate. It had been cleaned up and cleaned out, the floor polished, the paint fresh.

"This looks like somebody fixed it all up," I said.

"That's what I wanted to show you. Somebody who's thinking of selling you'd say."

"Right."

"So I called that niece of Amahl's that lives upstate, and she didn't know much, they weren't close, but she told me the will was still in, what do you call it—probate?—and ain't nothing can be done until that's fixed."

"Does she know this apartment has been cleaned out?"

"Sure. I told her. She said that was fine, Carver Lennox told her he was getting ready to sell it and he was a big help to her. He took care of everything."

"She's going to sell it to him?"

"She says she don't know, it's not clear who this place belongs to, seeing as Amahl didn't specify nobody in his will, he just went too fast to do it, so it's all in a kind of mess. But I'm sure Carver has his eye on it."

"You think Mr. Washington meant you to have it?"

"Could be," she said. "I'd rather have him alive, tell the truth."

"Anything else?"

Regina led me back to the kitchen and through the back door, into the hall near the back stairs. Right then I heard something; so did she. Somebody was coming toward us, along the hall. I could hear him talking on his cell phone. Fear crossed Regina's face.

"Go home," I said. "Just walk to the elevator like nothing happened, just go on. He won't hurt you. I'll be right here. I'll wait."

"I'm scared of that man," she said, as Lennox got closer, his voice louder.

"It will be fine. Go on."

"Too many old folk dying in this building," said Regina. "I don't want to die."

CHAPTER 50

Who was the guy I saw slip out of the Sugar Hill Club and into the ice-cold night? It was after I'd left Regina McGee at the Armstrong. I pulled up across the street from the club and I saw him, the figure in a dark jacket, hood up, emerging from the club door. In a spill of white from the streetlight, he appeared, looked pale as a ghost, then was gone into the shadow. Was he black? Hard to tell. The glistening tarmac, the ice, the light, played tricks. Light turned black people white and white people dark.

A thief in the night. The phrase came to me as I crossed the street. My head throbbed. I needed sleep, but I felt wide awake, adrenaline roaring through my body. If Carver Lennox showed, I'd get it out of him. It was him. He had killed Lionel Hutchison. He was involved with the others. He wanted the apartments. He wanted the building.

It was almost midnight when I got inside the club. The place was empty except for a young couple, her in a yellow sweater and sparkly earrings like little Christmas trees, him in a red plaid shirt, sitting at a table near the deserted bandstand, holding hands over a bottle of Pinot Grigio. Canned music came over the sound system. I didn't know the guy behind the bar, but at the far end, last seat near the wall, sat Carver Lennox.

He saw me and raised a hand in greeting.

I climbed on the stool next to his, wondering if this was the man who had murdered Lionel Hutchison.

When Lennox had found me earlier at Amahl Washington's apartment on the ninth floor, he had been cool about it. I had expected a fight, but he didn't ask why I was there, just told me he'd picked up the message I wanted to meet and asked if midnight worked for me. He wanted to help his daughter with her home-work. She was upstairs at his apartment, he said. Said the Sugar Hill Club was fine. He'd meet me.

Now he ordered a refill on his whiskey. "What would you like, Artie?"

"I'll get my own." I asked for a beer.

"How can I help?" said Lennox.

When the bartender put the bottle in front of me, I realized I was thirsty. My head hurt. I was dog tired.

"I've been thinking about all of the shit going down at the Arm-strong, and I figure you're the guy to paint me the picture," I said. "Open a window on it for me, Carver. You want to do that?"

Carver ignored my question. "You all right, man?" he said. "That beating you took in the storage room, I'm sorry about that. It's the kind of thing we have to change. That damn back door is always open, there's always people in and out for smokes, and garbage, and to get their cars. It's not the way you run a building, you know, I tell them over and over. Only Diaz gets it. But he can't do everything alone."

"Yeah?"

"Yes. You have a different impression?"

"He's very attentive."

"You mean he eavesdrops?" Lennox laughed.

"Isn't that what you pay him for?"

"I pay him to make my building a better place."

"Right."

"Help me here, Artie. You think Diaz has his hand out more than normal? I need to know."

I didn't answer for a minute. I downed the beer.

"I didn't come to talk about Diaz. Your problem," I said.

"What do you need?"

"You tell me."

He leaned close, arms on the bar, hand gripping the whiskey glass. His eyes were bloodshot. In the whites of his eyes were tiny threads of red. In the corners was more blood. I was so close to Lennox, I thought I could see the blood in his left eye leaking.

"You don't think I care that Lionel died?" Lennox said. He was pretty wasted. He had been drinking, a lot, I realized.

"Do you?"

"He was my friend, so I fucking care. It's also bad news for my building."

"Your building?"

"You fucking know what I mean," he said, his voice low now, but angry.

"What about Marianna Simonova? And Amahl Washington?"

"They were old, man. They were old and sick and they died."

I kept my mouth shut, and my silence got to him.

"You think they were murdered, too?" he said. "You think it's connected? Is that what you think?" The horror that crossed his face seemed real.

I ordered another beer.

"Should I have another drink?" It was rhetorical. He gestured for another, his third, he said. Or fourth. Raised it. Drank it.

"So how many apartments you got empty, Cal?"

"There's some," he said. "Why?"

"Let's say I'm a fucking financial idiot. You're planning to turn the Armstrong into a new co-op, call it the Barack Obama, that right?"

"You don't like our new president, man? That's your problem." Lennox sounded hostile.

"I'm guessing the way you got it structured, you need a majority of owners who will go along. Ready to play your game when you ask five grand for maintenance, or else sell up, right? You already got your hands on a few, isn't that right, Cal?"

"Shares, yeah."

"What?"

"You buy shares in a co-op, you don't buy the apartment."

"What-fucking-ever," I said. "And you and the new shareholders can run the board between you, that right?"

"I don't know what business it is of yours," he said. "Listen to me, man, just ask me what you want to know. I want Hutchison's murder solved, right? I loved that man. You listening?"

"Well, you'll get hold of his place now, won't you? I mean, his wife wants out, isn't that right? You have enough apartments now?"

"Plenty." He pushed his empty glass away and got up from the bar stool.

"Let me buy you one," I said, backing off. I figured I better ease up or I'd lose Lennox before I nailed him. "You mind if I ask you about Amahl Washington?"

"You can ask me any fucking thing you want, man. You understand?" He was drunk, but he was willing to talk.

Was this his game? I still had him figured for Hutchison's murder, but the longer I spent in the bar, the less sure I was.

"I was fucking sad, man," said Lennox. "I played basketball in high school, and Amahl was my hero. He was a great man. He did a lot for his people. He retired and he went on to the City Council."

"He died at the Armstrong. Your wife was his doctor."

"Please! Lucille is the straightest woman ever walked this planet. Her religion is what makes her tick, not fucking money. She was Amahl's doc because she's the best lung specialist at Presbyterian."

"Lionel Hutchison was her mentor, isn't that right? Isn't that why Simonova saw Lucille Bernard, too? You were friends with Mrs. Simonova?"

"I'm getting another drink," said Lennox. I signaled the bartender. I paid for it.

"You didn't like her?" I asked.

"Who?"

"Simonova."

"You have no idea." He turned so I couldn't see his face.

"You wouldn't be sad to get your hands on her apartment, would you? But it belongs to Marie Louise. Simonova left it to her, you must know that."

"Nice for Marie Louise.

Oddly, Lennox seemed glad for Marie Louise, and I wondered why

"You didn't want a shot at buying Simonova's apartment?"

"No way," he said, half to himself. "No fucking way."

"You were at Simonova's the night before she died. In fact, more than once last week."

"She asked me over," said Lennox. "She needed some help."

"What with? I noticed she had presents for you and your kids; what's that about?"

"She gave everybody presents. It was how she bribed people. Listen, man, you got anything to tell me about Lionel Hutchison? That's why I came out on this fucking miserable night, right?"

"You knew about Hutchison's obsession with pain relief, with assisted suicide?"

He snorted. "Everybody fucking knew. It was his religion. Times I was in the middle, Celestina saying Lionel wants to kill people, him shilling for his euthanasia thing."

"Celestina Hutchison said you offered to buy her out, that Lionel refused, but she wanted out. You gave her money. Said Lionel told you he'd never leave."

"I want you to do me a favor," said Lennox, his voice soft, even, almost needy. "I'm asking you. Please."

"What is it?"

"Tell Marie Louise I'm sorry I even suspected her, will you? Help her, if you can, if she needs an immigration lawyer or anything," said Lennox. "There's money in a safe behind the Warhol picture of Ali in my apartment—you've probably already seen it, you and your pal, Virgil? Just give it to her, tell her I'm sorry."

The regrets about Marie Louise, the apology, the instructions to give her money, all of it made me suspect Lennox more. There was something weird about it. He was getting ready to confess. He was feeling bad. He was slumped on that bar stool now, head in his hands. Suddenly, he looked up.

"You think I fucking killed these people to get their apartments?" Lennox said, angry again now. "That's what you've been thinking all along, isn't it? You think because I'm black, I have it in me to kill people?"

"You don't have to be black."

"But I am."

"Calm down," I said. "I'm sorry."

"You don't know anything."

"Then tell me something. Tell me about Marianna Simonova."

In his face I saw something I hadn't seen before. I saw how much he hated the Russian. I saw that she was somehow connected to all of it, at the bottom of it all.

It was quiet in the club. The bartender was waiting for us to finish. I could hear the clock over the bar tick. Could hear the cars outside.

"You want me to tell you about her?"

"She was a crazy woman who made up stories about her past," Lennox said. "Crazy like a fox. She tells everyone, 'I was Paul Robeson's girlfriend, I was an important person.' All the time she's saying how she just loves black people, seeing as how we're so oppressed, we're so fucking pure, we're so decent." He looked at me. "I couldn't stand her—what she said, even how she looked, the way she smelled. That stink of incense and cigarette smoke, the imperious way she had, ordering everyone around."

"Why didn't they tell her to fuck off?"

"She seduced everybody with those fucking stories. She'd tell you she was the mother of Jesus Christ if it would get her some attention."

Lennox's voice possessed the fury of somebody who'd been hurt really bad.

"What else?" I said.

"You should really listen to me," Lennox said. "I didn't kill anybody. I'm trying to tell you something and you're not hearing me. Hold on." He reached for his coat that was over the bar stool next to him. He pulled out a brown leather folder, the kind where you keep photographs.

"Nobody knows about this, man," said Lennox. "But I'm going to tell you, OK? I'm going to tell you some shit so you can go and solve your fucking crimes, you and that Virgil."

He had the look of a man who was going to confess, wanted to confess. Then he got up abruptly, stumbling over the bar stool.

"I have to get some air," he said. "I had too much to drink, I'm just wasted, man." He glanced at me and smiled slightly, but it was the sad smile of a man who knows he's washed up. "Don't worry," Lennox added. "I'll be back. You can come with me. Or you can watch me through the window, watch me puke, if you want."

My heart raced. I was sweating. I knew he was getting ready to talk. I wanted him to trust me. He waited for my permission.

I ordered another beer. I didn't drink it. The young couple left the club. The bartender wiped down the tables and looked at me. He wanted to close up.

The time seemed to drag.

"Go on," I said. "Get some air."

"You coming? Or you want to trust me?" He tossed some money on the bar.

I didn't have much time to think. I saw he was going to puke. I told him to go.

From where I was, standing close to the window, to the door, I could see the street. I saw Lennox bent double. Then I thought he was going to run after all, getting in position, a runner's position. He seemed to take a step. I got my gun, yelled at the bartender to call 911 for help.

I'd been a jerk. You didn't use psychology with a killer. The idea that my trusting him would make him talk had been crazy. He was a man in a rage. I ran.

For a split second, I lost sight of Lennox. There was a heavy velvet curtain over the door, the kind they put up in the winter to keep the cold out, and it obscured my view. By the time I got outside, it was too late.

CHAPTER 51

When I knelt beside Carver Lennox on the sidewalk outside the club, I saw he was bleeding bad.

"Carver?"

I could feel his breath, still warm, on my face. He was bleeding from his gut, from his face. It had happened so fast that he'd never had a chance. Somebody had put a knife in him before I got outside.

Near where he lay on the cold sidewalk was a long, curved knife. The attacker had left in a hurry. He had been distracted by something, startled enough to drop the knife. Next to it were Lennox's horn-rims.

"Carver?"

He didn't answer. I tried CPR as best I could. I wrapped my jacket over his wound.

The bartender had called 911, and now I heard sirens.

"Carver? Cal? You hear me?"

He tried to talk, wanted to say something, but he couldn't. His mouth was full of blood.

"Come on. Stay with me." I put my fingers against his neck.

He had known he was in trouble. Had been trying to tell me something in the club, trying to show me something. Was it the financial meltdown that had caught him in its claws? He owed money. Maybe the attack had come from somebody who wanted it back.

All over town, panicked, frantic people were doing bad deals, borrowing money, desperate to hang on to some piece of their lives. Carver Lennox was so invested in the life he had made for himself—Princeton, the job at Goldman, the kids in private school, most of all the Armstrong—it was hard to know what he'd do to hang on to it all. The building had a grip on everybody in it; its history, its presence, even the sheer glamour it had once represented. For Lennox, it was also the future.

Come on! Stay with me!

Was it about Hutchison's murder? Was that what he wanted to tell me? About the other deaths in the Armstrong?

I looked down now at the face. Without the glasses, he looked so young, the expression so placid, except for the blood. When he tried to speak again, blood poured from his mouth. Something he wanted to tell me. I leaned closer. He flicked his eyes to the left.

A spill of things was scattered on the ground, stuff that must have come from his pocket—keys, change, a billfold, the brown leather folder he had tried to show me in the club.

The sirens came closer, cars turned into the street. I looked up.

Out of nowhere, I saw him. A car went by, and in the headlights, I saw the guy who must have been hiding back of a truck farther along the avenue. The guy I had seen earlier when I arrived. Guy with a black jacket.

Now he was running north on St. Nicholas. A big man, light on his feet. In headlights from the cars, his hair looked white.

I got out my phone and called in his description, this big man with white hair, but I couldn't leave Carver. His hand was in mine. It was still warm. I could feel a faint pulse in the wrist. My other hand was still on his neck, pressing, blood coming out between my fingers. Then he said something, said something so softly I had to put my ear to his mouth.

"What is it?"

"Pictures," he whispered. I picked up the leather folder. He nodded. I held it out to him, but he couldn't raise his arm, and his eyes were closed now. I stuffed it in my jeans.

Medics emerged from the ambulance at the curb. They loaded Carver Lennox into it, took him to Presbyterian. I called Lucille Bernard at home. I left a message with her office, on her cell.

"Artie?" It was Virgil Radcliff, who had arrived at the scene a few minutes earlier, along with a couple of cops in uniform and Jimmy Wagner.

I was wet from the snow and ice, my shirt and pants were covered with blood. "Did you tell Jimmy we had made Lennox for the killer?" I asked Virgil.

"It wasn't him, Artie. I know that now. He had an alibi."

"Sure, but it was his daughter, wouldn't she lie for him?"

"Yeah, could be, but seems the daughter had a friend with her, and the friend had her dad with her. They arrived just after Lennox and his kid—I didn't pay attention to them on the tape at first because they didn't set off any alarm bells. But they were there and they stayed until early morning. Said they lived in Carroll Gardens, and it was too far to head back to Brooklyn after the party, so Lennox invited them to stay. We got them going in, leaving. The girl's father swore they were there all night."

"Would they lie for Lennox?"

"I don't think so. The man said they weren't even friends, it was just the two kids knew each other from school," said Virgil. "You get anything from Lennox?"

"I was with him in the club," I said. "He was trying to tell me something, but he said he needed air, he was going to throw up. He went out. The creep was waiting for him. I shouldn't have let him go."

"Did you see the killer?"

"I called in a description. I think I know who it was." I was shaking. A cop in uniform got a shock blanket from the back of his car and put it around me.

"Tell me," said Virgil.

"Guy with white hair, strange, albino hair. I sat next to him at the Christmas party," I said. "Jesus, he was right there. He told me he liked jazz. He got a good look at me, and everybody else, including Carver."

I was shaking so hard, I had to sit down on the steps of a brownstone next to the club.

Virgil lit up a cigarette and offered me one. I took it. I told him I realized now I'd seen the creep earlier, just before I met Lennox. I had seen him slip away into the dark. He must have known Lennox was in the club, must have waited for him outside.

"You OK, Art?" It was Jimmy Wagner, who hurried over to check on me. I told him what I'd seen at the club, the guy I'd seen who knifed Lennox.

"Give me one of them." Wagner reached for Virgil's smokes. Virgil held the lighter. In its flame I saw how sick Wagner was looking. Sick. Worried. Skin gray.

Then I remembered. Struggling, I got out my phone. I put the picture on the screen. My hand shook so hard, Virgil took the cell from me.

"Tolya took this at the Christmas party last night. I almost forgot. It's the Russian," I said.

"Lemme see that," said Wagner, looking over my shoulder. "Jesus, Mary, Mother of God. Christ. Fucking Christ."

"What is it?"

Around us cops checked the sidewalk for blood. There were forensics people and somebody from the ME.

I looked at Wagner. "Jimmy? What is it?"

He grabbed my cell out of Virgil's hand and peered at the screen again. "It's the fucker I let go. The creep we held for the homicide on that body we found in the cemetery with the piece of paper stuck to it." Jimmy sucked on his smoke. "This prick probably killed him, probably did the guy who bled out into the closet, too. Knifed them both, and I let him go. Fuck. Fuck. Four homicides. Two dead white men that nobody identified yet, maybe creeps themselves, maybe mob shit. But what's fucking worse is Hutchison, and now Lennox. They're going to say somebody is killing good black men in Harlem, and it's going to be my fucking fault, and maybe it fucking is. I didn't sleep in forty-eight. I'm too old. But we'll fucking get him." He tossed away his cigarette. "You sent that picture around, Art?"

I held my cell. "I'm doing it now."

"Anything else, Art, man? Anything you remember?"

"At the party, the guy kept pulling down the sleeve of his sweater, like he had eczema he wanted to hide, or some kind of scar."

"Like a tattoo?"

"Could be."

"It's him for sure," said Wagner again. "So he was covering his tats. I looked at those tats and they didn't mean dick to me. Jesus, fucking stupid asshole that I am," said Wagner, lighting up again, dragging on the cigarette, coughing. "I should have held him longer."

"I just thought of something," I said, shivering.

"You need some dry clothes," Wagner said. "What?"

"You remember when I came by yesterday to see you? I was waiting by the sergeant at your house, and I saw this guy in a hoodie and North Face leaving. I got a faint impression he was looking at me, taking a look, clocking who I was."

Wagner went to his car to get his own smokes. Virgil said to me, "I have to go." Without another word, he moved away from the scene, through the crowd that had formed on the sidewalk and disappeared.

I knew Virgil needed to work the case his way. I knew he would hunt down the creep who did the killings if it was the last thing he did. I sent him a text. Told him I'd keep on it on my end. Call if you need me. Call.

I put on a blue jacket Wagner brought me.

"I'm sure it's the same guy who beat me up in the Armstrong basement, too. What's his name?"

"Ivan," said Wagner, and snorted. "Yeah, it really is, I told you, Ivan Ivanov. Where's Radcliff?"

"He went to find the fucker. Let him be, Jimmy. He needs to do this. He has a lot invested."

"I gotta put more guys on it, though."

"You do that, but let Radcliff go for it."

"I don't want you wandering off, right, Artie? We're going to need a Russian speaker. I want you holding this together, you hear?"

"I'll be around."

"Your phone is ringing, man," said Wagner, as more cars arrived, the flashing red and blue lighting up the dark street.

I started for my car.

"Where am I gonna find you, Artie?" Jimmy said.

"I'll be on my phone, don't worry. It's just something I gotta do there, Jimmy. Something I gotta know."

MONDAY

CHAPTER 52

The lobby at Presbyterian had the strange, desolate look city hospitals have in the middle of the night. Carver Lennox was dead by the time I got there.

I didn't stick around. There was nothing I could do. I was wearing the dark blue jacket Jimmy Wagner had loaned me at the scene; everyone could make me for a cop. There was no time to change.

I was worried as hell about Lily. She was at the Armstrong. I had woken her up when I called. She was fine, she'd said sleepily. But I drove over. Ivan, if it was his real name, would have seen Lily and me at the Christmas party, and if he wanted to get at me, he might go for her. He knew his way around the building. He beat me up in the storage room. I was betting he killed the Hutchison dog. I had seen him talking to Diaz at the back door. I knew Diaz would let him in if there was cash.

On my way over, I got hold of Tolya's voice mail, asked him to send one of his guys to the Armstrong. I was in the Armstrong lobby when Tolya called back and said he'd send somebody.

"You want me to come?" he asked in Russian.

I told him it would scare Lily. Just send a guy, I said, and went upstairs. I let myself in to Lily's apartment with the keys she had given me. I took off my shoes and went to the bedroom.

She was on her side, fast asleep. I watched her breathing. I went around the bed and looked at her face. On it was a half smile. Lily was somewhere else, in a happy dream.

After I checked the rest of the apartment, I washed my face in the kitchen sink, got my shoes, went out, and locked the door. It was very late. Quiet, too quiet. The Hutchisons were gone, Lionel dead, Celestina at her sister's. Simonova was buried on Long Island. Carver Lennox was in the hospital morgue.

In the dead of night, when pretty much everybody was asleep, nobody talking, no kids yelling, no music playing, the building crackled with little noises you couldn't hear during the day: the drip of leaking water, the hiss of a radiator, floorboards that sagged and creaked under your feet, my own heartbeat as I went slowly down the stairs.

No one was on the desk. I knew Diaz or one of the others was supposed to cover all night, but no one was there. On a chair in the corner was a young patrolman, half asleep. I shook him. I yelled at him. "There's been a fucking homicide here," I said. "Just fucking stay awake."

In the basement, I kept my gun out. I heard noises—voices, the rattle of machinery, the flick of a cigarette lighter. I ran in the direction of the sounds. Nothing.

I went out the back door and into the parking area, where I saw a large guy I recognized as one of Tolya's guys. Russian. An ex-weight-lifter in jeans and a leather jacket.

He nodded at me.

I said I'd be back soon, then I hesitated. I didn't like leaving Lily. I looked at him. I got the feeling he knew what was at stake. I hoped he knew.

The metal gate was down over the front of the Russian store named Tolstoy in Washington Heights. It was four in the morning. I called the owner, the guy they called Goga. I left a message. Told him to meet me at his store. Fifteen minutes later, he showed.

"Get in," I said in Russian, holding open the car door. Goga's expression turned fearful. He saw the blood on my pants. The NYPD jacket. He had grown up in a country where the arrival of cops could only mean trouble.

As Goga edged into the seat next to mine, I reached over him and shut the car door.

"It's cold," I said, and got out my cell phone. "Thank you for coming."

"I am always here early, for food deliveries," he replied nervously. "This is no trouble for me, to arrive early."

I showed him the picture of Ivan. "You've seen him?"

Goga nodded. "Sure," he said. "Mr. Ivanov. Sure. Nice guy, good manners, comes to buy caviar, cookies, cheese. Nice clothes," he added, and said he thought Ivanov lived in Miami Beach.

"Did Mrs. Simonova ever talk to him?"

"Sure. Several times they happen to be here same time."

"What did they talk about?"

"I don't remember so good," said Goga. "Maybe weather. Maybe politics. They talk so I do not hear so well." He sounded uneasy. I pressed him. I tried to make him dredge up something, anything, from his memory. I said another detective would stop by later in case he remembered.

He told me he didn't know anything at all.

I was about to let him go when my phone rang.

CHAPTER 53

Virgil told me he got a tip-off from some guy he knew, homeless guy who lived up near the George Washington Bridge, guy who said he'd seen somebody in an alley behind the old synagogue nearby. Virgil went and he found Ivan, who beat him up pretty bad, but even while the creep was punching him, Virgil managed to hold on, get out his gun, and bring him in.

I got his call when I was finishing up at the Russian grocery store. I went to the station house. It was him. Same black jacket, same weird white hair. Same cultured voice, though he didn't talk much, not at first. Ivan Ivanov.

Between us, Virgil and me, we didn't get much out of him. We sat him in the interrogation room. He was a lot slicker than your usual Russki hood. Even sitting down, he seemed big—the big shoulders, the heavy chest and arms. His removed his jacket. In jeans and a sweater, he looked at ease, as if he knew his way around a police station. Swore his name was Ivan Ivanov and laughed as if it were a joke.

He had been at the club earlier. I had seen him run away after Lennox was knifed. We had to wait on prints, see if Ivanov's match the prints on the knife. Did Ivanov kill the others? The guy in the cemetery? In the closet of a brownstone? Did he push Lionel Hutchison?

The creep, this Ivanov, sat calmly at the table, watching me. He smoked when Virgil tossed him a pack of cigarettes. He ate the bologna sandwich we ordered for him. He drank the coffee. But he didn't talk. He pretended not to recognize me. He confirmed only that his name was Ivanov, and said he was Russian, a citizen of Russia with an American green card.

For half an hour, while I talked to him, Virgil sat at the table with me. I had tried to get him to go to the emergency room, but he'd stuck Band-Aids on his face and refused. Nothing broken, he said. Bastard didn't break anything.

"Wait a minute," said Virgil. He reached over, pushed up Ivan's sleeves. There were the tats.

"You can read this?" he said to me.

I read: WORKERS OF THE WORLD UNITE. Same tats as the dead guy who'd had the Communist Manifesto skewered to his heart.

"You're a true believer?" I said in Russian. He asked for cigarettes. "Tell me what you believe, then," I added. "I'm interested."

He shrugged.

"What about the dog?" I said. "You didn't have to kill the damn dog, did you? You enjoyed that?"

Ivan's face barely changed, but he said, very softly, "What dog?" Then he smiled slightly and pulled out a leather thong he wore around his neck and showed me the tooth on it. "Dog's tooth, to ward off evil eye," he said. "For luck."

"You killed the dog for that?"

He shrugged. I yanked the tooth off the thong and looked at it. It was old. It was too big for the dog.

"It's from a wolf," I said in Russian. "Don't play with me."

"I don't play," he said.

"Let's go," I said to Virgil.

"Where are you going?" Ivan said in English.

"What do you care?" I said.

In the corridor outside the room where we had left Ivan, Virgil said, "You think he did it? All of them?"

"I think you should put something on those cuts," I said. "At least go sit down."

"You want him to yourself, don't you, Artie?"

"He's yours. It's up to you."

"Go on, maybe he'll warm up to a fellow Russki." Virgil reached out his hand for a chair to steady himself.

"Listen to me. Go in back and lie down on that bunk for a while. I'll get you when he starts talking."

"You think he'll talk?"

I nodded. "If I have anything to do with it."

"Good, you came without the monkey," Ivan said in Russian when I went back into the interrogation room alone.

"Did you know Marianna Simonova?" I said.

Ivan looked up. In that split second, I saw he was startled. Then he shut down again. He still didn't ask for a lawyer. I figured he was illegal after all, in spite of his green card. It was probably a fake. I picked it up from the table.

"How much are these going for?"

"You need one?" he said.

"Talk to me about Simonova. You knew her, didn't you? She was one of your comrades," I said. "Bitch that she was."

"She was a good woman."

"She was a murderer."

"You're full of shit."

"Anyway, she's dead," I said, and seeing it upset him, added, "Good thing, she was crazy and bad and she still believed in fucking Stalin. Mad old woman." I added some choice Russian epithets. I saw it got to him. "You didn't know she was dead? No?"

"How would I know?" It was impossible to tell if he was lying. He shifted in his seat, and took a deep drag on his cigarette.

"You think she was a good woman? Why?"

"She was a patriot."

"That's why you have those tattoos? You're a patriot. You think you're a good Russian, a true Soviet comrade?"

"Perhaps."

"Listen, Ivan, if you didn't kill those two Russians, and you didn't kill Carver Lennox, tell me some more about Simonova. What's there to lose? Maybe I could help you out."

It was a gamble. I was pretty sure Ivan was good for Carver

Lennox and the other two homicides, that the prints would be a match. But Goga had also put him in the grocery store with Marianna Simonova. I was curious. It was a hunch. Maybe it was the Commie stuff that made me connect them. As soon as I saw him react, I knew I was onto something. Now the creep wanted to talk.

"She was a true comrade," he said. "She was not like those who just quit when bastard Gorbachev came to power. She remained true."

"You mean she was a spy? Who did she work for?"

"There is always somebody who continues to believe."

"Only assholes," I said.

"Things changed. We became nothing," said Ivan. "We were great empire. We became shitty little country. Putin has tried, he is big man, but all you hear is democracy, freedom." He snorted. "What does this mean, this 'democracy'?"

"You tell me."

"It means only money."

"So you kill people for your ideology?"

"Nothing is simple," he said.

"Why don't you tell me how you and Simonova were involved? Where did you meet her?"

"Suddenly, I don't remember." He leaned back and folded his arms.

"Try."

"No good. I don't remember." He closed his eyes.

I leaned close. "Fucking tell me what you know about her."

For three, four, five minutes, I listened to the clock on the wall tick. Ivan remained silent.

"What did Simonova tell you?"

He looked at me. "She tells me to be quiet, so this is what I will be."

He closed his eyes again.

The door banged opened and Virgil came in, rubbing his eyes.

"Can you take it from here?" I said.

"Sure. You leaving?"

"For a while. See if you can get it out of him who he worked for," I said, and looked at Ivan. "Do what you have to."

Gloria Lopez met me on her way to work. She emerged from the train station at 145th Street, and we sat in Starbucks and drank coffee. She was wearing a red winter coat and a white hat. In her hand was an envelope.

"I got you some stuff on those pills."

"Already?"

"I'm a fast worker," she said. "I also got hold of a friend at the ME's office and asked them to check on Dr. Hutchison. It's all in the envelope. I wasn't on a date last night, by the way. I was working the phone for you. I just wanted to make you jealous."

"Fair enough. Thank you. And you look great."

"Thanks. You look like shit. You get any sleep lately?"

"Not a lot. Listen, I know you had to call in something big for this."

"You have no idea, Artie. I have to go." She got up, kissed my cheek, and said, "Merry Christmas."

"I'll call you," I said.

She turned. "So is it Lily?"

I didn't answer. After Gloria left, I just sat, drinking black coffee and reading the notes the ME had faxed to her.

CHAPTER 54

Lionel Hutchison died from cyanide poisoning." I stood in Lily's doorway.

Lily, stared at me. "My God. Come in. Lucille is here. Take it easy when you tell her, will you? She loved Lionel."

I went into the apartment. Lucille Bernard got up from the kitchen counter.

"You OK?" I said. "I'm sorry about Carver. How are your kids doing, Dr. Bernard?" This time she said she'd like it if I called her Lucille.

"They're with my mother. You know, I'm really sorry about Carver, too. We were once in love, and we have the children," she said. "I came over to pick up some things they left at Carver's place. I didn't want them stopping by. They have their own keys, you see." Her eyes filled. "I'm sorry. I'm just so tired."

"Do you want something to drink, Artie? You look cold. Lucille?"

I nodded and Lily poured Scotch in three glasses. Lucille pushed aside her mug of tea and took the drink.

"How come you're wearing that jacket?" Lily said to me.

"He put his own jacket over Carver," Lucille said. "I heard. Thank you. I'll get it cleaned for you."

"It doesn't matter."

"You were there the whole time?" Lucille asked. "With Carver?"

"Yes."

"Did he say anything?"

"He couldn't speak much."

"You sat with him. He wasn't alone."

"I was with him until they took him to the hospital."

"Thank you," said Lucille.

"Tell her, Artie." Lily picked up her drink.

"Tell me what?"

"It was cyanide that killed Lionel Hutchison."

"My God," Lucille said. "How do you know?"

"This." I gave her the ME's notes.

"Was it Celestina?"

"It was Marianna Simonova," I said. "I think she switched some of her blood pressure pills for Lionel's. I think she opened the capsules and put them in his bottle. She could have borrowed some of his medications, they both took similar drugs."

"Tell me how you got the information."

"I took a stab. I have a friend who works for the city. She has friends at the ME's office."

"My God," Lily said. "There was something Marianna used to say. She used to say, 'In old days, hero is never taken alive.' In the old days, according to Marianna, soldiers and spies carried cyanide pills. If they were captured, they could bite on the tablet. It would kill them fast. 'Hero is never taken alive.' God, she loved saying that. I should have thought of it. But how do you get the stuff?"

"It's easy," said Lucille. "Do you remember the Tylenol scare? I think it was in 1982."

"Yes," Lily said.

"I was in high school. I remember," Lucille said. "Some nut put cyanide in Tylenol. People died. We had Tylenol at home, and my mother went bananas. She never used it again. It would be so damn easy. And Lionel was obsessive about his medication. He always always took it."

"Help me understand," Lily said.

"Let's say Simonova told Lionel she needed some extra pills, and she borrowed his bottle," Lucille said. "Or she switched the vials. Or she got the drugstore to deliver both their prescriptions to her. What difference would it make? Either way, she could get her hands on some of his pills, open the capsules, replace some of the medication with cyanide. Sooner or later, he'd take one with the poison. They borrowed from each other all the time, Lionel told me that once."

"Someone checked the prints on the bottle with the poisoned capsules," I said. "It had Lionel's name on the prescription and his prints, but also Simonova's. I took a glass from her apartment earlier. They made a match. But it had Lionel's prints as well as hers."

"It's cold in here," said Lily. "How would Marianna get the cyanide?"

"You can buy it online," said Lucille.

"But Lionel fell," Lily said.

"What are the effects of cyanide?" I asked Lucille. "Not counting death."

"The effects are similar to suffocation. Cyanide stops the body's cells from being able to use oxygen." She looked up. "It can produce dizziness, seizure. Acute ingestion has a very fast onset. The heart can collapse."

"He told me he sometimes took his meds along with his coffee and went outside really early, on the terrace or the roof, so he could smoke. What if he took the capsule with the cyanide early yesterday morning, when Celestina was still at her sister's. What if he got dizzy or had a seizure and fell?" I looked at Lucille.

"In that case, he wasn't pushed," she said.

"Cyanide works fast?"

"If you use the right dose."

"Marianna killed him," said Lily. "She did it in a way so nobody would ever know." She smashed her fist on the counter. "She killed him even after she was dead. Artie?"

"What?"

"I still don't understand," said Lily. "How come the medical examiner didn't spot it in Lionel right away?"

"They wouldn't look for it unless they knew what to look for," I said. "It's not part of the usual tox screen."

"And there's no other symptoms you can see?" Lily said, sounding desperate. She didn't want to believe what Marianna Simonova had done.

"Only one," Lucille said. "It can discolor the skin. Sometimes it makes it redden. It's one of the symptoms that makes you look for cyanide in an autopsy. But only in some people."

"Some?" I said.

"If you're black, chances are nobody will notice."

CHAPTER 55

There were red and green cupcakes on Lily's kitchen counter. I ate one.

"Amelie Smith brought those," said Lily. "They were taking them to a school fair with their kids. Everybody's out," she added. "The floor feels empty."

I told Lily about Ivan.

"Marianna knew a lot of people."

"Did you meet them? Russians?"

"Some. Some just in passing. A few when I took her to Washington Heights shopping. A few once I went with her to Brighton Beach. She had an address book where she wrote everything. She always took it with her, in a big, old-fashioned leather purse," Lily said, pouring more Scotch. "Take off that jacket, Artie, it makes you look like a cop."

I took it off. From my jeans I got Simonova's address book and put it on the counter.

"I took it from her apartment earlier," I said.

"Why?"

"Habit."

"Is this Ivan in it?"

"Yes." I opened the book. I showed her. Lily examined the names.

"I remember once Marianna wanted to call the grocery store, and I picked up that address book, and she got furious when I touched it. Artie, you want to lie down? You look terrible."

"I'm OK. But is there anything else I should know?" I held up the address book. "What about all these marks and stars and stuff beside the names? Was it some kind of code?"

"I guess she had some kind of system. Can you read it?"

I flipped through the pages. Some of the names had New York numbers and addresses. Some were in Moscow. Some both. Some had moved from Moscow to New York, the Moscow numbers crossed out. A few were in Florida and Los Angeles.

"Anything?" said Lily.

"Tell me what else you know about her."

"Artie?"

"What's that, honey?"

"Do you believe Marianna killed Lionel?"

"I'm sorry."

Lily got up and went into the other room. She came back with a cardboard box.

"What is it?"

"Some of the notes I made about Marianna. Some of the journals she gave me. There are a couple of video tapes. She didn't have a DVD player. I only looked at some of it. A lot's in Russian. I don't know, maybe I was trying to protect her, or let her keep her privacy or some fucking thing. Maybe I should have given this to you earlier, Artie."

"There wasn't time," I said. "Everything has happened so fast the past couple days."

"There's more in her apartment," Lily said. "In the study."

"I have to go back."

"I can't go in there."

"That's fine." I didn't want her with me. What I was going to do wasn't legal. I had to work fast. Lucille knew about the cyanide. I was gambling she figured I'd report it. I couldn't be sure. She might call Jimmy Wagner herself. As soon as it was out, there'd be cops crawling all over Simonova's apartment.

Lily gave me the keys. I put my arms around her. She didn't push me away.

It was so quiet in the building, I felt we were alone.

"Will you be OK?"

"Yes."

"Wait for me here."

"Hurry, Artie. Please. I just want all of this to end." Lily kissed me. "Just hurry."

"I love you," I said.

CHAPTER 56

My name is Marianna Simonova, I am born in USSR, and now I live here at Armstrong Building, Harlem, New York. Is that good, Lily, darling, is this where you want I start?"

Lily had shown me a tape of Simonova singing when I first got to the building on Friday. There had been another tape on top of the video player. I'd put it in and now the Russian stared at me out of the TV again, as she had that first morning.

I figured that Lily had shot it. Again I saw the jaunty Russian, her face made up, the eyes glittering. Only now I knew she was a killer. I knew she had killed Lionel Hutchison, but why? What was her motive? They had been friends.

The whole apartment was filled with the woman's books, letters, tapes, photographs. I was working against time. Virgil had called to say the ME had confirmed there was cyanide in Lionel Hutchison, enough to kill him. The fact that Lucille had produced bottles with Hutchison's name on one and Simonova's on another meant somebody was going to ask questions about the dead woman. And soon.

"How much time do I have?" I'd asked Virgil.

"It's the end of the day," he said. "There's plenty going on, everybody is busy as hell right now. I figure you've got a little window, Artie, but not a lot. You have to get out of there before morning, you hear me? I know Wagner is going to want me on this, and Dawes is asking questions. I think you should hurry up. I think you should get out of Simonova's apartment as fast as you can, and for God's sake, try not to leave anything. You don't want people to know you were looking around. I have to go." He hung up in a hurry, as if somebody had entered a room, heard him talking to me, and told him to kill the call.

The place and everything in it now belonged to Marie Louise. I had no business in here. Even by midnight, I still had work to do. Hurry, I thought.

I knew I should get out, but I couldn't. There was something holding me. And Lily had been involved with Simonova, more than she'd told me. I couldn't let go, not yet.

I pushed play again, and Simonova began talking about her life, looking up from time to time to see if Lily was happy with the tape. Her voice was harsh from cigarettes and disease, her English broken. She switched to Russian, answering Lily's questions, or just rambling. But she was lively, laughing.

From inside the old TV, from the tape, the dead woman talked at me. She painted an epic life.

Marianna Simonova was born in a provincial village near Perm in 1938. She was an orphan, no family. Only the Party gave her a life, she explained, but she explained it in terms of a glorious revolutionary spirit. Communism was her religion; the Party was her family.

"I was fantastic little Young Pioneer, I am so cute in my outfit," she says, looking out from the screen and singing a snatch of a song I knew from my own childhood.

No parents. I wondered if she had made them disappear, like some Soviet kids. If their parents had spoiled histories, if they had been enemies of the state, or had done time in Gulags, some children simply denied their own history, their own blood. Otherwise, you were doomed: no access to the best education, no access to decent housing, no access to a life that was worth anything at all. Some children made their parents disappear; others informed on them.

I wondered about Simonova. For a woman who had accumulated so much stuff, there was nothing about her own family, no pictures, no souvenirs, nothing at all.

I sat in the near dark, watching the tape, not wanting to put on the lights. Then I heard footsteps in the hall. I looked through the peephole in Simonova's door, but it was only Regina McGee, trudging home with her shopping bags.

I sat on the floor again and looked at the TV.

Simonova went on with her history. She grew up in a Soviet orphanage and somehow got herself to school in Moscow. She loved music. She heard Paul Robeson. She developed a passion for him and became determined to meet him. They had an affair, she claimed. I heard Lily's voice asking for dates; Simonova refused to answer, then she became defensive. Lily eased up. She just wanted the story.

On and on Simonova went, Lily rarely interrupting, as she spun her tales about the Soviet Union: of Yuri Gagarin in space, of the trans-Siberian railway, of her feats as a young gymnast, and the occasion when she presented Stalin with a bouquet of roses in Red Square. No detail was left out, not what she had worn or who she met. She had been looking for somebody who would take an interest in her tales, and in Lily she'd found a taker.

Marianna Simonova had touched something deep in Lily's past—the politics, the community of the left, her father. Simonova had exploited it.

On the tape she sang patriotic songs for Lily's benefit. In the background, I could hear Lily singing along.

Again, I stopped the tape. I had to get to the journals, the letters. I got up and glanced at the shelves of books, looking for anything that might give me a clue, but most were political tomes or Russian novels.

Near the sofa on the little table were the same two books I'd seen before: a copy of Chekhov's stories; and a book about Rasputin. Rasputin was poisoned with cyanide.

At the desk I looked through a pile of letters. Then I went into Simonova's bedroom, the bathroom, the study. My phone rang and I jumped. Lily said she was at Tolya's new brownstone now. Might sleep over. I was glad. She was safer with Tolya.

It was cold. I glanced at the bottle of vodka still on the table, and I took a swig. It burned my throat. Everything in the apartment felt cold to the touch, the boxes, the leather journals, the cassettes.

Against one wall was a small chest of drawers. It was stuffed with photographs.

There were photographs everywhere: on the mantel, in little Russian boxes, on every surface. Newspaper clippings with more pictures were piled in a cardboard box.

When you first start, you think the hard part about being a cop will be the streets, the creeps and crooks and killers. You think about the victims, the bodies, the blood, the morgue. If you're any kind of human being, the stuff, especially when it involves kids, makes you feel sick, makes you puke, gives you ulcers. You stop feeling sick, it's time to quit.

As bad for me is the history—the victim's, the killer's. You turn back page after page, interrogations, transcripts, confessions, diaries, letters, heart racing, stomach turning, cold sweat on your neck, knowing it will reveal something terrible, the grim hidden secrets.

I knew the only way to find out what had happened to Simonova was here. The lump on my head ached. I was hungry. In Simonova's kitchen I found Russian Christmas cookies. I ate some. Drank more of her vodka.

By ten that night, one lamp on, I had clippings and letters and photographs laid out on the worn purple Turkish rug. I laid them out like a hand of solitaire.

I'd finished with the video tapes, but in a drawer in the bedroom, I'd found audio cassettes and an old-fashioned player. Some of the tapes were marked with Lily's name. Most of what I heard, when I began to listen, was in Russian.

Were the tapes for a book Lily wanted to write? Did Simonova figure she'd get them translated? Did she want to leave a record? She knew she was sick, maybe dying. The dead woman had recorded her life.

While I listened, and a lot of it was propaganda, Simonova's philosophy, I went through more of her journals. I looked at newspaper clippings.

In Moscow she had worked in some obscure bureau. She clipped foreign magazines and sent the information to the KGB, to a low-level KGB apparatchik. She'd been a small-time librarian who could only afford to live in a communal apartment, but she had access to foreign magazines.

In her spare time, she had churned out papers she hoped to publish, papers written by a faithful Communist Party hack, which is what she had been. All she ever was.

Most of her clippings, most of the magazine articles she had saved for herself, were about black people in America. It had been her specialty. Her obsession. She had fallen for these exotics, as she saw them, the oppressed, the victims of American imperialism, of the racism she believed to be rife in the United States.

Paul Robeson featured in many of the articles, and there were copies of letters she had written to him. She had never met him.

I changed the audio tape. On this one, Simonova described how she had come to America.

"Lily, yes, this is working OK? Sure, so I continue," said Simonova. "I leave Moscow in 1972 after this Nixon-Brezhnev detente, when Jews are permitted to go to Israel, so I tell everybody I am Jewish, though I am not sure what I am. Still, I must go, so I make my way to New York with other so-called Jews. First time in history, many Russians pretend to be Jew. But not because I love America. I remain true socialist. I leave because I am pregnant. I meet American musician in Moscow, we spend one night, and so. Can I have water, please?"

She paused, to drink the water, I assumed, and then continued. "I live first in Brighton Beach, then in Washington Heights, I teach, I do translation, I even work as waitress."

In the first part of the tape, Simonova spoke in English. Then she switched to Russian. She told Lily to get the rest translated, but these were things she could say only in Russian.

She began.

I listened carefully, stopping and starting the tape. It wasn't completely clear if the KGB had contacted Simonova before she left Russia or after she had arrived in New York, but she became a very small time sleeper.

She wasn't activated until 1982, just before Brezhnev died and the Soviet Union was running out of steam—out of oil. There followed Andropov and Chernenko, then Gorbachev came in, the system collapsed, and Marianna Simonova was left stranded in the United States, without the KGB money or the contacts. She was on her own. Nobody was interested in a two-bit sleeper who had only done minor errands. She went freelance.

English again: "So, dear Lily, I come to Harlem, first to 131st Street, then Armstrong, where I make nice life. I tell people how I knew Comrade Robeson. I talk to them about people I know." Listening, I understood how she had made her myth, the kind that would enchant people like Lily.

What kind of work had she done in New York after the Soviet Union collapsed? I wasn't sure. She'd done translations, but she had lived well. Too well.

I burrowed in her papers, and I kept thinking: Where did she get the money?

I found receipts, scraps of paper with names, notes, lists. She had kept everything, the last shreds of reality, as if without all of it, she would cease to exist.

Then I found more tapes that had come from an old answering machine; somebody had set it up to record telephone calls. I found the machine in a closet and I sat and listened to her phone calls, most in Russian, and shuddered as I made notes. She had taped all her calls, perhaps by mistake, maybe on purpose. I couldn't know.

Her conversations in English, some with other people in the Armstrong, ran to arrangements for bridge or doctor's appointments. There was nothing much interesting.

The calls in Russian were also about social arrangements; many of the voices belonged to other women.

But there were two men who seemed to call Simonova frequently. She addressed them as Comrade. The same men, same voices, one with a crude accent, the other educated. Over and Over, they had called her.

The conversations cropped up at random times on a dozen different answering-machine tapes. I could date them by the events they discussed: Iraq, Putin, Obama. Both men professed a longing for the return of a regime like Stalin's. Both considered Putin an important man, a strong man, a truly Russian man. With Simonova, in Russian, they discussed the revival of the real men, who would fix things.

I thought of the tats on Ivan's arm: WORKERS OF THE WORLD UNITE, and of the Communist Manifesto skewered into the dead guy's heart. They were low-level thugs, but they still believed. Or maybe the new order had left them out in the cold, and they worked as thugs for hire as a kind of revenge.

The harder I listened to the men on the phone, the more I was convinced one of them was Ivan.

The specifics of the jobs they did and who they did them for were never mentioned. Simonova, the low-level KGB creep, had turned to the agency's successor, the FSB. She did anything she could get. It didn't seem to matter if it was political or just plain criminal. She wanted the money.

Like Nixon, she had been obsessed with taping things, making notes, scratching entries in one of her diaries every night—people she'd seen, talked to, played cards with, people she liked or had a beef with. Like Nixon, too, in the way she resented everybody, she was obsessed with her so-called enemies.

I was lost in her world now. Lost among her tapes and phone calls and address books, even a transcript from a CNN program. But I kept going back to the photographs.

I made coffee. I looked at the cluttered living room, the icons, the statues and books and paper, the sofa, the fancy chairs. I went through the pictures all over again, and then, finally, I found it, the thing I had been looking for, the thing that had been rattling around in my head.

On the table near the sofa was a small mirror, about six by eight. It was on the same table where she had kept things that seemed important—pills, vodka, cigarettes, the book about Rasputin. I picked it up on a hunch, and in it I saw my own reflection, tired, at the end of my rope. My hand on the back, I felt something loose.

I pried the glass from the frame. In the back were half a dozen more photographs. I sat back on my heels, staring down at them. I knew. My God, I thought. Now I understood.

I heard of a noise.

"Who's there?"

But it was only the wind blowing at the terrace door. Fucking wind, all weekend it had been rattling glass, sending me out of doors, prowling the terraces. Some of the time I'd felt I could hear the Armstrong itself moaning, the whole building wailing, its history, now the deaths.

I went out and looked around. I looked in the pail where Lionel Hutchison had tossed his cigarette butts the morning I'd seen him, Saturday morning. How many did he light up? Two, I remembered. There were four in the pail, and there was a piece of toast. It had stopped snowing Saturday night. Anything left out here before, would have been covered, but the two butts, the toast were visible, no snow covering them. Footprints too in snow that was now half a foot deep. There'd been no snow when I first met Hutchison. I leaned over to the Hutchison terrace. Prints there, too.

Did Lionel climb onto his friend's terrace? Did he bring his coffee and his meds out? Did he take the pill, get dizzy and fall off? I stared at the prints. Then I heard somebody.

Somebody was at Simonova's door.

CHAPTER 57

Virgil's face was bruised from the fight with Ivan. His hand was resting on an oxygen tank on wheels.

"I got it off Diaz." He dragged it into the apartment and shut the door. "Listen, you have to get out of here."

I looked around the room.

"I can't. Not yet. I'm not finished."

"Artie, listen to me. I talked to Dawes. He's taking over. He's going to work this building, the cases—Hutchison, Lennox. You have to go. He's not going to like your poring over this stuff. You don't have a warrant. I can't stop him."

"And he doesn't like me anyway, right?"

Virgil shrugged.

"Listen, you should know, I think Lionel Hutchison fell from the terrace here. There's evidence, if you look for it."

"Christ," said Virgil. "If Dawes finds out you were here and there's evidence on the terrace, he'll know you saw it. He'll go apeshit, Artie. He'll go ballistic. You should get out. You don't need the grief if Dawes finds you here, and we have plenty of dope on Ivan and the dead Russkis now. Go," Virgil said. He stumbled and sat hard on the arm of a chair. "What's all that?" He was looking at the photographs on the floor.

"Marianna Simonova was pregnant when she came to America. One-night stand in Moscow. Six months after she arrived, she gave birth to a boy. She named him Vladimir. His adopted parents changed his name. She only saw him once after that. Never tracked the father down."

"This is her?" Virgil picked up a photograph of Simonova in New York, when she was very young, and pretty.

"You'd never recognize her, would you?"

"No," said Virgil.

I wanted to see if he came up with the same thing I did. I put more pictures in a row. "These came from a leather folder Carver Lennox had on him when he was murdered. I had the feeling he wanted me to see them." I showed Virgil the picture of a little boy of about three.

He was facing the camera, peering through glasses, the kind that make a child look serious and sad. He had a round face. His suit was too big for him, as if it had been cut down, and the jacket was buttoned up tight. He was holding somebody's hand, but all you could see was her arm and hand—a woman's hand, from the look of the cuff of her dress and her glove. He was black. You couldn't tell about the woman. In the background was the Statue of Liberty.

"It's Carver, isn't it?" said Virgil. "You can see it."

"I also found this in Lennox's folder."

It was the same child, same suit, looking at the Statue of Liberty, his hand in a woman's gloved hand, but with his back to the camera. The woman was Marianna Simonova. It was the picture from her apartment, the one I had seen Saturday morning, the picture that had been missing when I went back.

"Jesus," said Virgil. "My God."

"I found these hidden behind one of Simonova's mirrors." I showed Virgil the photographs of the same little boy as a baby. I turned the pictures over. On each, written in Cyrillic with a blue fountain pen, were names and dates. "She called him Vladimir. His adoptive parents changed it to Carver."

"He was her son?" Virgil said. "Carver Lennox was Marianna Simonova's son?"

"Yes."

"Did Carver know?"

"Not until recently, far as I can tell. Maybe last week. I have more paper to get through. You need to go, Virgil. You don't want Dawes for an enemy."

"But she knew," he said. "Simonova knew it was her boy?"

"She knew almost as soon as she moved into the building years ago. And she watched. She had the photographs. She decided to make herself into a good mother, she decided to see what Carver needed and give it to him."

"You think she moved into the Armstrong by chance?"

"I can't prove it. I guess only Lionel suspected, but she moved in, same building, same floor. You have to think she knew. Anyway, she makes friends in the building, she hears what's going on with fixing the place up, she gets to know Carver and his part in it. He's her son."

"So she kept it to herself for years."

"I think, and I'm guessing, in her own cracked way she wanted to get it right, do something for him, make up for abandoning him, the way she saw it."

"She got to know everyone here?" said Virgil. "She knew it all."

"Yes, she makes herself the center of the action for the old folk in the building. Then she gives to Obama. Carver's a big supporter. That really gives her clout. She raises money, she holds debate-night parties, she goes to Obama headquarters when she can and makes phone calls. They're impressed. Here's this strange white Russian woman, and she's doing everything for their guy."

Virgil looked at the door suddenly.

"Let's get the fuck out of here."

"Not yet. I'm not finished. I think Lionel might have mentioned to Simonova that he was concerned about Amahl Washington's death. If she had been involved, that would give her another motive to get rid of Lionel."

"You're saying she had a part in that?" Virgil looked at me.

"I don't know."

"Did Lionel know about her and Lennox?"

"He was sharp. It's possible."

"When?"

"A week ago, two, I'm not sure."

"So she decided to get rid of Lionel? Isn't it hard to buy cyanide?"

I showed him the transcript I had just found; it was from CNN, a report by Sanjay Gupta, the network doc, on a cyanide case, a Maryland teenager who spiked his friend's drink with poison and killed him.

"Listen to this," I said, and read some of it out. "OK, so, Gupta says, 'It's remarkably easy to purchase cyanide online . . . We had some of our producers do it themselves . . . You can actually have it sent to your home.' There's more on how you can get it in pesticides, metal strippers, you can get it at hardware stores, things like that."

"Jesus, Artie," Virgil said.

"Yeah, she was reading up. I found a receipt for pesticides from a hardware store midtown. What did she need it for? She got Lionel Hutchison to prescribe extra pills for her, she put cyanide in the capsules and gave him the bottle back. That way she could be sure it would work. That day, the next day. There were five pills."

"Like Russian roulette?"

"You got it."

"But why? I mean, unless she was crazy, why do this?"

"For Carver Lennox. Her son."

"I'm still not sure I get it completely. Lay it out for me."

"She knew he wanted to take over the building. She knew he wanted those big apartments. And she would make it happen for him. Washington, Lionel Hutchison."

"Did she know she was dying when she fixed his pills?"

"It didn't matter to her. Either way, Lennox would get hold of the apartments. She knew Celestina had a soft spot for him; Carver would get her place, and he'd find a way to get Amahl Washington's."

"It still doesn't add up," said Virgil. "What about the guy who killed Carver? And how come she left everything to Marie Louise Semake?"

"I checked. She arranged it only two days before she died. On Wednesday. There was a tape with a phone call between her and Carver, telling him she had some wonderful news for him, a kind of Christmas gift."

"Go on."

"She told him she was his mother, she told him she had fixed for him to get Amahl Washington's apartment. She didn't say it outright, but he could have figured it out, he wasn't dumb. It's all on one of her phone tapes. He must have been horrified. He didn't want it. He told her he didn't want it."

"Do you think she mentioned that she had planned Lionel's death?"

"No. Carver would have stopped it."

"Why didn't he tell somebody about Washington?" Virgil asked.

"Maybe he intended to. But clearly, after her talk with Carver, she felt he had betrayed her, he rejected her gift, he rejected her, she made a new will. To spite him. And everyone else. And it was too late to change her plans; she had already put Lionel's death in place."

"She arranged for Carver's murder, too?"

"Yes," I said. "Before she died. She didn't know she was going to die when she did, but either way, Carver's death was in the works."

"The creep? Ivan?"

"Those tapes of her phone call, I found, I'm betting I'll find a call to Ivan. She had been a true believer, but when the Soviet system collapsed, she did favors for anyone she could—FSB, Russian mob, who the hell knows. Ivan was part of some two-bit mob who used the Commie Manifesto for tats, for a slogan."

"Ironic?"

"Who knows," I said, "but it was Ivan who beat me up. He killed the dog because it was barking too loud, maybe for fun, too, his kind of fun, and he killed Carver. All it took was a phone call from Simonova. Ivan owed her."

I told Virgil I was sure that during the previous six or seven months, as Simonova's health got worse, Carver Lennox had become her obsession. She was determined to be a good mother. She intended to leave him something. She knew about his ambition for the building.

For her son, she would make a little empire and leave it to him. Ironic, maybe, for an old Communist, she wrote in her diary. But he was her son. For him she would become a capitalist, for him, anything.

She had outlined her ambitions on paper, certain nobody would see her journals, not for a while. She knew she was dying. She had time, though. She would destroy everything first.

"Was she crazy, or just evil?" said Virgil.

"Is there a difference?"

Virgil went to the other side of the room to take a call, and when he came back, he said, "We really need to go. This is a damn crime scene," he added. "We've been doing a lot of breaking and entering, you and me. No warrant."

"You go. I'll go soon," I said. "Just go."

"Lily's not at home, by the way."

"I know that."

"Is she OK? Where is she?"

"She's with Tolya Sverdloff."

"Your pal."

"Right."

"I don't think you take it seriously, Lily and me," said Virgil. "Just so you know, Artie, I'm dead serious about her, I really am."

"You still want to fight a duel with me or something over her?"

"I'm not joking, since you ask. I'm going to win. I'm not letting go easy."

"How serious?"

"That's up to Lily."

"Demasiado."

The oxygen machine was in the middle of the apartment where Virgil had left it. It was a huge thing, all the dials and tubes. I stared at it. I remembered something Diaz had told me. Of Amahl Washington, he had said, "too much" in Spanish. What was the word? He had said you could die from too much oxygen. Demasaido. Too much.

Had somebody turned up Simonova's oxygen? Had she suffered a seizure? Did Hutchison find her like that and position, pose her so she looked at peace? My heart was jumping; cold sweat ran down my neck.

When I looked closely at the tank, I saw I was right. The dial was turned up to the highest setting. Somebody had turned it up high, and it had killed her, oxygen had flooded Simonova's brain, and poisoned her.

I took a picture of the machine with my phone. I scrambled now to read as much as I could. More paper. More journals.

Digging into the box Lily had given me, I finally found another audio tape. I put it on. Sat and listened. Lily's voice first: "This is for a book about Marianna Simonova." There followed an interview.

It was as if Simonova was daring Lily, speaking in Russian, then in English. Enough of this recording was in English that I knew Lily had understood it; for the rest, she had been waiting for somebody to translate the Russian. Waiting for me.

Was it Lily who had urged Lionel Hutchison to sign the death certificate? To get the case closed as fast as possible? I wasn't sure.

But Lily had been frantic when I first got here, to the building. She had called me to come. She had been beside herself, crying, scared, shaking. My fault, Artie, she had said. My fault.

I listened some more and realized Lily had put this tape in the box for me. She wanted me to hear, to know.

For a long time, most of a year, she had listened to Simonova's stories, had admired her, flattered her. Lily listened. Simonova began to trust her. She told her more and more, about her time in the KGB, how she had been sent to seduce young men, the epic adventures. Who could say if it was true?

Then, about a week before Simonova died, the tone of Lily's questions began to change. It was on this tape. I heard it.

Simonova expressed great trust in Lily. She said they were comrades and she could tell her anything. Maybe it was why she had written the last-minute letter leaving her apartment to Lily.

The last few days of Simonova's life, she had begun bragging to

Lily about loyalty, about the work she did, the way she was still in the service of her country, how the new Russians, oligarchs, officials, agents, needed her. And paid her well. The tape ended abruptly. I turned it over.

I pressed play again.

"Even now I am old, I give help to Russian government," Simonova said. "Last summer, they call and say, Marianna Simonova, we need you; we are concerned about this man who lives in New York City who is called Anatoly Sverdloff."

"How did you help?" a voice said. It was Lily. Even through the plastic box, I could hear Lily strain for calm, could feel how it had taken every ounce of self-possession for her to remain attentive. "How did you help?" she said again.

Simonova laughed triumphantly. "They congratulate me for my idea. I help them locate daughter of Anatoly Sverdloff. I say to them always best way to deal with father is through child. The name of girl is Valentina."

"When did you help them find Sverdloff's daughter?"

"Late in last spring," Simonova said.

It had been late last spring when Valentina Sverdloff was murdered.

So I knew.

Lily had wanted me to hear it. She had given me the box with the tapes. I knew now why Lily had wanted me to help her instead of Virgil. I knew why the oxygen had been turned too high. Simonova didn't die because Lily forgot her medications, or because Lionel Hutchison tried to keep her from suffering. She had died from too much oxygen, that and her need to boast of her triumphs. She bragged to Lily. It had been Simonova's big mistake.

I turned the dial on the oxygen down to a normal setting. I wiped it off. I pushed it in the closet.

In the kitchen I found a metal garbage can and a big black plastic bag. I took them out onto the terrace. I stuffed in everything—tapes, notes, the address book—everything with Lily's name or references to her. I put in the old cassette player, the answering machine.

I turned my back to the wind as best I could, lit a match and set fire to the leftovers of Simonova's life, and waited while it burned, praying nobody would notice. When the paper had turned to ash, the plastic melted, I took the whole mess, put it in the black bag and went back into the apartment.

I put on my jacket. I picked up the black bag. When I left the apartment, I took it all with me, all of it.

But noise came from the hall. The kind of uninhibited noise cops make. I went back outside. I climbed over the wall to the Hutchisons' terrace and then to Carver's. I waited. Somebody had decided to look around. If Simonova had poisoned Lionel Hutchison, that alone gave them plenty of reason. I looked into the hallway. The cops must have been inside Simonova's place.

I knew I had to get away. They'd smell the stink of ash. I had to find Lily. I called Tolya.

"She's not here," he said.

I ran into her apartment, managed to avoid anyone seeing me.

She was gone. Her clothes were gone, her computer, everything.

CHAPTER 58

I went home. I parked my car, saw Mike waving at me through the coffee shop window, saw him beckon to me, but I ignored him, and went upstairs. I was beat. Anxious as hell about Lily, and dead tired.

"Hello, Artie." She was sitting at the kitchen counter. "I borrowed your keys from Mike. I hope that was OK." Lily looked at me.

"Yes."

"I had to get out of that building for a while. I couldn't just stay with Tolya." She paused. "That's not true," she said. "I wanted to be here."

"I'm glad you came." I sat across from her.

"My own apartment is still sublet," she said.

"Stay here." I said. "Lily?"

"What?"

"The tape you used to record Simonova, the one you put in the box of her stuff—you wanted me to find it."

"Yes. I couldn't understand all the Russian, but there was plenty in English.

"So you know what she did to Valentina?"

"Yes."

"Artie, there's something I need to tell you."

I cut her off. "No. There's nothing at all. I know. Everything is fine. It's all taken care of. It's over."

"Thank you. What about the Russian? Ivan? Won't he talk? Say he had instructions from Marianna?"

"So what? Who will care what a pig like him says? Did you tell Virgil?"

"Not everything," said Lily. "He wouldn't have understood about Valentina and Tolya. He doesn't know that I loved Val, and you loved her, and how it is with Tolya and us."

"Why didn't you just tell me?"

"I wanted to, God, I really did. I was going to, but then you got there, and I was so crazy, it was as if I'd fallen over into some other universe. I didn't know if I should tell you the truth or try to mislead you, so I came up with that cockamamie story about forgetting Marianna's meds. I was scared. I freaked out. I'm so sorry."

"Don't apologize. Not to me. Never."

She reached in her bag and took out a CD. "I wanted to give you this," she said. "Lionel gave it to me for you."

I opened the brown envelope addressed to me in Lionel Hutchison's hand with his old Parker pen. In it was *Anniversary*, a Stan Getz album. I put it on my CD player. Then Lily and I sat on my couch and listened to "Blood Count," Billy Strayhorn's last song. We sat there for a long time, just listening.

Inauguration Day,
January 20, 2009

That morning I ran into Sam, the doorman at the building next to mine. He was getting a cab for a woman and her kid. Then he said hi and we stopped to talk for a minute.

"Great day," he said.

"Yeah," I said. "Yes."

"Never thought I'd live to see this day." Sam's eyes welled up. "Never in my whole damn life," he said.

Most of the time, Sam was a quiet man. Today he wanted to talk. He was wearing an Obama button.

"You know it's my birthday," said Sam, straightening his jacket. "Nice way to celebrate. I'm seventy years old today, Artie. My daughter went down to DC this morning. I said to her, 'I want you there, I want you to see it with your own eyes and tell me.'" Sam paused and smiled. "Bet they don't got anybody like Mr. Obama over in Russia."

"Not a chance." I don't know why I asked, but since he had mentioned the place where I was born, I said, "Where are you from?" I realized I didn't know. I had never asked Sam. I should have asked him.

We stood inside the front door of the building. He told me he was from Mississippi. Bad place, he said.

"Can I tell you something?" he asked.

"Sure."

"I was no more than six years old," said Sam. "I went out hunting for rabbits with my grandfather—I adored him; he raised me—and I got lost in the woods." He paused. "Lost my way, lost him. I just wandered around, and then I looked up, and he was hanging from a tree."

339

I didn't know what to say, so we just stood there for a while until Sam said, "I have to get going. Want to be at home for the speech."

In spite of having voted for McCain, Mike Rizzi had made fresh apple pie that morning, and I got Sonny Lippert over to eat breakfast with me. We sat, drinking coffee, chewing the fat. It was inauguration day. He told me he had fixed it with Jimmy Wagner to lose the tape that showed my car near the van on election night. For a while, Sonny told me, there had been talk that I'd pushed the van out of place, that somehow I was involved, that I could even be had up for some kind of involuntary manslaughter. But they found the bastard who left the hand brake off, and there wasn't much they had on me.

Lippert had fixed it with Wagner and I was grateful. I thought about the van, and how my finding a parking space meant I had made it to the election-night party where I'd seen Lily.

I knew Radcliff was probably still pissed off at me, thought I was trying to get Lily back. He was right. I wasn't sure I could survive without her.

Later that morning, when Obama was to be sworn in, I went over to Il Posto Acconto, my friend Beatrice's place on East Second Street, to eat and watch the big TV over the bar. Lily had said she'd come by at some point, no promise when, just that she'd come for a drink. She had moved back to her own apartment, and we had spoken a few times and met for a drink once or twice. I didn't ask about Virgil, not yet. It was none of my business. Yet.

Bea, the best Italian cook in town, is a glamorous Roman who can always cheer you up with her talk and her food, and she was there with Julio, her husband, who's a dead ringer for Dizzy Gillespie. I drank one of Bea's great Bloody Marys and watched the crowd in a frozen DC, and wished I had gone.

"She'll be here," Beatrice said, seeing me look out the glass door to the street. She knew I was waiting for Lily.

It was cold out. A few people dropped in to Beatrice's, everybody looking quiet and solemn and happy. Tolya showed up and sat next to me. We drank a bottle of good wine.

Bea turned up the TV. We stopped talking and watched.

And then Obama was sworn in, and Aretha Franklin, in a big hat, sang, and we sat and watched. And I waited.

Tolya raised his glass.

I looked at the young black man in front of the frozen Capitol, and I looked at Tolya. "Things are going to get better now, aren't they?" I said.